INTRODUCTION

OF the three novels collected here, *Rasselas* (1759) may be seen as the last stand of Augustanism, a Palladian façade of reason, before the liberation of the unconscious impulses in man's nature brought about the Romantic Revival. Only five years separates it from that landmark in English taste, *The Castle of Otranto* (1764). Twenty years later, with Beckford's *Vathek*, a forerunner of Hoffmann and Huysmans, we are in the full flood of Byronic romanticism. For the people of the later eighteenth century had begun to feel imprisoned within the regularity of the Augustan order, and premonitory rumblings of melancholy and disquiet can be heard in *Rasselas* itself.

Johnson wrote *Rasselas* during the evenings of a week to pay for his mother's funeral. Its general tone is set by the opening sentence: "Ye who listen with credulity to the whispers of fancy, and pursue with eagerness the phantoms of hope, who expect that age will perform the promises of youth, and that the deficiencies of the present day will be supplied by the morrow, attend to the history of Rasselas, Prince of Abyssinia." This "history" soon resolves itself into a disquisition on the limitations of life, a prose *Vanity of Human Wishes*. Reared in the Happy Valley, where every want is supplied, Rasselas longs to visit the outside world in order to learn how the rest of mankind live. "I have already enjoyed too much," he exclaims, "give me something to desire." But their experiences lead both the prince and his sister Nekayah to the conclusion that there is more in life to be endured than enjoyed and that the world holds little worth desiring. So the philosopher of truth and reason, unhinged by the death of his daughter, discovers too late that wisdom is not sufficient to arm the heart against calamity, though "he compared reason to the sun, of which the light is constant, uniform, and lasting; and fancy to a meteor, of bright but transitory lustre, irregular in its motion, and delusive in its direction." So, too, the hermit only realizes

towards the close of his life all he has lost by solitude, for if
"marriage has many pains, celibacy has no pleasures." And
among the more illusory philosophies of life ironically glanced
at is that of the natural man, or the life led according to nature.
Standing before the Great Pyramid, the philosopher Imlac
sagely observes: "It seems to have been erected only in compliance with that hunger of imagination which preys incessantly upon life. . . . He that has built for use, till use is
supplied, must begin to build for vanity, and extend his
plan to the uttermost power of human performance, that he
may not be soon reduced to form another wish." It is the
hunger of imagination, Johnson concludes, that is the cause of
our wretchedness, by continually making us long for that
which we have not got. So Rasselas and his sister return,
sadder and wiser, to the Happy Valley, for "of these wishes
that they had formed they well knew that none could be
obtained."

In *Rasselas* may be found many of the finest qualities of
Johnson's thought, illuminated with those brilliant generaliza-
tions that are never merely witty and clever, but the outcome
of profound experience. The slow and balanced periods are
built up and resolved with Handelian grace. Behind them one
hears the voice and feels the personality of Johnson himself,
with his sublime common sense and immense solidity of
character. Unlike its almost exact contemporary *Candide*,
Rasselas, if one of the wisest, is certainly one of the saddest
books ever written. Its noble melancholy is evidence that
of the great Augustan tradition only the long sunset glow now
remained.

To pass on to *The Castle of Otranto* is like going from the
reasonable order of Kew Gardens, with its lawns and
classical temples framed in trees, to the pretty rococo Gothic of
Strawberry Hill. *The Castle of Otranto* is a midsummer dream
of 1764. "Shall I even confess to you what was the origin of this
romance?" Walpole wrote to the Rev. William Cole in 1765.
"I waked one morning in the beginning of last June from a
dream, of which all I could recover was, that I had thought
myself in an ancient castle (a very natural dream for a head filled
like mine with Gothic story) and that on the uppermost
banister of a great staircase I saw a gigantic hand in armour.
In the evening I sat down and began to write, without knowing
in the least what I intended to say." The year before he had
visited Trinity College, Cambridge; on his next visit five years

EVERYMAN'S LIBRARY

856

FICTION

Everyman, I will go with thee, and be thy guide,
In thy most need to go by thy side

SAMUEL JOHNSON, born at Lichfield in 1709, the son of a bookseller. His poverty forced him to leave Oxford before taking a degree. Became a school teacher, and in 1735 married Mrs Elizabeth Porter. Went to London in 1737 and devoted himself to journalism and literature. Met Boswell in 1763. Died in 1784.

HORATIO, or HORACE, WALPOLE, fourth Earl of Orford, born in 1717 and educated at Eton and King's College, Cambridge. Travelled in France and Italy, 1739–41. M.P., 1741–67. Established a private press at his residence in Twickenham. Died in 1797.

WILLIAM BECKFORD, born at Fonthill in 1760. Educated privately, studying music under Mozart and painting under Alexander Cozens. Inherited a vast fortune at the age of nine. Made grand tour of Europe, 1780–1, and married Lady Margaret Gordon in 1783. Travelled in Portugal, Spain, and France till 1798, then secluded himself in Fonthill and afterwards in Bath. Died in 1844.

SHORTER NOVELS
OF THE
EIGHTEENTH CENTURY

EDITED BY
PHILIP HENDERSON

LONDON J. M. DENT & SONS LTD
NEW YORK E. P. DUTTON & CO INC

later he suddenly found himself in the courtyard of Otranto.
Trinity had supplied him unconsciously with the courtyard,
the great hall and several other features which his own house
at Strawberry Hill lacked.   The novel was, therefore, as Mr.
Ketton-Cremer observes in his biography of Walpole, "the
child of an incongruous marriage between Strawberry Hill
and Trinity Great Court."   The supernatural "machinery"
Walpole took from the romances of chivalry, but his story of
the usurper Manfred is founded, as Mr. Montague Summers
has shown, on an adaptation of the life of that Manfred of
Sicily (1233–66) who also bore the title of Prince of Otranto.
Walpole himself seems to have forgotten this, just as he had
forgotten about Trinity Great Court, for he chose the title
Otranto at random from a map of the kingdom of Naples
simply for its sonorous sound.

Walpole became so engrossed in his tale that he completed
it in two months, sometimes writing far into the night till he
grew too tired to hold his pen.   Fearing that it would be
laughed at, he pretended that it was a translation of an Italian
book found in the library of an old Catholic family in the north
of England.   But on its publication *The Castle of Otranto*
proved so successful (it was at first believed to be by Gray)
that the first edition was soon exhausted, and in his preface
to the second Walpole owned to the authorship and stated the
principles on which he had written it.   His aim was, he says,
to combine the marvellous with the real by blending the old
type of romance with the new.   "In the former, all was
imagination and improbability; in the latter, nature is always
intended to be, and sometimes has been, copied with success.
Invention has not been wanting; but the great resources of
fancy have been dammed up by a strict adherence to common
life."   In *Otranto*, he assures us, his rule is nature, his model
Shakespeare.   Walpole's contemporaries, thrilling with a
delicious sense of wonder and surprise, agreed that he had
created a new type of romance.

To people tiring of classical balance and repose, here were all
those elements of enthusiasm, heroical aspiration and Gothic
wildness they longed for.   Indeed, Walpole has a good claim
to be considered the first surrealist novelist.   For there is a
dream-like inconsequence about his story, with its vast helmet
falling from the skies upon the little prince at his marriage
ceremony, and the gigantic leg in the gallery, the gigantic
mailed hand on the banister, the sighing portrait that steps

from its frame to interrupt a seduction scene, and the final bursting asunder of the whole castle by the enormous spectral form of Alfonso, that has so alarmingly shadowed it at moments of crisis throughout the tale. *The Castle of Otranto* is particularly surrealist in its dialogue, and the juxtaposition of the language and sentiments of the *beau monde* with Gothic violence. Above all, it is significant as a portent of what was to come. As Professor Caroline Spurgeon has pointed out, Walpole must be given the credit for creating the Byronic hero. If the man that Byron tried to be was the invention of Mrs. Radcliffe, it is Walpole who gave the first sketch of the dark, melancholy, handsome hero, when Bianca describes her ideal lover "with large black eyes, a smooth white forehead and manly curling locks like jet." Again, Theodore eventually marries Isabella because with her he can indulge the melancholy that has taken possession of his soul.

The order and lucidity of Beckford's prose is evidence that he was very much a man of the eighteenth century, in control of his own romanticism, though strongly influenced by both the Gothic and the oriental tastes of his time. For *Vathek* was partly the outcome of *The Arabian Nights*, of Beckford's study as a very young man of Persian and Arabic manuscripts, and of the practices of magic and occultism, to which he was introduced by the painter Alexander Cozens. Its more immediate inspiration, however, came from those Christmas festivities at Fonthill in 1781, which left such an enduring impression on his imagination. This party, Beckford wrote fifty years later, was "the realization of romance in its most extravagant intensity. Immured we were *au pied de la lettre* for three days following—windows so strictly closed that neither common daylight nor commonplace visitors could get in or even peep in. . . . Our society was extremely youthful and lovely to look upon. . . . Whilst the wretched world without lay dark, and bleak, and howling the very air of summer seemed playing round us. . . . The glowing haze investing every object, the mystic look, the vastness, the intricacy of this vaulted labyrinth occasioned so bewildering an effect that it became almost impossible for any one to define—at the moment—where he stood, where he had been, or to whither he was wandering." Though the party took place in his father's Georgian mansion, from this account of it one would imagine that Beckford had his own Gothic abbey in mind. Among the guests were Louisa Beckford, his cousin's wife, with whom Beckford was

in love, and young William Courtenay, with whom he was soon
after involved in a public scandal. "I composed *Vathek*
immediately upon my return to London," the account continues, "thoroughly imbued with all that passed at Fonthill
during this voluptuous festival. It will be seen then that the
Kalifeh's adventures were written down, not at the age of
seventeen, as Lord Byron has chosen to fancy, but at the age
of twenty and two." Even so it is an astonishing work for
so young a man.

There is no direct evidence of what actually took place
during "this voluptuous festival" at Fonthill. But cryptic
references in Beckford's letters to Louisa suggest that a form
of the Black Mass was celebrated. His early letters to Cozens
admit of a similar interpretation. *Vathek* was begun at
12 Wimpole Street, with Louisa Beckford and William
Courtenay translated into the figures of Nouronihar and
Gulchenrouz and the mysterious Alexander Cozens cast, perhaps, as one of the many mages and sorcerers. The Egyptian
Hall at Fonthill became the Hall of Eblis, the Palace of
Subterranean Fire, and for the scenery Beckford drew upon
his memories of Switzerland and Italy. He worked fitfully at
his romance during the next three months, interrupted by the
distractions of the Christmas season in London. In May he
left for Italy, where *Vathek* was completed before the end of
the year. It was written in spare, economical French, in
conscious imitation of Voltaire, and on his return journey from
Naples to Leghorn Beckford began an English version which
he never completed. In a letter of January 1783 to Samuel
Henley, who was now translating the novel, Beckford first
mentions the *Episodes of Vathek*, which he intended to
have inserted as a series of narrations by the damned in the
Hall of Eblis, at the same time giving strict instructions that
his book should first be published in the original French.
Henley, however, issued his rendering surreptitiously, without
the *Episodes*, in June 1786, during Beckford's long absence
from England, as a translation from the Arabic. Beckford
at once published the original version at Lausanne and
Paris. In comparison to this, Henley's translation is heavy-
footed and Latinized.

At first it seems that *Vathek* is to be merely an amusing and
fantastic oriental tale; but, like his author, the caliph is
obsessed with the darker side of magic and renounces Mahomet
in order to visit the Palace of Subterranean Fire, a fatal place

from which he does not return. In his description of these scenes Beckford's novel achieves an unexpected grandeur. *Vathek* displays, as Mr. Guy Chapman remarks, the duality of Beckford's nature, "a brutally comic spirit and a sense of sin and guilt." Both Vathek and Nouronihar are punished for their "unrestrained passions," and throughout the *Episodes* it is the same pair of impetuous lovers and amateurs of witchcraft who are so magnificently damned. Like Marlowe's *Doctor Faustus*, *Vathek* is an allegory of "that blind curiosity, which would transgress those bounds the wisdom of the Creator has prescribed to human knowledge."

PHILIP HENDERSON.

For biographical notes on the authors and short bibliographies see the beginning of each story.

CONTENTS

THE HISTORY OF RASSELAS
PRINCE OF ABYSSINIA

BY
SAMUEL JOHNSON

SAMUEL JOHNSON

JOHNSON was born at Lichfield on 18 September, 1709, where his father was a small bookseller. Although "miserably poor" and subject to fits of melancholy that were at times divided only by a thin partition from madness, and cursed by a kind of St. Vitus's dance and a scrofulous affliction, which had disfigured his face and deprived him of the use of one eye, Johnson determined to "fight his way by his literature and his wit." Because of his poverty he was forced to leave Pembroke College, Oxford, after only four terms and became an under-master at a grammar school at Market Bosworth and, later, in Birmingham, supported himself by translating for the booksellers. At Birmingham he met Mrs. Elizabeth Porter, a widow twenty years his senior, whom he married in 1735. His wife brought him £800 and with this he opened a school for young gentlemen near Lichfield. But he never had more than eight pupils, of whom the Garrick brothers were two. In 1737 he went to London with Garrick and offered his tragedy *Irene* to Drury Lane without success. He became a contributor to the *Gentleman's Magazine* and its parliamentary reporter from 1740 to 1743. His poem *London* was published in 1738, and next year *The Vanity of Human Wishes*. In 1744 he wrote his powerful *Life of Savage*, followed a year later by his first contribution to Shakespeare criticism (*Miscellaneous Observations on Macbeth*). The *Plan* of his great Dictionary, inscribed to Lord Chesterfield, appeared in 1747. Two years later Garrick produced *Irene* at Drury Lane. His chief recreation being a good dinner enlivened by good talk, Johnson founded about this time his first club at the King's Head in Ivy Lane. Mrs. Johnson died in 1751, to be mourned for many years by her husband. In 1755 the Dictionary was ready for publication and Chesterfield, who had ignored the original prospectus, hailed Johnson in the *World* as the dictator of the English language. In reply Johnson sent him the famous letter on patronage. With the accession of George III in 1762, Johnson received a pension of £300 a year and was thenceforward no longer compelled to "write for bread." Next year he met James Boswell, his biographer. His edition of Shakespeare appeared in 1765 and the *Lives of the Poets* in ten volumes from 1779 to 1781. A tour of the Scottish Highlands in Boswell's company resulted in *A Journey to the Western Isles* (1775). His friendship with Henry Thrale began about 1759, and the Thrale's fine house at Streatham Park was, until 1782, Johnson's principal asylum. The Thrales, he said, "soothed twenty years of a life radically wretched." In 1782 his health rapidly declined, and he died after an attack of dropsy on 13 December, 1784, at Bolt Court, Fleet Street. He was buried in Westminster Abbey.

W. P. Courtney and D. Nichol Smith, *A Bibliography of Samuel Johnson*, 1915; supplemented by R. W. Chapman, 1938. Contemporary accounts ed. by Hugh Kingsmill, *Johnson Without Boswell*, 1940; Bertrand H. Bronson, *Johnson Agonistes*, 1946. Lives by: James Boswell, 1791; Leslie Stephen, 1878; Hugh Kingsmill, 1933; J. C. Bailey, 1944; C. E. Vulliamy, 1946.

CHAPTER I

DESCRIPTION OF A PALACE IN A VALLEY

YE who listen with credulity to the whispers of fancy, and pursue with eagerness the phantoms of hope, who expect that age will perform the promises of youth, and that the deficiencies of the present day will be supplied by the morrow, attend to the history of Rasselas, Prince of Abyssinia.

Rasselas was the fourth son of the mighty emperor, in whose dominions the Father of Waters begins his course; whose bounty pours down the streams of plenty, and scatters over half the world the harvests of Egypt.

According to the custom which has descended from age to age among the monarchs of the torrid zone, Rasselas was confined in a private palace, with the other sons and daughters of Abyssinian royalty, till the order of succession should call him to the throne.

The place which the wisdom or policy of antiquity had destined for the residence of the Abyssinian princes, was a spacious valley in the kingdom of Amhara, surrounded on every side by mountains, of which the summits overhang the middle part. The only passage by which it could be entered, was a cavern that passed under a rock, of which it has long been disputed whether it was the work of nature or of human industry. The outlet of the cavern was concealed by a thick wood, and the mouth which opened into the valley was closed with gates of iron, forged by the artificers of ancient days, so massy that no man could without the help of engines open or shut them.

From the mountains on every side, rivulets descended, that filled all the valley with verdure and fertility, and formed a lake in the middle, inhabited by fish of every species, and frequented by every fowl whom nature has taught to dip the wing in water. This lake discharged its superfluities by a stream, which entered a dark cleft of the mountain on the northern side, and fell with dreadful noise from precipice to precipice till it was heard no more.

3

The sides of the mountains were covered with trees; the banks of the brooks were diversified with flowers; every blast shook spices from the rocks, and every month dropped fruits upon the ground. All animals that bite the grass, or browse the shrub, whether wild or tame, wandered in this extensive circuit, secured from beasts of prey by the mountains which confined them. On one part were flocks and herds feeding in the pastures, on another all the beasts of chase frisking in the lawns; the sprightly kid was bounding on the rocks, the subtle monkey frolicking in the trees, and the solemn elephant reposing in the shade. All the diversities of the world were brought together; the blessings of nature were collected, and its evils extracted and excluded.

The valley, wide and fruitful, supplied its inhabitants with the necessaries of life, and all delights and superfluities were added at the annual visit which the emperor paid his children, when the iron gate was opened to the sound of music, and, during eight days, every one that resided in the valley was required to propose whatever might contribute to make seclusion pleasant, to fill up the vacancies of attention, and lessen the tediousness of time. Every desire was immediately granted. All the artificers of pleasure were called to gladden the festivity; the musicians exerted the power of harmony, and the dancers showed their activity before the princes, in hope that they should pass their lives in this blissful captivity, to which those only were admitted whose performance was thought able to add novelty to luxury. Such was the appearance of security and delight which this retirement afforded, that they to whom it was new always desired that it might be perpetual; and as those on whom the iron gate had once closed were never suffered to return, the effect of longer experience could not be known. Thus every year produced new schemes of delight, and new competitors for imprisonment.

The palace stood on an eminence, raised about thirty paces above the surface of the lake. It was divided into many squares or courts, built with greater or less magnificence, according to the rank of those for whom they were designed. The roofs were turned into arches of massy stone, joined by a cement that grew harder by time; and the building stood from century to century, deriding the solstitial rains and equinoctial hurricanes, without need of reparation.

This house, which was so large as to be fully known to none but some ancient officers who successively inherited the secrets of the place, was built as if suspicion herself had dictated the plan. To every room there was an open and secret passage; every square had a communication with the rest, either from the upper stories by private galleries, or by subterranean passages from the lower apartments. Many of the columns had unsuspected cavities, in which a long race of monarchs had reposited their treasures. They then closed up the opening with marble, which was never to be removed but in the utmost exigencies of the kingdom; and recorded their accumulations in a book, which was itself concealed in a tower, not entered but by the emperor, attended by the prince who stood next in succession.

CHAPTER II

THE DISCONTENT OF RASSELAS IN THE HAPPY VALLEY

HERE the sons and daughters of Abyssinia lived only to know the soft vicissitudes of pleasure and repose, attended by all that were skilful to delight, and gratified with whatever the senses can enjoy. They wandered in gardens of fragrance, and slept in the fortresses of security. Every art was practised to make them pleased with their own condition. The sages who instructed them told them of nothing but the miseries of public life, and described all beyond the mountains as regions of calamity, where discord was always raging, and where man preyed upon man.

To heighten their opinion of their own felicity, they were daily entertained with songs, the subject of which was the Happy Valley. Their appetites were excited by frequent enumerations of different enjoyments; and revelry and merriment was the business of every hour, from the dawn of morning to the close of even.

These methods were generally successful: few of the princes had ever wished to enlarge their bounds, but passed their lives in full conviction that they had all within their reach that art or nature could bestow, and pitied those whom fate had excluded from this seat of tranquillity, as the sport of chance and the slaves of misery.

Thus they rose in the morning and lay down at night, pleased with each other and with themselves, all but Rasselas, who, in the twenty-sixth year of his age, began to withdraw himself from their pastimes and assemblies, and to delight in solitary walks and silent meditation. He often sat before tables covered with luxury, and forgot to taste the dainties that were placed before him; he rose abruptly in the midst of the song, and hastily retired beyond the sound of music. His attendants observed the change, and endeavoured to renew his love of pleasure; he neglected their officiousness, repulsed their invitations, and spent day after day on the banks of rivulets sheltered with trees, where he sometimes listened to the birds in the branches, sometimes observed the fish playing in the stream, and anon cast his eyes upon the pastures and mountains filled with animals, of which some were biting the herbage, and some sleeping among the bushes.

This singularity of his humour made him much observed. One of the sages, in whose conversation he had formerly delighted, followed him secretly, in hope of discovering the cause of his disquiet. Rasselas, who knew not that any one was near him, having for some time fixed his eyes upon the goats that were browsing among the rocks, began to compare their condition with his own.

"What," said he, "makes the difference between man and all the rest of the animal creation? Every beast that strays beside me has the same corporal necessities with myself: he is hungry and crops the grass, he is thirsty and drinks the stream; his thirst and hunger are appeased, he is satisfied and sleeps; he rises again and is hungry; he is again fed and is at rest. I am hungry and thirsty like him, but when thirst and hunger cease I am not at rest; I am like him pained with want, but am not like him satisfied with fullness. The intermediate hours are tedious and gloomy; I long again to be hungry, that I may again quicken my attention. The birds peck the berries or the corn, and fly away to the groves, where they sit in seeming happiness on the branches, and waste their lives in tuning one unvaried series of sounds. I likewise can call the lutanist and the singer; but the sounds that pleased me yesterday weary me to-day, and will grow yet more wearisome to-morrow. I can discover within me no power of perception which is not glutted with its proper pleasure; yet I do not feel myself delighted. Man surely has some latent sense for which this place affords no gratification; or he has some desires distinct from sense, which must be satisfied before he can be happy."

After this he lifted up his head, and seeing the moon rising, walked towards the palace. As he passed through the fields, and saw the animals around him, "Ye," said he, "are happy, and need not envy me that walk thus among you, burdened with myself; nor do I, ye gentle beings, envy your felicity, for it is not the felicity of man. I have many distresses from which ye are free; I fear pain when I do not feel it; I sometimes shrink at evils recollected, and sometimes start at evils anticipated: surely the equity of providence has balanced peculiar sufferings with peculiar enjoyments."

With observations like these the prince amused himself as he returned, uttering them with a plaintive voice, yet with a look that discovered him to feel some complacence in his own perspicacity, and to receive some solace of the miseries of life, from consciousness of the delicacy with which he felt, and the eloquence with which he bewailed them. He mingled cheerfully in the diversions of the evening, and all rejoiced to find that his heart was lightened.

CHAPTER III

THE WANTS OF HIM THAT WANTS NOTHING

On the next day, his old instructor, imagining that he had now made himself acquainted with his disease of mind, was in hope of curing it by counsel, and officiously sought an opportunity of conference, which the prince, having long considered him as one whose intellects were exhausted, was not very willing to afford. "Why," said he, "does this man thus intrude upon me? shall I be never suffered to forget those lectures which pleased only while they were new, and to become new again must be forgotten?" He then walked into the wood, and composed himself to his usual meditations; when, before his thoughts had taken any settled form, he perceived his pursuer at his side, and was at first prompted by his impatience to go hastily away; but, being unwilling to offend a man whom he had once reverenced and still loved, he invited him to sit down with him on the bank.

The old man, thus encouraged, began to lament the change which had been lately observed in the prince, and to inquire why he so often retired from the pleasures of the palace to loneliness and silence. "I fly from pleasure," said the prince, "because pleasure has ceased to please; I am lonely, because

I am miserable, and am unwilling to cloud with my presence the happiness of others." "You, sir," said the sage, "are the first who has complained of misery in the Happy Valley. I hope to convince you that your complaints have no real cause. You are here in full possession of all that the Emperor of Abyssinia can bestow; here is neither labour to be endured nor danger to be dreaded, yet here is all that labour or danger can procure or purchase. Look round and tell me which of your wants is without supply: if you want nothing, how are you unhappy?"

"That I want nothing," said the prince, "or that I know not what I want, is the cause of my complaint; if I had any known want, I should have a certain wish; that wish would excite endeavour, and I should not then repine to see the sun move so slowly towards the western mountain, or lament when the day breaks and sleep will no longer hide me from myself. When I see the kids and the lambs chasing one another, I fancy that I should be happy if I had something to pursue. But possessing all that I can want, I find one day and one hour exactly like another, except that the latter is still more tedious than the former. Let your experience inform me how the day may now seem as short as in my childhood, while nature was yet fresh, and every moment showed me what I never had observed before. I have already enjoyed too much; give me something to desire."

The old man was surprised at this new species of affliction, and knew not what to reply, yet was unwilling to be silent. "Sir," said he, "if you had seen the miseries of the world, you would know how to value your present state." "Now," said the prince, "you have given me something to desire; I shall long to see the miseries of the world, since the sight of them is necessary to happiness."

CHAPTER IV

THE PRINCE CONTINUES TO GRIEVE AND MUSE

At this time the sound of music proclaimed the hour of repast, and the conversation was concluded. The old man went away sufficiently discontented to find that his reasonings had produced the only conclusion which they were intended to prevent. But in the decline of life shame and grief are of short duration: whether it be that we bear easily what we have borne long;

or that, finding ourselves in age less regarded, we less regard others; or, that we look with slight regard upon afflictions to which we know that the hand of death is about to put an end.

The prince, whose views were extended to a wider space, could not speedily quiet his emotions. He had been before terrified at the length of life which nature promised him, because he considered that in a long time much must be endured; he now rejoiced in his youth, because in many years much might be done.

This first beam of hope that had been ever darted into his mind, rekindled youth in his cheeks, and doubled the lustre of his eyes. He was fired with the desire of doing something, though he knew not yet with distinctness either end or means.

He was now no longer gloomy and unsocial; but, considering himself as master of a secret stock of happiness, which he could enjoy only by concealing it, he affected to be busy in all schemes of diversion, and endeavoured to make others pleased with the state of which he himself was weary. But pleasures never can be so multiplied or continued, as not to leave much of life unemployed; there were many hours, both of the night and day, which he could spend without suspicion in solitary thought. The load of life was much lightened: he went eagerly into the assemblies, because he supposed the frequency of his presence necessary to the success of his purposes; he retired gladly to privacy, because he had now a subject of thought.

His chief amusement was to picture to himself that world which he had never seen; to place himself in various conditions, to be entangled in imaginary difficulties, and to be engaged in wild adventures; but his benevolence always terminated his projects in the relief of distress, the detection of fraud, the defeat of oppression, and the diffusion of happiness.

Thus passed twenty months of the life of Rasselas. He busied himself so intensely in visionary bustle, that he forgot his real solitude, and, amidst hourly preparations for the various incidents of human affairs, neglected to consider by what means he should mingle with mankind.

One day, as he was sitting on a bank, he feigned to himself an orphan virgin robbed of her little portion by a treacherous lover, and crying after him for restitution and redress. So strongly was the image impressed upon his mind, that he started up in the maid's defence, and run forward to seize the plunderer, with all the eagerness of real pursuit. Fear naturally quickens the flight of guilt. Rasselas could not catch the fugitive with his utmost efforts; but resolving to weary by perseverance him whom he could not surpass in speed, he pressed on till the foot of the mountain stopped his course.

Here he recollected himself, and smiled at his own useless impetuosity. Then raising his eyes to the mountain, "This," said he, "is the fatal obstacle that hinders at once the enjoyment of pleasure, and the exercise of virtue. How long is it that my hopes and wishes have flown beyond this boundary of my life, which yet I never have attempted to surmount!"

Struck with this reflection, he sat down to muse; and remembered, that since he first resolved to escape from his confinement, the sun had passed twice over him in his annual course. He now felt a degree of regret with which he had never been before acquainted. He considered how much might have been done in the time which had passed and left nothing real behind it. He compared twenty months with the life of man. "In life," said he, "is not to be counted the ignorance of infancy, or imbecility of age. We are long before we are able to think, and we soon cease from the power of acting. The true period of human existence may be reasonably estimated at forty years, of which I have mused away the four-and-twentieth part. What I have lost was certain, for I have certainly possessed it; but of twenty months to come who can assure me?"

The consciousness of his own folly pierced him deeply, and he was long before he could be reconciled to himself. "The rest of my time," said he, "has been lost by the crime or folly of my ancestors, and the absurd institutions of my country; I remember it with disgust, yet without remorse: but the months that have passed since new light darted into my soul, since I formed a scheme of reasonable felicity, have been squandered by my own fault. I have lost that which can never be restored; I have seen the sun rise and set for twenty months, an idle gazer on the light of heaven: in this time the birds have left the nest of their mother, and committed themselves to the woods and to the skies; the kid has forsaken the teat, and learned by degrees to climb the rocks in quest of independent sustenance. I only have made no advances, but am still helpless and ignorant. The moon, by more than twenty changes, admonished me of the flux of life; the stream that rolled before my feet upbraided my inactivity. I sat feasting on intellectual luxury, regardless alike of the examples of the earth, and the instructions of the planets. Twenty months are passed; who shall restore them?"

These sorrowful meditations fastened upon his mind; he passed four months in resolving to lose no more time in idle resolves, and was awakened to more vigorous exertion, by hearing a maid, who had broken a porcelain cup, remark, that what cannot be repaired is not to be regretted.

This was obvious; and Rasselas reproached himself that he had not discovered it; having not known, or not considered, how many useful hints are obtained by chance, and how often the mind, hurried by her own ardour to distant views, neglects the truths that lie open before her. He for a few hours regretted his regret, and from that time bent his whole mind upon the means of escaping from the Valley of Happiness.

CHAPTER V

THE PRINCE MEDITATES HIS ESCAPE

He now found that it would be very difficult to effect that which it was very easy to suppose effected. When he looked round about him, he saw himself confined by the bars of nature, which had never yet been broken, and by the gate, through which none that once had passed it were ever able to return. He was now impatient as an eagle in a grate. He passed week after week in clambering the mountains, to see if there was any aperture which the bushes might conceal, but found all the summits inaccessible by their prominence. The iron gate he despaired to open; for it was not only secured with all the power of art, but was always watched by successive sentinels, and was by its position exposed to the perpetual observation of all the inhabitants.

He then examined the cavern through which the waters of the lake were discharged; and, looking down at a time when the sun shone strongly upon its mouth, he discovered it to be full of broken rocks, which, though they permitted the stream to flow through many narrow passages, would stop any body of solid bulk. He returned discouraged and dejected; but having now known the blessing of hope, resolved never to despair.

In these fruitless searches he spent ten months. The time, however, passed cheerfully away: in the morning he rose with new hope, in the evening applauded his own diligence, and in the night slept sound after his fatigue. He met a thousand amusements which beguiled his labour and diversified his thoughts. He discerned the various instincts of animals and properties of plants, and found the place replete with wonders, of which he purposed to solace himself with the contemplation, if he should never be able to accomplish his flight; rejoicing that his endeavours, though yet unsuccessful, had supplied him with a source of inexhaustible inquiry.

But his original curiosity was not yet abated; he resolved to obtain some knowledge of the ways of men. His wish still continued, but his hope grew less. He ceased to survey any longer the walls of his prison, and spared to search by new toils for interstices which he knew could not be found, yet determined to keep his design always in view, and lay hold on any expedient that time should offer.

CHAPTER VI

A DISSERTATION ON THE ART OF FLYING

AMONG the artists that had been allured into the Happy Valley, to labour for the accommodation and pleasure of its inhabitants, was a man eminent for his knowledge of the mechanic powers, who had contrived many engines both of use and recreation. By a wheel which the stream turned, he forced the water into a tower, whence it was distributed to all the apartments of the palace. He erected a pavilion in the garden, around which he kept the air always cool by artificial showers. One of the groves, appropriated to the ladies, was ventilated by fans, to which the rivulet that run through it gave a constant motion; and instruments of soft music were placed at proper distances, of which some played by the impulse of the wind, and some by the power of the stream.

This artist was sometimes visited by Rasselas, who was pleased with every kind of knowledge, imagining that the time would come when all his acquisitions should be of use to him in the open world. He came one day to amuse himself in his usual manner, and found the master busy in building a sailing chariot; he saw that the design was practicable upon a level surface, and with expressions of great esteem solicited its completion. The workman was pleased to find himself so much regarded by the prince, and resolved to gain yet higher honours. "Sir," said he, "you have seen but a small part of what the mechanic sciences can perform. I have been long of opinion, that instead of the tardy conveyance of ships and chariots, man might use the swifter migration of wings; that the fields of air are open to knowledge, and that only ignorance and idleness need crawl upon the ground."

This hint rekindled the prince's desire of passing the mountains; having seen what the mechanist had already performed, he was willing to fancy that he could do more; yet resolved to inquire further, before he suffered hope to afflict him by disappointment. "I am afraid," said he to the artist, "that your imagination prevails over your skill, and that you now tell me rather what you wish, than what you know. Every animal has his element assigned him; the birds have the air, and man and beasts the earth." "So," replied the mechanist, "fishes have the water, in which yet beasts can swim by nature, and men by art. He that can swim needs not despair to fly; to swim is to fly in a grosser fluid, and to fly is to swim in a subtler. We are only to proportion our power of resistance to the different density of matter through which we are to pass. You will be necessarily upborn by the air, if you can renew any impulse upon it faster than the air can recede from the pressure."

"But the exercise of swimming," said the prince, "is very laborious; the strongest limbs are soon wearied: I am afraid the act of flying will be yet more violent; and wings will be of no great use, unless we can fly further than we can swim."

"The labour of rising from the ground," said the artist, "will be great, as we see it in the heavier domestic fowls; but as we mount higher, the earth's attraction, and the body's gravity, will be gradually diminished, till we shall arrive at a region where the man will float in the air without any tendency to fall: no care will then be necessary but to move forwards, which the gentlest impulse will effect. You, sir, whose curiosity is so extensive, will easily conceive with what pleasure a philosopher, furnished with wings, and hovering in the sky, would see the earth, and all its inhabitants, rolling beneath him, and presenting to him successively, by its diurnal motion, all the countries within the same parallel. How must it amuse the pendent spectator to see the moving scene of land and ocean, cities and deserts! To survey with equal security the marts of trade, and the fields of battle; mountains infested by barbarians, and fruitful regions gladdened by plenty and lulled by peace! How easily shall we then trace the Nile through all his passage; pass over to distant regions, and examine the face of nature from one extremity of the earth to the other!"

"All this," said the prince, "is much to be desired; but I am afraid that no man will be able to breathe in these regions of speculation and tranquillity. I have been told that respiration is difficult upon lofty mountains; yet from these precipices, though so high as to produce great tenuity of air, it is very easy to fall; therefore I suspect that, from any height where life can be supported, there may be danger of too quick descent."

"Nothing," replied the artist, "will ever be attempted, if all possible objections must be first overcome. If you will favour my project, I will try the first flight at my own hazard. I have considered the structure of all volant animals, and find the folding continuity of the bat's wings most easily accommodated to the human form. Upon this model I shall begin my task to-morrow, and in a year expect to tower into the air beyond the malice and pursuit of man. But I will work only on this condition, that the art shall not be divulged, and that you shall not require me to make wings for any but ourselves."

"Why," said Rasselas, "should you envy others so great an advantage? All skill ought to be exerted for universal good; every man has owed much to others, and ought to repay the kindness that he has received."

"If men were all virtuous," returned the artist, "I should with great alacrity teach them all to fly. But what would be the security of the good, if the bad could at pleasure invade them from the sky? Against an army sailing through the clouds, neither walls, nor mountains, nor seas, could afford any security. A flight of northern savages might hover in the wind, and light at once with irresistible violence upon the capital of a fruitful region that was rolling under them. Even this valley, the retreat of princes, the abode of happiness, might be violated by the sudden descent of some of the naked nations that swarm on the coast of the southern sea."

The prince promised secrecy, and waited for the performance, not wholly hopeless of success. He visited the work from time to time, observed its progress, and remarked many ingenious contrivances to facilitate motion, and unite levity with strength. The artist was every day more certain that he should leave vultures and eagles behind him, and the contagion of his confidence seized upon the prince.

In a year the wings were finished; and, on a morning appointed, the maker appeared furnished for flight on a little promontory:

he waved his pinions awhile to gather air, then leaped from his
stand, and in an instant dropped into the lake. His wings,
which were of no use in the air, sustained him in the water, and
the prince drew him to land, half dead with terror and vexation.

CHAPTER VII

THE PRINCE FINDS A MAN OF LEARNING

THE prince was not much afflicted by this disaster, having
suffered himself to hope for a happier event, only because he had
no other means of escape in view. He still persisted in his
design to leave the happy valley by the first opportunity.

His imagination was now at a stand; he had no prospect of
entering into the world; and, notwithstanding all his endeavours
to support himself, discontent by degrees preyed upon him,
and he began again to lose his thoughts in sadness when the
rainy season, which in these countries is periodical, made it
inconvenient to wander in the woods.

The rain continued longer and with more violence than had
been ever known; the clouds broke on the surrounding mountains, and the torrents streamed into the plain on every side,
till the cavern was too narrow to discharge the water. The
lake overflowed its banks, and all the level of the valley was
covered with the inundation. The eminence on which the
palace was built, and some other spots of rising ground, were
all that the eye could now discover. The herds and flocks left
the pastures, and both the wild beasts and the tame retreated
to the mountains.

This inundation confined all the princes to domestic amusements; and the attention of Rasselas was particularly seized by
a poem, which Imlac rehearsed, upon the various conditions of
humanity. He commanded the poet to attend him in his
apartment, and recite his verses a second time; then entering
into familiar talk, he thought himself happy in having found
a man who knew the world so well, and could so skilfully paint
the scenes of life. He asked a thousand questions about things,
to which, though common to all other mortals, his confinement
from childhood had kept him a stranger. The poet pitied his
ignorance, and loved his curiosity, and entertained him from
day to day with novelty and instruction, so that the prince

regretted the necessity of sleep, and longed till the morning should renew his pleasure.

As they were sitting together, the prince commanded Imlac to relate his history, and to tell by what accident he was forced, or by what motive induced, to close his life in the Happy Valley. As he was going to begin his narrative, Rasselas was called to a concert, and obliged to restrain his curiosity till the evening.

CHAPTER VIII

THE HISTORY OF IMLAC

THE close of the day is, in the regions of the torrid zone, the only season of diversion and entertainment, and it was therefore midnight before the music ceased, and the princesses retired. Rasselas then called for his companion, and required him to begin the story of his life.

"Sir," said Imlac, "my history will not be long: the life that is devoted to knowledge passes silently away, and is very little diversified by events. To talk in public, to think in solitude, to read and to hear, to inquire and answer inquiries, is the business of a scholar. He wanders about the world without pomp or terror, and is neither known nor valued but by men like himself.

"I was born in the kingdom of Goiama, at no great distance from the fountain of the Nile. My father was a wealthy merchant, who traded between the inland countries of Afric and the ports of the Red Sea. He was honest, frugal, and diligent, but of mean sentiments and narrow comprehension: he desired only to be rich, and to conceal his riches, lest he should be spoiled by the governor of the province."

"Surely," said the prince, "my father must be negligent of his charge, if any man in his dominions dares take that which belongs to another. Does he not know that kings are accountable for injustice as well as done? If I were emperour, not the meanest of my subjects should be oppressed with impunity. My blood boils when I am told that a merchant durst not enjoy his honest gains, for fear of losing them by the rapacity of power. Name the governor who robbed the people, that I may declare his crimes to the emperor."

"Sir," said Imlac, "your ardour is the natural effect of virtue animated by youth: the time will come when you will acquit your father, and perhaps hear with less impatience of the governor. Oppression is, in the Abyssinian dominions, neither frequent nor tolerated; but no form of government has been yet discovered, by which cruelty can be wholly prevented. Subordination supposes power in one part, and subjection on the other; and if power be in the hands of men, it will some-times be abused. The vigilance of the supreme magistrate may do much, but much will still remain undone. He can never know all the crimes that are committed, and can seldom punish all that he knows."

"This," said the prince, "I do not understand; but I had rather hear thee than dispute. Continue thy narration."

"My father," proceeded Imlac, "originally intended that I should have no other education than such as might qualify me for commerce; and discovering in me great strength of memory and quickness of apprehension, often declared his hope that I should be some time the richest man in Abyssinia."

"Why," said the prince, "did thy father desire the increase of his wealth, when it was already greater than he durst discover or enjoy? I am unwilling to doubt thy veracity, yet incon-sistencies cannot both be true."

"Inconsistencies," answered Imlac, "cannot both be right, but, imputed to man, they may both be true. Yet diversity is not inconsistency. My father might expect a time of greater security. However, some desire is necessary to keep life in motion; and he whose real wants are supplied must admit those of fancy."

"This," said the prince, "I can in some measure conceive. I repent that I interrupted thee."

"With this hope," proceeded Imlac, "he sent me to school; but when I had once found the delight of knowledge, and felt the pleasure of intelligence and the pride of invention, I began silently to despise riches, and determined to disappoint the purpose of my father, whose grossness of conception raised my pity. I was twenty years old before his tenderness would expose me to the fatigue of travel, in which time I had been instructed, by successive masters, in all the literature of my native country. As every hour taught me something new, I lived in a continual course of gratifications; but, as I advanced towards manhood, I lost much of the reverence with which I had been used to look on my instructors; because, when the lesson was ended, I did not find them wiser or better than common men.

"At length my father resolved to initiate me in commerce, and opening one of his subterranean treasuries, counted out ten thousand pieces of gold. 'This, young man,' said he, 'is the stock with which you must negotiate. I began with less than the fifth part, and you see how diligence and parsimony have increased it. This is your own to waste or to improve. If you squander it by negligence or caprice, you must wait for my death before you will be rich; if in four years you double your stock, we will thenceforward let subordination cease, and live together as friends and partners; for he shall always be equal with me, who is equally skilled in the art of growing rich.'

"We laid our money upon camels, concealed in bales of cheap goods, and travelled to the shore of the Red Sea. When I cast my eye on the expanse of waters, my heart bounded like that of a prisoner escaped. I felt an unextinguishable curiosity kindle in my mind, and resolved to snatch this opportunity of seeing the manners of other nations, and of learning sciences unknown in Abyssinia.

"I remembered that my father had obliged me to the improvement of my stock, not by a promise which I ought not to violate, but by a penalty which I was at liberty to incur; and therefore determined to gratify my predominant desire, and, by drinking at the fountains of knowledge, to quench the thirst of curiosity.

"As I was supposed to trade without connexion with my father, it was easy for me to become acquainted with the master of a ship, and procure a passage to some other country. I had no motives of choice to regulate my voyage; it was sufficient for me that, wherever I wandered, I should see a country which I had not seen before. I therefore entered a ship bound for Surat, having left a letter for my father declaring my intention."

CHAPTER IX

THE HISTORY OF IMLAC CONTINUED

"When I first entered upon the world of waters, and lost sight of land, I looked round about me with pleasing terror, and thinking my soul enlarged by the boundless prospect, imagined that I could gaze round for ever without satiety; but in a short time I grew weary of looking on barren uniformity, where I could only see again what I had already seen. I then descended into the ship, and doubted for a while whether all my future pleasures would not end like this, in disgust and disappointment. Yet, surely, said I, the ocean and the land are very different; the only variety of water is rest and motion, but the earth has mountains and valleys, deserts and cities; it is inhabited by men of different customs and contrary opinions; and I may hope to find variety in life, though I should miss it in nature.

"With this thought I quieted my mind; and amused myself during the voyage, sometimes by learning from the sailors the art of navigation, which I have never practised, and sometimes by forming schemes for my conduct in different situations. in not one of which I have been ever placed.

"I was almost weary of my naval amusements when we landed safely at Surat. I secured my money, and purchasing some commodities for show, joined myself to a caravan that was passing into the inland country. My companions, for some reason or other conjecturing that I was rich, and, by my inquiries and admiration, finding that I was ignorant, considered me as a novice whom they had a right to cheat, and who was to learn at the usual expense the art of fraud. They exposed me to the theft of servants and the exaction of officers, and saw me plundered upon false pretences, without any advantage to themselves, but that of rejoicing in the superiority of their own knowledge."

"Stop a moment," said the prince. "Is there such depravity in man, as that he should injure another without benefit to himself? I can easily conceive that all are pleased with superiority; but your ignorance was merely accidental, which, being neither your crime nor your folly, could afford them no reason to applaud themselves; and the knowledge which they had, and which you wanted, they might as effectually have shown by warning as betraying you."

"Pride," said Imlac, "is seldom delicate, it will please itself with very mean advantages; and envy feels not its own happiness, but when it may be compared with the misery of others. They were my enemies, because they grieved to think me rich; and my oppressors, because they delighted to find me weak."

"Proceed," said the prince: "I doubt not of the facts which you relate, but imagine that you impute them to mistaken motives."

"In this company," said Imlac, "I arrived at Agra, the capital of Indostan, the city in which the Great Mogul commonly resides. I applied myself to the language of the country, and in a few months was able to converse with the learned men; some of whom I found morose and reserved, and others easy and communicative; some were unwilling to teach another what they had with difficulty learned themselves; and some showed that the end of their studies was to gain the dignity of instructing.

"To the tutor of the young princes I recommended myself so much, that I was presented to the emperor as a man of uncommon knowledge. The emperor asked me many questions concerning my country and my travels; and though I cannot now recollect anything that he uttered above the power of a common man, he dismissed me astonished at his wisdom, and enamoured of his goodness.

"My credit was now so high, that the merchants with whom I had travelled applied to me for recommendations to the ladies of the court. I was surprised at their confidence of solicitation, and gently reproached them with their practices on the road. They heard me with cold indifference, and showed no tokens of shame or sorrow.

"They then urged their request with the offer of a bribe; but what I would not do for kindness, I would not do for money, and refused them, not because they had injured me, but because I would not enable them to injure others; for I knew they would have made use of my credit to cheat those who should buy their wares.

"Having resided at Agra till there was no more to be learned, I travelled into Persia, where I saw many remains of ancient magnificence, and observed many new accommodations of life. The Persians are a nation eminently social, and their assemblies afforded me daily opportunities of remarking characters and manners, and of tracing human nature through all its variations.

"From Persia I passed into Arabia, where I saw a nation at once pastoral and warlike; who live without any settled habitation; whose only wealth is their flocks and herds; and who have yet carried on through all ages an hereditary war with all mankind, though they neither covet nor envy their possessions."

CHAPTER X

IMLAC'S HISTORY CONTINUED. A DISSERTATION UPON POETRY

"WHEREVER I went, I found that poetry was considered as the highest learning, and regarded with a veneration somewhat approaching to that which man would pay to the Angelic Nature. And yet it fills me with wonder, that, in almost all countries, the most ancient poets are considered as the best: whether it be that every other kind of knowledge is an acquisition gradually attained, and poetry is a gift conferred at once; or that the first poetry of every nation surprised them as a novelty, and retained the credit by consent, which it received by accident at first; or whether, as the province of poetry is to describe Nature and Passion, which are always the same, the first writers took possession of the most striking objects for description, and the most probable occurrences for fiction, and left nothing to those that followed them, but transcription of the same events, and new combinations of the same images. Whatever be the reason, it is commonly observed that the early writers are in possession of nature, and their followers of art; that the first excel in strength and invention, and the latter in elegance and refinement.

"I was desirous to add my name to this illustrious fraternity. I read all the poets of Persia and Arabia, and was able to repeat by memory the volumes that are suspended in the mosque of Mecca. But I soon found that no man was ever great by imitation. My desire of excellence impelled me to transfer my attention to nature and to life. Nature was to be my subject, and men to be my auditors: I could never describe what I had not seen; I could not hope to move those with delight or terror, whose interests and opinions I did not understand.

"Being now resolved to be a poet, I saw everything with a new purpose; my sphere of attention was suddenly magnified; no kind of knowledge was to be overlooked. I ranged mountains and deserts for images and resemblances, and pictured upon my mind every tree of the forest and flower of the valley. I observed with equal care the crags of the rock and the pinnacles of the palace. Sometimes I wandered along the mazes of the rivulet, and sometimes watched the changes of the summer clouds. To a poet nothing can be useless. Whatever is beautiful, and whatever is dreadful, must be familiar to his imagination:

he must be conversant with all that is awfully vast or elegantly little. The plants of the garden, the animals of the wood, the minerals of the earth, and meteors of the sky, must all concur to store his mind with inexhaustible variety: for every idea is useful for the enforcement or decoration of moral or religious truth; and he who knows most will have most power of diversifying his scenes, and of gratifying his reader with remote allusions and unexpected instruction.

"All the appearances of nature I was therefore careful to study; and every country which I have surveyed has contributed something to my poetical powers."

"In so wide a survey," said the prince, "you must surely have left much unobserved. I have lived, till now, within the circuit of these mountains, and yet cannot walk abroad without the sight of something which I had never beheld before, or never heeded."

"The business of a poet," said Imlac, "is to examine, not the individual, but the species; to remark general properties and large appearances. He does not number the streaks of the tulip, or describe the different shades in the verdure of the forest: he is to exhibit in his portraits of nature such prominent and striking features, as recall the original to every mind; and must neglect the minuter discriminations, which one may have remarked, and another have neglected, for those characteristics which are alike obvious to vigilance and carelessness.

"But the knowledge of nature is only half the task of a poet: he must be acquainted likewise with all the modes of life. His character requires that he estimate the happiness and misery of every condition, observe the power of all the passions in all their combinations, and trace the changes of the human mind as they are modified by various institutions and accidental influences of climate or custom, from the sprightliness of infancy to the despondence of decrepitude. He must divest himself of the prejudices of his age and country; he must consider right and wrong in their abstracted and invariable state; he must disregard present laws and opinions, and rise to general and transcendental truths, which will always be the same. He must therefore content himself with the slow progress of his name, contemn the applause of his own time, and commit his claims to the justice of posterity. He must write as the interpreter of nature, and the legislator of mankind, and consider himself as presiding over the thoughts and manners of future generations; as a being superior to time and place.

"His labour is not yet at an end; he must know many languages and many sciences; and, that his style may be worthy of his thoughts, must, by incessant practice, familiarize to himself every delicacy of speech and grace of harmony."

CHAPTER XI

IMLAC'S NARRATIVE CONTINUED. A HINT ON PILGRIMAGE

IMLAC now felt the enthusiastic fit, and was proceeding to aggrandize his own profession, when the prince cried out, "Enough! thou hast convinced me that no human being can ever be a poet. Proceed with thy narration."

"To be a poet," said Imlac, "is indeed very difficult."

"So difficult," returned the prince, "that I will at present hear no more of his labours. Tell me whither you went when you had seen Persia."

"From Persia," said the poet, "I travelled through Syria, and for three years resided in Palestine, where I conversed with great numbers of the northern and western nations of Europe; the nations which are now in possession of all power and all knowledge; whose armies are irresistible, and whose fleets command the remotest parts of the globe. When I compared these men with the natives of our own kingdom, and those that surround us, they appeared almost another order of beings. In their countries it is difficult to wish for anything that may not be obtained: a thousand arts, of which we never heard, are continually labouring for their convenience and pleasure; and whatever their own climate has denied them is supplied by their commerce."

"By what means," said the prince, "are the Europeans thus powerful? or why, since they can so easily visit Asia and Africa for trade or conquest, cannot the Asiatics and Africans invade their coasts, plant colonies in their ports, and give laws to their natural princes? The same wind that carries them back would bring us thither."

"They are more powerful, sir, than we," answered Imlac, "because they are wiser; knowledge will always predominate over ignorance, as man governs the other animals. But why their knowledge is more than ours, I know not what reason can be given, but the unsearchable will of the Supreme Being."

"When," said the prince with a sigh, "shall I be able to visit Palestine, and mingle with this mighty confluence of nations? Till that happy moment shall arrive, let me fill up the time with such representations as thou canst give me. I am not ignorant of the motive that assembles such numbers in that place, and cannot but consider it as the centre of wisdom and piety, to which the best and wisest men of every land must be continually resorting."

"There are some nations," said Imlac, "that send few visitants to Palestine; for many numerous and learned sects in Europe concur to censure pilgrimage as superstitious, or deride it as ridiculous."

"You know," said the prince, "how little my life has made me acquainted with diversity of opinions; it will be too long to hear the arguments on both sides; you, that have considered them, tell me the result."

"Pilgrimage," said Imlac, "like many other acts of piety, may be reasonable or superstitious, according to the principles upon which it is performed. Long journeys in search of truth are not commanded. Truth, such as is necessary to the regulation of life, is always found where it is honestly sought. Change of place is no natural cause of the increase of piety, for it inevitably produces dissipation of mind. Yet, since men go every day to view the fields where great actions have been performed, and return with stronger impressions of the event, curiosity of the same kind may naturally dispose us to view that country whence our religion had its beginning; and I believe no man surveys those awful scenes without some confirmation of holy resolutions. That the Supreme Being may be more easily propitiated in one place than in another, is the dream of idle superstition; but that some places may operate upon our own minds in an uncommon manner, is an opinion which hourly experience will justify. He who supposes that his vices may be more successfully combated in Palestine, will, perhaps, find himself mistaken; yet he may go thither without folly: he who thinks they will be more freely pardoned, dishonours at once his reason and religion."

"These," said the prince, "are European distinctions. I will consider them another time. What have you found to be the effect of knowledge? Are those nations happier than we?"

"There is so much infelicity," said the poet, "in the world, that scarce any man has leisure from his own distresses to estimate the comparative happiness of others. Knowledge is certainly one of the means of pleasure, as is confessed by the natural desire which every mind feels of increasing its ideas. Ignorance is mere privation, by which nothing can be produced: it is a vacuity in which the soul sits motionless and torpid for want of attraction; and without knowing why, we always rejoice when we learn, and grieve when we forget. I am therefore inclined to conclude, that if nothing counteracts the natural consequence of learning, we grow more happy as our minds take a wider range.

"In enumerating the particular comforts of life, we shall find many advantages on the side of the Europeans. They cure wounds and diseases with which we languish and perish. We suffer inclemencies of weather which they can obviate. They have engines for the dispatch of many laborious works, which we must perform by manual industry. There is such communication between distant places, that one friend can hardly be said to be absent from another. Their policy removes all public inconveniences; they have roads cut through their mountains, and bridges laid upon their rivers. And, if we descend to the privacies of life, their habitations are more commodious, and their possessions are more secure."

"They are surely happy," said the prince, "who have all these conveniences, of which I envy none so much as the facility with which separated friends interchange their thoughts."

"The Europeans," answered Imlac, "are less unhappy than we; but they are not happy. Human life is everywhere a state in which much is to be endured, and little to be enjoyed."

CHAPTER XII

THE STORY OF IMLAC CONTINUED

"I AM not yet willing," said the prince, "to suppose that happiness is so parsimoniously distributed to mortals; nor can believe but that, if I had the choice of life, I should be able to fill every day with pleasure. I would injure no man, and should provoke no resentment; I would relieve every distress, and should enjoy the benedictions of gratitude. I would choose my friends among the wise, and my wife among the virtuous; and therefore should be in no danger from treachery or unkindness. My children should, by my care, be learned and pious, and would repay to my age what their childhood had received. What would dare to molest him who might call on every side to thousands enriched by his bounty, or assisted by his power? And why should not life glide quietly away in the soft reciprocation of protection and reverence? All this may be done without the help of European refinements, which appear by their effects to be rather specious than useful. Let us leave them, and pursue our journey."

"From Palestine," said Imlac, "I passed through many regions of Asia; in the more civilized kingdoms as a trader, and among the barbarians of the mountains as a pilgrim. At last I began to long for my native country, that I might repose, after my travels and fatigues, in the places where I had spent my earliest years, and gladden my old companions with the recital of my adventures. Often did I figure to myself those with whom I had sported away the gay hours of dawning life, sitting round me in its evening, wondering at my tales, and listening to my counsels.

"When this thought had taken possession of my mind, I considered every moment as wasted which did not bring me nearer to Abyssinia. I hastened into Egypt, and, notwithstanding my impatience, was detained ten months in the contemplation of its ancient magnificence, and in inquiries after the remains of its ancient learning. I found in Cairo a mixture of all nations; some brought thither by the love of knowledge, some by the hope of gain, and many by the desire of living after their own manner without observation, and of lying hid in the obscurity of multitudes: for in a city, populous as Cairo, it is possible to obtain at the same time the gratifications of society, and the secrecy of solitude.

"From Cairo I travelled to Suez, and embarked on the Red Sea, passing along the coast till I arrived at the port from which I had departed twenty years before. Here I joined myself to a caravan, and re-entered my native country.

"I now expected the caresses of my kinsmen, and the congratulations of my friends, and was not without hope that my father, whatever value he had set upon riches, would own with gladness and pride a son who was able to add to the felicity and honour of the nation. But I was soon convinced that my thoughts were vain. My father had been dead fourteen years, having divided his wealth among my brothers, who were removed to some other provinces. Of my companions, the greater part was in the grave; of the rest, some could with difficulty remember me, and some considered me as one corrupted by foreign manners.

"A man used to vicissitudes is not easily dejected. I forgot, after a time, my disappointment, and endeavoured to recommend myself to the nobles of the kingdom; they admitted me to their tables, heard my story, and dismissed me. I opened a school, and was prohibited to teach. I then resolved to sit down in the quiet of domestic life, and addressed a lady that was fond of my conversation, but rejected my suit because my father was a merchant.

"Wearied at last with solicitation and repulses, I resolved to hide myself for ever from the world, and depend no longer on the opinion or caprice of others. I waited for the time when the gate of the Happy Valley should open, that I might bid farewell to hope and fear: the day came; my performance was distinguished with favour; and I resigned myself with joy to perpetual confinement."

"Hast thou here found happiness at last?" said Rasselas. "Tell me without reserve; art thou content with thy condition? or, dost thou wish to be again wandering and inquiring? All the inhabitants of this valley celebrate their lot, and, at the annual visit of the emperor, invite others to partake of their felicity."

"Great prince," said Imlac, "I shall speak the truth; I know not one of all your attendants who does not lament the hour when he entered this retreat. I am less unhappy than the rest, because I have a mind replete with images, which I can vary and combine at pleasure. I can amuse my solitude by the renovation of the knowledge which begins to fade from my memory, and by recollection of the accidents of my past life. Yet all this ends in the sorrowful consideration, that my acquirements are now useless, and that none of my pleasures can be again enjoyed. The rest, whose minds have no impression but of the present moment, are either corroded by malignant passions, or sit stupid in the gloom of perpetual vacancy."

"What passions can infest those," said the prince, "who have no rivals? We are in a place where impotence precludes malice, and where all envy is repressed by community of enjoyments."

"There may be community," said Imlac, "of material possessions, but there can never be community of love or of esteem. It must happen that one will please more than another; he that knows himself despised will always be envious; and still more envious and malevolent, if he is condemned to live in the presence of those who despise him. The invitations by which they allure others to a state which they feel to be wretched, proceed from the natural malignity of hopeless misery. They are weary of themselves and of each other, and expect to find relief in new companions. They envy the liberty which their folly has forfeited, and would gladly see all mankind imprisoned like themselves.

"From this crime, however, I am wholly free. No man can say that he is wretched by my persuasion. I look with pity on the crowds who are annually soliciting admission to captivity, and wish that it were lawful for me to warn them of their danger."

"My dear Imlac," said the prince, "I will open to thee my whole heart. I have long meditated an escape from the Happy Valley. I have examined the mountains on every side, but find myself insuperably barred: teach me the way to break my prison; thou shalt be the companion of my flight, the guide of my rambles, the partner of my fortune, and my sole director in the *choice of life.*"

"Sir," answered the poet, "your escape will be difficult, and, perhaps, you may soon repent your curiosity. The world, which you figure smooth and quiet as the lake in the valley, you will find a sea foaming with tempests and boiling with whirlpools: you will be sometimes overwhelmed by the waves of violence, and sometimes dashed against the rocks of treachery. Amidst wrongs and frauds, competitions and anxieties, you will wish a thousand times for these seats of quiet, and willingly quit hope to be free from fear."

"Do not seek to deter me from my purpose," said the prince; "I am impatient to see what thou hast seen; and, since thou art thyself weary of the valley, it is evident that thy former state was better than this. Whatever be the consequence of my experiment, I am resolved to judge with mine own eyes of the various conditions of men, and then to make deliberately my *choice of life.*"

"I am afraid," said Imlac, "you are hindered by stronger restraints than my persuasions; yet, if your determination is fixed, I do not counsel you to despair. Few things are impossible to diligence and skill."

CHAPTER XIII

RASSELAS DISCOVERS THE MEANS OF ESCAPE

THE prince now dismissed his favourite to rest; but the narrative of wonders and novelties filled his mind with perturbation. He revolved all that he had heard, and prepared innumerable questions for the morning.

Much of his uneasiness was now removed. He had a friend to whom he could impart his thoughts, and whose experience could assist him in his designs. His heart was no longer condemned to swell with silent vexation. He thought that even the Happy Valley might be endured with such a companion, and that if they could range the world together, he should have nothing further to desire.

In a few days the water was discharged, and the ground dried. The prince and Imlac then walked out together, to converse without the notice of the rest. The prince, whose thoughts were always on the wing, as he passed by the gate, said, with a countenance of sorrow, "Why art thou so strong, and why is man so weak?"

"Man is not weak," answered his companion; "knowledge is more than equivalent to force. The master of mechanics laughs at strength. I can burst the gate, but cannot do it secretly. Some other expedient must be tried."

As they were walking on the side of the mountain, they observed that the conies, which the rain had driven from their burrows, had taken shelter among the bushes, and formed holes behind them, tending upwards in an oblique line. "It has been the opinion of antiquity," said Imlac, "that human reason borrowed many arts from the instinct of animals; let us, therefore, not think ourselves degraded by learning from the coney. We may escape by piercing the mountain in the same direction. We will begin where the summit hangs over the middle part, and labour upward till we shall issue up beyond the prominence."

The eyes of the prince, when he heard this proposal, sparkled with joy. The execution was easy, and the success certain.

No time was now lost. They hastened early in the morning to choose a place proper for their mine. They clambered with great fatigue among crags and brambles, and returned without having discovered any part that favoured their design. The second and the third day were spent in the same manner, and with the same frustration. But, on the fourth, they found a small cavern, concealed by a thicket, where they resolved to make their experiment.

Imlac procured instruments proper to hew stone and remove earth, and they fell to their work on the next day with more eagerness than vigour. They were presently exhausted by their efforts, and sat down to pant upon the grass. The prince, for a moment, appeared to be discouraged. "Sir," said his companion, "practice will enable us to continue our labour for a longer time; mark, however, how far we have advanced, and you will find that our toil will some time have an end. Great works are performed, not by strength but perseverance: yonder palace was raised by single stones, yet you see its height and spaciousness. He that shall walk with vigour three hours a day, will pass in seven years a space equal to the circumference of the globe."

They returned to their work day after day, and, in a short time, found a fissure in the rock, which enabled them to pass far with very little obstruction. This Rasselas considered as a good omen. "Do not disturb your mind," said Imlac, "with other hopes or fears than reason may suggest: if you are pleased with prognostics of good, you will be terrified likewise with tokens of evil, and your whole life will be a prey to superstition. Whatever facilitates our work is more than an omen, it is a cause of success. This is one of those pleasing surprises which often happen to active resolution. Many things difficult to design prove easy to performance."

CHAPTER XIV

RASSELAS AND IMLAC RECEIVE AN UNEXPECTED VISIT

THEY had now wrought their way to the middle, and solaced their toil with the approach of liberty, when the prince, coming down to refresh himself with air, found his sister Nekayah standing before the mouth of the cavity. He started and stood confused, afraid to tell his design, and yet hopeless to conceal it. A few moments determined him to repose on her fidelity, and secure her secrecy by a declaration without reserve.

"Do not imagine," said the princess, "that I came hither as a spy: I had long observed from my window that you and

Imlac directed your walk every day towards the same point; but I did not suppose you had any better reason for the preference than a cooler shade, or more fragrant bank; nor followed you with any other design than to partake of your conversation. Since, then, not suspicion but fondness has detected you, let me not lose the advantage of my discovery. I am equally weary of confinement with yourself, and not less desirous of knowing what is done or suffered in the world. Permit me to fly with you from this tasteless tranquillity, which will yet grow more loathsome when you have left me. You may deny me to accompany you, but cannot hinder me from following."

The prince, who loved Nekayah above his other sisters, had no inclination to refuse her request, and grieved that he had lost an opportunity of showing his confidence by a voluntary communication. It was therefore agreed that she should leave the valley with them; and that, in the meantime, she should watch lest any other straggler should, by chance or curiosity, follow them to the mountain.

At length their labour was at an end; they saw light beyond the prominence, and, issuing to the top of the mountain, beheld the Nile, yet a narrow current, wandering beneath them.

The prince looked round with rapture, anticipated all the pleasures of travel, and in thought was already transported beyond his father's dominions. Imlac, though very joyful at his escape, had less expectation of pleasure in the world, which he had before tried, and of which he had been weary.

Rasselas was so much delighted with a wider horizon, that he could not soon be persuaded to return into the valley. He informed his sister that the way was open, and that nothing now remained but to prepare for their departure.

CHAPTER XV

THE PRINCE AND PRINCESS LEAVE THE VALLEY, AND SEE MANY WONDERS

THE prince and princess had jewels sufficient to make them rich whenever they came into a place of commerce, which, by Imlac's direction, they hid in their clothes; and, on the night of the next full moon, all left the valley. The princess was followed only by a single favourite, who did not know whither she was going.

They clambered through the cavity, and began to go down on the other side. The princess and her maid turned their eyes towards every part, and, seeing nothing to bound their prospect, considered themselves as in danger of being lost in a dreary vacuity. They stopped and trembled. "I am almost afraid," said the princess, "to begin a journey of which I cannot perceive an end, and to venture into this immense plain, where I may be approached on every side by men whom I never saw." The prince felt nearly the same emotions, though he thought it more manly to conceal them.

Imlac smiled at their terrors, and encouraged them to proceed; but the princess continued irresolute till she had been imperceptibly drawn forward too far to return.

In the morning they found some shepherds in the field, who set milk and fruits before them. The princess wondered that she did not see a palace ready for her reception, and a table spread with delicacies; but being faint and hungry, she drank the milk and ate the fruits, and thought them of a higher flavour than the products of the valley.

They travelled forward by easy journeys, being all unaccustomed to toil or difficulty, and knowing that, though they might be missed, they could not be pursued. In a few days they came into a more populous region, where Imlac was diverted with the admiration which his companions expressed at the diversity of manners, stations, and employments.

Their dress was such as might not bring upon them the suspicion of having anything to conceal; yet the prince, wherever he came, expected to be obeyed, and the princess was frighted because those that came into her presence did not prostrate themselves before her. Imlac was forced to observe them with great vigilance, lest they should betray their rank by their unusual behaviour, and detained them several weeks in the first village, to accustom them to the sight of common mortals.

By degrees the royal wanderers were taught to understand that they had for a time laid aside their dignity, and were to expect only such regard as liberality and courtesy could procure. And Imlac having, by many admonitions, prepared them to endure the tumults of a port, and the ruggedness of the commercial race, brought them down to the sea-coast.

The prince and his sister, to whom everything was new, were gratified equally at all places, and therefore remained for some months at the port, without any inclination to pass further. Imlac was content with their stay, because he did not think it safe to expose them, unpractised in the world, to the hazards of a foreign country.

At last he began to fear lest they should be discovered, and proposed to fix a day for their departure. They had no pretensions to judge for themselves, and referred the whole scheme to his direction. He therefore took passage in a ship to Suez; and, when the time came, with great difficulty prevailed on the princess to enter the vessel. They had a quick and prosperous voyage, and from Suez travelled by land to Cairo.

CHAPTER XVI

THEY ENTER CAIRO, AND FIND EVERY MAN HAPPY

As they approached the city, which filled the strangers with astonishment, "This," said Imlac to the prince, "is the place where travellers and merchants assemble from all the corners of the earth. You will here find men of every character and every occupation. Commerce is here honourable: I will act as a merchant, and you shall live as strangers who have no other end of travel than curiosity; it will soon be observed that we are rich; our reputation will procure us access to all whom we shall desire to know; you will see all the conditions of humanity, and enable yourself at leisure to make your *choice of life.*"

They now entered the town, stunned by the noise and offended by the crowds. Instruction had not yet so prevailed over habit, but that they wondered to see themselves pass undistinguished along the street, and met by the lowest of the people without reverence or notice. The princess could not at first bear the thought of being levelled with the vulgar, and for some days continued in her chamber, where she was served by her favourite Pekuah as in the palace of the valley.

Imlac, who understood traffic, sold part of the jewels the next day, and hired a house, which he adorned with such magnificence that he was immediately considered as a merchant of great wealth. His politeness attracted many acquaintance, and his generosity made him courted by many dependants. His table was crowded by men of every nation, who all admired his knowledge and solicited his favour. His companions, not being able to mix in the conversation, could make no discovery of their ignorance or surprise, and were gradually initiated in the world as they gained knowledge of the language.

The prince had, by frequent lectures, been taught the use and nature of money; but the ladies could not, for a long time, comprehend what the merchants did with small pieces of gold and silver, or why things of so little use should be received as equivalent to the necessaries of life.

They studied the language two years, while Imlac was preparing to set before them the various ranks and conditions of mankind. He grew acquainted with all who had anything uncommon in their fortune or conduct. He frequented the voluptuous and the frugal, the idle and the busy, the merchants and the men of learning.

The prince being now able to converse with fluency, and having learned the caution necessary to be observed in his intercourse with strangers, began to accompany Imlac to places of resort, and to enter into all assemblies, that he might make his *choice of life*.

For some time he thought choice needless, because all appeared to him equally happy. Wherever he went he met gaiety and kindness, and heard the song of joy or the laugh of carelessness. He began to believe that the world overflowed with universal plenty, and that nothing was withheld either from want or merit; that every hand showered liberality, and every heart melted with benevolence; "and who then," says he, "will be suffered to be wretched?"

Imlac permitted the pleasing delusion, and was unwilling to crush the hope of inexperience, till one day, having sat awhile silent, "I know not," said the prince, "what can be the reason that I am more unhappy than any of our friends. I see them perpetually and unalterably cheerful, but feel my own mind restless and uneasy. I am unsatisfied with those pleasures which I seem most to court. I live in the crowds of jollity, not so much to enjoy company as to shun myself, and am only loud and merry to conceal my sadness."

"Every man," said Imlac, "may, by examining his own mind, guess what passes in the minds of others; when you feel that your own gaiety is counterfeit, it may justly lead you to suspect that of your companions not to be sincere. Envy is commonly reciprocal. We are long before we are convinced that happiness is never to be found; and each believes it possessed by others, to keep alive the hope of obtaining it for himself. In the assembly where you passed the last night, there appeared such sprightliness of air and volatility of fancy, as might have suited beings of a higher order, formed to inhabit serener regions inaccessible to care or sorrow; yet, believe me, prince, there was not one who did not dread the moment when solitude should deliver him to the tyranny of reflection."

"This," said the prince, "may be true of others, since it is true of me; yet, whatever be the general infelicity of man, one condition is more happy than another, and wisdom surely directs us to take the least evil in the *choice of life*."

"The causes of good and evil," answered Imlac, "are so various and uncertain, so often entangled with each other, so diversified by various relations, and so much subject to accidents which cannot be foreseen, that he who would fix his condition upon incontestable reasons of preference must live and die inquiring and deliberating."

"But surely," said Rasselas, "the wise men, to whom we listen with reverence and wonder, chose that mode of life for themselves which they thought most likely to make them happy."

"Very few," said the poet, "live by choice. Every man is placed in his present condition by causes which acted without his foresight, and with which he did not always willingly co-operate; and therefore you will rarely meet one who does not think the lot of his neighbour better than his own."

"I am pleased to think," said the prince, "that my birth has given me at least one advantage over others, by enabling me to determine for myself. I have here the world before me; I will review it at leisure: surely happiness is somewhere to be found."

CHAPTER XVII

THE PRINCE ASSOCIATES WITH YOUNG MEN OF SPIRIT AND GAIETY

RASSELAS rose next day, and resolved to begin his experiments upon life. "Youth," cried he, "is the time of gladness: I will join myself to the young men whose only business is to gratify their desires, and whose time is all spent in a succession of enjoyments."

To such societies he was readily admitted; but a few days brought him back weary and disgusted. Their mirth was without images; their laughter without motive; their pleasures were gross and sensual, in which the mind had no part; their conduct was at once wild and mean: they laughed at order and at law; but the frown of power dejected, and the eye of wisdom abashed them.

The prince soon concluded that he should never be happy in a course of life of which he was ashamed. He thought it unsuitable to a reasonable being to act without a plan, and to be sad or cheerful only by chance. "Happiness," said he, "must be something solid and permanent, without fear and without uncertainty."

But his young companions had gained so much of his regard by their frankness and courtesy, that he could not leave them without warning and remonstrance. "My friends," said he, "I have seriously considered our manners and our prospects, and find that we have mistaken our own interest. The first years of man must make provision for the last. He that never thinks never can be wise. Perpetual levity must end in ignorance; and intemperance, though it may fire the spirits for an hour, will make life short or miserable. Let us consider that youth is of no long duration, and that in maturer age, when the enchantments of fancy shall cease, and phantoms of delight dance no more about us, we shall have no comforts but the esteem of wise men, and the means of doing good. Let us, therefore, stop, while to stop is in our power: let us live as men who are some time to grow old, and to whom it will be the most dreadful of all evils not to count their past years but by follies, and to be reminded of their former luxuriance of health only by the maladies which riot has produced."

They stared awhile in silence one upon another, and at last drove him away by a general chorus of continued laughter.

The consciousness that his sentiments were just, and his intentions kind, was scarcely sufficient to support him against the horror of derision. But he recovered his tranquillity, and pursued his search.

CHAPTER XVIII

THE PRINCE FINDS A WISE AND HAPPY MAN

As he was one day walking in the street, he saw a spacious building, which all were, by the open doors, invited to enter. He followed the stream of people, and found it a hall or school of declamation, in which professors read lectures to their auditory. He fixed his eye upon a sage raised above the rest, who discoursed with great energy on the government of the passions. His look was venerable, his action graceful, his pronunciation clear, and his diction elegant. He showed, with great strength of sentiment and variety of illustration, that human nature is degraded and debased when the lower faculties predominate over the higher; that when fancy, the parent of passion, usurps the dominion of the mind, nothing ensues but the natural effect of unlawful government, perturbation and confusion; that she betrays the fortresses of the intellect to rebels, and excites her children to sedition against reason, their lawful sovereign. He compared reason to the sun, of which the light is constant, uniform, and lasting; and fancy to a meteor, of bright but transitory lustre, irregular in its motion, and delusive in its direction.

He then communicated the various precepts given from time to time for the conquest of passion, and displayed the happiness of those who had obtained the important victory, after which man is no longer the slave of fear, nor the fool of hope; is no more emaciated by envy, inflamed by anger, emasculated by tenderness, or depressed by grief; but walks on calmly through the tumults or privacies of life, as the sun pursues alike his course through the calm or the stormy sky.

He enumerated many examples of heroes immovable by pain or pleasure, who looked with indifference on those modes or accidents to which the vulgar give the names of good and evil. He exhorted his hearers to lay aside their prejudices, and arm themselves against the shafts of malice or misfortune by invulnerable patience; concluding, that this state only was happiness, and that this happiness was in every one's power.

Rasselas listened to him with the veneration due to the instructions of a superior being, and waiting for him at the door, humbly implored the liberty of visiting so great a master of true wisdom. The lecturer hesitated a moment, when Rasselas put a purse of gold into his hand, which he received with a mixture of joy and wonder.

"I have found," said the prince at his return to Imlac, "a man who can teach all that is necessary to be known, who, from the unshaken throne of rational fortitude, looks down on the scenes of life changing beneath him. He speaks, and attention watches his lips; he reasons, and conviction closes his periods. This man shall be my future guide: I will learn his doctrines, and imitate his life."

"Be not too hasty," said Imlac, "to trust or to admire the teachers of morality: they discourse like angels, but they live like men."

Rasselas, who could not conceive how any man could reason so forcibly without feeling the cogency of his own arguments, paid his visit in a few days, and was denied admission. He had now learned the power of money, and made his way by a piece of gold to the inner apartment, where he found the philosopher, in a room half darkened, with his eyes misty, and his face pale. "Sir," said he, "you are come at a time when all human friendship is useless: what I suffer cannot be remedied; what I have lost cannot be supplied. My daughter, my only daughter, from whose tenderness I expected all the comforts of my age, died last night of a fever. My views, my purposes, my hopes are at an end: I am now a lonely being disunited from society."

"Sir," said the prince, "mortality is an event by which a wise man can never be surprised: we know that death is always near, and it should therefore always be expected."

"Young man," answered the philosopher, "you speak like one that has never felt the pangs of separation." "Have you then forgot the precepts," said Rasselas, "which you so powerfully enforced? Has wisdom no strength to arm the heart against calamity? Consider that external things are naturally variable, but truth and reason are always the same." "What comfort," said the mourner, "can truth and reason afford me? Of what effect are they now, but to tell me that my daughter will not be restored?"

The prince, whose humanity would not suffer him to insult misery with reproof, went away convinced of the emptiness of rhetorical sound, and the inefficacy of polished periods and studied sentences.

CHAPTER XIX

A GLIMPSE OF PASTORAL LIFE

HE was still eager upon the same inquiry; and having heard of a hermit, that lived near the lowest cataract of the Nile, and filled the whole country with the fame of his sanctity, resolved to visit his retreat, and inquire whether that felicity which public life could not afford was to be found in solitude; and whether a man whose age and virtue made him venerable could teach any peculiar art of shunning evils or enduring them.

Imlac and the princess agreed to accompany him; and, after

the necessary preparations, they began their journey. Their way lay through the fields, where shepherds tended their flocks, and the lambs were playing upon the pasture. "This," said the poet, "is the life which has been often celebrated for its innocence and quiet; let us pass the heat of the day among the shepherds' tents, and know whether all our searches are not to terminate in pastoral simplicity."

The proposal pleased him, and they induced the shepherds, by small presents and familiar questions, to tell their opinion of their own state. They were so rude and ignorant, so little able to compare the good with the evil of the occupation, and so indistinct in their narratives and descriptions, that very little could be learned from them; but it was evident that their hearts were cankered with discontent, that they considered themselves as condemned to labour for the luxury of the rich, and looked up with stupid malevolence toward those that were placed above them.

The princess pronounced with vehemence, that she would never suffer these envious savages to be her companions, and that she should not soon be desirous of seeing any more specimens of rustic happiness; but could not believe that all the accounts of primeval pleasures were fabulous, and was yet in doubt, whether life had anything that could be justly preferred to the placid gratifications of fields and woods. She hoped that the time would come, when, with a few virtuous and elegant companions, she should gather flowers planted by her own hand, fondle the lambs of her own ewe, and listen without care, among brooks and breezes, to one of her maidens reading in the shade.

CHAPTER XX

THE DANGER OF PROSPERITY

On the next day they continued their journey, till the heat compelled them to look round for shelter. At a small distance they saw a thick wood, which they no sooner entered than they perceived that they were approaching the habitations of men. The shrubs were diligently cut away, to open walks where the shades were darkest; the boughs of opposite trees were artificially interwoven; seats of flowery turf were raised in vacant spaces; and a rivulet, that wantoned along the side of a winding path, had its banks sometimes opened into small basins, and its stream sometimes obstructed by little mounds of stone, heaped together to increase its murmurs.

They passed slowly through the wood, delighted with such unexpected accommodations, and entertained each other with conjecturing what or who he could be, that, in those rude and unfrequented regions, had leisure and art for such harmless luxury.

As they advanced, they heard the sound of music, and saw youths and virgins dancing in the grove; and going still further, beheld a stately palace built upon a hill, surrounded with woods. The laws of eastern hospitality allowed them to enter, and the master welcomed them like a man liberal and wealthy.

He was skilful enough in appearances soon to discern that they were no common guests, and spread his table with magnificence. The eloquence of Imlac caught his attention, and the lofty courtesy of the princess excited his respect. When they offered to depart, he entreated their stay, and was the next day still more unwilling to dismiss them than before. They were easily persuaded to stop, and civility grew up in time to freedom and confidence.

The prince now saw all the domestics cheerful, and all the face of nature smiling round the place, and could not forbear to hope that he should find here what he was seeking; but when he was congratulating the master upon his possessions, he answered with a sigh, "My condition has indeed the appearance of happiness, but appearances are delusive. My prosperity puts my life in danger; the Bassa of Egypt is my enemy, incensed only by my wealth and popularity. I have been hitherto protected against him by the princes of the country; but as the favour of the great is uncertain, I know not how soon my defenders may be persuaded to share the plunder with the Bassa. I have sent my treasures into a distant country, and, upon the first alarm, am prepared to follow them. Then will my enemies riot in my mansion, and enjoy the gardens which I have planted."

They all joined in lamenting his danger, and deprecating his exile; and the princess was so much disturbed with the tumult of grief and indignation, that she retired to her apartment.

They continued with their kind inviter a few days longer, and then went forward to find the hermit.

CHAPTER XXI

THE HAPPINESS OF SOLITUDE.   THE HERMIT'S HISTORY

THEY came on the third day, by the direction of the peasants, to the hermit's cell: it was a cavern in the side of a mountain, overshadowed with palm trees; at such a distance from the cataract, that nothing more was heard than a gentle uniform murmur, such as composed the mind to pensive meditation, especially when it was assisted by the wind whistling among the branches. The first rude essay of nature had been so much improved by human labour, that the cave contained several apartments appropriated to different uses, and often afforded lodging to travellers, whom darkness or tempests happened to overtake.

The hermit sat on a bench at the door, to enjoy the coolness of the evening.   On one side lay a book with pens and papers, on the other mechanical instruments of various kinds.   As they approached him unregarded, the princess observed that he had not the countenance of a man that had found, or could teach, the way to happiness.

They saluted him with great respect, which he repaid like a man not unaccustomed to the forms of courts.   "My children," said he, "if you have lost your way, you shall be willingly supplied with such conveniences for the night as this cavern will afford.   I have all that nature requires, and you will not expect delicacies in a hermit's cell."

They thanked him, and, entering, were pleased with the neatness and regularity of the place.   The hermit set flesh and wine before them, though he fed only upon fruits and water.   His discourse was cheerful without levity, and pious without enthusiasm.   He soon gained the esteem of his guests, and the princess repented of her hasty censure.

At last Imlac began thus: "I do not now wonder that your reputation is so far extended.   We have heard at Cairo of your wisdom, and came hither to implore your direction for this young man and maiden in the *choice of life*."

"To him that lives well," answered the hermit, "every form of life is good; nor can I give any other rule for choice, than to remove from all apparent evil."

"He will remove most certainly from evil," said the prince, "who shall devote himself to that solitude which you have recommended by your example."

"I have indeed lived fifteen years in solitude," said the hermit,
"but have no desire that my example should gain any imitators.
In my youth I professed arms, and was raised by degrees to the
highest military rank. I have traversed wide countries at the
head of my troops, and seen many battles and sieges. At last,
being disgusted by the preferments of a younger officer, and
feeling that my vigour was beginning to decay, I was resolved
to close my life in peace, having found the world full of snares,
discord, and misery. I had once escaped from the pursuit of
the enemy by the shelter of this cavern, and therefore chose it
for my final residence. I employed artificers to form it into
chambers, and stored it with all that I was likely to want.

"For some time after my retreat, I rejoiced like a tempest-
beaten sailor at his entrance into the harbour, being delighted
with the sudden change of the noise and hurry of war to stillness and repose. When the pleasure of novelty went away,
I employed my hours in examining the plants which grow in
the valley, and the minerals which I collected from the rocks.
But that inquiry is now grown tasteless and irksome. I have
been for some time unsettled and distracted: my mind is disturbed with a thousand perplexities of doubt and vanities of
imagination, which hourly prevail upon me, because I have no
opportunities of relaxation or diversion. I am sometimes
ashamed to think that I could not secure myself from vice, but
by retiring from the exercise of virtue, and begin to suspect
that I was rather impelled by resentment, than led by devotion,
into solitude. My fancy riots in scenes of folly, and I lament
that I have lost so much and have gained so little. In solitude,
if I escape the example of bad men, I want likewise the counsel
and conversation of the good. I have been long comparing
the evils with the advantages of society, and resolve to return
into the world to-morrow. The life of a solitary man will be
certainly miserable, but not certainly devout."

They heard his resolution with surprise, but after a short
pause offered to conduct him to Cairo. He dug up a considerable treasure which he had hid among the rocks, and accompanied them to the city, on which, as he approached it, he gazed
with rapture.

CHAPTER XXII

THE HAPPINESS OF A LIFE LED ACCORDING TO NATURE

RASSELAS went often to an assembly of learned men, who met at stated times to unbend their minds and compare their opinions. Their manners were somewhat coarse, but their conversation was instructive, and their disputations acute, though sometimes too violent, and often continued till neither controvertist remembered upon what question they began. Some faults were almost general among them: every one was desirous to dictate to the rest, and every one was pleased to hear the genius or knowledge of another depreciated.

In this assembly Rasselas was relating his interview with the hermit, and the wonder with which he heard him censure a course of life which he had so deliberately chosen, and so laudably followed. The sentiments of the hearers were various. Some were of opinion that the folly of his choice had been justly punished by condemnation to perpetual perseverance. One of the youngest among them, with great vehemence, pronounced him an hypocrite. Some talked of the right of society to the labour of individuals, and considered retirement as a desertion of duty. Others readily allowed that there was a time when the claims of the public were satisfied, and when a man might properly sequester himself, to review his life and purify his heart.

One, who appeared more affected with the narrative than the rest, thought it likely that the hermit would, in a few years, go back to his retreat, and perhaps, if shame did not restrain or death intercept him, return once more from his retreat into the world: "For the hope of happiness," said he, "is so strongly impressed, that the longest experience is not able to efface it. Of the present state, whatever it be, we feel, and are forced to confess, the misery; yet, when the same state is again at a distance, imagination paints it as desirable. But the time will surely come, when desire will be no longer our torment, and no man shall be wretched but by his own fault."

"This," said a philosopher, who had heard him with tokens of great impatience, "is the present condition of a wise man. The time is already come, when none are wretched but by their own fault. Nothing is more idle than to inquire after happiness, which nature has kindly placed within our reach. The way to be happy is to live according to nature, in obedience to that universal and unalterable law with which every heart is originally impressed; which is not written on it by precept, but engraven by destiny, not instilled by education, but infused at our nativity. He that lives according to nature will suffer nothing from the delusions of hope, or importunities of desire; he will receive and reject with equability of temper, and act or suffer as the reason of things shall alternately prescribe. Other men may amuse themselves with subtle definitions, or intricate ratiocinations. Let them learn to be wise by easier means: let them observe the hind of the forest, and the linnet of the grove; let them consider the life of animals, whose motions are regulated by instinct: they obey their guide, and are happy. Let us therefore, at length, cease to dispute, and learn to live; throw away the encumbrance of precepts, which they who utter them with so much pride and pomp do not understand, and carry with us this simple and intelligible maxim: that deviation from nature is deviation from happiness."

When he had spoken, he looked round him with a placid air, and enjoyed the consciousness of his own beneficence. "Sir," said the prince with great modesty, "as I, like all the rest of mankind, am desirous of felicity, my closest attention has been fixed upon your discourse; I doubt not the truth of a position which a man so learned has so confidently advanced. Let me only know what it is to live according to nature."

"When I find young men so humble and so docile," said the philosopher, "I can deny them no information which my studies have enabled me to afford. To live according to nature, is to act always with due regard to the fitness arising from the relations and qualities of causes and effects; to concur with the great and unchangeable scheme of universal felicity; to co-operate with the general disposition and tendency of the present system of things."

The prince soon found that this was one of the sages whom he should understand less as he heard him longer. He therefore bowed and was silent; and the philosopher, supposing him satisfied, and the rest vanquished, rose up, and departed with the air of a man that had co-operated with the present system.

CHAPTER XXIII

THE PRINCE AND HIS SISTER DIVIDE BETWEEN THEM THE WORK OF OBSERVATION

RASSELAS returned home full of reflections, doubtful how to direct his future steps. Of the way to happiness he found the learned and simple equally ignorant; but, as he was yet young, he flattered himself that he had time remaining for more experiments and further inquiries. He communicated to Imlac his observations and his doubts, but was answered by him with new doubts, and remarks that gave him no comfort. He therefore discoursed more frequently and freely with his sister, who had yet the same hope with himself, and always assisted him to give some reason why, though he had been hitherto frustrated, he might succeed at last.

"We have hitherto," said she, "known but little of the world: we have never yet been either great or mean. In our own country, though we had royalty, we had no power; and in this, we have not yet seen the private recesses of domestic peace. Imlac favours not our search, lest we should in time find him mistaken. We will divide the task between us: you shall try what is to be found in the splendour of courts, and I will range the shades of humbler life. Perhaps command and authority may be the supreme blessings, as they afford most opportunities of doing good; or, perhaps, what this world can give may be found in the modest habitations of middle fortune, too low for great designs, and too high for penury and distress."

CHAPTER XXIV

THE PRINCE EXAMINES THE HAPPINESS OF HIGH STATIONS

RASSELAS applauded the design, and appeared next day with a splendid retinue at the court of the Bassa. He was soon distinguished for his magnificence, and admitted, as a prince whose curiosity had brought him from distant countries, to an intimacy with the great officers, and frequent conversation with the Bassa himself.

He was at first inclined to believe, that the man must be pleased with his own condition whom all approached with reverence and heard with obedience, and who had the power to extend his edicts to a whole kingdom. "There can be no pleasure," said he, "equal to that of feeling at once the joy of thousands all made happy by wise administration. Yet since by the law of subordination this sublime delight can be in one nation but the lot of one, it is surely reasonable to think that there is some satisfaction more popular and accessible, and that millions can hardly be subjected to the will of a single man, only to fill his particular breast with incommunicable content."

These thoughts were often in his mind, and he found no solution of the difficulty. But as presents and civilities gained him more familiarity, he found that almost every man who stood high in employment hated all the rest, and was hated by them, and that their lives were a continual succession of plots and detections, stratagems and escapes, faction and treachery. Many of those who surrounded the Bassa were sent only to watch and report his conduct; every tongue was muttering censure, and every eye was searching for a fault.

At last the letters of revocation arrived, the Bassa was carried in chains to Constantinople, and his name was mentioned no more.

"What are we now to think of the prerogatives of power?" said Rasselas to his sister; "is it without any efficacy to good? or, is the subordinate degree only dangerous, and the supreme safe and glorious? Is the Sultan the only happy man in his dominions? or, is the Sultan himself subject to the torments of suspicion and the dread of enemies?"

In a short time the second Bassa was deposed; the Sultan that had advanced him was murdered by the Janizaries, and his successor had other views and different favourites.

CHAPTER XXV

THE PRINCESS PURSUES HER INQUIRY WITH MORE DILIGENCE THAN SUCCESS

THE princess, in the meantime, insinuated herself into many families; for there are few doors through which liberality, joined with good humour, cannot find its way. The daughters of many houses were airy and cheerful; but Nekayah had been too long accustomed to the conversation of Imlac and her brother to be much pleased with childish levity, and prattle which had no meaning. She found their thoughts narrow, their wishes low, and their merriment often artificial. Their pleasures, poor as they were, could not be preserved pure, but were embittered by petty competitions and worthless emulation. They were always jealous of the beauty of each other; of a quality to which solicitude can add nothing, and from which detraction can take nothing away. Many were in love with triflers like themselves, and many fancied that they were in love when in truth they were only idle. Their affection was seldom fixed on sense or virtue, and therefore seldom ended but in vexation. Their grief, however, like their joy, was transient; everything floated in their mind unconnected with the past or future, so that one desire easily gave way to another, as a second stone cast into the water effaces and confounds the circles of the first.

With these girls she played as with inoffensive animals, and found them proud of her countenance, and weary of her company.

But her purpose was to examine more deeply, and her affability easily persuaded the hearts that were swelling with sorrow to discharge their secrets in her ear; and those whom hope flattered, or prosperity delighted, often courted her to partake their pleasures.

The princess and her brother commonly met in the evening, in a private summer-house on the bank of the Nile, and related to each other the occurrences of the day. As they were sitting together, the princess cast her eyes upon the river that flowed before her. "Answer," said she, "great father of waters, thou that rollest thy floods through eighty nations, to the invocations of the daughter of the native king. Tell me if thou waterest, through all thy course, a single habitation from which thou dost not hear the murmurs of complaint?"

"You are, then," said Rasselas, "not more successful in private houses than I have been in courts." "I have, since the last partition of our provinces," said the princess, "enabled myself to enter familiarly into many families, where there was the fairest show of prosperity and peace, and know not one house that is not haunted by some fury that destroys their quiet.

"I did not seek ease among the poor, because I concluded that there it could not be found. But I saw many poor, whom I had supposed to live in affluence. Poverty has, in large cities, very different appearances: it is often concealed in splendour, and often in extravagance. It is the care of a very great part of mankind to conceal their indigence from the rest; they support themselves by temporary expedients, and every day is lost in contriving for the morrow.

"This, however, was an evil, which, though frequent, I saw with less pain, because I could relieve it. Yet some have refused my bounties; more offended with my quickness to detect their wants, than pleased with my readiness to succour them; and others, whose exigencies compelled them to admit my kindness, have never been able to forgive their benefactress. Many, however, have been sincerely grateful, without the ostentation of gratitude, or the hope of other favours."

CHAPTER XXVI

THE PRINCESS CONTINUES HER REMARKS UPON PRIVATE LIFE

NEKAYAH, perceiving her brother's attention fixed, proceeded in her narrative.

"In families, where there is or is not poverty, there is commonly discord: if a kingdom be, as Imlac tells us, a great family, a family likewise is a little kingdom, torn with factions and exposed to revolutions. An unpractised observer expects the love of parents and children to be constant and equal; but this kindness seldom continues beyond the years of infancy: in a short time the children become rivals to their parents; benefits are allayed by reproaches, and gratitude debased by envy.

"Parents and children seldom act in concert: each child endeavours to appropriate the esteem or fondness of the parents, and the parents, with yet less temptation, betray each other to their children; thus, some place their confidence in the father, and some in the mother, and by degrees the house is filled with artifices and feuds.

"The opinions of children and parents, of the young and the old, are naturally opposite, by the contrary effects of hope and despondence, of expectation and experience, without crime or folly on either side. The colours of life in youth and age appear different, as the face of nature in spring and winter. And how can children credit the assertions of parents, which their own eyes show them to be false?

"Few parents act in such a manner as much to enforce their

maxims by the credit of their lives. The old man trusts wholly to slow contrivance and gradual progression; the youth expects to force his way by genius, vigour, and precipitance. The old man pays regard to riches, and the youth reverences virtue. The old man deifies prudence; the youth commits himself to magnanimity and chance. The young man, who intends no ill, believes that none is intended, and therefore acts with openness and candour; but his father, having suffered the injuries of fraud, is impelled to suspect, and too often allured to practise it. Age looks with anger on the temerity of youth, and youth with contempt on the scrupulosity of age. Thus parents and children, for the greatest part, live on to love less and less; and, if those whom nature has thus closely united are the torments of each other, where shall we look for tenderness and consolation?"

"Surely," said the prince, "you must have been unfortunate in your choice of acquaintance: I am unwilling to believe, that the most tender of all relations is thus impeded in its effects by natural necessity."

"Domestic discord," answered she, "is not inevitably and fatally necessary; but yet it is not easily avoided. We seldom see that a whole family is virtuous; the good and evil cannot well agree; and the evil can yet less agree with one another; even the virtuous fall sometimes to variance, when their virtues are of different kinds, and tending to extremes. In general, those parents have most reverence who most deserve it; for he that lives well cannot be despised.

"Many other evils infest private life. Some are the slaves of servants whom they have trusted with their affairs. Some are kept in continual anxiety by the caprice of rich relations, whom they cannot please and dare not offend. Some husbands are imperious, and some wives perverse: and, as it is always more easy to do evil than good, though the wisdom or virtue of one can very rarely make many happy, the folly or vice of one may often make many miserable."

"If such be the general effect of marriage," said the prince, "I shall, for the future, think it dangerous to connect my interest with that of another, lest I should be unhappy by my partner's fault."

"I have met," said the princess, "with many who live single for that reason; but I never found that their prudence ought to raise envy. They dream away their time without friendship, without fondness, and are driven to rid themselves of the day, for which they have no use, by childish amusements or vicious delights. They act as beings under the constant sense of some known inferiority, that fills their minds with rancour and their tongues with censure. They are peevish at home, and malevolent abroad; and, as the outlaws of human nature, make it their business and their pleasure to disturb that society which debars them from its privileges. To live without feeling or exciting sympathy, to be fortunate without adding to the felicity of others, or afflicted without tasting the balm of pity, is a state more gloomy than solitude: it is not retreat, but exclusion from mankind. Marriage has many pains, but celibacy has no pleasures."

"What then is to be done?" said Rasselas; "the more we inquire, the less we can resolve. Surely he is most likely to please himself that has no other inclination or regard."

CHAPTER XXVII

DISQUISITION UPON GREATNESS

THE conversation had a short pause. The prince, having considered his sister's observations, told her, that she had surveyed life with prejudice, and supposed misery where she did not find it. "Your narrative," says he, "throws yet a darker gloom upon the prospects of futurity; the predictions of Imlac were but faint sketches of the evils painted by Nekayah. I have been lately convinced that quiet is not the daughter of grandeur or of power: that her presence is not to be bought by wealth, nor enforced by conquest. It is evident, that as any man acts in a wider compass, he must be more exposed to opposition from enmity, or miscarriage from chance; who-ever has many to please or to govern, must use the ministry of many agents, some of whom will be wicked, and some ignorant; by some he will be misled, and by others betrayed. If he gratifies one he will offend another; those that are not favoured will think themselves injured; and, since favours can be conferred but upon few, the greater number will be always discontented."

"The discontent," said the princess, "which is thus un-reasonable, I hope that I shall always have spirit to despise, and you power to repress."

"Discontent," answered Rasselas, "will not always be without reason, under the most just and vigilant administration of public affairs. None, however attentive, can always discover that merit which indigence or faction may happen to obscure; and none, however powerful, can always reward it. Yet he that sees inferior desert advanced above him will naturally impute that preference to partiality or caprice; and, indeed, it can scarcely be hoped that any man, however magnanimous by nature, or exalted by condition, will be able to persist for ever in the fixed and inexorable justice of distribution: he will sometimes indulge his own affections, and sometimes those of his favourites; he will permit some to please him who can never serve him; he will discover in those whom he loves, qualities which in reality they do not possess; and to those from whom he receives pleasure, he will in his turn endeavour to give it. Thus will recommendations sometimes prevail which were purchased by money, or by the more destructive bribery of flattery and servility.

"He that has much to do will do something wrong, and of that wrong must suffer the consequences; and, if it were possible that he should always act rightly, yet when such numbers are to judge of his conduct, the bad will censure and obstruct him by malevolence, and the good sometimes by mistake.

"The highest stations cannot therefore hope to be the abodes of happiness, which I would willingly believe to have fled from thrones and palaces to seats of humble privacy and placid obscurity. For what can hinder the satisfaction, or intercept the expectations, of him whose abilities are adequate to his employments, who sees with his own eyes the whole circuit of his influence, who chooses by his own knowledge all whom he trusts, and whom none are tempted to deceive by hope or fear? Surely he has nothing to do but to love and to be loved, to be virtuous and to be happy."

"Whether perfect happiness would be procured by perfect goodness," said Nekayah, "this world will never afford an opportunity of deciding. But this, at least, may be maintained, that we do not always find visible happiness in proportion to visible virtue. All natural and almost all political evils are incident alike to the bad and good: they are confounded in the misery of a famine, and not much distinguished in the fury of a faction; they sink together in a tempest, and are driven together from their country by invaders. All that virtue can afford is quietness of conscience and a steady prospect of a happier state; this may enable us to endure calamity with patience; but remember that patience must suppose pain."

CHAPTER XXVIII

RASSELAS AND NEKAYAH CONTINUE THEIR CONVERSATION

"DEAR princess," said Rasselas, "you fall into the common errors of exaggeratory declamation, by producing, in a familiar disquisition, examples of national calamities, and scenes of extensive misery, which are found in books rather than in the world, and which, as they are horrid, are ordained to be rare. Let us not imagine evils which we do not feel, nor injure life by misrepresentations. I cannot bear that querulous eloquence which threatens every city with a siege like that of Jerusalem, that makes famine attend on every flight of locusts, and suspends pestilence on the wing of every blast that issues from the south.

"On necessary and inevitable evils which overwhelm kingdoms at once, all disputation is vain: when they happen they must be endured. But it is evident, that these bursts of universal distress are more dreaded than felt; thousands and ten thousands flourish in youth and wither in age, without the knowledge of any other than domestic evils, and share the same pleasures and vexations, whether their kings are mild or cruel, whether the armies of their country pursue their enemies or retreat before them. While courts are disturbed with intestine competitions, and ambassadors are negotiating in foreign countries, the smith still plies his anvil, and the husband-man drives his plough forward; the necessaries of life are required and obtained; and the successive business of the seasons continues to make its wonted revolutions.

"Let us cease to consider what, perhaps, may never happen, and what, when it shall happen, will laugh at human speculation. We will not endeavour to modify the motions of the elements, or to fix the destiny of kingdoms. It is our business to consider what beings like us may perform; each labouring for his own happiness, by promoting within his circle, however narrow, the happiness of others.

"Marriage is evidently the dictate of nature; men and women are made to be companions of each other; and therefore I cannot be persuaded but that marriage is one of the means of happiness."

"I know not," said the princess, "whether marriage be more than one of the innumerable modes of human misery. When I see and reckon the various forms of connubial infelicity, the unexpected causes of lasting discord, the diversities of temper, the oppositions of opinion, the rude collisions of contrary desire where both are urged by violent impulses, the obstinate contests of disagreeing virtues where both are supported by consciousness of good intention, I am sometimes disposed to think with the severer casuists of most nations, that marriage is rather permitted than approved, and that none, but by the instigation of a passion too much indulged, entangle themselves with indissoluble compacts."

"You seem to forget," replied Rasselas, "that you have, even now, represented celibacy as less happy than marriage. Both conditions may be bad, but they cannot both be worst. Thus it happens when wrong opinions are entertained, that they mutually destroy each other, and leave the mind open to truth."

"I did not expect," answered the princess, "to hear that imputed to falsehood which is the consequence only of frailty. To the mind, as to the eye, it is difficult to compare with exactness objects vast in their extent, and various in their parts. Where we see or conceive the whole at once, we readily note the discriminations, and decide the preference; but of two systems, of which neither can be surveyed by any human being in its full compass of magnitude and multiplicity of complication, where is the wonder that, judging of the whole by parts, I am alternately affected by one and the other, as either presses on my memory or fancy? We differ from ourselves, just as we differ from each other, when we see only part of the question, as in the multifarious relations of politics and morality; but when we perceive the whole at once, as in numerical computations, all agree in one judgment, and none ever varies his opinion."

"Let us not add," said the prince, "to the other evils of life the bitterness of controversy, nor endeavour to vie with each other in subtleties of argument. We are employed in a search, of which both are equally to enjoy the success, or suffer by the miscarriage. It is therefore fit that we assist each other. You surely conclude too hastily from the infelicity of marriage against its institution: will not the misery of life prove equally that life cannot be the gift of heaven? The world must be peopled by marriage, or peopled without it."

"How the world is to be peopled," returned Nekayah, "is not my care, and needs not be yours. I see no danger that the present generation should omit to leave successors behind them: we are not now inquiring for the world, but for ourselves."

CHAPTER XXIX

THE DEBATE OF MARRIAGE CONTINUED

"The good of the whole," said Rasselas, "is the same with the good of all its parts. If marriage be best for mankind, it must be evidently best for individuals; or a permanent and necessary duty must be the cause of evil, and some must be inevitably sacrificed to the convenience of others. In the estimate which you have made of the two states, it appears that the incommodities of a single life are, in a great measure, necessary and certain, but those of the conjugal state accidental and avoidable.

"I cannot forbear to flatter myself, that prudence and benevolence will make marriage happy. The general folly of mankind is the cause of general complaint. What can be expected but disappointment and repentance from a choice made in the immaturity of youth, in the ardour of desire, without judgment, without foresight, without inquiry after conformity of opinions, similarity of manners, rectitude of judgment, or purity of sentiment?

"Such is the common process of marriage. A youth and maiden, meeting by chance or brought together by artifice, exchange glances, reciprocate civilities, go home, and dream of one another. Having little to divert attention, or diversify thought, they find themselves uneasy when they are apart, and therefore conclude that they shall be happy together. They marry, and discover what nothing but voluntary blindness before had concealed: they wear out life in altercations, and charge nature with cruelty.

"From those early marriages proceeds likewise the rivalry of parents and children. The son is eager to enjoy the world before the father is willing to forsake it, and there is hardly room at once for two generations. The daughter begins to bloom before the mother can be content to fade, and neither can forbear to wish for the absence of the other.

"Surely all these evils may be avoided by that deliberation and delay which prudence prescribes to irrevocable choice. In the variety and jollity of youthful pleasures, life may be well enough supported without the help of a partner. Longer time will increase experience, and wider views will allow better opportunities of inquiry and selection: one advantage, at least, will be certain; the parents will be visibly older than their children."

"What reason cannot collect," said Nekayah, "and what experiment has not yet taught, can be known only from the report of others. I have been told that late marriages are not eminently happy. This is a question too important to be neglected, and I have often proposed it to those whose accuracy of remark, and comprehensiveness of knowledge, made their suffrages worthy of regard. They have generally determined that it is dangerous for a man and woman to suspend their fate upon each other, at a time when opinions are fixed, and habits are established; when friendships have been contracted on both sides; when life has been planned into method, and the mind has long enjoyed the contemplation of its own prospects.

"It is scarcely possible that two, travelling through the world under the conduct of chance, should have been both directed to the same path, and it will not often happen that either will quit the track which custom has made pleasing. When the desultory levity of youth has settled into regularity, it is soon succeeded by pride ashamed to yield, or obstinacy delighting to contend. And even though mutual esteem produces mutual desire to please, time itself, as it modifies unchangeably the external mien, determines likewise the direction of the passions, and gives an inflexible rigidity to the manners. Long customs are not easily broken: he that attempts to change the course of his own life very often labours in vain: and how shall we do that for others, which we are seldom able to do for ourselves?"

"But surely," interposed the prince, "you suppose the chief motive of choice forgotten or neglected. Whenever I shall seek a wife, it shall be my first question, whether she be willing to be led by reason."

"Thus it is," said Nekayah, "that philosophers are deceived. There are a thousand familiar disputes which reason never can decide; questions that elude investigation, and make logic ridiculous; cases where something must be done, and where little can be said. Consider the state of mankind, and inquire how few can be supposed to act upon any occasions, whether small or great, with all the reasons of action present to their minds. Wretched would be the pair above all names of wretchedness, who should be doomed to adjust by reason, every morning, all the minute detail of a domestic day.

"Those who marry at an advanced age will probably escape

the encroachments of their children; but, in diminution of this advantage, they will be likely to leave them, ignorant and helpless, to a guardian's mercy; or, if that should not happen, they must at least go out of the world before they see those whom they love best either wise or great.

"From their children, if they have less to fear, they have less also to hope, and they lose, without equivalent, the joys of early love, and the convenience of uniting with manners pliant, and minds susceptible of new impressions, which might wear away their dissimilitudes by long cohabitation, as soft bodies, by continual attrition, conform their surfaces to each other.

"I believe it will be found that those who marry late are best pleased with their children, and those who marry early, with their partners."

"The union of these two affections," said Rasselas, "would produce all that could be wished. Perhaps there is a time when marriage might unite them, a time neither too early for the father, nor too late for the husband."

"Every hour," answered the princess, "confirms my prejudice in favour of the position so often uttered by the mouth of Imlac, 'That nature sets her gifts on the right hand and on the left.' Those conditions which flatter hope and attract desire are so constituted that, as we approach one, we recede from another. There are goods so opposed that we cannot seize both, but, by too much prudence, may pass between them at too great a distance to reach either. This is often the fate of long consideration: he does nothing who endeavours to do more than is allowed to humanity. Flatter not yourself with contrarieties of pleasure. Of the blessings set before you, make your choice, and be content. No man can taste the fruits of autumn while he is delighting his scent with the flowers of the spring: no man can, at the same time, fill his cup from the source and from the mouth of the Nile."

CHAPTER XXX

IMLAC ENTERS AND CHANGES THE CONVERSATION

HERE Imlac entered, and interrupted them. "Imlac," said Rasselas, "I have been taking from the princess the dismal history of private life, and am almost discouraged from further search."

"It seems to me," said Imlac, "that while you are making the choice of life, you neglect to live. You wander about a single city, which, however large and diversified, can now afford few novelties, and forget that you are in a country, famous among the earliest monarchies for the power and wisdom of its inhabitants; a country where the sciences first dawned that illuminate the world, and beyond which the arts cannot be traced of civil society or domestic life.

"The old Egyptians have left behind them monuments of industry and power, before which all European magnificence is confessed to fade away. The ruins of their architecture are the schools of modern builders, and from the wonders which time has spared, we may conjecture, though uncertainly, what it has destroyed."

"My curiosity," said Rasselas, "does not very strongly lead me to survey piles of stone, or mounds of earth; my business is with man. I came hither not to measure fragments of temples, or trace choked aqueducts, but to look upon the various scenes of the present world."

"The things that are now before us," said the princess, "require attention, and deserve it. What have I to do with the heroes or the monuments of ancient times? with times which never can return, and heroes whose form of life was different from all that the present condition of mankind requires or allows?"

"To know anything," returned the poet, "we must know its effects; to see men we must see their works, that we may learn what reason has dictated, or passion has incited, and find what are the most powerful motives of action. To judge rightly on the present, we must oppose it to the past; for all judgment is comparative, and of the future nothing can be known. The truth is, that no mind is much employed upon the present; recollection and anticipation fill up almost all our moments. Our passions are joy and grief, love and hatred, hope and fear. Of joy and grief the past is the object, and the future of hope and fear: even love and hatred respect the past, for the cause must have been before the effect.

"The present state of things is the consequence of the former, and it is natural to inquire what were the sources of the good that we enjoy, or the evil that we suffer. If we act only for ourselves, to neglect the study of history is not prudent; if we are entrusted with the care of others, it is not just. Ignorance, when it is voluntary, is criminal; and he may properly be charged with evil, who refused to learn how he might prevent it.

"There is no part of history so generally useful as that which relates the progress of the human mind, the gradual improvement of reason, the successive advances of science, the vicissitudes of learning and ignorance, which are the light and darkness of thinking beings, the extinction and resuscitation of arts, and the revolutions of the intellectual world. If accounts of battles and invasions are peculiarly the business of princes, the useful or elegant arts are not to be neglected; those who have kingdoms to govern have understandings to cultivate.

"Example is always more efficacious than precept. A soldier is formed in war, and a painter must copy pictures. In this, contemplative life has the advantage: great actions are seldom seen, but the labours of art are always at hand for those who desire to know what art has been able to perform.

"When the eye or the imagination is struck with any uncommon work, the next transition of an active mind is to the means by which it was performed. Here begins the true use of such contemplation; we enlarge our comprehension by new ideas, and perhaps recover some art lost to mankind, or learn what is less perfectly known in our own country. At least we compare our own with former times, and either rejoice at our improvements, or, what is the first motion towards good, discover our defects."

"I am willing," said the prince, "to see all that can deserve my search." "And I," said the princess, "shall rejoice to learn something of the manners of antiquity."

"The most pompous monument of Egyptian greatness, and one of the most bulky works of manual industry," said Imlac, "are the Pyramids; fabrics raised before the time of history, and of which the earliest narratives afford us only uncertain traditions. Of these the greatest is still standing, very little injured by time."

"Let us visit them to-morrow," said Nekayah. "I have often heard of the Pyramids, and shall not rest till I have seen them within and without with my own eyes."

CHAPTER XXXI

THEY VISIT THE PYRAMIDS

THE resolution being thus taken, they set out the next day. They laid tents upon their camels, being resolved to stay among the Pyramids till their curiosity was fully satisfied. They travelled gently, turned aside to everything remarkable, stopped from time to time and conversed with the inhabitants, and observed the various appearances of towns ruined and inhabited, of wild and cultivated nature.

When they came to the Great Pyramid, they were astonished at the extent of the base and the height of the top. Imlac explained to them the principles upon which the pyramidal form was chosen for a fabrick intended to co-extend its duration with that of the world: he showed that its gradual diminution gave it such stability as defeated all the common attacks of the elements, and could scarcely be overthrown by earthquakes themselves, the least resistible of natural violence. A concussion that should shatter the Pyramid would threaten the dissolution of the continent.

They measured all its dimensions, and pitched their tents at its foot. Next day they prepared to enter its exterior apartments, and having hired the common guides, climbed up to the first passage, when the favourite of the princess, looking into the cavity, stepped back and trembled. "Pekuah," said the princess, "of what art thou afraid?" "Of the narrow entrance," answered the lady, "and of the dreadful gloom. I dare not enter a place which must surely be inhabited by unquiet souls. The original possessors of these dreadful vaults will start up before us, and perhaps shut us in for ever." She spoke, and threw her arms round the neck of her mistress.

"If all your fear be of apparitions," said the prince, "I will promise you safety: there is no danger from the dead: he that is once buried will be seen no more."

"That the dead are seen no more," said Imlac, "I will not undertake to maintain, against the concurrent and unvaried testimony of all ages, and of all nations. There is no people, rude or learned, among whom apparitions of the dead are not related and believed. This opinion, which perhaps prevails as far as human nature is diffused, could become universal only by its truth: those that never heard of one another would not have agreed in a tale which nothing but experience can make credible. That it is doubted by single cavillers, can very little weaken the general evidence; and some who deny it with their tongues confess it by their fears.

"Yet I do not mean to add new terrors to those which have already seized upon Pekuah. There can be no reason why spectres should haunt the Pyramid more than other places, or why they should have power or will to hurt innocence and purity. Our entrance is no violation of their privileges; we can take nothing from them, how then can we offend them?"

"My dear Pekuah," said the princess, "I will always go before you, and Imlac shall follow you. Remember that you are the companion of the Princess of Abyssinia."

"If the princess is pleased that her servant should die," returned the lady, "let her command some death less dreadful than enclosure in this horrid cavern. You know I dare not disobey you: I must go if you command me; but, if I once enter, I never shall come back."

The princess saw that her fear was too strong for expostulation or reproof, and embracing her, told her that she should stay in the tent till their return. Pekuah was yet not satisfied, but entreated the princess not to pursue so dreadful a purpose as that of entering the recesses of the Pyramid. "Though I cannot teach courage," said Nekayah, "I must not learn cowardice; nor leave at last undone what I came hither only to do."

CHAPTER XXXII

THEY ENTER THE PYRAMID

PEKUAH descended to the tents, and the rest entered the Pyramid: they passed through the galleries, surveyed the vaults of marble, and examined the chest in which the body of the founder is supposed to have been reposited. They then sat down in one of the most spacious chambers to rest awhile before they attempted to return.

"We have now," said Imlac, "gratified our minds with an exact view of the greatest work of man, except the wall of China.

"Of the wall it is very easy to assign the motive. It secured a wealthy and timorous nation from the incursions of barbarians, whose unskilfulness in arts made it easier for them to supply their wants by rapine than by industry, and who from time to time poured in upon the habitations of peaceful commerce, as vultures descend upon domestic fowl. Their celerity and fierceness made the wall necessary, and their ignorance made it efficacious.

"But for the Pyramids no reason has ever been given adequate to the cost and labour of the work. The narrowness of the chambers proves that it could afford no retreat from enemies, and treasures might have been reposited at far less expense with equal security. It seems to have been erected only in compliance with that hunger of imagination which preys incessantly upon life, and must be always appeased by some employment. Those who have already all that they can enjoy must enlarge their desires. He that has built for use, till use is supplied, must begin to build for vanity, and extend his plan to the utmost power of human performance, that he may not be soon reduced to form another wish.

"I consider this mighty structure as a monument of the insufficiency of human enjoyments. A king whose power is unlimited, and whose treasures surmount all real and imaginary wants, is compelled to solace, by the erection of a Pyramid, the satiety of dominion and tastelessness of pleasures, and to amuse the tediousness of declining life, by seeing thousands labouring without end, and one stone, for no purpose, laid upon another. Whoever thou art that, not content with a moderate condition, imaginest happiness in royal magnificence, and dreamest that command or riches can feed the appetite of novelty with perpetual gratifications, survey the Pyramids, and confess thy folly!"

CHAPTER XXXIII

THE PRINCESS MEETS WITH AN UNEXPECTED MISFORTUNE

THEY rose up, and returned through the cavity at which they had entered, and the princess prepared for her favourite a long narrative of dark labyrinths and costly rooms, and of the different impressions which the varieties of the way had made upon her. But when they came to their train, they found every one silent and dejected; the men discovered shame and fear in their countenances, and the women were weeping in the tents.

What had happened they did not try to conjecture, but immediately inquired. "You had scarcely entered into the Pyramid," said one of the attendants, "when a troop of Arabs rushed upon us; we were too few to resist them, and too slow to escape. They were about to search the tents, set us on our camels, and drive us along before them, when the approach of some Turkish horsemen put them to flight; but they seized the Lady Pekuah with her two maids, and carried them away. The Turks are now pursuing them by our instigation, but I fear they will not be able to overtake them."

The princess was overpowered with surprise and grief. Rasselas, in the first heat of his resentment, ordered his servants to follow him, and prepared to pursue the robbers with his sabre in his hand. "Sir," said Imlac, "what can you hope from violence or valour? the Arabs are mounted on horses trained to battle and retreat; we have only beasts of burden. By leaving our present station we may lose the princess, but cannot hope to regain Pekuah."

In a short time the Turks returned, having not been able to reach the enemy. The princess burst out into new lamentations, and Rasselas could scarcely forbear to reproach them with cowardice; but Imlac was of opinion that the escape of the Arabs was no addition to their misfortune, for perhaps they would have killed their captives rather than have resigned them.

CHAPTER XXXIV

THEY RETURN TO CAIRO WITHOUT PEKUAH

THERE was nothing to be hoped from longer stay. They returned to Cairo, repenting of their curiosity, censuring the negligence of the government, lamenting their own rashness which had neglected to procure a guard, imagining many expedients by which the loss of Pekuah might have been prevented, and resolving to do something for her recovery, though none could find anything proper to be done.

Nekayah retired to her chamber, where her women attempted to comfort her by telling her that all had their troubles, and that Lady Pekuah had enjoyed much happiness in the world for a long time, and might reasonably expect a change of fortune.

They hoped that some good would befall her wheresoever she was, and that their mistress would find another friend who might supply her place.

The princess made them no answer, and they continued the form of condolence, not much grieved in their hearts that the favourite was lost.

Next day the prince presented to the Bassa a memorial of the wrong which he had suffered, and a petition for redress. The Bassa threatened to punish the robbers, but did not attempt to catch them; nor indeed could any account or description be given by which he might direct the pursuit.

It soon appeared that nothing would be done by authority. Governors, being accustomed to hear of more crimes than they can punish, and more wrongs than they can redress, set themselves at ease by indiscriminate negligence, and presently forget the request when they lose sight of the petitioner.

Imlac then endeavoured to gain some intelligence by private agents. He found many who pretended to an exact knowledge of all the haunts of the Arabs, and to regular correspondence with their chiefs, and who readily undertook the recovery of Pekuah. Of these, some were furnished with money for their journey, and came back no more; some were liberally paid for accounts which a few days discovered to be false. But the princess would not suffer any means, however improbable, to be left untried. While she was doing something, she kept her hope alive. As one expedient failed, another was suggested; when one messenger returned unsuccessful, another was dispatched to a different quarter.

Two months had now passed, and of Pekuah nothing had been heard; the hopes which they had endeavoured to raise in each other grew more languid, and the princess, when she saw nothing more to be tried, sunk down inconsolable in hopeless dejection. A thousand times she reproached herself with the easy compliance by which she permitted her favourite to stay behind her. "Had not my fondness," said she, "lessened my authority, Pekuah had not dared to talk of her terrors. She ought to have feared me more than spectres. A severe look would have overpowered her; a peremptory command would have compelled obedience. Why did foolish indulgence prevail upon me? Why did I not speak, and refuse to hear?"

"Great princess," said Imlac, "do not reproach yourself for your virtue, or consider that as blameable by which evil has accidentally been caused. Your tenderness for the timidity of Pekuah was generous and kind. When we act according to our duty, we commit the event to Him by whose laws our actions are governed, and who will suffer none to be finally punished for obedience. When, in prospect of some good, whether natural or moral, we break the rules prescribed us, we withdraw from the direction of superior wisdom, and take all consequences upon ourselves. Man cannot so far know the connexion of causes and events, as that he may venture to do wrong in order to do right. When we pursue our end by lawful means, we may always console our miscarriage by the hope of future recompense. When we consult only our own policy, and attempt to find a nearer way to good, by overleaping the settled boundaries of right and wrong, we cannot be happy even by success, because we cannot escape the consciousness of our fault: but if we miscarry, the disappointment is irremediably embittered. How comfortless is the sorrow of him who feels at once the pangs of guilt, and the vexation of calamity which guilt has brought upon him!

"Consider, princess, what would have been your condition, if the Lady Pekuah had entreated to accompany you, and being compelled to stay in the tents, had been carried away; or how would you have borne the thought, if you had forced her into the pyramid, and she had died before you in agonies of terror."

"Had either happened," said Nekayah, "I could not have endured life till now: I should have been tortured to madness by the remembrance of such cruelty, or must have pined away in abhorrence of myself."

"This at least," said Imlac, "is the present reward of virtuous conduct, that no unlucky consequence can oblige us to repent it."

CHAPTER XXXV

THE PRINCESS LANGUISHES FOR WANT OF PEKUAH

NEKAYAH, being thus reconciled to herself, found that no evil is insupportable, but that which is accompanied with consciousness of wrong. She was from that time delivered from the violence of tempestuous sorrow, and sunk into silent pensiveness and gloomy tranquillity. She sat from morning to evening recollecting all that had been done or said by her Pekuah, treasured up with care every trifle on which Pekuah had set an accidental value, and which might recall to mind any little incident or careless conversation. The sentiments of her whom she now expected to see no more, were treasured in her memory as rules of life, and she deliberated to no other end than to conjecture, on any occasion, what would have been the opinion and counsel of Pekuah.

The women by whom she was attended knew nothing of her real condition, and therefore she could not talk to them but with caution and reserve. She began to remit her curiosity, having no great care to collect notions which she had no convenience of uttering. Rasselas endeavoured first to comfort, and afterwards to divert her; he hired musicians, to whom she seemed to listen, but did not hear them, and procured masters to instruct her in various arts, whose lectures, when they visited her again, were again to be repeated. She had lost her taste of pleasure, and her ambition of excellence. And her mind, though forced into short excursions, always recurred to the image of her friend.

Imlac was every morning earnestly enjoined to renew his inquiries, and was asked every night whether he had yet heard of Pekuah, till not being able to return the princess the answer that she desired, he was less and less willing to come into her presence. She observed his backwardness, and commanded him to attend her. "You are not," said she, "to confound impatience with resentment, or to suppose that I charge you with negligence, because I repine at your unsuccessfulness. I do not much wonder at your absence; I know that the unhappy are never pleasing, and that all naturally avoid the contagion of misery. To hear complaints is wearisome alike to the wretched and the happy; for who would cloud, by adventitious grief, the short gleams of gaiety which life allows us? or who, that is struggling under his own evils, will add to them the miseries of another?

"The time is at hand, when none shall be disturbed any longer by the sighs of Nekayah; my search after happiness is now at an end. I am resolved to retire from the world with all its flatteries and deceits, and will hide myself in solitude, without any other care than to compose my thoughts, and regulate my hours by a constant succession of innocent occupations, till with a mind purified from all earthly desires, I shall enter into that state to which all are hastening, and in which I hope again to enjoy the friendship of Pekuah."

"Do not entangle your mind," said Imlac, "by irrevocable

determinations, nor increase the burden of life by a voluntary accumulation of misery: the weariness of retirement will continue or increase when the loss of Pekuah is forgotten. That you have been deprived of one pleasure is no very good reason for rejection of the rest."

"Since Pekuah was taken from me," said the princess, "I have no pleasure to reject or to retain. She that has no one to love or trust has little to hope. She wants the radical principle of happiness. We may, perhaps, allow that what satisfaction this world can afford must arise from the conjunction of wealth, knowledge, and goodness: wealth is nothing but as it is bestowed, and knowledge nothing but as it is communicated; they must therefore be imparted to others, and to whom could I now delight to impart them? Goodness affords the only comfort which can be enjoyed without a partner, and goodness may be practised in retirement."

"How far solitude may admit goodness or advance it, I shall not," replied Imlac, "dispute at present. Remember the confession of the pious hermit. You will wish to return into the world, when the image of your companion has left your thoughts." "That time," said Nekayah, "will never come. The generous frankness, the modest obsequiousness, and the faithful secrecy of my dear Pekuah, will always be more missed, as I shall live longer to see vice and folly."

"The state of a mind oppressed with a sudden calamity," said Imlac, "is like that of the fabulous inhabitants of the new-created earth, who, when the first night came upon them, supposed that day would never return. When the clouds of sorrow gather over us, we see nothing beyond them, nor can imagine how they will be dispelled; yet a new day succeeded to the night, and sorrow is never long without a dawn of ease. But they who restrain themselves from receiving comfort do as the savages would have done, had they put out their eyes when it was dark. Our minds, like our bodies, are in continual flux; something is hourly lost, and something acquired. To lose much at once is inconvenient to either, but while the vital powers remain uninjured, nature will find the means of reparation. Distance has the same effect on the mind as on the eye, and while we glide along the stream of time, whatever we leave behind us is always lessening, and that which we approach increasing, in magnitude. Do not suffer life to stagnate; it will grow muddy for want of motion; commit yourself again to the current of the world; Pekuah will vanish by degrees: you will meet in your way some other favourite, or learn to diffuse yourself in general conversation."

"At least," said the prince, "do not despair before all remedies have been tried; the inquiry after the unfortunate lady is still continued, and shall be carried on with yet greater diligence, on condition that you will promise to wait a year for the event, without any unalterable resolution."

Nekayah thought this a reasonable demand, and made the promise to her brother, who had been advised by Imlac to require it. Imlac had, indeed, no great hope of regaining Pekuah; but he supposed, that if he could secure the interval of a year, the princess would be then in no danger of a cloister.

CHAPTER XXXVI

PEKUAH IS STILL REMEMBERED. THE PROGRESS OF SORROW

NEKAYAH, seeing that nothing was omitted for the recovery of her favourite, and having, by her promise, set her intention of retirement at a distance, began imperceptibly to return to common cares and common pleasures. She rejoiced without her own consent at the suspension of her sorrows, and sometimes caught herself with indignation in the act of turning away her mind from the remembrance of her, whom yet she resolved never to forget.

She then appointed a certain hour of the day for meditation on the merits and fondness of Pekuah, and for some weeks retired constantly at the time fixed, and returned with her eyes swollen and her countenance clouded. By degrees she grew less scrupulous, and suffered any important and pressing avocation to delay the tribute of daily tears. She then yielded to less occasions; sometimes forgot what she was indeed afraid to remember, and at last wholly released herself from the duty of periodical affliction.

Her real love of Pekuah was yet not diminished. A thousand occurrences brought her back to memory, and a thousand wants, which nothing but the confidence of friendship can supply, made her frequently regretted. She therefore solicited Imlac never to desist from inquiry, and to leave no art of intelligence untried, that at least she might have the comfort of knowing that she did not suffer by negligence or sluggishness. "Yet what," said she, "is to be expected from our pursuit of happiness, when we find the state of life to be such, that happiness itself is the cause of misery? Why should we endeavour to attain that of which the possession cannot be secured? I shall henceforward fear to yield my heart to excellence however bright, or to fondness however tender, lest I should lose again what I have lost in Pekuah."

CHAPTER XXXVII

THE PRINCESS HEARS NEWS OF PEKUAH

IN seven months, one of the messengers, who had been sent away upon the day when the promise was drawn from the princess, returned, after many unsuccessful rambles, from the borders of Nubia, with an account that Pekuah was in the hands of an Arab chief, who possessed a castle or fortress on the extremity of Egypt. The Arab, whose revenue was plunder, was willing to restore her, with her two attendants, for two hundred ounces of gold.

The price was no subject of debate. The princess was in ecstasies, when she heard that her favourite was alive, and might so cheaply be ransomed. She could not think of delaying for a moment Pekuah's happiness or her own, but entreated her brother to send back the messenger with the sum required. Imlac, being consulted, was not very confident of the veracity of the relater, and was still more doubtful of the Arab's faith, who might, if he were too liberally trusted, detain at once the money and the captives. He thought it dangerous to put themselves in the power of the Arab, by going into his district, and could not expect that the rover would so much expose himself as to come into the lower country, where he might be seized by the forces of the Bassa.

It is difficult to negotiate where neither will trust. But Imlac, after some deliberation, directed the messenger to propose that Pekuah should be conducted by ten horsemen to the monastery of St. Antony, which is situated in the deserts of Upper Egypt, where she should be met by the same number, and her ransom should be paid.

That no time might be lost, as they expected that the proposal would not be refused, they immediately began their journey to the monastery; and when they arrived, Imlac went forward with the former messenger to the Arab's fortress. Rasselas was desirous to go with them, but neither his sister nor Imlac would consent. The Arab, according to the custom of his nation, observed the laws of hospitality with great exactness to those who put themselves into his power, and, in a few days, brought Pekuah with her maids, by easy journeys, to their place appointed, where, receiving the stipulated price, he restored her with great respect to liberty and her friends, and undertook to conduct them back towards Cairo, beyond all danger of robbery or violence.

The princess and her favourite embraced each other with transport too violent to be expressed, and went out together to pour the tears of tenderness in secret, and exchange professions of kindness and gratitude. After a few hours they returned into the refectory of the convent, where, in the presence of the prior and his brethren, the prince required of Pekuah the history of her adventures.

CHAPTER XXXVIII

THE ADVENTURES OF THE LADY PEKUAH

"At what time and in what manner I was forced away," said Pekuah, "your servants have told you. The suddenness of the event struck me with surprise, and I was at first rather stupefied than agitated with any passion of either fear or sorrow. My confusion was increased by the speed and tumult of our flight, while we were followed by the Turks, who, as it seemed, soon despaired to overtake us, or were afraid of those whom they made a show of menacing.

"When the Arabs saw themselves out of danger, they slackened their course; and as I was less harassed by external violence, I began to feel more uneasiness in my mind. After some time, we stopped near a spring shaded with trees in a pleasant meadow, where we were set upon the ground, and offered such refreshments as our masters were partaking. I was suffered to sit with my maids apart from the rest, and none attempted to comfort or insult us. Here I first began to feel the full weight of my misery. The girls sat weeping in silence, and from time to time looked on me for succour. I knew not to what condition we were doomed, nor could conjecture where would be the place of our captivity, or whence to draw any hope of deliverance. I was in the hands of robbers and savages, and had no reason to suppose that their pity was more than their justice, or that they would forbear the gratification of any ardour of desire, or caprice of cruelty. I, however, kissed my maids, and endeavoured to pacify them by remarking that we were yet treated with decency, and that, since we were now carried beyond pursuit, there was no danger of violence to our lives.

"When we were to be set again on horseback, my maids clung round me, and refused to be parted; but I commanded them not to irritate those who had us in their power. We travelled the remaining part of the day through an unfrequented and pathless country, and came by moonlight to the side of a hill, where the rest of the troop were stationed. Their tents were pitched and their fires kindled, and our chief was welcomed as a man much beloved by his dependants.

"We were received into a large tent, where we found women who had attended their husbands in the expedition. They set before us the supper which they had provided, and I ate rather to encourage my maids, than to comply with any appetite of my own. When the meat was taken away, they spread the carpets for repose. I was weary, and hoped to find in sleep that remission of distress which nature seldom denies. Ordering myself therefore to be undressed, I observed that the women looked very earnestly upon me, not expecting, I suppose, to see me so submissively attended. When my upper vest was taken off, they were apparently struck with the splendour of my clothes, and one of them timorously laid her hand upon the embroidery. She then went out, and in a short time came back with another woman, who seemed to be of higher rank and greater authority. She did, at her entrance, the usual act of reverence, and taking me by the hand, placed me in a smaller tent, spread with finer carpets, where I spent the night quietly with my maids.

"In the morning, as I was sitting on the grass, the chief of the troop came towards me. I rose up to receive him, and he bowed with great respect. 'Illustrious lady,' said he, ' my fortune is better than I had presumed to hope: I am told by my women that I have a princess in my camp.' 'Sir,' answered I, 'your women have deceived themselves and you; I am not a princess, but an unhappy stranger, who intended soon to have left this country, in which I am now to be imprisoned for ever.' 'Whoever or whencesoever you are,' returned the Arab, 'your dress, and that of your servants, show your rank to be high and your wealth to be great. Why should you, who can so easily procure your ransom, think yourself in danger of perpetual captivity? The purpose of my incursions is to increase my riches, or, more properly, to gather tribute. The sons of Ishmael are the natural and hereditary lords of this part of the continent, which is usurped by late invaders and low-born tyrants, from whom we are compelled to take by the sword what is denied to justice. The violence of war admits no distinction; the lance that is lifted at guilt and power will sometimes fall on innocence and gentleness.'

"'How little,' said I, 'did I expect that yesterday it should have fallen upon me!'

"'Misfortunes,' answered the Arab, 'should always be expected. If the eye of hostility could learn reverence or pity, excellence like yours had been exempt from injury. But the angels of affliction spread their toils alike for the virtuous and the wicked, for the mighty and the mean. Do not be disconsolate: I am not one of the lawless and cruel rovers of the desert; I know the rules of civil life; I will fix your ransom, give a passport to your messenger, and perform my stipulation with nice punctuality.'

"You will easily believe that I was pleased with his courtesy: and finding that his predominant passion was desire of money, I began now to think my danger less, for I knew that no sum would be thought too great for the release of Pekuah. I told him that he should have no reason to charge me with ingratitude, if I was used with kindness, and that any ransom which could be expected for a maid of common rank would be paid; but that he must not persist to rate me as a princess. He said he would consider what he should demand, and then smiling, bowed and retired.

"Soon after, the women came about me, each contending to be more officious than the other, and my maids themselves were served with reverence. We travelled onward by short journeys. On the fourth day, the chief told me that my ransom must be two hundred ounces of gold; which I not only promised him, but told him that I would add fifty more, if I and my maids were honourably treated.

"I never knew the power of gold before. From that time I was the leader of the troop. The march of every day was longer or shorter as I commanded, and the tents were pitched where I chose to rest. We now had camels and other conveniences for travel; my own women were always at my side; and I amused myself with observing the manners of the vagrant nations, and with viewing remains of ancient edifices, with which these deserted countries appear to have been, in some distant age, lavishly embellished.

"The chief of the band was a man far from illiterate: he was able to travel by the stars or the compass, and had marked, in his erratic expeditions, such places as are most worthy the notice of a passenger. He observed to me, that buildings are always best preserved in places little frequented and difficult of access: for, when once a country declines from its primitive splendour, the more inhabitants are left, the quicker ruin will be made. Walls supply stones more easily than quarries, and palaces and temples will be demolished, to make stables of granite and cottages of porphyry."

CHAPTER XXXIX

THE ADVENTURES OF PEKUAH CONTINUED

"WE wandered about in this manner for some weeks, whether, as our chief pretended, for my gratification, or, as I rather suspected, for some convenience of his own. I endeavoured to appear contented, where sullenness and resentment would have been of no use, and that endeavour conduced much to the calmness of my mind; but my heart was always with Nekayah, and the troubles of the night much overbalanced the amusements of the day. My women, who threw all their cares upon their mistress, set their minds at ease from the time when they saw me treated with respect, and gave themselves up to the incidental alleviations of our fatigue without solicitude or sorrow. I was pleased with their pleasure, and animated with their confidence. My condition had lost much of its terror, since I found that the Arab ranged the country merely to get riches. Avarice is an uniform and tractable vice: other intellectual distempers are different in different constitutions of mind; that which soothes the pride of one will offend the pride of another; but to the favour of the covetous there is a ready way; bring money, and nothing is denied.

"At last we came to the dwelling of our chief, a strong and spacious house built with stone in an island of the Nile, which lies, as I was told, under the tropic. 'Lady,' said the Arab, 'you shall rest after your journey a few weeks in this place, where you are to consider yourself as sovereign. My occupation is war: I have therefore chosen this obscure residence, from which I can issue unexpected, and to which I can retire unpursued. You may now repose in security; here are few pleasures, but here is no danger.' He then led me into the inner apartments, and seating me on the richest couch, bowed to the ground. His women, who considered me as a rival, looked on me with malignity; but being soon informed that I was a great lady detained only for my ransom, they began to vie with each other in obsequiousness and reverence.

"Being again comforted with new assurances of speedy liberty, I was for some days diverted from impatience by the novelty of the place. The turrets overlooked the country to a great distance, and afforded a view of many windings of the stream. In the day I wandered from one place to another as the course of the sun varied the splendour of the prospect, and saw many things which I had never seen before. The crocodiles and river-horses are common in this unpeopled region, and I often looked upon them with terror, though I knew that they could not hurt me. For some time I expected to see mermaids and tritons, which, as Imlac has told me, the European travellers have stationed in the Nile; but no such beings ever appeared, and the Arab, when I inquired after them, laughed at my credulity.

"At night the Arab always attended me to a tower set apart for celestial observations, where he endeavoured to teach me the names and courses of the stars. I had no great inclination to this study, but an appearance of attention was necessary to please my instructor, who valued himself for his skill; and, in a little while, I found some employment requisite to beguile the tediousness of time, which was to be passed always amidst the same objects. I was weary of looking in the morning on things from which I had turned away weary in the evening; I therefore was at last willing to observe the stars rather than do nothing, but could not always compose my thoughts, and was very often thinking on Nekayah, when others imagined me contemplating the sky. Soon after, the Arab went upon another expedition, and then my only pleasure was to talk with my maids about the accident by which we were carried away, and the happiness that we should all enjoy at the end of our captivity."

"There were women in your Arab's fortress," said the princess: "why did you not make them your companions, enjoy their conversation, and partake their diversions? In a place where they found business or amusement, why should you alone sit corroded with idle melancholy? or why could not you bear for a few months that condition to which they were condemned for life?"

"The diversions of the women," answered Pekuah, "were only childish play, by which the mind accustomed to stronger operations could not be kept busy. I could do all which they delighted in doing, by powers merely sensitive, while my intellectual faculties were flown to Cairo. They ran from room to room, as a bird hops from wire to wire in his cage. They danced for the sake of motion, as lambs frisk in a meadow. One sometimes pretended to be hurt, that the rest might be alarmed; or hid herself, that another might seek her. Part of their time passed in watching the progress of light bodies that floated on the river, and part in marking the various forms into which clouds broke in the sky.

"Their business was only needlework, in which I and my maids sometimes helped them; but you know that the mind will easily straggle from the fingers, nor will you suspect that captivity and absence from Nekayah could receive solace from silken flowers.

"Nor was much satisfaction to be hoped from their conversation: for of what could they be expected to talk? They had seen nothing, for they had lived from early youth in that narrow spot; of what they had not seen they could have no knowledge, for they could not read. They had no ideas but of the few things that were within their view, and had hardly names for anything but their clothes and their food. As I bore a superior character, I was often called to terminate their quarrels, which I decided as equitably as I could. If it could have amused me to hear the complaints of each against the rest, I might have been often detained by long stories; but the motives of their animosity were so small, that I could not listen without intercepting the tale."

"How," said Rasselas, "can the Arab, whom you represented as a man of more than common accomplishments, take any pleasure in his seraglio, when it is filled only with women like these? Are they exquisitely beautiful?"

"They do not," said Pekuah, "want that unaffecting and ignoble beauty which may subsist without sprightliness or sublimity, without energy of thought or dignity of virtue. But to a man like the Arab such beauty was only a flower casually plucked and carelessly thrown away. Whatever pleasures he might find among them, they were not those of friendship or society. When they were playing about him, he looked on them with inattentive superiority; when they vied for his regard, he sometimes turned away disgusted. As they had no knowledge, their talk could take nothing from the tediousness of life; as they had no choice, their fondness, or appearance of fondness, excited in him neither pride nor gratitude; he was not exalted in his own esteem by the smiles of a woman who saw no other man, nor was much obliged by that regard, of which he could never know the sincerity, and which he might often perceive to be exerted, not so much to delight him as to pain a rival. That which he gave and they received as love, was only a careless distribution of superfluous time, such love as man can bestow upon that which he despises, such as has neither hope nor fear, neither joy nor sorrow."

"You have reason, lady, to think yourself happy," said Imlac, "that you have been thus easily dismissed. How could a mind, hungry for knowledge, be willing, in an intellectual famine, to lose such a banquet as Pekuah's conversation?"

"I am inclined to believe," answered Pekuah, "that he was for some time in suspense; for, notwithstanding his promise, whenever I proposed to dispatch a messenger to Cairo, he found some excuse for delay. While I was detained in his house, he made many incursions into the neighbouring countries; and perhaps he would have refused to discharge me, had his plunder been equal to his wishes. He returned always courteous, related his adventures, delighted to hear my observations, and endeavoured to advance my acquaintance with the stars. When I importuned him to send away my letters, he soothed me with professions of honour and sincerity; and, when I could be no longer decently denied, put his troop again in motion, and left me to govern in his absence. I was much afflicted by this studied procrastination, and was sometimes afraid that I should be forgotten; that you would leave Cairo, and I must end my days in an island of the Nile.

"I grew at last hopeless and dejected, and cared so little to entertain him, that he for a while more frequently talked with my maids. That he should fall in love with them or with me might have been equally fatal, and I was not much pleased with the growing friendship. My anxiety was not long;

for, as I recovered some degree of cheerfulness, he returned to me, and I could not forbear to despise my former uneasiness.

"He still delayed to send for my ransom, and would, perhaps, never have determined, had not your agent found his way to him. The gold, which he would not fetch, he could not reject when it was offered. He hastened to prepare for our journey hither, like a man delivered from the pain of an intestine conflict. I took leave of my companions in the house, who dismissed me with cold indifference."

Nekayah, having heard her favourite's relation, rose and embraced her, and Rasselas gave her an hundred ounces of gold, which she presented to the Arab for the fifty that were promised.

CHAPTER XL

THE HISTORY OF A MAN OF LEARNING

THEY returned to Cairo, and were so well pleased at finding themselves together, that none of them went much abroad. The prince began to love learning, and one day declared to Imlac, that he intended to devote himself to science, and pass the rest of his days in literary solitude.

"Before you make your final choice," answered Imlac, "you ought to examine its hazards, and converse with some of those who are grown old in the company of themselves. I have just left the observatory of one of the most learned astronomers in the world, who has spent forty years in unwearied attention to the motions and appearances of the celestial bodies, and has drawn out his soul in endless calculations. He admits a few friends once a month, to hear his deductions and enjoy his discoveries. I was introduced as a man of knowledge worthy of his notice. Men of various ideas and fluent conversation are commonly welcome to those whose thoughts have been long fixed upon a single point, and who find the images of other things stealing away. I delighted him with my remarks; he smiled at the narrative of my travels, and was glad to forget the constellations, and descend for a moment into the lower world.

"On the next day of vacation I renewed my visit, and was so fortunate as to please him again. He relaxed from that time the severity of his rule, and permitted me to enter at my own choice. I found him always busy, and always glad to be relieved. As each knew much which the other was desirous of learning, we exchanged our notions with great delight. I perceived that I had every day more of his confidence, and always found new cause of admiration in the profundity of his mind. His comprehension is vast, his memory capacious and retentive, his discourse is methodical, and his expression clear.

"His integrity and benevolence are equal to his learning. His deepest researches and most favourite studies are willingly interrupted for any opportunity of doing good by his counsel or his riches. To his closest retreat, at his most busy moments, all are admitted that want his assistance: 'For though I exclude idleness and pleasure, I will never,' says he, 'bar my doors against charity. To man is permitted the contemplation of the skies, but the practice of virtue is commanded.'"

"Surely," said the princess, "this man is happy."

"I visited him," said Imlac, "with more and more frequency, and was every time more enamoured of his conversation; he was sublime without haughtiness, courteous without formality, and communicative without ostentation. I was at first, great princess, of your opinion, thought him the happiest of mankind, and often congratulated him on the blessing that he enjoyed. He seemed to hear nothing with indifference but the praises of his condition, to which he always returned a general answer, and diverted the conversation to some other topic.

"Amidst this willingness to be pleased and labour to please, I had quickly reason to imagine that some painful sentiment pressed upon his mind. He often looked up earnestly towards the sun, and let his voice fall in the midst of his discourse. He would sometimes, when we were alone, gaze upon me in silence, with the air of a man who longed to speak what he was yet resolved to suppress. He would often send for me with vehement injunctions of haste, though, when I came to him, he had nothing extraordinary to say; and sometimes, when I was leaving him, would call me back, pause a few moments, and then dismiss me."

CHAPTER XLI

THE ASTRONOMER DISCOVERS THE CAUSE OF HIS UNEASINESS

"At last the time came when the secret burst his reserve. We were sitting together last night in the turret of his house, watching the emersion of a satellite of Jupiter. A sudden tempest clouded the sky, and disappointed our observation. We sat awhile silent in the dark, and then he addressed himself to me in these words: 'Imlac, I have long considered thy friendship as the greatest blessing of my life. Integrity without knowledge is weak and useless, and knowledge without integrity is dangerous and dreadful. I have found in thee all the qualities requisite for trust, benevolence, experience, and fortitude. I have long discharged an office which I must soon quit at the call of nature, and shall rejoice in the hour of imbecility and pain to devolve it upon thee.'

"I thought myself honoured by this testimony, and protested, that whatever could conduce to his happiness would add likewise to mine.

"'Hear, Imlac, what thou wilt not without difficulty credit. I have possessed for five years the regulation of weather, and the distribution of the seasons; the sun has listened to my dictates, and passed from tropic to tropic by my direction; the clouds, at my call, have poured their waters, and the Nile has overflowed at my command; I have restrained the rage of the dog-star, and mitigated the fervours of the Crab. The winds alone, of all the elemental powers, have hitherto refused my authority, and multitudes have perished by equinoctial tempests, which I found myself unable to prohibit or restrain. I have administered this great office with exact justice, and made to the different nations of the earth an impartial dividend of rain and sunshine. What must have been the misery of half the globe, if I had limited the clouds to particular regions, or confined the sun to either side of the equator?'"

CHAPTER XLII

THE OPINION OF THE ASTRONOMER IS EXPLAINED AND JUSTIFIED

"I suppose he discovered in me, through the obscurity of the room, some tokens of amazement and doubt, for, after a short pause, he proceeded thus:

"'Not to be easily credited will neither surprise nor offend me; for I am, probably, the first of human beings to whom this trust has been imparted. Nor do I know whether to deem this distinction a reward or punishment; since I have possessed it, I have been far less happy than before, and nothing but the consciousness of good intention could have enabled me to support the weariness of unremitted vigilance.'

"'How long, sir,' said I, 'has this great office been in your hands?'

"'About ten years ago,' said he, 'my daily observations of the changes of the sky led me to consider, whether, if I had the power of the seasons, I could confer greater plenty upon the inhabitants of the earth. This contemplation fastened on my mind, and I sat days and nights in imaginary dominion, pouring upon this country and that the showers of fertility, and seconding every fall of rain with a due proportion of sunshine. I had yet only the will to do good, and did not imagine that I should ever have the power.

"'One day, as I was looking on the fields withering with heat, I felt in my mind a sudden wish that I could send rain on the southern mountains, and raise the Nile to an inundation. In the hurry of my imagination I commanded rain to fall; and by comparing the time of my command with that of the inundation, I found that the clouds had listened to my lips.'

"'Might not some other cause,' said I, 'produce this concurrence? the Nile does not always rise on the same day.'

"'Do not believe,' said he with impatience, 'that such objections could escape me: I reasoned long against my own conviction, and laboured against truth with the utmost obstinacy. I sometimes suspected myself of madness, and should not have dared to impart this secret but to a man like you, capable of distinguishing the wonderful from the impossible, and the incredible from the false.'

"'Why, sir,' said I, 'do you call that incredible, which you know, or think you know, to be true?'

"'Because,' said he, 'I cannot prove it by any external evidence; and I know too well the laws of demonstration to think that my conviction ought to influence another, who cannot like me be conscious of its force. I therefore shall not attempt to gain credit by disputation. It is sufficient that I feel this power, that I have long possessed, and every day exerted it. But the life of man is short, the infirmities of age increase upon me, and the time will soon come, when the regulator of the year must mingle with the dust. The care of appointing a successor has long disturbed me; the night and the day have been spent in comparisons of all the characters which have come to my knowledge, and I have yet found none so worthy as thyself."

CHAPTER XLIII

THE ASTRONOMER LEAVES IMLAC HIS DIRECTIONS

"'Hear, therefore, what I shall impart, with attention such as the welfare of a world requires. If the task of a king be considered as difficult, who has the care only of a few millions, to whom he cannot do much good or harm, what must be the anxiety of him on whom depends the action of the elements, and the great gifts of light and heat! Hear me therefore with attention.

"'I have diligently considered the position of the earth and sun, and formed innumerable schemes in which I changed their situation. I have sometimes turned aside the axis of the earth, and sometimes varied the ecliptic of the sun; but I have found it impossible to make a disposition by which the world may be advantaged; what one region gains, another loses, by any imaginable alteration, even without considering the distant parts of the solar system with which we are unacquainted. Do not, therefore, in thy administration of the year, indulge thy pride by innovation; do not please thyself with thinking that thou canst make thyself renowned to all future ages by disordering the seasons. The memory of mischief is no desirable fame. Much less will it become thee to let kindness or interest prevail. Never rob other countries of rain to pour it on thine own. For us the Nile is sufficient.'

"I promised, that when I possessed the power, I would use it with inflexible integrity; and he dismissed me, pressing my hand. 'My heart,' said he, 'will be now at rest, and my benevolence will no more destroy my quiet; I have found a man of wisdom and virtue, to whom I can cheerfully bequeath the inheritance of the sun.'"

The prince heard this narration with very serious regard; but the princess smiled, and Pekuah convulsed herself with laughter. "Ladies," said Imlac, "to mock the heaviest of human afflictions is neither charitable nor wise. Few can attain this man's knowledge, and few practise his virtues;

but all may suffer his calamity. Of the uncertainties of our present state, the most dreadful and alarming is the uncertain continuance of reason."

The princess was recollected, and the favourite was abashed. Rasselas, more deeply affected, inquired of Imlac, whether he thought such maladies of the mind frequent, and how they were contracted.

CHAPTER XLIV

THE DANGEROUS PREVALENCE OF IMAGINATION

"DISORDERS of intellect," answered Imlac, "happen much more often than superficial observers will easily believe. Perhaps, if we speak with rigorous exactness, no human mind is in its right state. There is no man whose imagination does not sometimes predominate over his reason, who can regulate his attention wholly by his will, and whose ideas will come and go at his command. No man will be found in whose mind airy notions do not sometimes tyrannize, and force him to hope or fear beyond the limits of sober probability. All power of fancy over reason is a degree of insanity; but while this power is such as we can control and repress, it is not visible to others, nor considered as any depravation of the mental faculties: it is not pronounced madness but when it becomes ungovernable and apparently influences speech or action.

"To indulge the power of fiction, and send imagination out upon the wing, is often the sport of those who delight too much in silent speculation. When we are alone we are not always busy; the labour of excogitation is too violent to last long; the ardour of inquiry will sometimes give way to idleness or satiety. He who has nothing external that can divert him, must find pleasure in his own thoughts, and must conceive himself what he is not; for who is pleased with what he is? He then expatiates in boundless futurity, and culls from all imaginable conditions that which for the present moment he should most desire, amuses his desires with impossible enjoyments, and confers upon his pride unattainable dominion. The mind dances from scene to scene, unites all pleasures in all combinations, and riots in delights, which nature and fortune, with all their bounty, cannot bestow.

"In time some particular train of ideas fixes the attention;

all other intellectual gratifications are rejected; the mind, in weariness or leisure, recurs constantly to the favourite conception, and feasts on the luscious falsehood whenever she is offended with the bitterness of truth. By degrees the reign of fancy is confirmed; she grows first imperious, and in time despotic. Then fictions begin to operate as realities, false opinions fasten upon the mind, and life passes in dreams of rapture or of anguish.

"This, sir, is one of the dangers of solitude, which the hermit has confessed not always to promote goodness, and the astronomer's misery has proved to be not always propitious to wisdom."

"I will no more," said the favourite, "imagine myself the queen of Abyssinia. I have often spent the hours which the princess gave to my own disposal, in adjusting ceremonies and regulating the court; I have repressed the pride of the powerful and granted the petitions of the poor; I have built new palaces in more happy situations, planted groves upon the tops of mountains, and have exulted in the beneficence of royalty, till, when the princess entered, I had almost forgotten to bow down before her."

"And I," said the princess, "will not allow myself any more to play the shepherdess in my waking dreams. I have often soothed my thoughts with the quiet and innocence of pastoral employments, till I have in my chamber heard the winds whistle, and the sheep bleat; sometimes freed the lamb entangled in the thicket, and sometimes with my crook encountered the wolf. I have a dress like that of the village maids, which I put on to help my imagination, and a pipe on which I play softly, and suppose myself followed by my flocks."

"I will confess," said the prince, "an indulgence of fantastic delight more dangerous than yours. I have frequently endeavoured to image the possibility of a perfect government, by which all wrong should be restrained, all vice reformed, and all the subjects preserved in tranquillity and innocence. This thought produced innumerable schemes of reformation, and dictated many useful regulations and salutary edicts. This has been the sport, and sometimes the labour, of my solitude; and I start when I think with how little anguish I once supposed the death of my father and my brothers."

"Such," says Imlac, "are the effects of visionary schemes. When we first form them, we know them to be absurd, but familiarize them by degrees, and in time lose sight of their folly."

CHAPTER XLV

THEY DISCOURSE WITH AN OLD MAN

THE evening was now far past, and they rose to return home. As they walked along the bank of the Nile, delighted with the beams of the moon quivering on the water, they saw at a small distance an old man, whom the prince had often heard in the assembly of the sages. "Yonder," said he, "is one whose years have calmed his passions, but not clouded his reason; let us close the disquisitions of the night, by inquiring what are his sentiments of his own state, that we may know whether youth alone is to struggle with vexation, and whether any better hope remains for the latter part of life."

Here the sage approached and saluted them. They invited him to join their walk, and prattled awhile, as acquaintance that had unexpectedly met one another. The old man was cheerful and talkative, and the way seemed short in his company. He was pleased to find himself not disregarded, accompanied them to their house, and, at the prince's request, entered with them. They placed him in the seat of honour, and set wine and conserves before him.

"Sir," said the princess, "an evening walk must give to a man of learning, like you, pleasures which ignorance and youth can hardly conceive. You know the qualities and the causes of all that you behold, the laws by which the river flows, the periods in which the planets perform their revolutions. Everything must supply you with contemplation, and renew the consciousness of your own dignity."

"Lady," answered he, "let the gay and the vigorous expect pleasure in their excursions; it is enough that age can obtain ease. To me the world has lost its novelty: I look round, and see what I remember to have seen in happier days. I rest against a tree, and consider, that in the same shade I once disputed upon the annual overflow of the Nile with a friend who is now silent in the grave. I cast my eyes upwards, fix them on the changing moon, and think with pain on the vicissitudes of life. I have ceased to take much delight in physical truth; for what have I to do with those things which I am soon to leave?"

"You may at least recreate yourself," said Imlac, "with the recollection of an honourable and useful life, and enjoy the praise which all agree to give you."

"Praise," said the sage with a sigh, "is to an old man an empty sound. I have neither mother to be delighted with the reputation of her son, nor wife to partake the honours of her husband. I have outlived my friends and my rivals. Nothing is now of much importance; for I cannot extend my interest beyond myself. Youth is delighted with applause, because it is considered as the earnest of some future good, and because the prospect of life is far extended; but to me, who am now declining to decrepitude, there is little to be feared from the malevolence of men, and yet less to be hoped from their affection or esteem. Something they may yet take away, but they can give me nothing. Riches would now be useless, and high employment would be pain. My retrospect of life recalls to my view many opportunities of good neglected, much time squandered upon trifles, and more lost in idleness and vacancy. I leave many great designs unattempted, and many great attempts unfinished. My mind is burdened with no heavy crime, and therefore I compose myself to tranquillity; endeavour to abstract my thoughts from hopes and cares, which, though reason knows them to be vain, still try to keep their old possession of the heart; expect, with serene humility, that hour which nature cannot long delay; and hope to possess, in a better state, that happiness which here I could not find, and that virtue which here I have not attained."

He rose and went away, leaving his audience not much elated with the hope of long life. The prince consoled himself with remarking, that it was not reasonable to be disappointed by this account, for age had never been considered as the season of felicity, and if it was possible to be easy in decline and weakness, it was likely that the days of vigour and alacrity might be happy; that the noon of life might be bright, if the evening could be calm.

The princess suspected that age was querulous and malignant, and delighted to repress the expectations of those who had newly entered the world. She had seen the possessors of estates look with envy on their heirs, and known many who enjoyed pleasure no longer than they can confine it to themselves.

Pekuah conjectured that the man was older than he appeared, and was willing to impute his complaints to delirious dejection; or else supposed that he had been unfortunate, and was therefore discontented: "For nothing," said she, "is more common, than to call our own condition the condition of life."

Imlac, who had no desire to see them depressed, smiled at

the comforts which they could so readily procure to themselves, and remembered, that at the same age he was equally confident of unmingled prosperity, and equally fertile of consolatory expedients. He forbore to force upon them unwelcome knowledge, which time itself would too soon impress. The princess and her lady retired; the madness of the astronomer hung upon their minds, and they desired Imlac to enter upon his office, and delay next morning the rising of the sun.

CHAPTER XLVI

THE PRINCESS AND PEKUAH VISIT THE ASTRONOMER

THE princess and Pekuah having talked in private of Imlac's astronomer, thought his character at once so amiable and so strange, that they could not be satisfied without a nearer knowledge; and Imlac was requested to find the means of bringing them together.

This was somewhat difficult: the philosopher had never received any visits from women, though he lived in a city that had in it many Europeans, who followed the manners of their own countries, and many from other parts of the world, that lived there with European liberty. The ladies would not be refused, and several schemes were proposed for the accomplishment of their design. It was proposed to introduce them as strangers in distress, to whom the sage was always accessible; but, after some deliberation, it appeared that by this artifice no acquaintance could be formed, for their conversation would be short, and they could not decently importune him often. "This," said Rasselas, "is true; but I have yet a stronger objection against the misrepresentation of your state. I have always considered it as treason against the great republic of human nature, to make any man's virtues the means of deceiving him, whether on great or little occasions. All imposture weakens confidence, and chills benevolence. When the sage finds that you are not what you seemed, he will feel the resentment natural to a man who, conscious of great abilities, discovers that he has been tricked by understandings meaner than his own, and, perhaps, the distrust which he can never afterwards wholly lay aside, may stop the voice of counsel and close the hand of charity; and where will you find the power of restoring his benefactions to mankind, or his peace to himself?"

To this no reply was attempted, and Imlac began to hope that their curiosity would subside; but, next day, Pekuah told him, she had now found an honest pretence for a visit to the astronomer, for she would solicit permission to continue under him the studies in which she had been initiated by the Arab, and the princess might go with her either as a fellow-student, or because a woman could not decently come alone. "I am afraid," said Imlac, "that he will be soon weary of your company; men advanced far in knowledge do not love to repeat the elements of their art, and I am not certain that even of the elements, as he will deliver them, connected with inferences and mingled with reflections, you are a very capable auditress." "That," said Pekuah, "must be my care; I ask of you only to take me thither. My knowledge is, perhaps, more than you imagine it; and, by concurring always with his opinions, I shall make him think it greater than it is."

The astronomer, in pursuance of this resolution, was told that a foreign lady, travelling in search of knowledge, had heard of his reputation, and was desirous to become his scholar. The uncommonness of the proposal raised at once his surprise and curiosity; and when, after a short deliberation, he consented to admit her, he could not stay without impatience till the next day.

The ladies dressed themselves magnificently, and were attended by Imlac to the astronomer, who was pleased to see himself approached with respect by persons of so splendid an appearance. In the exchange of the first civilities he was timorous and bashful; but when the talk became regular, he recollected his powers, and justified the character which Imlac had given. Inquiring of Pekuah what could have turned her inclination towards astronomy, he received from her a history of her adventure at the Pyramid, and of the time passed in the Arab's island. She told her tale with ease and elegance, and her conversation took possession of his heart. The discourse was then turned to astronomy: Pekuah displayed what she knew: he looked upon her as a prodigy of genius, and entreated her not to desist from a study which she had so happily begun.

They came again and again, and were every time more welcome than before. The sage endeavoured to amuse them, that they might prolong their visits, for he found his thoughts grow brighter in their company; the clouds of solicitude vanished by degrees, as he forced himself to entertain them, and he grieved when he was left at their departure to his old employment of regulating the seasons.

The princess and her favourite had now watched his lips for several months, and could not catch a single word from which they could judge whether he continued, or not, in the opinion of his preternatural commission. They often contrived to bring him to an open declaration; but he easily eluded all their attacks, and, on which side soever they pressed him, escaped from them to some other topic.

As their familiarity increased, they invited him often to the house of Imlac, where they distinguished him by extraordinary respect. He began gradually to delight in sublunary pleasures. He came early, and departed late; laboured to recommend himself by assiduity and compliance; excited their curiosity after new arts, that they might still want his assistance; and when they made any excursion of pleasure or inquiry, entreated to attend them.

By long experience of his integrity and wisdom, the prince and his sister were convinced that he might be trusted without danger; and lest he should draw any false hopes from the civilities which he received, discovered to him their condition, with the motives of their journey, and required his opinion on the choice of life.

"Of the various conditions which the world spreads before you, which you shall prefer," said the sage, "I am not able to instruct you. I can only tell that I have chosen wrong. I have passed my time in study without experience; in the attainment of sciences which can, for the most part, be but remotely useful to mankind. I have purchased knowledge at the expense of all the common comforts of life; I have missed the endearing elegance of female friendship, and the happy commerce of domestic tenderness. If I have obtained any prerogatives above other students, they have been accompanied with fear, disquiet, and scrupulosity; but even of these prerogatives, whatever they were, I have, since my thoughts have been diversified by more intercourse with the world, begun to question the reality. When I have been for a few days lost in pleasing dissipation, I am always tempted to think that my inquiries have ended in error, and that I have suffered much and suffered it in vain."

Imlac was delighted to find that the sage's understanding

was breaking through its mists, and resolved to detain him from the planets till he should forget his task of ruling them, and reason should recover its original influence.

From this time the astronomer was received into familiar friendship, and partook of all their projects and pleasures; his respect kept him attentive, and the activity of Rasselas did not leave much time unengaged. Something was always to be done: the day was spent in making observations which furnished talk for the evening, and the evening was closed with a scheme for the morrow.

The sage confessed to Imlac, that since he had mingled in the gay tumults of life, and divided his hours by a succession of amusements, he found the conviction of his authority over the skies fade gradually from his mind, and began to trust less to an opinion which he never could prove to others, and which he now found subject to variation, from causes in which reason had no part. "If I am accidentally left alone for a few hours," said he, "my inveterate persuasion rushes upon my soul, and my thoughts are chained down by some irresistible violence; but they are soon disentangled by the prince's conversation, and instantaneously released at the entrance of Pekuah. I am like a man habitually afraid of spectres, who is set at ease by a lamp, and wonders at the dread which harassed him in the dark; yet, if his lamp be extinguished, feels again the terrors which he knows that when it is light he shall feel no more. But I am sometimes afraid lest I indulge my quiet by criminal negligence, and voluntarily forget the great charge with which I am entrusted. If I favour myself in a known error, or am determined by my own ease in a doubtful question of this importance, how dreadful is my crime!"

"No disease of the imagination," answered Imlac, "is so difficult of cure as that which is complicated with the dread of guilt; fancy and conscience then act interchangeably upon us, and so often shift their places, that the illusions of one are not distinguished from the dictates of the other. If fancy presents images not moral or religious, the mind drives them away when they give it pain; but when melancholic notions take the form of duty, they lay hold on the faculties without opposition, because we are afraid to exclude or banish them. For this reason the superstitious are often melancholy, and the melancholy almost always superstitious.

"But do not let the suggestions of timidity overpower your better reason: the danger of neglect can be but as the probability of the obligation, which, when you consider it with freedom, you find very little, and that little growing every day less. Open your heart to the influence of the light which from time to time breaks in upon you; when scruples importune you, which you in your lucid moments know to be vain, do not stand to parley, but fly to business, or to Pekuah, and keep this thought always prevalent, that you are only one atom of the mass of humanity, and have neither such virtue nor vice, as that you should be singled out for supernatural favours or afflictions."

CHAPTER XLVII

THE PRINCE ENTERS, AND BRINGS A NEW TOPIC

"ALL this," said the astronomer, "I have often thought, but my reason has been so long subjugated by an uncontrollable and overwhelming idea, that it durst not confide in its own decisions. I now see how fatally I betrayed my quiet, by suffering chimeras to prey upon me in secret; but melancholy shrinks from communication, and I never found a man before to whom I could impart my troubles, though I had been certain of relief. I rejoice to find my own sentiments confirmed by yours, who are not easily deceived, and can have no motive or purpose to deceive. I hope that time and variety will dissipate the gloom that has so long surrounded me, and the latter part of my days will be spent in peace."

"Your learning and virtue," said Imlac, "may justly give you hopes."

Rasselas then entered with the princess and Pekuah, and inquired, whether they had contrived any new diversion for the next day. "Such," said Nekayah, "is the state of life, that none are happy but by the anticipation of change: the change itself is nothing; when we have made it, the next wish is to change again. The world is not yet exhausted; let me see something to-morrow which I never saw before."

"Variety," said Rasselas, "is so necessary to content, that even the Happy Valley disgusted me by the recurrence of its luxuries; yet I could not forbear to reproach myself with impatience, when I saw the monks of St. Anthony support, without complaint, a life, not of uniform delight, but uniform hardship."

"Those men," answered Imlac, "are less wretched in their silent convent than the Abyssinian princes in their prison of pleasure. Whatever is done by the monks is incited by an adequate and reasonable motive. Their labour supplies them with necessaries; it therefore cannot be omitted, and is certainly rewarded. Their devotion prepares them for another state, and reminds them of its approach while it fits them for it. Their time is regularly distributed: one duty succeeds another, so that they are not left open to the distraction of unguided choice, nor lost in the shades of listless inactivity. There is a certain task to be performed at an appropriated hour; and their toils are cheerful, because they consider them as acts of piety by which they are always advancing towards endless felicity."

"Do you think," said Nekayah, "that the monastic rule is a more holy and less imperfect state than any other? May not he equally hope for future happiness who converses openly with mankind, who succours the distressed by his charity, instructs the ignorant by his learning, and contributes by his industry to the general system of life; even though he should omit some of the mortifications which are practised in the cloister, and allow himself such harmless delights as his condition may place within his reach?"

"This," said Imlac, "is a question which has long divided the wise, and perplexed the good. I am afraid to decide on either part. He that lives well in the world is better than he that lives well in a monastery. But, perhaps, every one is not able to stem the temptations of public life; and if he cannot conquer, he may properly retreat. Some have little power to do good, and have likewise little strength to resist evil. Many are weary of their conflicts with adversity, and are willing to eject those passions which have long busied them in vain. And many are dismissed by age and diseases from the more laborious duties of society. In monasteries, the weak and timorous may be happily sheltered, the weary may repose, and the penitent may meditate. Those retreats of prayer and contemplation have something so congenial to the mind of man, that, perhaps, there is scarcely one that does not purpose to close his life in pious abstraction, with a few associates serious as himself."

"Such," said Pekuah, "has often been my wish, and I have heard the princess declare, that she could not willingly die in a crowd."

"The liberty of using harmless pleasures," proceeded Imlac,

"will not be disputed; but it is still to be examined what pleasures are harmless. The evil of any pleasure that Nekayah can image, is not in the act itself, but in its consequences. Pleasure, in itself harmless, may become mischievous, by endearing to us a state which we know to be transient and probatory, and withdrawing our thoughts from that of which every hour brings us nearer to the beginning, and of which no length of time will bring us to the end. Mortification is not virtuous in itself, nor has any other use, but that it disengages us from the allurements of sense. In the state of future perfection, to which we all aspire, there will be pleasure without danger, and security without restraint."

The princess was silent; and Rasselas, turning to the astronomer, asked him, whether he could not delay her retreat, by showing her something which she had not seen before.

"Your curiosity," said the sage, "has been so general, and your pursuit of knowledge so vigorous, that novelties are not now very easily to be found; but what you can no longer procure from the living may be given by the dead. Among the wonders of this country are the Catacombs, or the ancient repositories in which the bodies of the earliest generations were lodged, and where, by the virtue of the gums which embalmed them, they yet remain without corruption."

"I know not," said Rasselas, "what pleasure the sight of the Catacombs can afford; but, since nothing else offered, I am resolved to view them, and shall place this with many other things, which I have done because I would do something."

They hired a guard of horsemen, and the next day visited the Catacombs. When they were about to descend into the sepulchral caves, "Pekuah," said the princess, "we are now again invading the habitations of the dead; I know that you will stay behind; let me find you safe when I return." "No; I will not be left," answered Pekuah, "I will go down between you and the prince."

They then all descended, and roved with wonder through the labyrinth of subterraneous passages, where the bodies were laid in rows on either side.

CHAPTER XLVIII

IMLAC DISCOURSES ON THE NATURE OF THE SOUL

"WHAT reason," said the prince, "can be given, why the Egyptians should thus expensively preserve those carcasses, which some nations consume with fire, others lay to mingle with the earth, and all agree to remove from their sight as soon as decent rites can be performed?"

"The original of ancient customs," said Imlac, "is commonly unknown, for the practice often continues when the cause has ceased; and concerning superstitious ceremonies it is vain to conjecture, for what reason did not dictate reason cannot explain. I have long believed that the practice of embalming arose only from tenderness to the remains of relations or friends, and to this opinion I am more inclined, because it seems impossible that this care should have been general: had all the dead been embalmed, their repositories must in time have been more spacious than the dwellings of the living. I suppose only the rich or honourable were secured from corruption, and the rest left to the course of nature.

"But it is commonly supposed, that the Egyptians believed the soul to live as long as the body continued undissolved, and therefore tried this method of eluding death."

"Could the wise Egyptians," said Nekayah, "think so grossly of the soul? If the soul could once survive its separation, what could it afterwards receive or suffer from the body?"

"The Egyptians would doubtless think erroneously," said the astronomer, "in the darkness of heathenism, and the first dawn of philosophy. The nature of the soul is still disputed, amidst all our opportunities of clearer knowledge: some yet say that it may be material, who, nevertheless, believe it to be immortal."

"Some," answered Imlac, "have indeed said that the soul is material, but I can scarcely believe that any man has thought it, who knew how to think; for all the conclusions of reason enforce the immateriality of mind, and all the notices of sense and investigations of science concur to prove the unconsciousness of matter.

"It was never supposed that cogitation is inherent in matter, or that every particle is a thinking being. Yet, if any part of matter be devoid of thought, what part can we suppose to think? Matter can differ from matter only in form, density, bulk, motion, and direction of motion: to which of these, however varied or combined, can consciousness be annexed? To be round or square, to be solid or fluid, to be great or little, to be moved slowly or swiftly one way or another, are modes of material existence, all equally alien from the nature of cogitation. If matter be once without thought, it can only be made to think by some new modification; but all the modifications which it can admit are equally unconnected with cogitative powers."

"But the materialists," said the astronomer, "urge that matter may have qualities with which we are unacquainted."

"He who will determine," returned Imlac, "against that which he knows, because there may be something which he knows not,—he that can set hypothetical possibility against acknowledged certainty,—is not to be admitted among reasonable beings. All that we know of matter is, that matter is inert, senseless, and lifeless; and if this conviction cannot be opposed but by referring us to something that we know not, we have all the evidence that human intellect can admit. If that which is known may be overruled by that which is unknown, no being, not omniscient, can arrive at certainty."

"Yet let us not," said the astronomer, "too arrogantly limit the Creator's power."

"It is no limitation of omnipotence," replied the poet, "to suppose that one thing is not consistent with another, that the same proposition cannot be at once true and false, that the same number cannot be even and odd, that cogitation cannot be conferred on that which is created incapable of cogitation."

"I know not," said Nekayah, "any great use of this question. Does that immateriality, which in my opinion you have sufficiently proved, necessarily include eternal duration?"

"Of immateriality," said Imlac, "our ideas are negative, and therefore obscure. Immateriality seems to imply a natural power of perpetual duration as a consequence of exemption from all causes of decay; whatever perishes is destroyed by the solution of its contexture, and separation of its parts; nor can we conceive how that which has no parts, and therefore admits no solution, can be naturally corrupted or impaired."

"I know not," said Rasselas, "how to conceive anything without extension; what is extended must have parts, and you allow that whatever has parts may be destroyed."

"Consider your own conceptions," replied Imlac, "and the

difficulty will be less. You will find substance without extension. An ideal form is no less real than material bulk; yet an ideal form has no extension. It is no less certain, when you think on a pyramid, that your mind possesses the idea of a pyramid, than that the pyramid itself is standing. What space does the idea of a pyramid occupy more than the idea of a grain of corn? or how can either idea suffer laceration? As is the effect, such is the cause: as thought, such is the power that thinks; a power impassive and indiscerptible."

"But the Being," said Nekayah, "whom I fear to name, the Being which made the soul, can destroy it."

"He surely can destroy it," answered Imlac, "since, however unperishable, it receives from a superior nature its power of duration. That it will not perish by any inherent cause of decay, or principle of corruption, may be shown by philosophy; but philosophy can tell no more. That it will not be annihilated by Him that made it, we must humbly learn from higher authority." The whole assembly stood a while silent and collected. "Let us return," said Rasselas, "from this scene of mortality. How gloomy would be these mansions of the dead to him who did not know that he should never die, that what now acts shall continue its agency, and what now thinks shall think on for ever. Those that lie here stretched before us, the wise and the powerful of ancient times, warn us to remember the shortness of our present state: they were, perhaps, snatched away while they were busy like us in the choice of life."

"To me," said the princess, "the choice of life is become less important; I hope hereafter to think only on the choice of eternity."

They then hastened out of the caverns, and under the protection of their guard returned to Cairo.

CHAPTER XLIX

THE CONCLUSION, IN WHICH NOTHING IS CONCLUDED

It was now the time of the inundation of the Nile: a few days after their visit to the Catacombs, the river began to rise.

They were confined to their house. The whole region being under water gave them no invitation to any excursions, and being well supplied with material for talk, they diverted themselves with comparisons of the different forms of life which they had observed, and with various schemes of happiness which each of them had formed.

Pekuah was never so much charmed with any place as the convent of St. Anthony, where the Arab restored her to the princess, and wished only to fill it with pious maidens, and to be made prioress of the order; she was weary of expectation and disgust, and would gladly be fixed in some unvariable state.

The princess thought, that of all sublunary things knowledge was the best: she desired first to learn all sciences, and then proposed to found a college of learned women, in which she would preside, that, by conversing with the old, and educating the young, she might divide her time between the acquisition and communication of wisdom, and raise up for the next age models of prudence, and patterns of piety.

The prince desired a little kingdom, in which he might administer justice in his own person, and see all the parts of government with his own eyes; but he could never fix the limits of his dominion, and was always adding to the number of his subjects.

Imlac and the astronomer were contented to be driven along the stream of life, without directing their course to any particular port.

Of these wishes that they had formed they well knew that none could be obtained. They deliberated awhile what was to be done, and resolved, when the inundation should cease, to return to Abyssinia.

THE CASTLE OF OTRANTO:

A GOTHIC STORY

BY

HORACE WALPOLE, EARL OF ORFORD

HORACE WALPOLE

HORACE, the fourth son of Sir Robert Walpole, was born at 17 Arlington Street, London, on 24 September, 1717. He spent the greater part of his boyhood at his father's house in Chelsea, a building that is now incorporated in Chelsea Hospital. At Eton Walpole did not distinguish himself in any way. After leaving King's College, Cambridge, in 1737, his father appointed him Inspector of Imports and Exports in the Customs House and, in the following year, Usher to the Exchequer. In 1739 he began the usual grand tour of the Continent, in company with the poet Gray, returning to England in 1741. His father died in 1745 and, in 1747, Walpole settled at "a little plaything house" close to the river at Twickenham, which, with the assistance of John Chute and Richard Bentley (and later Wyatt), he transformed into "a little Gothic castle." These alterations, begun in 1748, were completed by 1776. Of all the Gothic Revival buildings in England, Strawberry Hill was the most influential and remains the most charming. Here Walpole installed a private printing press, from which he issued many of his own works and Thomas Gray's *The Bard*. Although never really interested in politics, he stood for Callington in 1741, a seat which he exchanged for that of Castle Rising in 1753. In 1757 he attempted to save the life of the unfortunate Admiral Byng, and in the same year became a member for King's Lynn. Between 1764 and 1767 he acted as advisor to his cousin, the Hon. H. S. Conway. He went to Paris in 1765, where he formed a friendship with Madame du Deffand, his most exquisite correspondent. His comedy *Nature Will Prevail* was acted with considerable success at the Haymarket Theatre. He never married. Strawberry Hill remained the passion of his life. His voluminous and vivacious correspondence gives an unrivalled picture of his age. He became the fourth Earl of Orford in 1791 and died at what was then 40 Berkeley Square on 2 March, 1797.

Among his books printed at Strawberry Hill are: *A Letter from Xo Ho*, 1757; *A Catalogue of the Royal and Noble Authors of England*, 1758; *Fugitive Pieces in Verse and Prose*, 1758; *Anecdotes of Painting in England*, 1762; *The Mysterious Mother*, A Tragedy, 1768; *A Description and Inventory of the Villa of Horace Walpole*, 1774; *Essay on Modern Gardening*, 1785.

A. T. Hazen, *A Bibliography of Horace Walpole*, 1948; *Letters*, ed. by Mrs. Paget Toynbee, 16 vols., 1903–5, with three supplementary vols. ed. by Paget Toynbee, 1918–25; the Yale Edition of the *Correspondence*, ed. by W. S. Lewis, 16 vols., 1937–52; *Selected Letters*, ed. by W. Hadley (Everyman's Library), 1926; also selected edition by W. S. Lewis, Folio Society, 1951.

The Castle of Otranto, ed. by Caroline Spurgeon, 1907; by Montague Summers, 1924; by Osward Doughty, 1929. Lives by: Austin Dobson, 1890; Stephen Gwynn, 1932; R. W. Ketton-Cremer, 1940. See also Sir Walter Scott, *Lives of the Novelists*; Montague Summers, *The Gothic Quest*, 1938.

PREFACE TO THE FIRST EDITION

THE following work was found in the library of an ancient
Catholic family in the north of England. It was printed at
Naples, in the black letter, in the year 1529. How much
sooner it was written does not appear. The principal incidents
are such as were believed in the darkest ages of Christianity;
but the language and conduct have nothing that savours of
barbarism. The style is of the purest Italian. If the story was
written near the time when it is supposed to have happened,
it must have been between 1095, the era of the first crusade,
and 1243, the date of the last, or not long afterwards. There
is no other circumstance in the work that can lead us to guess
at the period in which the scene is laid; the names of the actors
are evidently fictitious, and probably disguised on purpose;
yet the Spanish names of the domestics seem to indicate, that
this work was not composed until the establishment of the
Arragonian kings in Naples had made Spanish appellations
familiar in that country. The beauty of the diction, and the
zeal of the author (moderated, however, by singular judgment),
concur to make me think that the date of the composition was
little antecedent to that of the impression. Letters were then
in the most flourishing state in Italy, and contributed to dispel
the empire of superstition, at that time so forcibly attacked by
the reformers. It is not unlikely that an artful priest might
endeavour to turn their own arms on the innovators; and might
avail himself of his abilities as an author to confirm the populace
in their ancient errors and superstitions. If this was his view,
he has certainly acted with signal address. Such a work as
the following would enslave a hundred vulgar minds beyond
half the books of controversy that have been written from the
days of Luther to the present hour.

This solution of the author's motives is, however, offered as
a mere conjecture. Whatever his views were, or whatever
effects the execution of them might have, his work can only
be laid before the public at present as a matter of entertainment. Even as such some apology for it is necessary. Miracles,

visions, necromancies, dreams, and other preternatural events, are exploded now even from romances. That was not the case when our author wrote; much less when the story itself is supposed to have happened. Belief in every kind of prodigy was so established in those dark ages, that an author would not be faithful to the manners of the times who should omit all mention of them. He is not bound to believe them himself, but he must represent his actors as believing them.

If this air of the miraculous is excused, the reader will find nothing else unworthy of his perusal. Allow the possibility of the facts, and all the actors comport themselves as persons would do in their situation. There is no bombast, no similes, flowers, digressions, or unnecessary descriptions. Everything tends directly to the catastrophe. Never is the reader's attention relaxed. The rules of the drama are almost observed throughout the conduct of the piece. The characters are well drawn and still better maintained. Terror, the author's principal engine, prevents the story from ever languishing; and it is so often contrasted by pity, that the mind is kept up in a constant vicissitude of interesting passions.

Some persons may, perhaps, think the characters of the domestics too little serious for the general cast of the story; but, besides their opposition to the principal personages, the art of the author is very observable in his conduct of the subalterns. They discover many passages essential to the story, which could not be well brought to light but by their *naïveté* and simplicity: in particular, the womanish terror and foibles of Bianca, in the last chapter, conduce essentially towards advancing the catastrophe.

It is natural for a translator to be prejudiced in favour of his adopted work. More impartial readers may not be so much struck with the beauties of this piece as I was. Yet I am not blind to my author's defects. I could wish he had grounded his plan on a more useful moral than this; that *the sins of the fathers are visited on their children to the third and fourth generation*. I doubt whether, in his time, any more than at present, ambition curbed its appetite of dominion from the dread of so remote a punishment. And yet this moral is weakened by that less direct insinuation, that even such anathema may be diverted by devotion to St. Nicholas. Here the interest of the monk plainly gets the better of the judgment of the author. However, with all its faults, I have no doubt but the English reader will be pleased with a sight of this performance. The piety that reigns throughout, the lessons of virtue that are inculcated, and the rigid purity of the sentiments, exempt this work from the censure to which romances are but too liable. Should it meet with the success I hope for, I may be encouraged to reprint the original Italian, though it will tend to depreciate my own labour. Our language falls far short of the charms of the Italian, both for variety and harmony. The latter is peculiarly excellent for simple narrative. It is difficult in English *to relate* without falling too low or rising too high; a fault obviously occasioned by the little care taken to speak pure language in common conversation. Every Italian or Frenchman, of any rank, piques himself on speaking his own tongue correctly and with choice. I cannot flatter myself with having done justice to my author in this respect: his style is as elegant as his conduct of the passions is masterly. It is pity that he did not apply his talents to what they were evidently proper for—the theatre.

I will detain the reader no longer, but to make one short remark. Though the machinery is invention, and the names of the actors imaginary, I cannot but believe that the ground-work of the story is founded on truth. The scene is undoubtedly laid in some real castle. The author seems frequently, without design, to describe particular parts. *The chamber*, says he, *on the right hand ; the door on the left hand ; the distance from the chapel to Conrad's apartment :* these, and other passages, are strong presumptions that the author had some certain building in his eye. Curious persons, who have leisure to employ in such researches, may possibly discover in the Italian writers the foundation on which our author has built. If a catastrophe, at all resembling that which he describes, is believed to have given rise to this work, it will contribute to interest the reader, and will make THE CASTLE OF OTRANTO a still more moving story.

PREFACE TO THE SECOND EDITION

THE favourable manner in which this little piece has been received by the public calls upon the author to explain the grounds on which he composed it. But before he opens those motives, it is fit that he should ask pardon of his readers for having offered his work to them under the borrowed personage of a translator. As diffidence of his own abilities, and the novelty of the attempt, were the sole inducements to assume that disguise, he flatters himself he shall appear excusable. He resigned his performance to the impartial judgment of the public; determined to let it perish in obscurity, if disapproved; nor meaning to avow such a trifle, unless better judges should pronounce that he might own it without a blush.

It was an attempt to blend the two kinds of romance: the ancient and the modern. In the former, all was imagination and improbability; in the latter, nature is always intended to be, and sometimes has been, copied with success. Invention has not been wanting; but the great resources of fancy have been dammed up, by a strict adherence to common life. But if in the latter species nature has cramped imagination, she did but take her revenge, having been totally excluded from old romances. The actions, sentiments, conversations, of the heroes and heroines of ancient days, were as unnatural as the machines employed to put them in motion.

The author of the following pages thought it possible to reconcile the two kinds. Desirous of leaving the powers of fancy at liberty to expatiate through the boundless realms of invention, and thence of creating more interesting situations, he wished to conduct the mortal agents in his drama according to the rules of probability; in short, to make them think, speak, and act, as it might be supposed mere men and women would do in extraordinary positions. He had observed, that in all inspired writings, the personages under the dispensation of miracles, and witnesses to the most stupendous phenomena, never lose sight of their human character; whereas, in the productions of romantic story, an improbable event never fails to be attended by an absurd dialogue. The actors seem to lose their senses, the moment the laws of nature have lost their tone. As the public have applauded the attempt, the author must not say he was entirely unequal to the task he had undertaken; yet if the new route he has struck out shall have paved a road for men of brighter talents, he shall own with pleasure and modesty, that he was sensible the plan was capable of receiving greater embellishments than his imagination or conduct of the passions could bestow on it.

With regard to the deportment of the domestics, on which I have touched in the former preface, I will beg leave to add a few words. The simplicity of their behaviour, almost tending to excite smiles, which at first seems not consonant to the serious cast of the work, appeared to me not only not improper, but was marked designedly in that manner. My rule was nature. However grave, important, or even melancholy, the sensations of princes and heroes may be, they do not stamp the same affections on their domestics; at least the latter do not, or should not be made to express their passions in the same dignified tone. In my humble opinion, the contrast between the sublime of the one and the *naïveté* of the other, sets the pathetic of the former in a stronger light. The very impatience which a reader feels while delayed by the coarse pleasantries of vulgar actors from arriving at the knowledge of the important catastrophe he expects, perhaps heightens, certainly proves, that he has been artfully interested in the depending event. But I had higher authority than my own opinion for this conduct. That great master of nature, Shakespeare, was the model I copied. Let me ask if his tragedies of *Hamlet* and *Julius Cæsar* would not lose a considerable share of their spirit and wonderful beauties, if the humour of the grave-diggers, the fooleries of Polonius, and the clumsy jests of the Roman citizens, were omitted, or vested in heroics? Is not the eloquence of Antony, the nobler and affectingly unaffected oration of Brutus, artificially exalted by the rude outbursts of nature from the mouths of their auditors? These touches remind one of the Grecian sculptor, who, to convey the idea of a Colossus within the dimensions of a seal, inserted a little boy measuring his thumb.

No, says Voltaire, in his edition of Corneille, this mixture of buffoonery and solemnity is intolerable.—Voltaire is a genius— but not of Shakespeare's magnitude. Without recurring to disputable authority, I appeal from Voltaire to himself. I

shall not avail myself of his former encomiums on our mighty
poet, though the French critic has twice translated the same
speech in *Hamlet*, some years ago in admiration, latterly in
derision; and I am sorry to find that his judgment grows weaker
when it ought to be farther matured. But I shall make use of
his own words, delivered on the general topic of the theatre,
when he was neither thinking to recommend or decry Shakespeare's practice; consequently at a moment when Voltaire was
impartial. In the preface to his *Enfant Prodigue*, that exquisite
piece, of which I declare my admiration, and which, should I
live twenty years longer, I trust I shall never attempt to ridicule,
he has these words, speaking of comedy (but equally applicable
to tragedy, if tragedy is, as surely it ought to be, a picture of
human life; nor can I conceive why occasional pleasantry ought
more to be banished from the tragic scene, than pathetic serious-
ness from the comic): "*On y voit un melange de serieux et de
plaisanterie, de comique et de touchant;* souvent meme une
seule avanture *produit tous ces contrastes. Rien n'est si commun
qu'une maison dans laquelle* un pere gronde, une fille occupée
de sa passion pleure; *le fils se moque des deux, et quelques parens
prennent part differemment à la scene, etc. Nous n'inferons pas
de là que toute comedie doive avoir des scenes de bouffonerie et des
scenes attendrissantes : il y a beaucoup de tres bonnes pièces où
il ne regne que de la gayeté ; d'autres toutes serieuses ; d'autres
melangées : d'autres où l'attendrissement va jusqu'aux larmes :*
il ne faut donner l'exclusion à aucun genre *: et si l'on me deman-
doit quel genre est le meilleur, je repondrois, celui qui est le mieux
traité.*" Surely if a comedy may be *toute serieuse*, tragedy
may now and then, soberly, be indulged in a smile. Who shall
proscribe it? shall the critic, who, in self-defence, declares that
no kind ought to be excluded from comedy, give laws to
Shakespeare?

I am aware that the preface from whence I have quoted these
passages does not stand in Monsieur de Voltaire's name, but
in that of his editor; yet who doubts that the editor and author
were the same person? or where is the editor who has so happily
possessed himself of his author's style and brilliant ease of argument? These passages were indubitably the genuine sentiments of that great writer. In his epistle to Maffei, prefixed to
his *Merope*, he delivers almost the same opinion, though I
doubt with a little irony. I will repeat his words, and then
give my reason for quoting them. After translating a passage
in Maffei's *Merope*, Monsieur de Voltaire adds, "*Tous ces traits*

sont naïfs : tout y est convenable à ceux que vous introduisez sur la scene, et aux mœurs que vous leur donnez. Ces familiarités naturelles eussent été, à ce que je crois, bien reçues dans Athenes ; mais Paris et notre parterre veulent une autre espece de simplicité." I doubt, I say, whether there is not a grain of sneer in this and other passages of that epistle; yet the force of truth is not damaged by being tinged with ridicule. Maffei was to represent a Grecian story: surely the Athenians were as competent judges of Grecian manners and of the propriety of introducing them, as the parterre of Paris. On the contrary, says Voltaire (and I cannot but admire his reasoning), there were but ten thousand citizens at Athens, and Paris has near eight hundred thousand inhabitants, among whom one may reckon thirty thousand judges of dramatic works.—Indeed! but, allowing so numerous a tribunal, I believe this is the only instance in which it was ever pretended, that thirty thousand persons, living near two thousand years after the era in question, were, upon the mere face of the poll, declared better judges than the Grecians themselves of what ought to be the manners of a tragedy written on a Grecian story.

I will not enter into a discussion of the *espece de simplicité*, which the parterre of Paris demands, nor of the shackles with which *the thirty thousand judges* have cramped their poetry, the chief merit of which, as I gather from repeated passages in *The New Commentary on Corneille*, consists in vaulting in spite of those fetters; a merit which, if true, would reduce poetry, from the lofty effort of imagination, to a puerile and most contemptible labour—*difficiles nugæ* with a witness! I cannot, however, help mentioning a couplet, which, to my English ears, always sounded as the flattest and most trifling instance of circumstantial propriety: but which Voltaire, who has dealt so severely with nine parts in ten of Corneille's works, has singled out to defend in Racine:

> De son appartement cette porte est prochaine,
> Et cette autre conduit dans celui de la reine.

In English :

> To Cæsar's closet through this door you come,
> And t'other leads to the queen's drawing-room.

Unhappy Shakespeare! hadst thou made Rosencrantz inform his compeer, Guildenstern, of the ichnography of the palace of Copenhagen, instead of presenting us with a moral dialogue between the Prince of Denmark and the grave-digger, the illuminated pit of Paris would have been instructed *a second time* to adore thy talents.

The result of all I have said is, to shelter my own daring under the canon of the brightest genius this country, at least, has produced. I might have pleaded, that having created a new species of romance, I was at liberty to lay down what rules I thought fit for the conduct of it: but I should be more proud of having imitated, however faintly, weakly, and at a distance, so masterly a pattern, than to enjoy the entire merit of invention, unless I could have marked my work with genius as well as with originality. Such as it is, the public have honoured it sufficiently, whatever rank their suffrages allot to it.

SONNET

TO THE RIGHT HONOURABLE

LADY MARY COKE

THE gentle maid, whose hapless tale
    These melancholy pages speak
Say, gracious lady, shall she fail
    To draw the tear adown thy cheek?

No; never was thy pitying breast
    Insensible to human woes;
Tender, though firm, it melts distrest
    For weaknesses it never knows.

Oh! guard the marvels I relate
Of fell ambition scourg'd by fate,
    From reason's peevish blame.
Blest with thy smile, my dauntless sail
I dare expand to fancy's gale,
    For sure thy smiles are fame.

H. W.

CHAPTER I

MANFRED, Prince of Otranto, had one son and one daughter: the latter, a most beautiful virgin, aged eighteen, was called Matilda. Conrad, the son, was three years younger, a homely youth, sickly, and of no promising disposition; yet he was the darling of his father, who never showed any symptoms of affection to Matilda. Manfred had contracted a marriage for his son with the Marquis of Vicenza's daughter, Isabella; and she had already been delivered by her guardians into the hands of Manfred, that he might celebrate the wedding as soon as Conrad's infirm state of health would permit. Manfred's impatience for this ceremonial was remarked by his family and neighbours. The former, indeed, apprehending the severity of their prince's disposition, did not dare to utter their surmises on this precipitation. Hippolita, his wife, an amiable lady, did sometimes venture to represent the danger of marrying their only son so early, considering his great youth, and greater infirmities; but she never received any other answer than reflections on her own sterility, who had given him but one heir. His tenants and subjects were less cautious in their discourses: they attributed this hasty wedding to the prince's dread of seeing accomplished an ancient prophecy, which was said to have pronounced, that *the castle and lordship of Otranto should pass from the present family, whenever the real owner should be grown too large to inhabit it*. It was difficult to make any sense of this prophecy; and still less easy to conceive what it had to do with the marriage in question. Yet these mysteries, or contradictions, did not make the populace adhere the less to their opinion.

Young Conrad's birthday was fixed for his espousals. The company was assembled in the chapel of the castle, and everything ready for beginning the divine office, when Conrad himself was missing. Manfred, impatient of the least delay, and who had not observed his son retire, dispatched one of his attendants to summon the young prince. The servant, who had not stayed long enough to have crossed the court to Conrad's apartment, came running back breathless, in a frantic manner, his eyes staring, and foaming at the mouth. He said nothing, but pointed to the court. The company were struck with terror and amazement. The Princess Hippolita, without know-ing what was the matter, but anxious for her son, swooned away. Manfred, less apprehensive than enraged at the pro-crastination of the nuptials, and at the folly of his domestic, asked imperiously what was the matter? The fellow made no answer, but continued pointing towards the court-yard; and, at last, after repeated questions put to him, cried out:

"Oh! the helmet! the helmet!"

In the mean time, some of the company had run into the court, from whence was heard a confused noise of shrieks, horror, and surprise. Manfred, who began to be alarmed at not seeing his son, went himself to get information of what occasioned this strange confusion. Matilda remained endea-vouring to assist her mother, and Isabella stayed for the same purpose, and to avoid showing any impatience for the bride-groom, for whom, in truth, she had conceived little affection.

The first thing that struck Manfred's eyes was a group of his servants endeavouring to raise something that appeared to him a mountain of sable plumes. He gazed without believing his sight. "What are ye doing?" cried Manfred, wrathfully. "Where is my son?"

A volley of voices replied, "Oh! my lord! the prince! the prince! the helmet! the helmet!"

Shocked with these lamentable sounds, and dreading he knew not what, he advanced hastily—but, what a sight for a father's eyes!—he beheld his child dashed to pieces, and almost buried under an enormous helmet, a hundred times more large than any casque ever made for human being, and shaded with a proportionable quantity of black feathers.

The horror of the spectacle, the ignorance of all around how this misfortune had happened, and, above all, the tremendous phenomenon before him, took away the prince's speech. Yet his silence lasted longer than even grief could occasion. He fixed his eyes on what he wished in vain to believe a vision; and seemed less attentive to his loss, than buried in meditation on the stupendous object that had occasioned it. He touched, he examined, the fatal casque; nor could even the bleeding, mangled remains of the young prince divert the eyes of Manfred from the portent before him. All who had known his partial fondness for young Conrad were as much surprised at their prince's insensibility, as thunderstruck themselves at the miracle of the helmet. They conveyed the disfigured corpse into the hall, without receiving the least direction from Manfred. As little was he attentive to the ladies who remained in the chapel; on the contrary, without mentioning the unhappy princesses, his wife and daughter, the first sounds that dropped from Manfred's lips were, "Take care of the Lady Isabella."

The domestics, without observing the singularity of this direction, were guided by their affection to their mistress to consider it as peculiarly addressed to her situation, and flew to her assistance. They conveyed her to her chamber more dead than alive, and indifferent to all the strange circumstances she heard, except the death of her son. Matilda, who doted on her mother, smothered her own grief and amazement, and thought of nothing but assisting and comforting her afflicted parent. Isabella, who had been treated by Hippolita like a daughter, and who returned that tenderness with equal duty and affection, was scarce less assiduous about the princess; at the same time endeavouring to partake and lessen the weight of sorrow which she saw Matilda strove to suppress, for whom she had conceived the warmest sympathy of friendship. Yet her own situation could not help finding its place in her thoughts. She felt no concern for the death of young Conrad, except commiseration; and she was not sorry to be delivered from a marriage which had promised her little felicity, either from her destined bridegroom, or from the severe temper of Manfred, who, though he had distinguished her by great indulgence, had impressed her mind with terror, from his causeless rigour to such amiable princesses as Hippolita and Matilda.

While the ladies were conveying the wretched mother to her bed, Manfred remained in the court, gazing on the ominous casque, and regardless of the crowd which the strangeness of the event had now assembled around him. The few words he articulated tended solely to inquiries, whether any man knew from whence it could have come? Nobody could give him the least information. However, as it seemed to be the sole object of his curiosity, it soon became so to the rest of the spectators, whose conjectures were as absurd and improbable, as the catastrophe itself was unprecedented. In the midst of their senseless guesses, a young peasant, whom rumour had drawn thither from a neighbouring village, observed, that the miraculous helmet was exactly like that on the figure in black marble of Alfonso the Good, one of their former princes, in the church of St. Nicholas.

"Villain! what sayest thou?" cried Manfred, starting from his trance in a tempest of rage, and seizing the young man by the collar; "how darest thou utter such treason? thy life shall pay for it."

The spectators, who as little comprehended the cause of the prince's fury as all the rest they had seen, were at a loss to unravel this new circumstance. The young peasant himself was still more astonished, not conceiving how he had offended the prince; yet, recollecting himself, with a mixture of grace and humility, he disengaged himself from Manfred's gripe, and then, with an obeisance which discovered more jealousy of innocence than dismay, he asked, with respect, of what he was guilty? Manfred, more enraged at the vigour, however decently exerted, with which the young man had shaken off his hold, than appeased by his submission, ordered his attendants to seize him, and, if he had not been withheld by his friends, whom he had invited to the nuptials, would have poniarded the peasant in their arms.

During this altercation, some of the vulgar spectators had run to the great church, which stood near the castle, and came back open-mouthed, declaring that the helmet was missing from Alfonso's statue. Manfred, at this news, grew perfectly frantic; and, as if he sought a subject on which to vent the tempest within him, he rushed again on the young peasant, crying, "Villain! monster! sorcerer! 'tis thou hast done this! 'tis thou hast slain my son!"

The mob, who wanted some object within the scope of their capacities, on whom they might discharge their bewildered reasonings, caught the words from the mouth of their lord, and re-echoed, "Ay, ay; 'tis he, 'tis he! he has stolen the helmet from good Alfonso's tomb, and dashed out the brains of our young prince with it," never reflecting how enormous the disproportion was between the marble helmet that had been in the church, and that of steel before their eyes; nor how impossible it was for a youth, seemingly not twenty, to wield a piece of armour of so prodigious a weight.

The folly of these ejaculations brought Manfred to himself: yet, whether provoked at the peasant having observed the resemblance between the two helmets, and thereby led to the farther discovery of the absence of that in the church, or wishing to bury any fresh rumour under so impertinent a supposition, he gravely pronounced that the young man was certainly a necromancer; and that till the Church could take cognizance of he affair, he would have the magician, whom they had thus detected, kept prisoner under the helmet itself, which he ordered his attendants to raise, and place the young man under it; declaring he should be kept there without food, with which his own infernal art might furnish him.

It was in vain for the youth to represent against this preposterous sentence: in vain did Manfred's friends endeavour to divert him from this savage and ill-grounded resolution. The generality were charmed with their lord's decision, which to their apprehensions carried great appearance of justice, as the magician was to be punished by the very instrument with which he had offended; nor were they struck with the least compunction at the probability of the youth being starved, for they firmly believed that, by his diabolical skill, he could easily supply himself with nutriment.

Manfred thus saw his commands even cheerfully obeyed; and appointing a guard, with strict orders to prevent any food being conveyed to the prisoner, he dismissed his friends and attendants, and retired to his own chamber, after locking the gates of the castle, in which he suffered none but his domestics to remain.

In the meantime, the care and zeal of the young ladies had brought the Princess Hippolita to herself, who, amidst the transports of her own sorrow, frequently demanded news of her lord, would have dismissed her attendants to watch over him, and at last enjoined Matilda to leave her, and visit and comfort her father. Matilda, who wanted not affectionate duty to Manfred, though she trembled at his austerity, obeyed the orders of Hippolita, whom she tenderly recommended to Isabella; and inquiring of the domestics of her father, was informed that he was retired to his chamber, and had commanded that nobody should have admittance to him. Concluding that he was immersed in sorrow for the death of her brother, and fearing to renew his tears by the sight of his sole remaining child, she hesitated whether she should break in upon his affliction: yet solicitude for him, backed by the commands of her mother, encouraged her to venture disobeying the orders he had given; a fault she had never been guilty of before. The gentle timidity of her nature made her pause for some minutes at his door. She heard him traverse his chamber backwards and forwards with disordered steps; a mood which increased her apprehensions. She was however just going to beg admittance, when Manfred suddenly opened the door; and as it was now twilight,

concurring with the disorder of his mind, he did not distinguish
the person, but asked angrily, who it was? Matilda replied
trembling, "My dearest father, it is I, your daughter."

Manfred, stepping back hastily, cried, "Begone, I do not want
a daughter"; and, flinging back abruptly, clapped the door
against the terrified Matilda.

She was too well acquainted with her father's impetuosity to
venture a second intrusion. When she had a little recovered
the shock of so bitter a reception, she wiped away her tears
to prevent the additional stab that the knowledge of it would
give to Hippolita, who questioned her in the most anxious terms
on the health of Manfred, and how he bore his loss. Matilda
assured her he was well, and supported his misfortune with
manly fortitude.

"But will he not let me see him?" said Hippolita, mournfully; "will he not permit me to blend my tears with his, and
shed a mother's sorrows in the bosom of her lord? Or do you
deceive me, Matilda? I know how Manfred doted on his son:
is not the stroke too heavy for him? has he not sunk under it.
You do not answer me:—alas! I dread the worst!—raise me
my maidens; I will, I will see my lord. Bear me to him instantly:
He is dearer to me even than my children."

Matilda made signs to Isabella to prevent Hippolita's rising;
and both those lovely young women were using their gentle
violence to stop and calm the princess, when a servant, on the
part of Manfred, arrived, and told Isabella that his lord demanded
to speak with her.

"With me!" cried Isabella.

"Go," said Hippolita, relieved by a message from her lord,
"Manfred cannot support the sight of his own family. He
thinks you less disordered than we are, and dreads the shock
of my grief. Console him, dear Isabella, and tell him I will
smother my own anguish rather than add to his."

As it was now evening, the servant who conducted Isabella
bore a torch before her. When they came to Manfred, who
was walking impatiently about the gallery, he started, and
said hastily:

"Take away that light, and begone." Then shutting the
door impetuously, he flung himself upon a bench against the
wall, and bade Isabella sit by him. She obeyed trembling.

"I sent for you, lady," said he, and then stopped, under
great appearance of confusion.

"My lord!"

"Yes, I sent for you on a matter of great moment," resumed he: "dry your tears, young lady:—you have lost your bridegroom. Yes, cruel fate! and I have lost the hopes of my race! but Conrad was not worthy of your beauty."

"How! my lord," said Isabella; "sure you do not suspect me of not feeling the concern I ought! my duty and affection would have always——"

"Think no more of him," interrupted Manfred: "he was a sickly, puny child; and Heaven has perhaps taken him away, that I might not trust the honours of my house on so frail a foundation. The line of Manfred calls for numerous supports. My foolish fondness for that boy blinded the eyes of my prudence—but it is better as it is. I hope, in a few years, to have reason to rejoice at the death of Conrad."

Words cannot paint the astonishment of Isabella. At first she apprehended that grief had disordered Manfred's understanding. Her next thought suggested that this strange discourse was designed to ensnare her: she feared that Manfred had perceived her indifference for his son; and in consequence of that idea she replied:

"Good my lord, do not doubt my tenderness: my heart would have accompanied my hand. Conrad would have engrossed all my care; and wherever fate shall dispose of me, I shall always cherish his memory, and regard your highness and the virtuous Hippolita as my parents."

"Curse on Hippolita!" cried Manfred: "forget her from this moment, as I do. In short, lady, you have missed a husband undeserving of your charms: they shall now be better disposed of. Instead of a sickly boy, you shall have a husband in the prime of his age, who will know how to value your beauties, and who may expect a numerous offspring."

"Alas! my lord," said Isabella, "my mind is too sadly engrossed by the recent catastrophe in your family to think of another marriage. If ever my father returns, and it shall be his pleasure, I shall obey, as I did when I consented to give my hand to your son; but, until his return, permit me to remain under your hospitable roof, and employ the melancholy hours in assuaging yours, Hippolita's, and the fair Matilda's affliction."

"I desired you once before," said Manfred, angrily, "not to name that woman: from this hour she must be a stranger to you, as she must be to me:—in short, Isabella, since I cannot give you my son, I offer you myself."

E 856

"Heavens!" cried Isabella, waking from her delusion, "what do I hear? You, my lord! You! my father-in-law, the father of Conrad! the husband of the virtuous and tender Hippolita!"

"I tell you," said Manfred imperiously, "Hippolita is no longer my wife; I divorce her from this hour. Too long has she cursed me by her unfruitfulness. My fate depends on having sons, and this night I trust will give a new date to my hopes."

At those words he seized the cold hand of Isabella, who was half dead with fright and horror. She shrieked and started from him. Manfred rose to pursue her, when the moon, which was now up and gleamed in at the opposite casement, presented to his sight the plumes of the fatal helmet, which rose to the height of the windows, waving backwards and forwards in a tempestuous manner, and accompanied with a hollow and rustling sound. Isabella, who gathered courage from her situation, and who dreaded nothing so much as Manfred's pursuit of his declaration, cried:

"Look, my lord! see, Heaven itself declares against your impious intentions!"

"Heaven nor hell shall impede my designs," said Manfred, advancing again to seize the princess. At that instant the portrait of his grandfather, which hung over the bench where they had been sitting, uttered a deep sigh, and heaved its breast. Isabella, whose back was turned to the picture, saw not the motion, nor whence the sound came but started, and said:

"Hark, my lord! what sound was that?" and at the same time made towards the door. Manfred, distracted between the flight of Isabella, who had now reached the stairs, and yet unable to keep his eyes from the picture, which began to move, had, however, advanced some steps after her, still looking backwards on the portrait, when he saw it quit its panel, and descend on the floor with a grave and melanchoy air.

"Do I dream?" cried Manfred, returning; "or are the devils themselves in league against me? Speak, infernal spectre! or, if thou art my grandsire, why dost thou, too, conspire against thy wretched descendant, who too dearly pays for——" Ere he could finish the sentence, the vision sighed again, and made a sign to Manfred to follow him.

"Lead on!" cried Manfred: "I will follow thee to the gulf of perdition." The spectre marched sedately, but dejected, to the end of the gallery, and turned into a chamber on the right hand. Manfred accompanied him at a little distance, full of anxiety and horror, but resolved. As he would have entered the chamber, the door was clapped to with violence by an invisible hand. The prince, collecting courage from this delay, would have forcibly burst open the door with his foot, but found that it resisted his utmost efforts.

"Since hell will not satisfy my curiosity," said Manfred, "I will use the human means in my power for preserving my race; Isabella shall not escape me."

That lady, whose resolution had given way to terror the moment she had quitted Manfred, continued her flight to the bottom of the principal staircase. There she stopped, not knowing whither to direct her steps, nor how to escape from the impetuosity of the prince. The gates of the castle she knew were locked, and guards placed in the court. Should she, as her heart prompted her, go and prepare Hippolita for the cruel destiny that awaited her, she did not doubt but Manfred would seek her there, and that his violence would incite him to double the injury he meditated, without leaving room for them to avoid the impetuosity of his passions. Delay might give him time to reflect on the horrid measures he had conceived, or produce some circumstance in her favour, if she could, for that night at least, avoid his odious purpose. Yet where conceal herself? how avoid the pursuit he would infallibly make throughout the castle? As these thoughts passed rapidly through her mind, she recollected a subterraneous passage which led from the vaults of the castle to the church of St. Nicholas. Could she reach the altar before she was overtaken, she knew even Manfred's violence would not dare to profane the sacredness of the place; and she determined, if no other means of deliverance offered, to shut herself up for ever among the holy virgins, whose convent was contiguous to the cathedral. In this resolution, she seized a lamp that burned at the foot of the staircase, and hurried towards the secret passage.

The lower part of the castle was hollowed into several intricate cloisters; and it was not easy for one under so much anxiety to find the door that opened into the cavern. An awful silence reigned throughout those subterraneous regions, except now and then some blasts of wind that shook the doors she had passed, and which, grating on the rusty hinges, were re-echoed through that long labyrinth of darkness. Every murmur struck her with new terror;—yet more she dreaded to hear the wrathful voice of Manfred urging his domestics to pursue her. She trod as softly as impatience would give her leave,—yet frequently stopped, and listened to hear if she was followed. In one of those moments she thought she heard a sigh. She shuddered, and recoiled a few paces. In a moment she thought she heard the step of some person. Her blood curdled: she concluded it was Manfred. Every suggestion that horror could inspire rushed into her mind. She condemned her rash flight, which had thus exposed her to his rage in a place where her cries were not likely to draw anybody to her assistance. Yet the sound seemed not to come from behind: if Manfred knew where she was, he must have followed her: she was still in one of the cloisters, and the steps she had heard were too distinct to proceed from the way she had come. Cheered with this reflection, and hoping to find a friend in whoever was not the prince, she was going to advance, when a door that stood ajar, at some distance to the left, was opened gently; but ere her lamp, which she held up, could discover who opened it, the person retreated precipitately on seeing the light.

Isabella, whom every incident was sufficient to dismay, hesitated whether she should proceed. Her dread of Manfred soon outweighed every other terror. The very circumstance of the person avoiding her, gave her a sort of courage. It could only be, she thought, some domestic belonging to the castle. Her gentleness had never raised her an enemy, and conscious innocence made her hope that, unless sent by the prince's order to seek her, his servants would rather assist than prevent her flight. Fortifying herself with these reflections, and believing, by what she could observe, that she was near the mouth of the subterraneous cavern, she approached the door that had been opened; but a sudden gust of wind, that met her at the door, extinguished her lamp, and left her in total darkness.

Words cannot paint the horror of the princess's situation. Alone, in so dismal a place, her mind impressed with all the terrible events of the day, hopeless of escaping, expecting every moment the arrival of Manfred, and far from tranquil on knowing she was within reach of somebody, she knew not whom, who for some cause seemed concealed thereabouts; all these thoughts crowded on her distracted mind, and she was ready to sink under her apprehensions. She addressed herself to every saint in heaven, and inwardly implored their assistance. For a considerable time she remained in an agony of despair. At last, as softly as was possible, she felt for the door, and having found it, entered trembling into the vault from whence she had heard the sigh and steps. It gave her a kind of momentary joy to perceive an imperfect ray of clouded moon-shine gleam from the roof of the vault, which seemed to be fallen in, and from whence hung a fragment of earth or building, she could not distinguish which, that appeared to have been crushed inwards. She advanced eagerly towards this chasm, when she discerned a human form standing close against the wall.

She shrieked, believing it the ghost of her betrothed Conrad. The figure, advancing, said in a submissive voice, "Be not alarmed, lady, I will not injure you."

Isabella, a little encouraged by the words and tone of voice of the stranger, and recollecting that this must be the person who had opened the door, recovered her spirits enough to reply, "Sir, whoever you are, take pity on a wretched princess, standing on the brink of destruction: assist me to escape from this fatal castle, or, in a few moments, I may be made miserable for ever."

"Alas!" said the stranger, "what can I do to assist you? I will die in your defence; but I am unacquainted with the castle, and want——"

"Oh!" said Isabella, hastily interrupting him, "help me but to find a trap-door that must be hereabout, and it is the greatest service you can do me, for I have not a minute to lose." Saying these words, she felt about on the pavement, and directed the stranger to search likewise, for a smooth piece of brass enclosed in one of the stones. "That," said she, "is the lock which opens with a spring, of which I know the secret. If we can find that, I may escape; if not, alas! courteous stranger, I fear I shall have involved you in my misfortunes. Manfred will suspect you for the accomplice of my flight, and you will fall a victim to his resentment."

"I value not my life," said the stranger; "and it will be some comfort to lose it, in trying to deliver you from his tyranny."

"Generous youth!" said Isabella, "how shall I ever requite——"

As she uttered these words, a ray of moonshine, streaming through a cranny of the ruin above, shone directly on the lock they sought.—"Oh! transport!" said Isabella, "here is the trap-door"; and, taking out the key, she touched the spring, which, starting aside, discovered an iron ring. "Lift up the door," said the princess. The stranger obeyed; and beneath appeared some stone steps descending into a vault totally dark. "We must go down here," said Isabella: "follow me; dark and dismal as it is, we cannot miss our way; it leads directly to the church of St. Nicholas—but, perhaps," added the princess, modestly, "you have no reason to leave the castle, nor have I farther occasion for your service; in a few minutes I shall be safe from Manfred's rage—only let me know to whom I am so much obliged."

"I will never quit you," said the stranger eagerly, "until I have placed you in safety—nor think me, princess, more generous than I am; though you are my principal care——"

The stranger was interrupted by a sudden noise of voices that seemed approaching, and they soon distinguished these words: "Talk not to me of necromancers; I tell you she must be in the castle; I will find her in spite of enchantment."

"Oh, heavens!" cried Isabella, "it is the voice of Manfred; make haste, or we are ruined! and shut the trap-door after you." Saying this, she descended the steps precipitately; and as the stranger hastened to follow her, he let the door slip out of his hands: it fell, and the spring closed over it. He tried in vain to open it, not having observed Isabella's method of touching the spring; nor had he many moments to make an essay. The noise of the falling door had been heard by Manfred, who, directed by the sound, hastened thither, attended by his servants with torches.

"It must be Isabella," cried Manfred, before he entered the vault: "she is escaping by the subterraneous passage, but she cannot have got far." What was the astonishment of the prince, when, instead of Isabella, the light of the torches discovered to him the young peasant, whom he thought confined under the fatal helmet. "Traitor!" said Manfred, "how camest thou here? I thought thee in durance above in the court."

"I am no traitor," replied the young man boldly, "nor am I answerable for your thoughts."

"Presumptuous villain!" cried Manfred, "dost thou provoke my wrath? Tell me; how hast thou escaped from above? Thou hast corrupted thy guards, and their lives shall answer it."

"My poverty," said the peasant calmly, "will disculpate them: though the ministers of a tyrant's wrath, to thee they are faithful, and but too willing to execute the orders which you unjustly imposed upon them."

"Art thou so hardy as to dare my vengeance?" said the prince; "but tortures shall force the truth from thee. Tell me; I will know thy accomplices."

"There was my accomplice!" said the youth, smiling and pointing to the roof.

Manfred ordered the torches to be held up, and perceived that one of the cheeks of the enchanted casque had forced its way through the pavement of the court, as his servants had let it fall over the peasant, and had broken through into the vault, leaving a gap through which the peasant had pressed himself some minutes before he was found by Isabella. "Was that the way by which thou didst descend?" said Manfred.

"It was," said the youth.

"But what noise was that," said Manfred, "which I heard, as I entered the cloister?"

"A door clapped," said the peasant; "I heard it as well as you."

"What door?" said Manfred hastily.

"I am not acquainted with your castle," said the peasant: "this is the first time I ever entered it; and this vault the only part of it within which I ever was."

"But I tell thee," said Manfred, wishing to find out if the youth had discovered the trap-door, "it was this way I heard the noise; my servants heard it too."

"My lord," interrupted one of them officiously, "to be sure it was the trap-door, and he was going to make his escape."

"Peace! blockhead," said the prince angrily; "if he was going to escape, how should he come on this side? I will know from his own mouth what noise it was I heard. Tell me truly, thy life depends on thy veracity."

"My veracity is dearer to me than my life," said the peasant; "nor would I purchase the one by forfeiting the other."

"Indeed, young philosopher!" said Manfred, contemptuously; "tell me, then, what was that noise I heard?"

"Ask me, what I can answer," said he, "and put me to death instantly, if I tell you a lie."

Manfred, growing impatient at the steady valour and indifference of the youth, cried, "Well, then, thou man of truth! answer; was it the fall of the trap-door that I heard?"

"It was," said the youth.

"It was!" said the prince; "and how didst thou come to know there was a trap-door here?"

"I saw the plate of brass by a gleam of moonshine," replied he.

"But what told thee it was a lock?" said Manfred; "how didst thou discover the secret of opening it?"

"Providence, that delivered me from the helmet, was able to direct me to the spring of a lock," said he.

"Providence should have gone a little farther, and have

placed thee out of the reach of my resentment," said Manfred: "when Providence had taught thee to open the lock, it abandoned thee for a fool, who did not know how to make use of its favours. Why didst thou not pursue the path pointed out for thy escape? Why didst thou shut the trap-door before thou hadst descended the steps?"

"I might ask you, my lord," said the peasant, "how I, totally unacquainted with your castle, was to know that those steps led to any outlet? but I scorn to evade your questions. Wherever those steps led to, perhaps, I should have explored the way. I could not be in a worse situation than I was. But the truth is, I let the trap-door fall: your immediate arrival followed. I had given the alarm—what imported it to me whether I was seized a minute sooner or a minute later?"

"Thou art a resolute villain for thy years," said Manfred; "yet, on reflection, I suspect thou dost but trifle with me: thou hast not yet told me how thou didst open the lock."

"That I will show you, my lord," said the peasant; and, taking up a fragment of stone that had fallen from above, he laid himself on the trap-door, and began to beat on the piece of brass that covered it; meaning to gain time for the escape of the princess. This presence of mind, joined to the frankness of the youth, staggered Manfred. He even felt a disposition towards pardoning one who had been guilty of no crime. Manfred was not one of those savage tyrants who wanton in cruelty unprovoked. The circumstances of his fortune had given an asperity to his temper, which was naturally humane; and his virtues were always ready to operate, when his passions did not obscure his reason.

While the prince was in this suspense, a confused noise of voices echoed through the distant vaults. As the sound approached, he distinguished the clamours of some of his domestics, whom he had dispersed through the castle in search of Isabella, calling out, "Where is my lord? where is the prince?"

"Here I am," said Manfred, as they came nearer; "have you found the princess?"

The first that arrived replied, "Oh, my lord, I am glad we have found you."

"Found me!" said Manfred; "have you found the princess?"

"We thought we had, my lord," said the fellow, looking terrified; "but——"

"But what?" cried the prince; "has she escaped?"

"Jaquez and I, my lord——"

"Yes, I and Diego," interrupted the second, who came up in still greater consternation.

"Speak one of you at a time," said Manfred; "I ask you, where is the princess?"

"We do not know," said they both together; "but we are frightened out of our wits."

"So I think, blockheads," said Manfred; "what is it has scared you thus?"

"Oh, my lord," said Jaquez, "Diego has seen such a sight! your highness would not believe your eyes."

"What new absurdity is this?" cried Manfred; "give me a direct answer, or by Heaven——"

"Why, my lord, if it please your highness to hear me," said the poor fellow, "Diego and I——"

"Yes, I and Jaquez," cried his comrade.

"Did not I forbid you to speak both at a time?" said the prince: "you, Jaquez, answer; for the other fool seems more distracted than thou art: what is the matter?"

"My gracious lord," said Jaquez, "if it please your highness to hear me, Diego and I, according to your highness's orders, went to search for the young lady; but being apprehensive that we might meet the ghost of my young lord, your highness's son, God rest his soul! as he has not received Christian burial——"

"Sot!" cried Manfred, in a rage, "is it only a ghost, then, that thou hast seen?"

"Oh, worse! worse! my lord," cried Diego: "I had rather have seen ten whole ghosts."

"Grant me patience!" said Manfred; "those blockheads distract me. Out of my sight, Diego; and thou, Jaquez, tell me, in one word, art thou sober? art thou raving? thou wast wont to have some sense; has the other sot frightened himself and thee too? speak; what is it he fancies he has seen?"

"Why, my lord," replied Jaquez, trembling. "I was going to tell your highness, that since the calamitous misfortune of my young lord, God rest his precious soul! not one of us, your highness's faithful servants, indeed we are, my lord, though poor men; I say, not one of us has dared to set a foot about the castle, but two together: so Diego and I, thinking that my young lady might be in the great gallery, went up there to look for her, and tell her your highness wanted something to impart to her."

"O blundering fools!" cried Manfred; "and in the mean-

*E 856

time she has made her escape, because you were afraid of goblins! Why, thou knave! she left me in the gallery; I came from thence myself."

"For all that, she may be there still for aught I know," said Jaquez; "but the devil shall have me before I seek her there again: poor Diego! I do not believe he will ever recover it."

"Recover what?" said Manfred; "am I never to learn what it is has terrified these rascals? But I lose my time; follow me, slave; I will see if she is in the gallery."

"For Heaven's sake, my dear good lord," cried Jaquez, "do not go to the gallery! Satan himself, I believe, is in the chamber next to the gallery."

Manfred, who hitherto had treated the terror of his servants as an idle panic, was struck at this new circumstance. He recollected the apparition of the portrait, and the sudden closing of the door at the end of the gallery—his voice faltered, and he asked with disorder, "What is in the great chamber?"

"My lord," said Jaquez, "when Diego and I came into the gallery, he went first, for he said he had more courage than I;— so, when we came into the gallery, we found nobody. We looked under every bench and stool; and still we found nobody."

"Were all the pictures in their places?" said Manfred.

"Yes, my lord," answered Jaquez; "but we did not think of looking behind them."

"Well, well," said Manfred, "proceed."

"When we came to the door of the great chamber," continued Jaquez, "we found it shut."

"And could not you open it?" said Manfred.

"Oh yes, my lord; would to Heaven we had not!" replied he: "nay, it was not I neither, it was Diego: he was grown fool-hardy, and would go on, though I advised him not: if ever I open a door that is shut again!"

"Trifle not," said Manfred, shuddering, "but tell me what you saw in the great chamber, on opening the door."

"I! my lord!" said Jaquez, "I saw nothing: I was behind Diego; but I heard the noise."

"Jaquez," said Manfred, in a solemn tone of voice; "tell me, I adjure thee by the souls of my ancestors, what was it thou sawest? what was it thou heardest?"

"It was Diego saw it, my lord, it was not I," replied Jaquez; "I only heard the noise. Diego had no sooner opened the door, than he cried out, and ran back—I ran back too, and said, 'Is it the ghost?'—'The ghost! no, no,' said Diego, and his hair stood an end—'it is a giant, I believe: he is all clad in armour, for I saw his foot and part of his leg, and they are as large as the helmet below in the court.' As he said these words, my lord, we heard a violent motion, and the rattling of armour, as if the giant was rising, for Diego has told me since that he believes the giant was lying down, for the foot and leg were stretched at length on the floor. Before we could get to the end of the gallery, we heard the door of the great chamber clap behind us, but we did not dare turn back to see if the giant was following us—yet, now I think on it, we must have heard him if he pursued us; but for Heaven's sake, good my lord, send for the chaplain, and have the castle exorcized, for, for certain, it is enchanted."

"Ay, pray do, my lord," cried all the servants at once, "or we must leave your highness's service."

"Peace, dotards!" said Manfred, "and follow me; I will know what all this means."

"We! my lord?" cried they, with one voice; "we would not go up to the gallery for your highness's revenue."

The young peasant, who had stood silent, now spoke. "Will your highness," said he, "permit me to try this adventure? my life is of consequence to nobody; I fear no bad angel, and have offended no good one."

"Your behaviour is above your seeming," said Manfred, viewing him with surprise and admiration: "hereafter I will reward your bravery; but now," continued he with a sigh, "I am so circumstanced, that I dare trust no eyes but my own. However, I give you leave to accompany me."

Manfred, when he first followed Isabella from the gallery, had gone directly to the apartment of his wife, concluding the princess had retired thither. Hippolita, who knew his step, rose with anxious fondness to meet her lord, whom she had not seen since the death of her son. She would have flown in a transport, mixed of joy and grief, to his bosom, but he pushed her rudely off, and said, "Where is Isabella?"

"Isabella, my lord!" said the astonished Hippolita.

"Yes, Isabella," cried Manfred imperiously; "I want Isabella."

"My lord," replied Matilda, who perceived how much his behaviour had shocked her mother, "she has not been with us since your highness summoned her to your apartment."

"Tell me where she is," said the prince; "I do not want to know where she has been."

"My good lord," says Hippolita, "your daughter tells you

the truth: Isabella left us by your command, and has not
returned since; but, my good lord, compose yourself: retire to
your rest; this dismal day has disordered you. Isabella shall
wait your orders in the morning."

"What, then, you know where she is?" cried Manfred. "Tell
me directly, for I will not lose an instant; and you, woman,"
speaking to his wife, "order your chaplain to attend me
forthwith."

"Isabella," said Hippolita, calmly, "is retired, I suppose to
her chamber: she is not accustomed to watch at this late hour.
Gracious my lord," continued she, "let me know what has
disturbed you. Has Isabella offended you?"

"Trouble me not with questions," said Manfred, "but tell
me where she is."

"Matilda shall call her," said the princess. "Sit down, my
lord, and resume your wonted fortitude."

"What! art thou jealous of Isabella?" replied he, "that you
wish to be present at our interview?"

"Good heavens! my lord," said Hippolita; "what is it your
highness means?"

"Thou wilt know ere many minutes are passed," said the
cruel prince. "Send your chaplain to me, and wait my pleasure
here." At these words he flung out of the room in search of
Isabella, leaving the amazed ladies thunderstruck with his
words and frantic deportment, and lost in vain conjectures on
what he was meditating.

Manfred was now returning from the vault, attended by the
peasant and a few of his servants, whom he had obliged to
accompany him. He ascended the staircase without stopping,
till he arrived at the gallery, at the door of which he met Hippolita and her chaplain. When Diego had been dismissed by
Manfred, he had gone directly to the princess's apartment
with the alarm of what he had seen. That excellent lady,
who no more than Manfred doubted of the reality of the vision,
yet affected to treat it as a delirium of the servants. Willing,
however, to save her lord from any additional shock, and
prepared by a series of grief not to tremble at any accession to
it, she determined to make herself the first sacrifice, if fate had
marked the present hour for their destruction. Dismissing the
reluctant Matilda to her rest, who in vain sued for leave to
accompany her mother, and attended only by her chaplain,
Hippolita had visited the gallery and great chamber; and now,
with more serenity of soul than she had felt for many hours, she

met her lord, and assured him that the vision of the gigantic leg and foot was all a fable; and no doubt an impression made by fear, and the dark and dismal hour of the night, on the minds of his servants. She and the chaplain had examined the chamber, and found everything in the usual order.

Manfred, though persuaded, like his wife, that the vision had been no work of fancy, recovered a little from the tempest of mind into which so many strange events had thrown him. Ashamed, too, of his inhuman treatment of a princess, who returned every injury with new marks of tenderness and duty, he felt returning love forcing itself into his eyes; but not less ashamed of feeling remorse towards one against whom he was inwardly meditating a yet more bitter outrage, he curbed the yearnings of his heart, and did not dare to lean even towards pity. The next transition of his soul was to exquisite villainy. Presuming on the unshaken submission of Hippolita, he flattered himself that she would not only acquiesce with patience to a divorce, but would obey, if it was his pleasure, in endeavouring to persuade Isabella to give him her hand—but ere he could indulge this horrid hope, he reflected that Isabella was not to be found. Coming to himself, he gave orders that every avenue to the castle should be strictly guarded, and charged his domestics, on pain of their lives, to suffer nobody to pass out. The young peasant to whom he spoke favourably, he ordered to remain in a small chamber on the stairs, in which there was a pallet-bed, and the key of which he took away himself, telling the youth he would talk with him in the morning. Then dismissing his attendants, and bestowing a sullen kind of half-nod on Hippolita, he retired to his own chamber.

CHAPTER II

MATILDA, who, by Hippolita's order, had retired to her apartment, was ill-disposed to take any rest. The shocking fate of her brother had deeply affected her. She was surprised at not seeing Isabella; but the strange words which had fallen from her father, and his obscure menace to the princess, his wife, accompanied by the most furious behaviour, had filled her gentle mind with terror and alarm. She waited anxiously for the return of Bianca, a young damsel that attended her, whom she had sent to learn what was become of Isabella.

Bianca soon appeared, and informed her mistress of what she had gathered from the servants, that Isabella was nowhere to be found. She related the adventure of the young peasant who had been discovered in the vault, though with many simple additions from the incoherent accounts of the domestics; and she dwelt principally on the gigantic leg and foot which had been seen in the gallery-chamber. This last circumstance had terrified Bianca so much, that she was rejoiced when Matilda told her that she would not go to rest, but would watch till the princess should rise.

The young princess wearied herself in conjectures on the flight of Isabella, and on the threats of Manfred to her mother. "But what business could he have so urgent with the chaplain?" said Matilda. "Does he intend to have my brother's body interred privately in the chapel?"

"Oh, madam," said Bianca, "now I guess. As you are become his heiress, he is impatient to have you married. He has always been raving for more sons; I warrant he is now impatient for grandsons. As sure as I live, madam, I shall see you a bride at last. Good madam, you won't cast off your faithful Bianca: you won't put Donna Rossara over me, now you are a great princess!"

"My poor Bianca," said Matilda, "how fast your thoughts ramble! I a great princess! What hast thou seen in Manfred's behaviour since my brother's death that bespeaks any increase of tenderness to me? No, Bianca; his heart was ever a stranger to me—but he is my father, and I must not complain. Nay, if Heaven shuts my father's heart against me, it overpays my little merit in the tenderness of my mother.—O that dear mother! Yes, Bianca, 'tis there I feel the rugged temper of Manfred. I can support his harshness to me with patience; but it wounds my soul when I am witness to his causeless severity towards her."

"Oh, madam," said Bianca, "all men use their wives so, when they are weary of them."

"And yet you congratulated me but now," said Matilda, "when you fancied my father intended to dispose of me!"

"I would have you a great lady," replied Bianca, "come what will. I do not wish to see you moped in a convent, as you would be if you had your will, and if my lady, your mother, who knows that a bad husband is better than no husband at all, did not hinder you.—Bless me! what noise is that? St. Nicholas forgive me! I was but in jest."

"It is the wind," said Matilda, "whistling through the battlements in the tower above. You have heard it a thousand times."

"Nay," said Bianca, "there was no harm neither in what I said: it is no sin to talk of matrimony—and so, madam, as I was saying, if my Lord Manfred should offer you a handsome young prince for a bridegroom, you would drop him a curtsy, and tell him you would rather take the veil?"

"Thank Heaven! I am in no such danger," said Matilda: "you know how many proposals for me he has rejected."

"And you thank him like a dutiful daughter, do you, madam? —but come, madam; suppose to-morrow morning he was to send for you to the great council-chamber, and there you should find at his elbow a lovely young prince, with large black eyes, a smooth white forehead, and manly curling locks like jet; in short, madam, a young hero resembling the picture of the good Alfonso in the gallery, which you sit and gaze at for hours together."

"Do not speak lightly of that picture," interrupted Matilda, sighing: "I know the adoration with which I look at that picture is uncommon—but I am not in love with a coloured panel. The character of that virtuous prince, the veneration with which my mother has inspired me for his memory, the orisons which, I know not why, she has enjoined me to pour forth at his tomb, all have concurred to persuade me that, somehow or other, my destiny is linked with something relating to him."

"Lord, madam! how should that be?" said Bianca: "I have always heard that your family was no way related to his; and I am sure I cannot conceive why my lady, the princess, sends you in a cold morning or a damp evening to pray at his tomb: he is no saint by the almanac. If you must pray, why does she not bid you address yourself to our great St. Nicholas? I am sure he is the saint I pray to for a husband."

"Perhaps my mind would be less affected," said Matilda, "if my mother would explain her reasons to me; but it is the mystery she observes, that inspires me with this—I know not what to call it. As she never acts from caprice, I am sure there is some fatal secret at bottom—nay, I know there is. In her agony of grief for my brother's death she dropped some words that intimated as much."

"Oh, dear madam," cried Bianca, "what were they?"

"No," said Matilda, "if a parent lets fall a word, and wishes it recalled, it is not for a child to utter it."

"What! was she sorry for what she had said?" asked Bianca. "I am sure, madam, you may trust me."

"With my own little secrets, when I have any, I may," said Matilda; "but never with my mother's. A child ought to have no ears or eyes, but as a parent directs."

"Well, to be sure, madam, you were born to be a saint," said Bianca, "and there is no resisting one's vocation: you will end in a convent at last. But there is my Lady Isabella would not be so reserved to me: she will let me talk to her of young men; and when a handsome cavalier has come to the castle, she has owned to me that she wished your brother Conrad resembled him."

"Bianca," said the princess, "I do not allow you to mention my friend disrespectfully. Isabella is of a cheerful disposition, but her soul is as pure as virtue itself. She knows your idling, babbling humour, and perhaps has now and then encouraged it, to divert melancholy, and enliven the solitude in which my father keeps us."

"Blessed Mary!" said Bianca, starting, "there it is again! Dear madam, do you hear nothing? The castle is certainly haunted!"

"Peace!" said Matilda, "and listen! I did think I heard a voice—but it must be fancy; your terrors, I suppose, have infected me."

"Indeed! indeed! madam," said Bianca, half weeping with agony, "I am sure I heard a voice."

"Does anybody lie in the chamber beneath?" said the princess.

"Nobody has dared to lie there," answered Bianca, "since the great astrologer, that was your brother's tutor, drowned himself. For certain, madam, his ghost and the young prince's are now met in the chamber below; for Heaven's sake let us fly to your mother's apartment!"

"I charge you not to stir," said Matilda. "If they are spirits in pain, we may ease their sufferings by questioning them. They can mean no hurt to us, for we have not injured them; and if they should, shall we be more safe in one chamber than in another? Reach me my beads; we will say a prayer, and then speak to them."

"Oh, dear lady, I would not speak to a ghost for the world," cried Bianca. As she said these words, they heard the case-ment of the little chamber below Matilda's open. They listened attentively, and in a few minutes thought they heard a person sing, but could not distinguish the words.

"This can be no evil spirit," said the princess, in a low voice: "it is undoubtedly one of the family—open the window, and we shall know the voice."

"I dare not, indeed, madam," said Bianca.

"Thou art a very fool," said Matilda, opening the window gently herself. The noise that the princess made was, however, heard by the person beneath, who stopped, and they concluded had heard the casement open.

"Is anybody below?" said the princess: "if there is, speak."

"Yes," said an unknown voice.

"Who is it?" said Matilda.

"A stranger," replied the voice.

"What stranger?" said she, "and how didst thou come here at this unusual hour, when all the gates of the castle are locked?"

"I am not here willingly," answered the voice; "but pardon me, lady, if I have disturbed your rest: I knew not that I was overheard. Sleep has forsaken me: I left a restless couch, and came to waste the irksome hours with gazing on the fair approach of morning, impatient to be dismissed from this castle."

"Thy words and accents," said Matilda, "are of a melancholy cast: if thou art unhappy, I pity thee. If poverty afflicts thee, let me know it: I will mention thee to the princess, whose beneficent soul ever melts for the distressed; and she will relieve thee."

"I am, indeed, unhappy," said the stranger, "and I know not what wealth is; but I do not complain of the lot which Heaven has cast for me. I am young and healthy and am not ashamed of owing my support to myself; yet think me not proud, or that I disdain your generous offers. I will remember you in my orisons, and I will pray for blessings on your gracious self and your noble mistress—if I sigh, lady, it is for others, not for myself."

"Now I have it, madam," said Bianca, whispering the princess. "This is certainly the young peasant; and, by my conscience, he is in love:—well, this is a charming adventure! Do, madam, let us sift him. He does not know you, but takes you for one of my Lady Hippolita's women."

"Art thou not ashamed, Bianca?" said the princess. "What right have we to pry into the secrets of this young man's heart? He seems virtuous and frank, and tells us he is unhappy. Are those circumstances that authorize us to make a property of him? How are we entitled to his confidence?"

"Lord! madam, how little you know of love!" replied Bianca: "why, lovers have no pleasure equal to talking of their mistress."

"And would you have me become a peasant's confidant?" said the princess.

"Well, then, let me talk to him," said Bianca: "though I have the honour of being your highness's maid of honour, I was not always so great. Besides, if love levels ranks, it raises them too: I have a respect for a young man in love."

"Peace, simpleton," said the princess. "Though he said he was unhappy, it does not follow that he must be in love. Think of all that has happened to-day, and tell me, if there are no misfortunes but what love causes.—Stranger," resumed the princess, "if thy misfortunes have not been occasioned by thy own fault, and are within the compass of the Princess Hippolita's power to redress, I will take upon me to answer that she will be thy protectress. When thou art dismissed from this castle, repair to holy Father Jerome, at the convent adjoining to the church of St. Nicholas, and make thy story known to him, as far as thou thinkest meet. He will not fail to inform the princess, who is the mother of all that want her assistance. Farewell! It is not seemly for me to hold further converse with a man at this unwonted hour."

"May the saints guard thee, gracious lady!" replied the peasant; "but, oh! if a poor and worthless stranger might presume to beg a minute's audience further—am I so happy? —the casement is not shut—might I venture to ask——"

"Speak quickly," said Matilda; "the morning dawns apace; should the labourers come into the fields and perceive us— what wouldst thou ask?"

"I know not how—I know not if I dare," said the young stranger, faltering; "yet the humanity with which you have spoken to me emboldens—lady, dare I trust you?"

"Heavens," said Matilda, "what dost thou mean? with what wouldst thou trust me?—speak boldly, if thy secret is fit to be entrusted to a virtuous breast."

"I would ask," said the peasant, recollecting himself, "whether what I have heard from the domestics is true, that the princess is missing from the castle."

"What imports it to thee to know?" replied Matilda: "thy first words bespoke a prudent and becoming gravity. Dost thou come hither to pry into the secrets of Manfred? Adieu. I have been mistaken in thee." Saying these words, she shut the casement hastily, without giving the young man time to reply.

"I had acted more wisely," said the princess to Bianca, with some sharpness, "if I had let thee converse with this peasant: his inquisitiveness seems of a piece with thy own."

"It is not fit for me to argue with your highness," replied Bianca; "but perhaps the questions I should have put to him would have been more to the purpose than those you have been pleased to ask him."

"Oh, no doubt," said Matilda; "you are a very discreet personage! may I know what you would have asked him?"

"A bystander often sees more of the game than those that play," answered Bianca. "Does your highness think, madam, that his question about my Lady Isabella was the result of mere curiosity? No, no, madam; there is more in it than you great folks are aware of. Lopez told me, that all the servants believe this young fellow contrived my Lady Isabella's escape —now, pray, madam, observe—you and I both know that my Lady Isabella never much fancied the prince your brother— well, he is killed just in the critical minute—I accuse nobody. A helmet falls from the moon—so my lord, your father, says; but Lopez and all the servants say, that this young spark is a magician, and stole it from Alfonso's tomb."

"Have done with this rhapsody of impertinence," said Matilda.

"Nay, madam, as you please," cried Bianca; "yet it is very particular, though, that my Lady Isabella should be missing the very same day, and that this young sorcerer should be found at the mouth of the trap-door—I accuse nobody—but if my young lord came honestly by his death——"

"Dare not, on thy duty," said Matilda, "to breathe a suspicion on the purity of my dear Isabella's fame."

"Purity or not purity," said Bianca, "gone she is—a stranger is found that nobody knows. You question him yourself. He tells you he is in love, or unhappy, it is the same thing—nay, he owned he was unhappy about others; and is anybody unhappy about another unless they are in love with them? and at the very next word he asks innocently, poor soul, if my Lady Isabella is missing."

"To be sure," said Matilda, "thy observations are not totally without foundation; Isabella's flight amazes me. The curiosity of the stranger is very particular; yet Isabella never concealed a thought from me."

"So she told you," said Bianca, "to fish out your secrets; but who knows, madam, but this stranger may be some prince in disguise? Do, madam, let me open the window, and ask him a few questions."

"No," replied Matilda, "I will ask him myself: if he knows aught of Isabella, he is not worthy that I should converse farther with him." She was going to open the casement, when they heard the bell ring at the postern gate of the castle, which is on the right hand of the tower where Matilda lay. This prevented the princess from renewing the conversation with the stranger.

After continuing silent for some time, "I am persuaded," said she to Bianca, "that whatever be the cause of Isabella's flight, it had no unworthy motive. If this stranger was accessory to it, she must be satisfied of his fidelity and worth. I observed, did not you, Bianca? that his words were tinctured with an uncommon infusion of piety. It was no ruffian's speech: his phrases were becoming a man of gentle birth."

"I told you, madam," said Bianca, "that I was sure he was some prince in disguise."

"Yet," said Matilda, "if he was privy to her escape how will you account for his not accompanying her in her flight? Why expose himself unnecessarily and rashly to my father's resentment?"

"As for that, madam," replied she, "if he could get from under the helmet, he will find ways of eluding your father's anger. I do not doubt but he has some talisman or other about him."

"You resolve everything into magic," said Matilda; "but a man who has any intercourse with infernal spirits does not dare to make use of those tremendous and holy words which he uttered. Didst thou not observe with what fervour he vowed to remember me to Heaven in his prayers? yes; Isabella was undoubtedly convinced of his piety."

"Commend me to the piety of a young fellow and a damsel that consult to elope!" said Bianca. "No, no, madam; my Lady Isabella is of another guess-mould than you take her for. She used, indeed, to sigh and lift up her eyes in your company, because she knows you are a saint; but when your back was turned——"

"You wrong her," said Matilda. "Isabella is no hypocrite: she has a due sense of devotion, but never affected a call she has not. On the contrary, she always combated my inclination for the cloister; and though I own the mystery she has made to me of her flight confounds me—though it seems inconsistent with the friendship between us—I cannot forget the disinterested warmth with which she always opposed my taking the veil: she wished to see me married, though my dower would have been a loss to her and my brother's children. For her sake, I will believe well of this young peasant."

"Then you do think there is some liking between them?" said Bianca. While she was speaking, a servant came hastily into the chamber, and told the princess that the Lady Isabella was found.

"Where?" said Matilda.

"She has taken sanctuary in St. Nicholas's church," replied the servant: "Father Jerome has brought the news himself; he is below with his highness."

"Where is my mother?" said Matilda.

"She is in her own chamber, madam, and has asked for you."

Manfred had risen at the first dawn of light, and gone to Hippolita's apartment, to inquire if she knew aught of Isabella. While he was questioning her, word was brought that Jerome demanded to speak with him. Manfred, little suspecting the cause of the friar's arrival, and knowing he was employed by Hippolita in her charities, ordered him to be admitted, intending to leave them together, while he pursued his search after Isabella.

"Is your business with me or the princess?" said Manfred.

"With both," replied the holy man. "The Lady Isabella——"

"What of her?" interrupted Manfred, eagerly.

"Is at St. Nicholas's altar," replied Jerome.

"That is no business of Hippolita's," said Manfred with confusion: "let us retire to my chamber, father, and inform me how she came thither."

"No, my lord," replied the good man with an air of firmness and authority, that daunted even the resolute Manfred, who could not help revering the saint-like virtues of Jerome, "my commission is to both; and, with your highness's good liking, in the presence of both, I shall deliver it: but first, my lord, I must interrogate the princess, whether she is acquainted with the cause of the Lady Isabella's retirement from your castle."

"No, on my soul," said Hippolita: "does Isabella charge me with being privy to it?"

"Father," interrupted Manfred, "I pay due reverence to your holy profession; but I am sovereign here, and will allow no meddling priest to interfere in the affairs of my domestic. If you have aught to say, attend me to my chamber. I do not use to let my wife be acquainted with the secret affairs of my state: they are not within a woman's province."

"My lord," said the holy man, "I am no intruder into the secrets of families. My office is to promote peace, to heal divisions, to preach repentance, and teach mankind to curb their headstrong passions. I forgive your highness's uncharitable apostrophe: I know my duty, and am the minister of a mightier prince than Manfred. Hearken to him who speaks through my organs."

Manfred trembled with rage and shame. Hippolita's countenance declared her astonishment and impatience to know where this would end: her silence more strongly spoke her observance of Manfred.

"The Lady Isabella," resumed Jerome, "commends herself to both your highnesses: she thanks both for the kindness with which she has been treated in your castle: she deplores the loss of your son, and her own misfortune in not becoming the daughter of such wise and noble princes, whom she shall always respect as parents: she prays for uninterrupted union and felicity between you (Manfred's colour changed); but, as it is no longer possible for her to be allied to you, she entreats your consent to remain in sanctuary till she can learn news of her father, or, by the certainty of his death, be at liberty, by the approbation of her guardians, to dispose of herself in suitable marrriage."

"I shall give no such consent," said the prince; "but insist on her return to the castle without delay: I am answerable for her person to her guardians, and will not brook her being in any hands but my own."

"Your highness will recollect whether that can any longer be proper," replied the friar.

"I want no monitor," said Manfred, colouring: "Isabella's conduct leaves room for strange suspicions; and that young villain, who was at least the accomplice of her flight, if not the cause of it——"

"The cause!" interrupted Jerome; "was a *young* man the cause?"

"This is not to be borne!" cried Manfred. "Am I to be bearded in my own palace by an insolent monk? thou art privy, I guess, to their amours."

"I would pray to Heaven to clear up your uncharitable surmises," said Jerome, "if your highness were not satisfied in your conscience how unjustly you accuse me. I do pray to Heaven to pardon that uncharitableness; and I implore your highness to leave the princess at peace in that holy place, where she is not liable to be disturbed by such vain and worldly fantasies as discourses of love from any man."

"Cant not to me," said Manfred, "but return and bring the princess to her duty."

"It is my duty to prevent her return hither," said Jerome. "She is where orphans and virgins are safest from the snares and wiles of this world; and nothing but a parent's authority shall take her thence."

"I am her parent," cried Manfred, "and demand her."

"She wished to have you for her parent," said the friar: "but Heaven, that forbade that connection, has for ever dissolved all ties betwixt you: and I announce to your highness——"

"Stop! audacious man," said Manfred, "and dread my displeasure."

"Holy father," said Hippolita, "it is your office to be no respecter of persons: you must speak as your duty prescribes; but it is my duty to hear nothing that it pleases not my lord I should hear. Attend the prince to his chamber. I will retire to my oratory, and pray to the blessed Virgin to inspire you with her holy counsels, and to restore the heart of my gracious lord to its wonted peace and gentleness."

"Excellent woman!" said the friar.—"My lord, I attend your pleasure."

Manfred, accompanied by the friar, passed to his own apartment, where, shutting the door, "I perceive, father," said he, "that Isabella has acquainted you with my purpose. Now hear my resolve, and obey. Reasons of state, most urgent reasons, my own and the safety of my people, demand that I should have a son. It is in vain to expect an heir from Hippolita; I have made choice of Isabella. You must bring her back, and you must do more. I know the influence you have with Hippolita: her conscience is in your hands. She is, I allow, a faultless woman: her soul is set on heaven, and scorns the little grandeur of this world: you can withdraw her from it entirely. Persuade her to consent to the dissolution of our marriage, and to retire into a monastery: she shall endow one if she will; and shall have the means of being as liberal to your order as she or you can wish. Thus you will divert the calamities that are hanging over our heads, and have the merit of saving the principality of Otranto from destruction. You are a prudent man, and, though the warmth of my temper betrayed me into some unbecoming expressions, I honour your virtue, and wish to be indebted to you for the repose of my life and the preservation of my family."

"The will of Heaven be done," said the friar. "I am but its worthless instrument. It makes use of my tongue to tell thee, prince, of thy unwarrantable designs. The injuries of the virtuous Hippolita have mounted to the throne of pity. By me thou art reprimanded for thy adulterous intention of repudiating her: by me thou art warned not to pursue the incestuous design on thy contracted daughter. Heaven, that delivered her from thy fury, when the judgments so recently fallen on thy house ought to have inspired thee with other thoughts, will continue to watch over her. Even I, a poor and despised friar, am able to protect her from thy violence. I, sinner as I am, and uncharitably reviled by your highness as an accomplice of I know not what amours, scorn the allurements with which it has pleased thee to tempt mine honesty. I love my order; I honour devout souls; I respect the piety of thy princess; but I will not betray the confidence she reposes in me, nor serve even the cause of religion by foul and sinful compliances: but, forsooth, the welfare of the state depends on your highness having a son! Heaven mocks the short-sighted views of man. But yester-morn, whose house was so great, so flourishing as Manfred's? Where is young Conrad now? My lord, I respect your tears, but I mean not to check them: let them flow, prince! they will weigh more with Heaven towards the welfare of thy subjects, than a marriage which, founded on lust or policy, could never prosper. The sceptre which passed from the race of Alfonso to thine cannot be preserved by a match which the Church will never allow. If it is the will of the Most High that Manfred's name must perish, resign yourself, my lord, to its decrees; and thus deserve a crown that can never pass away. Come, my lord, I like this sorrow; let us return to the princess; she is not apprised of your cruel intentions; nor did I mean more than to alarm you. You saw with what gentle patience, with what efforts of love, she heard, she rejected hearing, the extent of your guilt. I know she longs to fold you in her arms, and assure you of her unalterable affection."

"Father," said the prince, "you mistake my compunction. True, I honour Hippolita's virtues; I think her a saint; and wish it were for my soul's health to tie faster the knot that has united us; but, alas, father, you know not the bitterest of my pangs; it is some time that I have had scruples on the legality of our union: Hippolita is related to me in the fourth degree—it is true, we had a dispensation: but I have been informed, that she had also been contracted to another. This it is that sits heavy at my heart; to this state of unlawful wedlock I impute the visitation that has fallen on me in the death of Conrad. Ease my conscience of this burden, dissolve our marriage, and accomplish the work of godliness which your divine exhortations have commenced in my soul."

How cutting was the anguish which the good man felt, when he perceived this turn in the wily prince! He trembled for Hippolita, whose ruin he saw was determined; and he feared if Manfred had no hope of recovering Isabella, that his impatience for a son would direct him to some other object who might not be equally proof against the temptation of Manfred's rank. For some time the holy man remained absorbed in thought. At length, conceiving some hopes from delay, he thought the wisest conduct would be to prevent the prince from despairing of recovering Isabella. Her the friar knew he could dispose, from her affection to Hippolita, and from the aversion she had expressed to him for Manfred's addresses, to second his views till the censures of the Church could be fulminated against a divorce. With this intention, as if struck with the prince's scruples, he at length said:

"My lord, I have been pondering on what your highness has said; and if in truth it is delicacy of conscience that is the real motive of your repugnance to your virtuous lady, far be it from me to endeavour to harden your heart. The Church is an indulgent mother; unfold your griefs to her; she alone can administer comfort to your soul, either by satisfying your conscience, or, upon examination of your scruples, by setting you at liberty, and indulging you in the lawful means of continuing your lineage. In the latter case, if the Lady Isabella can be brought to consent——"

Manfred, who concluded that he had either over-reached the good man, or that his first warmth had been but a tribute paid to appearance, was overjoyed at this sudden turn, and repeated the most magnificent promises, if he should succeed by the friar's mediation. The well-meaning priest suffered him to deceive himself, fully determined to traverse his views, instead of seconding them.

"Since we now understand one another," resumed the prince, "I expect, father, that you satisfy me in one point. Who is the youth that I found in the vault? He must have been privy to Isabella's flight. Tell me truly, is he her lover? or is he an agent for another's passion? I have often suspected Isabella's indifference to my son; a thousand circumstances crowd on my mind that confirm that suspicion. She herself was so conscious of it, that while I discoursed her in the gallery she outran my suspicions, and endeavoured to justify herself from coolness to Conrad."

The friar, who knew nothing of the youth but what he had learnt occasionally from the princess, ignorant what was become of him, and not sufficiently reflecting on the impetuosity of Manfred's temper, conceived that it might not be amiss to sow the seeds of jealousy in his mind: they might be turned to some use hereafter, either by prejudicing the prince against Isabella, if he persisted in that union; or, by diverting his attention to a wrong scent, and employing his thoughts on a visionary intrigue, prevent his engaging in any new pursuit. With this unhappy policy, he answered in a manner to confirm Manfred in the belief of some connection between Isabella and the youth. The prince, whose passions wanted little fuel to throw them into a blaze, fell into a rage at the idea of what the friar had suggested.

"I will fathom to the bottom of this intrigue," cried he; and quitting Jerome abruptly, with a command to remain there till his return, he hastened to the great hall of the castle, and ordered the peasant to be brought before him.

"Thou hardened young impostor," said the prince, as soon as he saw the youth; "what becomes of thy boasted veracity now? It was Providence, was it, and the light of the moon, that discovered the lock of the trap-door to thee? Tell me, audacious boy, who thou art, and how long thou hast been acquainted with the princess; and take care to answer with less equivocation than thou didst last night, or tortures shall wring the truth from thee."

The young man, perceiving that his share in the flight of the princess was discovered, and concluding that anything he should say could no longer be of service or detriment to her, replied, "I am no impostor, my lord, nor have I deserved opprobrious language. I answered to every question your highness put to me last night with the same veracity that I shall speak now; and that will not be from fear of your tortures, but because my soul abhors a falsehood. Please to repeat your questions, my lord; I am ready to give you all the satisfaction in my power."

"You know my questions," replied the prince, "and only want time to prepare an evasion. Speak directly; who art thou, and how long hast thou been known to the princess?"

"I am a labourer at the next village," said the peasant; "my name is Theodore. The princess found me in the vault last night; before that hour I never was in her presence."

"I may believe as much or as little as I please of this," said Manfred; "but I will hear thy own story, before I examine into the truth of it. Tell me, what reason did the princess give thee for making her escape? Thy life depends on thy answer."

"She told me," replied Theodore, "that she was on the brink of destruction, and that if she could not escape from the castle, she was in danger in a few moments of being made miserable for ever."

"And on this slight foundation, on a silly girl's report," said Manfred, "thou didst hazard my displeasure!"

"I fear no man's displeasure," said Theodore, "when a woman in distress puts herself under my protection."

During this examination Matilda was going to the apartment of Hippolita. At the upper end of the hall, where Manfred sat, was a boarded gallery, with latticed windows, through which Matilda and Bianca were to pass. Hearing her father's voice, and seeing the servants assembled round him, she stopped to learn the occasion. The prisoner soon drew her attention: the steady and composed manner in which he answered, and the gallantry of his last reply, which were the first words she heard distinctly, interested her in his favour. His person was noble, handsome, and commanding, even in that situation, but his countenance soon engrossed her whole care.

"Heavens! Bianca," said the princess softly, "do I dream, or is not that youth the exact resemblance of Alfonso's picture in the gallery?" She could say no more, for her father's voice grew louder at every word.

"This bravado," said he, "surpasses all thy former insolence. Thou shalt experience the wrath with which thou darest to trifle. Seize him," continued Manfred, "and bind him—the first news the princess hears of her champion shall be, that he has lost his head for her sake."

"The injustice of which thou art guilty towards me," said Theodore, "convinces me that I have done a good deed in delivering the princess from thy tyranny. May she be happy, whatever becomes of me!"

"This is a lover," cried Manfred, in a rage; "a peasant within sight of death is not animated by such sentiments. Tell me, tell me, rash boy, who thou art, or the rack shall force thy secret from thee."

"Thou hast threatened me with death already," said the youth, "for the truth I have told thee; if that is all the encouragement I am to expect for sincerity, I am not tempted to indulge thy vain curiosity further."

"Then thou wilt not speak?" said Manfred.

"I will not," replied he.

"Bear him away into the court-yard," said Manfred; "I will see his head this instant severed from his body."

Matilda fainted at hearing those words. Bianca shrieked and cried, "Help, help! the princess is dead!" Manfred started at this ejaculation, and demanded what was the matter. The young peasant, who heard it too, was struck with horror, and asked eagerly the same question; but Manfred ordered him to be hurried into the court, and kept there for execution, till he had informed himself of the cause of Bianca's shrieks. When he learned the meaning, he treated it as a womanish panic, and ordering Matilda to be carried to her apartment, he rushed into the court, and calling for one of his guards, bade Theodore kneel down and prepare to receive the fatal blow.

The undaunted youth received the bitter sentence with a resignation that touched every heart but Manfred's. He wished earnestly to know the meaning of the words he had heard relating to the princess; but fearing to exasperate the tyrant more against her, he desisted. The only boon he deigned to ask was, that he might be permitted to have a confessor, and make his peace with Heaven. Manfred, who hoped by the confessor's means to come at the youth's history, readily granted his request; and being convinced that Father Jerome was now in his interest, he ordered him to be called and shrive the prisoner. The holy man, who had little foreseen the catastrophe that his imprudence occasioned, fell on his knees to the prince, and adjured him in the most solemn manner not to shed innocent blood. He accused himself in the bitterest terms for his indiscretion, endeavoured to exculpate the youth, and left no method untried to soften the tyrant's rage. Manfred, more incensed than appeased by Jerome's intercession, whose retraction now made him suspect he had been imposed upon by both, commanded the friar to do his duty, telling him he would not allow the prisoner many minutes for confession.

"Nor do I ask many, my lord," said the unhappy young

man. "My sins, thank Heaven, have not been numerous; nor exceed what might be expected at my years. Dry your tears, good father, and let us dispatch: this is a bad world; nor have I had cause to leave it with regret."

"Oh, wretched youth!" said Jerome, "how canst thou bear the sight of me with patience? I am thy murderer! it is I have brought this dismal hour upon thee!"

"I forgive thee from my soul," said the youth, "as I hope Heaven will pardon me. Hear my confession, father, and give me thy blessing."

"How can I prepare thee for thy passage as I ought?" said Jerome. "Thou canst not be saved without pardoning thy foes, and canst thou forgive that impious man there?"

"I can," said Theodore; "and do."

"And does not this touch thee, cruel prince?" said the friar.

"I sent for thee to confess him," said Manfred, sternly; "not to plead for him. Thou didst first incense me against him; his blood be upon thy head."

"It will, it will!" said the good man, in an agony of sorrow. "Thou and I must never hope to go where this blessed youth is going."

"Dispatch," said Manfred; "I am no more to be moved by the whining of priests than by the shrieks of women."

"What!" said the youth; "is it possible that my fate could have occasioned what I heard? Is the princess, then, again in thy power?"

"Thou dost but remember me of my wrath," said Manfred; "prepare thee, for this moment is thy last."

The youth, who felt his indignation rise, and who was touched with the sorrow which he saw he had infused into all the spectators, as well as into the friar, suppressed his emotions, and putting off his doublet, and unbuttoning his collar, knelt down to his prayers. As he stooped, his shirt slipped down below his shoulder, and discovered the mark of a bloody arrow.

"Gracious Heaven!" cried the holy man, starting, "what do I see? It is my child, my Theodore!"

The passions that ensued must be conceived; they cannot be painted. The tears of the assistants were suspended by wonder, rather than stopped by joy. They seemed to inquire into the eyes of their lord what they ought to feel. Surprise, doubt, tenderness, respect, succeeded each other in the countenance of the youth. He received with modest submission the effusion of the old man's tears and embraces; yet, afraid of giving a loose to hope, and suspecting, from what had passed, the inflexibility of Manfred's temper, he cast a glance towards the prince, as if to say, Canst thou be unmoved at such a scene as this?

Manfred's heart was capable of being touched. He forgot his anger in his astonishment; yet his pride forbade his owning himself affected. He even doubted whether this discovery was not a contrivance of the friar to save the youth. "What may this mean?" said he; "how can he be thy son? Is it consistent with thy profession or reputed sanctity to avow a peasant's offspring for the fruit of thy irregular amours?"

"Oh God!" said the holy man, "dost thou question his being mine? Could I feel the anguish I do, if I were not his father? Spare him, good prince! spare him! and revile me as thou pleasest."

"Spare him! spare him!" cried the attendants, "for this good man's sake."

"Peace!" said Manfred, sternly; "I must know, ere I am disposed to pardon. A saint's bastard may be no saint himself."

"Injurious lord!" said Theodore; "add not insult to cruelty. If I am this venerable man's son, though no prince, as thou art, know, the blood that flows in my veins——"

"Yes," said the friar, interrupting him, "his blood is noble; nor is he that abject thing, my lord, you speak him. He is my lawful son; and Sicily can boast of few houses more ancient than that of Falconara—but, alas! my lord, what is blood? what is nobility? We are all reptiles, miserable, sinful creatures. It is piety alone that can distinguish us from the dust whence we sprung, and whither we must return."

"Truce to your sermon," said Manfred; "you forget you are no longer Friar Jerome, but the Count of Falconara. Let me know your history: you will have time enough to moralize hereafter, if you should not happen to obtain the grace of that sturdy criminal there."

"Mother of God!" said the friar, "is it possible my lord can refuse a father the life of his only, his long-lost child? Trample me, my lord, scorn, afflict me, accept my life for his, but spare my son!"

"Thou canst feel, then," said Manfred, "what it is to lose an only son! A little hour ago thou didst preach up resignation to me: *my* house, if fate so pleased, must perish—but the Count of Falconara——"

"Alas! my lord," said Jerome, "I confess I have offended;

but aggravate not an old man's sufferings. I boast not of my family, nor think of such vanities; it is nature that pleads for this boy; it is the memory of the dear woman that bore him—is she, Theodore, is she dead?"

"Her soul has long been with the blessed," said Theodore.

"Oh! how?" cried Jerome; "tell me—no—she is happy! Thou art all my care now. Most dread lord! will you—will you grant me my poor boy's life?"

"Return to thy convent," answered Manfred; "conduct the princess hither; obey me in what else thou knowest, and I promise thee the life of thy son."

"Oh, my lord!" said Jerome, "is my honesty the price I must pay for this dear youth's safety?"

"For me!" cried Theodore; "let me die a thousand deaths, rather than stain thy conscience. What is it the tyrant would exact of thee? Is the princess still safe from his power? Protect her, thou venerable old man, and let all the weight of his wrath fall on me."

Jerome endeavoured to check the impetuosity of the youth; and ere Manfred could reply, the trampling of horses was heard, and a brazen trumpet, which hung without the gate of the castle, was suddenly sounded. At the same instant the sable plumes on the enchanted helmet, which still remained at the other end of the court, were tempestuously agitated, and nodded thrice, as if bowed by some invisible wearer.

CHAPTER III

MANFRED's heart misgave him when he beheld the plumage on the miraculous casque shaken in concert with the sounding of the brazen trumpet. "Father," said he to Jerome, whom he now ceased to treat as Count of Falconara, "what mean these portents? If I have offended"—the plumes were shaken with greater violence than before. "Unhappy prince that I am!" cried Manfred. "Holy father, will you not assist me with your prayers?"

"My lord," replied Jerome, "Heaven is no doubt displeased with your mockery of its servants. Submit yourself to the Church, and cease to persecute her ministers. Dismiss this innocent youth, and learn to respect the holy character I wear:

Heaven will not be trifled with. You see"— the trumpet sounded again.

"I acknowledge I have been too hasty," said Manfred. "Father, do you go to the wicket, and demand who is at the gate."

"Do you grant me the life of Theodore?" replied the friar.

"I do," said Manfred; "but inquire who is without."

Jerome, falling on the neck of his son, discharged a flood of tears, that spoke the fullness of his soul.

"You promised to go to the gate," said Manfred.

"I thought," replied the friar, "your highness would excuse my thanking you first in this tribute of my heart."

"Go, dearest sir," said Theodore, "obey the prince; I do not deserve that you should delay his satisfaction for me."

Jerome, inquiring who was without, was answered, "A herald."

"From whom?" said he.

"From the Knight of the Gigantic Sabre," said the herald; "and I must speak with the usurper of Otranto."

Jerome returned to the prince, and did not fail to repeat the message in the very words it had been uttered. The first sounds struck Manfred with terror; but when he heard himself styled usurper, his rage rekindled, and all his courage revived.

"Usurper!—insolent villain!" cried he; "who dares to question my title? Retire, father; this is no business for monks: I will meet this presumptuous man myself. Go to your convent, and prepare the princess's return; your son shall be a hostage for your fidelity: his life depends on your obedience."

"Good Heaven! my lord," cried Jerome, "your highness did but this instant freely pardon my child. Have you so soon forgot the interposition of Heaven?"

"Heaven," replied Manfred, "does not send heralds to question the title of a lawful prince. I doubt whether it even notifies its will through friars; but that is your affair, not mine. At present you know my pleasure; and it is not a saucy herald that shall save your son, if you do not return with the princess."

It was in vain for the holy man to reply. Manfred commanded him to be conducted to the postern gate, and shut out from the castle; and he ordered some of his attendants to carry Theodore to the top of the Black Tower, and guard him strictly scarce permitting the father and son to exchange a hasty embrace at parting. He then withdrew to the hall, and seating himself in princely state, ordered the herald to be admitted to his presence.

"Well, thou insolent!" said the prince, "what wouldst thou with me?"

"I come," replied he, "to thee, Manfred, usurper of the principality of Otranto, from the renowned and invincible knight, the Knight of the Gigantic Sabre: in the name of his lord, Frederic Marquis of Vicenza, he demands the Lady Isabella, daughter of that prince, whom thou hast basely and traitorously got into thy power, by bribing her false guardians during his absence; and he requires thee to resign the principality of Otranto, which thou hast usurped from the said Lord Frederic, the nearest of blood to the last rightful lord, Alfonso the Good. If thou dost not instantly comply with these just demands, he defies thee to single combat to the last extremity." And so saying the herald cast down his warder.

"And where is this braggart who sends thee?" said Manfred.

"At the distance of a league," said the herald: "he comes to make good his lord's claim against thee, as he is a true knight, and thou an usurper and ravisher."

Injurious as this challenge was, Manfred reflected that it was not his interest to provoke the marquis. He knew how well founded the claim of Frederic was, nor was this the first time he had heard of it. Frederic's ancestors had assumed the style of Princes of Otranto, from the death of Alfonso the Good without issue; but Manfred, his father, and grandfather, had been too powerful for the house of Vicenza to dispossess them. Frederic, a martial, amorous young prince, had married a beautiful young lady, of whom he was enamoured, and who had died in childbed of Isabella. Her death affected him so much, that he had taken the cross and gone to the Holy Land, where he was wounded in an engagement against the infidels, made prisoner, and reported to be dead. When the news reached Manfred's ears, he bribed the guardians of the Lady Isabella to deliver her up to him as a bride for his son Conrad, by which alliance he had proposed to unite the claims of the two houses. This motive, on Conrad's death, had co-operated to make him so suddenly resolve on espousing her himself; and the same reflection determined him now to endeavour at obtaining the consent of Frederic to this marriage. A like policy inspired him with the thought of inviting Frederic's champion into his castle, lest he should be informed of Isabella's flight, which he strictly enjoined his domestics not to disclose to any of the knight's retinue.

"Herald," said Manfred, as soon as he had digested these reflections, "return to thy master, and tell him, ere we liquidate our differences by the sword, Manfred would hold some converse with him. Bid him welcome to my castle, where, by my faith, as I am a true knight, he shall have courteous reception, and full security for himself and followers. If we cannot adjust our quarrel by amicable means, I swear he shall depart in safety, and shall have full satisfaction according to the laws of arms. So help me God and his Holy Trinity!" The herald made three obeisances, and retired.

During this interview, Jerome's mind was agitated by a thousand contrary passions. He trembled for the life of his son, and his first thought was to persuade Isabella to return to the castle. Yet he was scarce less alarmed at the thought of her union with Manfred. He dreaded Hippolita's unbounded submission to the will of her lord; and though he did not doubt but he could alarm her piety not to consent to a divorce, if he could get access to her, yet, should Manfred discover that the obstruction came from him, it might be equally fatal to Theodore. He was impatient to know whence came the herald, who, with so little management, had questioned the title of Manfred; yet he did not dare absent himself from the convent, lest Isabella should leave it, and her flight be imputed to him. He returned disconsolately to the monastery, uncertain on what conduct to resolve. A monk, who met him in the porch, and observed his melancholy air, said, "Alas! brother, is it then true that we have lost our excellent Princess Hippolita?"

The holy man started, and cried, "What meanest thou, brother? I came this instant from the castle, and left her in perfect health."

"Martelli," replied the other friar, "passed by the convent but a quarter of an hour ago, on his way from the castle, and reported that her highness was dead. All our brethren are gone to the chapel to pray for her happy transit to a better life, and willed me to wait thy arrival. They know thy holy attachment to that good lady, and are anxious for the affliction it will cause thee—indeed we have all reason to weep; she was a mother to our house. But this life is but a pilgrimage; we must not murmur—we shall all follow her: may our end be like hers!"

"Good brother, thou dreamest," said Jerome; "I tell thee I

come from the castle, and left the princess well:—where is the Lady Isabella?"

"Poor gentlewoman," replied the friar, "I told her the sad news, and offered her spiritual comfort; I reminded her of the transitory condition of mortality, and advised her to take the veil: I quoted the example of the holy Princess Sanchia of Arragon."

"Thy zeal was laudable," said Jerome, impatiently; "but at present it was unnecessary. Hippolita is well—at least I trust in the Lord she is; I heard nothing to the contrary—yet methinks, the prince's earnestness—well, brother, but where is the Lady Isabella?"

"I know not," said the friar: "she wept much, and said she would retire to her chamber."

Jerome left his comrade abruptly, and hastened to the princess, but she was not in her chamber. He inquired of the domestics of the convent, but could learn no news of her. He searched in vain throughout the monastery and the church, and dispatched messengers round the neighbourhood, to get intelligence if she had been seen, but to no purpose. Nothing could equal the good man's perplexity. He judged that Isabella, suspecting Manfred of having precipitated his wife's death, had taken the alarm, and withdrawn herself to some more secret place of concealment. This new flight would probably carry the prince's fury to the height. The report of Hippolita's death, though it seemed almost incredible, increased his consternation; and though Isabella's escape bespoke her aversion of Manfred for a husband, Jerome could feel no comfort from it while it endangered the life of his son. He determined to return to the castle, and made several of his brethren accompany him, to attest his innocence to Manfred, and, if necessary, join their intercessions with his for Theodore.

The prince, in the meantime, had passed into the court, and ordered the gates of the castle to be flung open for the reception of the stranger knight and his train. In a few minutes the cavalcade arrived. First came two harbingers with wands; next a herald, followed by two pages and two trumpeters; then a hundred foot-guards. These were attended by as many horse. After them fifty footmen, clothed in scarlet and black, the colours of the knight; then a led horse. Two heralds on each side of a gentleman on horseback, bearing a banner, with the arms of Vicenza and Otranto quarterly—a circumstance that much offended Manfred, but he stifled his resentment. Two more pages; the knight's confessor telling his beads; fifty more footmen clad as before; two knights habited in complete armour, their beavers down, comrades to the principal knight; the squires of the two knights, carrying their shields and devices; the knight's own squire; a hundred gentlemen bearing an enormous sword, and seeming to faint under the weight of it. The knight himself, on a chestnut steed, in complete armour, his lance in the rest, his face entirely concealed by his visor, which was surmounted by a large plume of scarlet and black feathers. Fifty foot-guards, with drums and trumpets, closed the procession, which wheeled off to the right and left, to make room for the principal knight.

As soon as he approached the gate, he stopped; and the herald, advancing, read again the words of the challenge. Manfred's eyes were fixed on the gigantic sword, and he scarce seemed to attend to the cartel; but his attention was soon diverted by a tempest of wind that rose behind him: he turned, and beheld the plumes of the enchanted helmet agitated in the same extraordinary manner as before. It required intrepidity like Manfred's not to sink under a concurrence of circumstances that seemed to announce his fate. Yet, scorning in the presence of strangers to betray the courage he had always manifested, he said boldly:

"Sir Knight, whoever thou art, I bid thee welcome. If thou art of mortal mould, thy valour shall meet its equal; and if thou art a true knight, thou wilt scorn to employ sorcery to carry thy point. Be these omens from heaven or hell, Manfred trusts to the righteousness of his cause, and to the aid of St. Nicholas, who has ever protected his house. Alight, Sir Knight, and repose thyself; to-morrow thou shalt have a fair field; and Heaven befriend the juster side!"

The knight made no reply, but, dismounting, was conducted by Manfred to the great hall of the castle. As they traversed the court, the knight stopped to gaze on the miraculous casque; and, kneeling down, seemed to pray inwardly for some minutes. Rising, he made a sign to the prince to lead on. As soon as they entered the hall, Manfred proposed to the stranger to disarm, but the knight shook his head in token of refusal. "Sir Knight," said Manfred, "this is not courteous: but by my good faith I will not cross thee; nor shalt thou have cause to complain of the Prince of Otranto. No treachery is designed on my part; I hope none is intended on thine; here, take my gage," giving him his ring, "your friends and you shall enjoy the laws of hospitality. Rest here until refreshments are brought; I will but give orders for the accommodation of your train, and return to you."

The three knights bowed, as accepting his courtesy. Manfred directed the stranger's retinue to be conducted to an adjacent hospital, founded by the Princess Hippolita for the reception of pilgrims. As they made the circuit of the court to return towards the gate, the gigantic sword burst from the supporters, and falling to the ground opposite to the helmet, remained immovable. Manfred, almost hardened to preternatural appearances, surmounted the shock of this new prodigy; and returning to the hall, where by this time the feast was ready, he invited his silent guests to take their places. Manfred, however ill his heart was at ease, endeavoured to inspire the company with mirth. He put several questions to them, but was answered only by signs. They raised their visors but sufficiently to feed themselves, and that but sparingly.

"Sirs," said the prince, "ye are the first guests I ever treated within these walls, who scorned to hold any intercourse with me; nor has it oft been customary, I ween, for princes to hazard their state and dignity against strangers and mutes. You say you come in the name of Frederic of Vicenza; I have ever heard that he was a gallant and courteous knight; nor would he, I am bold to say, think it beneath him to mix in social converse with a prince who is his equal, and not unknown by deeds in arms.—Still ye are silent—well, be it as it may, by the laws of hospitality and chivalry, ye are masters under this roof: ye shall do your pleasure—but come, give me a goblet of wine; ye will not refuse to pledge me to the healths of your fair mistresses." The principal knight sighed and crossed himself, and was rising from the board. "Sir Knight," said Manfred, "what I said was but in sport; I shall constrain you in nothing. Use your good liking; since mirth is not your mood, let us be sad. Business may hit your fancies better; let us withdraw, and hear if what I have to unfold may be better relished than the vain efforts I have made for your pastime."

Manfred then conducting the three knights into an inner chamber, shut the door, and inviting them to be seated, began thus, addressing himself to the chief personage:

"You come, Sir Knight, as I understand, in the name of the Marquis of Vicenza, to re-demand the Lady Isabella, his daughter, who has been contracted, in the face of Holy Church, to my son, by the consent of her legal guardians; and to require

me to resign my dominions to your lord, who gives himself
for the nearest of blood to Prince Alfonso, whose soul God rest!
I shall speak to the latter article of your demands first. You
must know, your lord knows, that I enjoy the principality of
Otranto from my father Don Manuel, as he received it from his
father Don Ricardo. Alfonso, their predecessor, dying child-
less in the Holy Land, bequeathed his estates to my grandfather, Don Ricardo, in consideration of his faithful services."
—The stranger shook his head.—"Sir Knight," said Manfred,
warmly, "Ricardo was a valiant and upright man; he was a
pious man; witness his munificent foundation of the adjoining
church and two convents. He was peculiarly patronized by
St. Nicholas—my grandfather was incapable—I say, sir, Don
Ricardo was incapable—excuse me, your interruption has disordered me.—I venerate the memory of my grandfather.—Well!
sirs, he held this estate; he held it by his good sword and by the
favour of St. Nicholas—so did my father; and so, sirs, will I,
come what come will.—But Frederic, your lord, is nearest in
blood.—I have consented to put my title to the issue of the
sword—does that imply a vicious title?—I might have asked,
where is Frederic, your lord? Report speaks him dead in captivity. You say, your actions say, he lives—I question it not
—I might, sirs, I might, but I do not. Other princes would
bid Frederic take his inheritance by force, if he can: they
would not stake their dignity on a single combat: they would
not submit it to the decision of unknown mutes!—Pardon me,
gentlemen, I am too warm; but suppose yourselves in my
situation: as ye are stout knights, would it not move your
choler to have your own and the honour of your ancestors
called in question?—But to the point: ye require me to deliver
up the Lady Isabella.—Sirs, I must ask if ye are authorized to
receive her?"—The knight nodded.—"Receive her!" continued
Manfred: "well, you are authorized to receive her—but, gentle
knight, may I ask if you have full powers?"—The knight
nodded.—"'Tis well," said Manfred. "Then hear what I have
to offer.—Ye see, gentlemen, before you the most unhappy of
men (he began to weep); afford me your compassion; I am
entitled to it; indeed I am. Know, I have lost my only hope,
my joy, the support of my house—Conrad died yester-morning."
—The knights discovered signs of surprise.—"Yes, sirs, fate
has disposed of my son. Isabella is at liberty."

"Do you then restore her?" cried the chief knight, breaking
silence.

"Afford me your patience," said Manfred. "I rejoice to find, by this testimony of your good will, that this matter may be adjusted without bloodshed. It is no interest of mine dictates what little I have farther to say. Ye behold in me a man disgusted with the world; the loss of my son has weaned me from earthly cares. Power and greatness have no longer any charms in my eyes. I wished to transmit the sceptre I had received from my ancestors with honour to my son—but that is over! Life itself is so indifferent to me, that I accepted your defiance with joy: a good knight cannot go to the grave with more satisfaction than when falling in his vocation. Whatever is the will of Heaven I submit; for, alas! sirs, I am a man of many sorrows. Manfred is no object of envy—but no doubt you are acquainted with my story."—The knight made signs of ignorance, and seemed curious to have Manfred proceed.— "Is it possible, sirs," continued the prince, "that my story should be a secret to you? Have you heard nothing relating to me and the Princess Hippolita?"—They shook their heads.— "No! thus, then sirs, it is. You think me ambitious: ambition alas! is composed of more rugged materials. If I were ambitious, I should not for so many years have been a prey to all the hell of conscientious scruples—but I weary your patience: I will be brief. Know, then, that I have long been troubled in mind on my union with the Princess Hippolita.—Oh, sirs, if ye were acquainted with that excellent woman! if ye knew that I adore her like a mistress, and cherish her as a friend—but man was not born of perfect happiness! She shares my scruples, and with her consent I have brought this matter before the Church, for we are related within the forbidden degrees. I expect every hour the definitive sentence that must separate us for ever— I am sure you feel for me—I see you do—pardon these tears!" —The knights gazed on each other, wondering where this would end. Manfred continued:—"The death of my son betiding while my soul was under this anxiety, I thought of nothing but resigning my dominions, and retiring for ever from the sight of mankind. My only difficulty was to fix on a successor, who would be tender of my people, and to dispose of the Lady Isabella, who is dear to me as my own blood. I was willing to restore the line of Alfonso, even in his most distant kindred; and though, pardon me, I am satisfied it was his will that Ricardo's lineage should take place of his own relations, yet where was I to search for those relations? I knew of none but Frederic, your lord: he was a captive to the infidels, or dead;

and were he living, and at home, would he quit the flourishing
state of Vicenza for the inconsiderable principality of Otranto?
If he would not, could I bear the thought of seeing a hard
unfeeling viceroy set over my poor faithful people?—for, sirs, I
love my people, and, thank Heaven, am beloved by them.   But
ye will ask, whither tends this long discourse? briefly, then,
thus, sirs.   Heaven in your arrival seems to point out a remedy
for these difficulties and my misfortunes.   The Lady Isabella
is at liberty; I shall soon be so—I would submit to anything
for the good of my people—were it not the best, the only way
to extinguish the feuds between our families if I was to take
the Lady Isabella to wife—you start—but though Hippolita's
virtues will ever be dear to me, a prince must not consider
himself; he is born for his people."—A servant at that instant
entering the chamber, apprised Manfred that Jerome and
several of his brethren demanded immediate access to him.

The prince, provoked at this interruption, and fearing that
the friar would discover to the strangers that Isabella had taken
sanctuary, was going to forbid Jerome's entrance.   But recollecting that he was certainly arrived to notify the princess's
return, Manfred began to excuse himself to the knights for
leaving them for a few moments, but was prevented by the
arrival of the friars.   Manfred angrily reprimanded them for
their intrusion, and would have forced them back from the
chamber; but Jerome was too much agitated to be repulsed.
He declared aloud the flight of Isabella, with protestations of
his own innocence.   Manfred, distracted at the news, and not
less at its coming to the knowledge of the strangers, uttered
nothing but incoherent sentences, now upbraiding the friar,
now apologizing to the knights; earnest to know what was
become of Isabella, yet equally afraid of their knowing; impatient to pursue her, yet dreading to have them join in the
pursuit.   He offered to dispatch messengers in quest of her—but
the chief knight, no longer keeping silence, reproached Manfred
in bitter terms for his dark and ambiguous dealing, and demanded the cause of Isabella's first absence from the castle.
Manfred, casting a stern look at Jerome, implying a command
of silence, pretended that on Conrad's death he had placed her
in sanctuary until he could determine how to dispose of her.
Jerome, who trembled for his son's life, did not dare contradict
this falsehood, but one of his brethren, not under the same
anxiety, declared frankly that she had fled to their church in
the preceding night.   The prince in vain endeavoured to stop

this discovery, which overwhelmed him with shame and confusion. The principal stranger, amazed at the contradictions he heard, and more than half persuaded that Manfred had secreted the princess, notwithstanding the concern he expressed at her flight, rushing to the door, said,—"Thou traitor-prince! Isabella shall be found." Manfred endeavoured to hold him, but the other knights assisting their comrade, he broke from the prince, and hastened into the court, demanding his attendants. Manfred, finding it vain to divert him from the pursuit, offered to accompany him; and summoning his attendants, and taking Jerome and some of the friars to guide them, they issued from the castle; Manfred privately giving orders to have the knight's company secured, while to the knight he affected to dispatch a messenger to require their assistance.

The company had no sooner quitted the castle, than Matilda, who felt herself deeply interested for the young peasant, since she had seen him condemned to death in the hall, and whose thoughts had been taken up with concerting measures to save him, was informed by some of the female attendants that Manfred had dispatched all his men various ways in pursuit of Isabella. He had in his hurry given this order in general terms, not meaning to extend it to the guard he had set upon Theodore, but forgetting it. The domestics, officious to obey so peremptory a prince, and urged by their own curiosity and love of novelty to join in any precipitate chase, had to a man left the castle. Matilda disengaged herself from her women, stole up to the Black Tower, and unbolting the door, presented herself to the astonished Theodore. "Young man," said she, "though filial duty and womanly modesty condemn the step I am taking, yet holy charity, surmounting all other ties, justifies this act. Fly; the doors of thy prison are open; my father and his domestics are absent; but they may soon return; begone in safety; and may the angels of heaven direct thy course!"

"Thou art surely one of those angels!" said the enraptured Theodore: "none but a blessed saint could speak, could act, could look like thee! May I not know the name of my divine protectress? Methought thou namedst thy father: is it possible? can Manfred's blood feel holy pity? Lovely lady, thou answerest not—but how art thou here thyself? why dost thou neglect thy own safety, and waste a thought on a wretch like Theodore? Let us fly together. The life thou bestowest shall be dedicated to thy defence."

*F 856

"Alas! thou mistakest," said Matilda, sighing: "I am Manfred's daughter, but no dangers await me."

"Amazement!" said Theodore; "but last night I blessed myself for yielding thee the service thy gracious compassion so charitably returns me now."

"Still thou art in error," said the princess; "but this is no time for explanation. Fly, virtuous youth, while it is in my power to save thee. Should my father return, thou and I both should indeed have cause to tremble."

"How?" said Theodore. "thinkest thou, charming maid, that I will accept of life at the hazard of aught calamitous to thee? better I endure a thousand deaths."

"I run no risk," said Matilda, "but by thy delay. Depart; it cannot be known that I assisted thy flight."

"Swear by the saints above," said Theodore, "that thou canst not be suspected; else here I vow to wait whatever can befall me."

"Oh, thou art too generous," said Matilda; "but rest assured that no suspicion can alight on me."

"Give me thy beauteous hand in token that thou dost not deceive me," said Theodore; "and let me bathe it with the warm tears of gratitude."

"Forbear," said the princess; "this must not be."

"Alas!" said Theodore, "I have never known but calamity until this hour—perhaps shall never know other fortune again: suffer the chaste raptures of holy gratitude: 'tis my soul would print its effusions on thy hand."

"Forbear, and be gone," said Matilda; "how would Isabella approve of seeing thee at my feet?"

"Who is Isabella?" said the young man with surprise.

"Ah me! I fear," said the princess, "I am serving a deceitful one;—hast thou forgot thy curiosity this morning?"

"Thy looks, thy actions, all thy beauteous self, seem an emanation of divinity," said Theodore; "but thy words are dark and mysterious:—speak, lady; speak to thy servant's comprehension."

"Thou understandest but too well!" said Matilda. "But once more, I command thee to be gone: thy blood, which I may preserve, will be on my head, if I waste the time in vain discourse."

"I go, lady," said Theodore, "because it is thy will, and because I would not bring the grey hairs of my father with sorrow to the grave. Say but, adored lady, that I have thy gentle pity."

"Stay," said Matilda; "I will conduct thee to the subterraneous vault by which Isabella escaped; it will lead thee to the church of St. Nicholas, where thou mayest take sanctuary."

"What!" said Theodore, "was it another, and not thy lovely self, that I assisted to find the subterraneous passage?"

"It was," said Matilda; "but ask no more; I tremble to see thee still abide here: fly to the sanctuary."

"To sanctuary!" said Theodore; "no, princess, sanctuaries are for helpless damsels, or for criminals. Theodore's soul is free from guilt, nor will wear the appearance of it. Give me a sword, lady, and thy father shall learn that Theodore scorns an ignominious flight."

"Rash youth!" said Matilda, "thou wouldst not dare to lift thy presumptuous arm against the Prince of Otranto?"

"Not against thy father; indeed, I dare not," said Theodore: "excuse me, lady; I had forgotten—but could I gaze on thee, and remember thou art sprung from the tyrant Manfred?—but he is thy father, and from this moment my injuries are buried in oblivion." A deep and hollow groan, which seemed to come from above, startled the princess and Theodore. "Good Heavens! we are overheard!" said the princess. They listened, but perceived no farther noise: they both concluded it the effect of pent-up vapours. And the princess, preceding Theodore softly, carried him to her father's armoury, where equipping him with a complete suit, he was conducted by Matilda to the postern-gate.

"Avoid the town," said the princess, "and all the western side of the castle: 'tis there the search must be making by Manfred and the strangers; but hie thee to the opposite quarter. Yonder, behind that forest to the east, is a chain of rocks, hollowed into a labyrinth of caverns that reach to the sea-coast. There thou mayest lie concealed till thou canst make signs to some vessel to put on shore and take thee off. Go; Heaven by thy guide!—and sometimes in thy prayers remember —Matilda!" Theodore flung himself at her feet; and seizing her lily hand, which with struggles she suffered him to kiss, he vowed on the earliest opportunity to get himself knighted, and fervently entreated her permission to swear himself eternally her knight. Ere the princess could reply, a clap of thunder was suddenly heard that shook the battlements. Theodore, regardless of the tempest, would have urged his suit, but the princess, dismayed, retreated hastily into the castle, and commanded the youth to be gone with an air that would not be disobeyed. He sighed and retired, but with eyes fixed on the gate until Matilda, closing it, put an end to an interview in which the hearts of both had drunk so deeply of a passion, which both now tasted for the first time.

Theodore went pensively to the convent, to acquaint his father with his deliverance. There he learned the absence of Jerome, and the pursuit that was making after the Lady Isabella, with some particulars of whose story he now first became acquainted. The generous gallantry of his nature prompted him to wish to assist her; but the monks could lend him no lights to guess at the route she had taken. He was not tempted to wander far in search of her, for the idea of Matilda had imprinted itself so strongly on his heart, that he could not bear to absent himself at much distance from her abode. The tenderness Jerome had expressed for him concurred to confirm this reluctance; and he even persuaded himself that filial affection was the chief cause of his hovering between the castle and monastery, until Jerome should return at night. Theodore at length determined to repair to the forest that Matilda had pointed out to him. Arriving there, he sought the gloomiest shades, as best suited to the pleasing melancholy that reigned in his mind. In this mood he roved insensibly to the caves which had formerly served as a retreat to hermits, and were now reported round the country to be haunted by evil spirits. He recollected to have heard this tradition; and being of a brave and adventurous disposition, he willingly indulged his curiosity in exploring the secret recesses of this labyrinth. He had not penetrated far before he thought he heard the steps of some person who seemed to retreat before him. Theodore, though firmly grounded in all our holy faith enjoins to be believed, had no apprehension that good men were abandoned without cause to the malice of the powers of darkness. He thought the place more likely to be infested by robbers than by those infernal agents who are reported to molest and bewilder travellers. He had long burned with impatience to approve his valour: drawing his sabre, he marched sedately onwards, still directing his steps, as the imperfect rustling round before him led the way. The armour he wore was a like indication to the person who avoided him. Theodore, now convinced that he was not mistaken, redoubled his pace, and evidently gained on the person that fled, whose haste increasing, Theodore came up just as a woman fell breathless before him. He hasted to raise her; but her terror was so great that he appre-

hended she would faint in his arms. He used every gentle
word to dispel her alarms, and assured her that, far from injuring,
he would defend her at the peril of his life. The lady recovering
her spirits from his courteous demeanour, and gazing on her
protector, said, "Sure, I have heard that voice before!"

"Not to my knowledge," replied Theodore, "unless, as I
conjecture, thou art the Lady Isabella."

"Merciful Heaven!" cried she, "thou art not sent in quest
of me, art thou?" And saying these words she threw herself
at his feet, and besought him not to deliver her up to Manfred.

"To Manfred!" cried Theodore; "no, lady, I have once already
delivered thee from his tyranny, and it shall fare hard with me
now, but I will place thee out of the reach of his daring."

"Is it possible," said she, "that thou shouldst be the generous
unknown whom I met last night in the vault of the castle?
Sure thou art not a mortal, but my guardian angel. On my
knees let me thank——"

"Hold, gentle princess," said Theodore, "nor demean thyself
before a poor and friendless young man. If Heaven has selected
me for thy deliverer, it will accomplish its work, and strengthen
my arm in thy cause: but come, lady, we are too near the mouth
of the cavern; let us seek its inmost recesses; I can have
no tranquillity till I have placed thee beyond the reach of
danger."

"Alas, what mean you, sir?" said she. "Though all your
actions are noble, though your sentiments speak the purity of
your soul, is it fitting that I should accompany you alone in
these perplexed retreats? should we be found together, what
would a censorious world think of my conduct?"

"I respect your virtuous delicacy," said Theodore; "nor
do you harbour a suspicion that wounds my honour. I meant
to conduct you into the most private cavity of these rocks,
and then, at the hazard of my life, to guard their entrance
against every living thing. Besides, lady," continued he,
drawing a deep sigh, "beauteous and all perfect as your form
is, and though my wishes are not guiltless of aspiring, know,
my soul is dedicated to another; and although——" A sudden
noise prevented Theodore from proceeding. They soon distinguished these sounds, "Isabella! what ho! Isabella!"
The trembling princess relapsed into her former agony of
fear. Theodore endeavoured to encourage her, but in vain.
He assured her he would rather die than suffer her to return
under Manfred's power, and begging her to remain concealed,

he went forth to prevent the person in search of her from approaching.

At the mouth of the cavern he found an armed knight discoursing with a peasant, who assured him he had seen a lady enter the passes of the rock. The knight was preparing to seek her, when Theodore, placing himself in his way, with his sword drawn, sternly forbade him at his peril to advance.

"And who art thou who darest to cross my way?" said the knight haughtily.

"One who does not dare more than he will perform," said Theodore.

"I seek the Lady Isabella," said the knight, "and understand she has taken refuge among these rocks. Impede me not, or thou wilt repent having provoked my resentment."

"Thy purpose is as odious as thy resentment is contemptible," said Theodore: "return whence thou camest, or we shall soon know whose resentment is most terrible."

The stranger, who was the principal knight that had arrived from the Marquis of Vicenza, had galloped from Manfred as he was busied in getting information of the princess, and giving various orders to prevent her falling into the power of the three knights. Their chief had suspected Manfred of being privy to the princess's absconding; and this insult from a man who, he concluded, was stationed by that prince to secrete her, confirming his suspicions, he made no reply, but discharging a blow with his sabre at Theodore, would soon have removed all obstruction, if Theodore, who took him for one of Manfred's captains, and who had no sooner given the provocation than he prepared to support it, had not received the stroke on his shield. The valour that had so long been smothered in his breast broke forth at once; he rushed impetuously on the knight, whose pride and wrath were not less powerful incentives to hardy deeds. The combat was furious, but not long: Theodore wounded the knight in three several places, and at last disarmed him, as he fainted by the loss of blood. The peasant, who had fled on the first onset, had given the alarm to some of Manfred's domestics, who, by his orders, were dispersed through the forest in pursuit of Isabella. They came up as the knight fell, whom they soon discovered to be the noble stranger. Theodore, notwithstanding his hatred to Manfred, could not behold the victory he had gained without emotions of pity and generosity. But he was more touched when he learned the quality of his adversary, and was informed that he was no retainer, but an enemy af Manfred. He assisted the servants of the latter in disarming the knight, and in endeavouring to stanch the blood that flowed from his wounds. The knight recovering his speech, said, in a faint and faltering voice, "Generous foe, we have both been in an error: I took thee for an instrument of the tyrant: I perceive thou hast made the like mistake: it is too late for excuses—I faint—if Isabella is at hand, call her; I have important secrets to——"

"He is dying," said one of the attendants; "has nobody a crucifix about them? Andrea, do thou pray over him."

"Fetch some water," said Theodore, "and pour it down his throat, while I hasten to the princess." Saying this, he flew to Isabella, and in few words told her modestly, that he had been so unfortunate by mistake as to wound a gentleman from her father's court, who wished, ere he died, to impart something of consequence to her. The princess, who had been transported at hearing the voice of Theodore, as he called to her to come forth, was astonished at what she heard. Suffering herself to be conducted by Theodore, the new proof of whose valour recalled her dispersed spirits, she came where the bleeding knight lay speechless on the ground—but her fears returned when she beheld the domestics of Manfred. She would again have fled, if Theodore had not made her observe that they were unarmed, and had not threatened them with instant death if they should dare to seize the princess. The stranger, opening his eyes, and beholding a woman, said, "Art thou—pray tell me truly—art thou Isabella of Vicenza?"

"I am," said she. "Good Heaven restore thee!"

"Then thou——then thou——" said the knight, struggling for utterance, "seest—thy father. Give me one——"

"Oh, amazement! horror! what do I hear? what do I see?" cried Isabella. "My father! you my father! how came you here, sir? for Heaven's sake speak!—Oh, run for help, or he will expire!"

"'Tis most true," said the wounded knight, exerting all his force; "I am Frederic thy father—yes, I came to deliver thee —it will not be—give me a parting kiss, and take——"

"Sir," said Theodore," do not exhaust yourself: suffer us to convey you to the castle."

"To the castle!" said Isabella; "is there no help nearer than the castle? would you expose my father to the tyrant? if he goes thither, I cannot accompany him—and yet, can I leave him?"

"My child," said Frederic, "it matters not to me whither I am carried: a few minutes will place me beyond danger—but while I have eyes to dote on thee, forsake me not, dear Isabella! This brave knight, I know not who he is, will protect thy innocence.—Sir, you will not abandon my child, will you?"

Theodore, shedding tears over his victim, and vowing to guard the princess at the expense of his life, persuaded Frederic to suffer himself to be conducted to the castle. They placed him on a horse belonging to one of the domestics, after binding up his wounds as well as they were able. Theodore marched by his side, and the afflicted Isabella, who could not bear to quit him, followed mournfully behind.

CHAPTER IV

THE sorrowful troop no sooner arrived at the castle than they were met by Hippolita and Matilda, whom Isabella had sent one of the domestics before to advertise of their approach. The ladies, causing Frederic to be conveyed into the nearest chamber, retired, while the surgeons examined his wounds. Matilda blushed at seeing Theodore and Isabella together; but endeavoured to conceal it by embracing the latter, and condoling with her on her father's mischance. The surgeons soon came to acquaint Hippolita that none of the marquis's wounds were dangerous, and that he was desirous of seeing his daughter and the princesses. Theodore, under pretence of expressing his joy at being freed from his apprehensions of the combat being fatal to Frederic, could not resist the impulse of following Matilda. Her eyes were so often cast down on meeting his, that Isabella, who regarded Theodore as attentively as he gazed on Matilda, soon divined who the object was that he had told her in the cave engaged his affections. While this mute scene passed, Hippolita demanded of Frederic the cause of his having taken that mysterious course for reclaiming his daughter; and threw in various apologies to excuse her lord for the match contracted between their children. Frederic, however incensed against Manfred, was not insensible to the courtesy and benevolence of Hippolita; but he was still more struck with the lovely form of Matilda. Wishing to detain them by his bedside, he informed Hippolita of his story. He told her, that, while prisoner to the infidel, he had dreamed that his daughter, of whom he had learned no news since his captivity, was detained

in a castle, where she was in danger of the most dreadful misfortunes; and that if he obtained his liberty, and repaired to a
wood near Joppa, he would learn more. Alarmed at this dream,
and incapable of obeying the direction given by it, his chains
became more grievous than ever. But while his thoughts were
occupied on the means of obtaining his liberty, he received the
agreeable news that the confederate princes, who were warring
in Palestine, had paid his ransom. He instantly set out for the
wood that had been marked in his dream. For three days he
and his attendants had wandered in the forest without seeing
a human form; but on the evening of the third they came to a
cell, in which they found a venerable hermit in the agonies of
death. Applying rich cordials, they brought the saint-like
man to his speech. "My sons," said he, "I am bounden to your
charity—but it is in vain—I am going to my eternal rest—yet I
die with the satisfaction of performing the will of Heaven.
When first I repaired to this solitude, after seeing my country
become a prey to unbelievers—it is, alas! above fifty years since
I was witness to that dreadful scene—St. Nicholas appeared to
me, and revealed a secret, which he bade me never disclose to
mortal man, but on my death-bed. This is that tremendous
hour, and ye are no doubt the chosen warriors to whom I was
ordered to reveal my trust. As soon as ye have done the last
offices to this wretched corse, dig under the seventh tree on the
left hand of this poor cave, and your pains will—— Oh, good
Heaven, receive my soul!" With those words the devout man
breathed his last.

"By break of day," continued Frederic, "when we had
committed the holy relics to earth, we dug according to direction; but what was our astonishment, when, about the depth
of six feet, we discovered an enormous sabre—the very weapon
yonder in the court. On the blade, which was then partly out
of the scabbard, though since closed by our efforts in removing
it, were written the following lines—no; excuse me, madam,"
added the marquis, turning to Hippolita, "if I forbear to repeat
them: I respect your sex and rank, and would not be guilty of
offending your ear with sounds injurious to aught that is dear
to you."

He paused — Hippolita trembled. She did not doubt but
Frederic was destined by Heaven to accomplish the fate
that seemed to threaten her house. Looking with anxious
fondness at Matilda, a silent tear stole down her cheek;
but recollecting herself, she said, "Proceed, my lord, Heaven

does nothing in vain; mortals must receive its divine behests with lowliness and submission. It is our part to deprecate its wrath, or bow to its decrees. Repeat the sentence, my lord; we listen resigned."

Frederic was grieved that he had proceeded so far. The dignity and patient firmness of Hippolita penetrated him with respect; and the tender, silent affection with which the princess and her daughter regarded each other melted him almost to tears. Yet apprehensive that his forbearance to obey would be more alarming, he repeated, in a faltering and low voice, the following lines:

> Where'er a casque that suits this sword is found,
> With perils is thy daughter compass'd round;
> Alfonso's blood alone can save the maid,
> And quiet a long-restless prince's shade.

"What is there in these lines," said Theodore, impatiently, "that affects these princesses? Why were they to be shocked by a mysterious delicacy, that has so little foundation?"

"Your words are rude, young man," said the marquis; "and though fortune has favoured you once——"

"My honoured lord," said Isabella, who resented Theodore's warmth, which she perceived was dictated by his sentiments for Matilda, "discompose not yourself for the glozing of a peasant's son: he forgets the reverence he owes you; but he is not accustomed——"

Hippolita, concerned at the heat that had arisen, checked Theodore for his boldness, but with an air acknowledging his zeal; and changing the conversation, demanded of Frederic where he had left her lord?

As the marquis was going to reply, they heard a noise without, and rising to inquire the cause, Manfred, Jerome, and part of the troop, who had met an imperfect rumour of what had happened, entered the chamber. Manfred advanced hastily towards Frederic's bed to condole with him on his misfortune, and to learn the circumstances of the combat, when, starting in an agony of terror and amazement, he cried:

"Ah! what art thou? Thou dreadful spectre! Is my hour come?"

"My dearest, gracious lord," cried Hippolita, clasping him in her arms, "what is it you see? Why do you fix your eyeballs thus?"

"What," cried Manfred, breathless, "dost thou see nothing,

Hippolita? Is this ghastly phantom sent to me alone—to me, who did not——"

"For mercy's sweetest self, my lord," said Hippolita, "resume your soul, command your reason; there are none here, but us, your friends."

"What, is not that Alfonso?" cried Manfred; "dost thou not see him? Can it be my brain's delirium?"

"This! my lord," said Hippolita: "this is Theodore, the youth who has been so unfortunate."

"Theodore," said Manfred mournfully, and striking his forehead—"Theodore, or a phantom, he has unhinged the soul of Manfred. But how comes he here? and how comes he in armour?"

"I believe he went in search of Isabella," said Hippolita.

"Of Isabella," said Manfred, relapsing into rage. "Yes, yes, that is not doubtful—but how did he escape from durance, in which I left him? Was it Isabella, or this hypocritical old friar, that procured his enlargement?"

"And would a parent be criminal, my lord," said Theodore, "if he meditated the deliverance of his child?"

Jerome, amazed to hear himself in a manner accused by his son, and without foundation, knew not what to think. He could not comprehend how Theodore had escaped—how he came to be armed, and to encounter Frederic. Still he would not venture to ask any questions that might tend to inflame Manfred's wrath against his son. Jerome's silence convinced Manfred that he had contrived Theodore's release.

"And is it thus, thou ungrateful old man," said the prince, addressing himself to the friar, "that thou repayest mine and Hippolita's bounties? And not content with traversing my heart's nearest wishes, thou armest thy bastard, and bringest him into my own castle to insult me!"

"My lord," said Theodore, "you wrong my father: nor he nor I are capable of harbouring a thought against your peace. Is it insolence thus to surrender myself to your highness's pleasure?" added he, laying his sword respectfully at Manfred's feet. "Behold my bosom; strike, my lord, if you suspect that a disloyal thought is lodged there. There is not a sentiment engraven on my heart that does not venerate you and yours."

The grace and fervour with which Theodore uttered these words interested every person present in his favour. Even Manfred was touched; yet still possessed with his resemblance to Alfonso, his admiration was dashed with secret horror.

"Rise," said he; "thy life is not my present purpose. But tell me thy history, and how thou camest connected with this old traitor here."

"My lord——" said Jerome, eagerly.

"Peace! impostor," said Manfred; "I will not have him prompted."

"My lord," said Theodore, "I want no assistance: my story is very brief. I was carried at five years of age to Algiers with my mother, who had been taken by corsairs from the coast of Sicily. She died of grief in less than a twelvemonth." The tears gushed from Jerome's eyes, on whose countenance a thousand anxious passions stood expressed. "Before she died," continued Theodore, "she bound a writing about my arm under my garments, which told me I was the son of the Count Falconara."

"It is most true," said Jerome; "I am that wretched father."

"Again I enjoin thee silence," said Manfred. "Proceed."

"I remained in slavery," said Theodore, "until within these two years; when, attending on my master in his cruises, I was delivered by a Christian vessel which overpowered the pirate; and discovering myself to the captain, he generously put me on shore in Sicily:—but, alas! instead of finding a father, I learned that his estate, which was situated on the coast, had, during his absence, been laid waste by the rover, who had carried my mother and me into captivity; that his castle had been burnt to the ground, and that my father, on his return, had sold what remained, and was retired into religion in the kingdom of Naples, but where, no man could inform me. Destitute and friendless, hopeless almost of attaining the transport of a parent's embrace, I took the first opportunity of setting sail for Naples; from whence, within these six days, I wandered into this province, still supporting myself by the labour of my hands: nor until yester-morn did I believe that Heaven had reserved any lot for me but peace of mind and contented poverty. This, my lord, is Theodore's story. I am blessed beyond my hope in finding a father; I am unfortunate beyond my desert in having incurred your highness's displeasure."

He ceased. A murmur of approbation gently arose from the audience.

"This is not all," said Frederic: "I am bound in honour to add what he suppresses. Though he is modest, I must be generous—he is one of the bravest youths on Christian ground. He is warm too; and from the short knowledge I have of him.

I will pledge myself for his veracity; if what he reports of him-self were not true, he would not utter it.—And for me, youth, I honour a frankness which becomes thy birth. But now, and thou didst offend me; yet the noble blood which flows in thy veins may well be allowed to boil out, when it has so recently traced itself to its source.—Come, my lord," turning to Man-fred, "if I can pardon him, surely you may: it is not the youth's fault, if you took him for a spectre."

This bitter taunt galled the soul of Manfred. "If beings from another world," replied he haughtily, "have power to impress my mind with awe, it is more than living man can do: nor could a stripling's arm——"

"My lord," interrupted Hippolita, "your guest has occasion for repose: shall we not leave him to his rest?" Saying this, and taking Manfred by the hand, she took leave of Frederic, and led the company forth. The prince, not sorry to quit a conversation which recalled to mind the discovery he had made of his most secret sensations, suffered himself to be conducted to his own apartment, after permitting Theodore, though under engagement to return to the castle on the morrow (a condition the young man gladly accepted), to retire with his father to the convent. Matilda and Isabella were too much occupied with their own reflections, and too little content with each other, to wish for farther converse that night. They separated, each to her chamber, with more expressions of ceremony and fewer of affection than had passed between them since their childhood.

If they parted with small cordiality, they did but meet with greater impatience, as soon as the sun was risen. Their minds were in a situation that excluded sleep, and each recollected a thousand questions which she wished she had put to the other overnight. Matilda reflected that Isabella had been twice delivered by Theodore in very critical situations, which she could not believe accidental. His eyes, it was true, had been fixed on her in Frederic's chamber; but that might have been to disguise his passion for Isabella from the fathers of both. It were better to clear this up. She wished to know the truth, lest she should wrong her friend by entertaining a passion for Isabella's lover. Thus jealousy prompted, and at the same time borrowed, an excuse from friendship to justify its curiosity.

Isabella, not less restless, had better foundation for her suspicions. Both Theodore's tongue and eyes had told her his heart was engaged—it was true—yet perhaps Matilda might not correspond to his passion; she had ever appeared insensible to love: all her thoughts were set on heaven. "Why did I dissuade her?" said Isabella to herself: "I am punished for my generosity; but when did they meet? where? It cannot be. I have deceived myself; perhaps last night was the first time they beheld each other; it must be some other object that has prepossessed his affections. If it is, I am not so unhappy as I thought; if it is not my friend Matilda—how! can I stoop to wish for the affection of a man who rudely and unnecessarily acquainted me with his indifference? and that at the very moment in which common courtesy demanded at least expressions of civility? I will go to my dear Matilda, who will confirm me in this becoming pride—man is false—I will advise with her on taking the veil: she will rejoice to find me in this disposition; and I will acquaint her that I no longer oppose her inclination for the cloister." In this frame of mind, and determined to open her heart entirely to Matilda, she went to that princess's chamber, whom she found already dressed, and leaning pensively on her arm. This attitude, so correspondent to what she felt herself, revived Isabella's suspicions, and destroyed the confidence she had purposed to place in her friend. They blushed at meeting, and were too much novices to disguise their sensations with address. After some unmeaning questions and replies, Matilda demanded of Isabella the cause of her flight. The latter, who had almost forgotten Manfred's passion, so entirely was she occupied by her own, concluding that Matilda referred to her last escape from the convent, which had occasioned the events of the preceding evening, replied, "Martelli brought word to the convent that your mother was dead——"

"Oh!" said Matilda, interrupting her, "Bianca has explained that mistake to me: on seeing me faint, she cried, 'The princess is dead'; and Martelli, who had come for the usual dole to the castle——"

"And what made you faint?" said Isabella, indifferent to the rest.

Matilda blushed, and stammered, "My father—he was sitting in judgment on a criminal."

"What criminal?" said Isabella, eagerly.

"A young man," said Matilda:—"I believe—I think it was that young man that——"

"What, Theodore?" said Isabella.

"Yes," answered she; "I never saw him before; I do not know how he had offended my father—but as he has been of service to you, I am glad my lord has pardoned him."

"Served me!" replied Isabella; "do you term it serving me, to wound my father, and almost occasion his death? Though it is but since yesterday that I am blessed with knowing a parent, I hope Matilda does not think I am such a stranger to filial tenderness as not to resent the boldness of that audacious youth, and that it is impossible for me ever to feel any affection for one who dared to lift his arm against the author of my being. No, Matilda, my heart abhors him; and if you still retain the friendship for me that you have vowed from your infancy, you will detest the man who has been on the point of making me miserable for ever."

Matilda held down her head, and replied, "I hope my dearest Isabella does not doubt her Matilda's friendship: I never beheld that youth until yesterday; he is almost a stranger to me: but as the surgeons have pronounced your father out of danger, you ought not to harbour uncharitable resentment against one, who, I am persuaded, did not know the marquis was related to you."

"You plead his cause very pathetically," said Isabella, "considering he is so much a stranger to you! I am mistaken, or he returns your charity."

"What mean you?" said Matilda.

"Nothing," said Isabella, repenting that she had given Matilda a hint of Theodore's inclination for her. Then, changing the discourse, she asked Matilda what occasioned Manfred to take Theodore for a spectre?

"Bless me," said Matilda, "did you not observe his extreme resemblance to the portrait of Alfonso in the gallery? I took notice of it to Bianca even before I saw him in armour; but with the helmet on he is the very image of that picture."

"I do not much observe pictures," said Isabella: "much less have I examined this young man so attentively as you seem to have done. Ah, Matilda, your heart is in danger; but let me warn you as a friend—he has owned to me that he is in love; it cannot be with you, for yesterday was the first time you ever met—was it not?"

"Certainly," replied Matilda; "but why does my dearest Isabella conclude from anything I have said, that"—she paused—then continuing: "he saw you first, and I am far from having the vanity to think that my little portion of charms could engage a heart devoted to you—may you be happy, Isabella, whatever is the fate of Matilda!"

"My lovely friend," said Isabella, whose heart was too honest to resist a kind expression, "it is you that Theodore admires; I saw it; I am persuaded of it; nor shall a thought of my own happiness suffer me to interfere with yours." This frankness drew tears from the gentle Matilda; and jealousy, that for a moment had raised a coolness between these amiable maidens, soon gave way to the natural sincerity and candour of their souls. Each confessed to the other the impression that Theodore had made on her; and this confidence was followed by a struggle of generosity, each insisting on yielding her claim to her friend. At length the dignity of Isabella's virtue reminding her of the preference which Theodore had almost declared for her rival, made her determine to conquer her passion, and cede the beloved object to her friend.

During this contest of amity, Hippolita entered her daughter's chamber.

"Madam," said she to Isabella, "you have so much tenderness for Matilda, and interest yourself so kindly in whatever affects our wretched house, that I can have no secrets with my child which are not proper for you to hear." The princesses were all attention and anxiety.

"Know then, madam," continued Hippolita, "and you, my dearest Matilda, that being convinced by all the events of these two last ominous days that Heaven purposes the sceptre of Otranto should pass from Manfred's hands into those of the Marquis Frederic; I have been perhaps inspired with the thought of averting our total destruction by the union of our rival houses. With this view I have been proposing to Manfred, my lord, to tender this dear, dear child to Frederic your father."

"Me to Lord Frederic!" cried Matilda. "Good heavens! my gracious mother, and have you named it to my father?"

"I have," said Hippolita: "he listened benignly to my proposal, and is gone to break it to the marquis."

"Ah! wretched princess," cried Isabella, "what hast thou done? what ruin has thy inadvertent goodness been preparing for thyself, for me, and for Matilda!"

"Ruin from me, to you, and to my child!" said Hippolita; "what can this mean?"

"Alas!" said Isabella, "the purity of your own heart prevents your seeing the depravity of others. Manfred, your lord, that impious man——"

"Hold!" said Hippolita, "you must not, in my presence, young lady, mention Manfred with disrespect; he is my lord and husband, and——"

"Will not long be so," said Isabella, "if his wicked purposes can be carried into execution."

"This language amazes me," said Hippolita. "Your feeling, Isabella, is warm: but until this hour I never knew it betray you into intemperance. What deed of Manfred authorizes you to treat him as a murderer, an assassin?"

"Thou virtuous, and too credulous princess!" replied Isabella; "it is not thy life he aims at—it is to separate himself from thee! to divorce thee! to——"

"To divorce me!"—"To divorce my mother!" cried Hippolita and Matilda at once.

"Yes," said Isabella; "and, to complete his crime, he meditates —I cannot speak it!"

"What can surpass what thou hast already uttered?" said Matilda.

Hippolita was silent. Grief choked her speech; and the recollection of Manfred's late ambiguous discourses confirmed what she heard.

"Excellent, dear lady!—madam! mother!" cried Isabella, flinging herself at Hippolita's feet in a transport of passion; "trust me, believe me, I will die a thousand deaths sooner than consent to injure you, than yield to so odious——"

"Oh, this is too much!" cried Hippolita. "What crimes does one crime suggest! Rise, dear Isabella; I do not doubt your virtue. Oh, Matilda, this stroke is too heavy for thee! weep not, my child; and not a murmur, I charge thee. Remember, he is *thy* father still!"

"But you are my mother, too," said Matilda, fervently; "and *you* are virtuous, *you* are guiltless! Oh, must not I, must not I complain?"

"You must not," said Hippolita; "come, all will be well. Manfred, in the agony for the loss of thy brother, knew not what he said; perhaps Isabella misunderstood him: his heart is good—and, my child, thou knowest not all. There is a destiny hangs over us: the hand of Providence is stretched out. Oh, could I but save thee from the wreck.—Yes," continued she, in a firmer tone, "perhaps the sacrifice of myself may atone for all; I will go and offer myself to this divorce—it boots not what becomes of me. I will withdraw into the neighbouring monastery, and waste the remainder of life in prayers and tears for my child and—the prince."

"Thou art as much too good for this world," said Isabella, "as Manfred is execrable—but think not, lady, that thy weakness shall determine for me. I swear, hear me all ye angels——"

"Stop, I adjure thee," cried Hippolita: "remember thou dost not depend on thyself; thou hast a father——"

"My father is too pious, too noble," interrupted Isabella, "to command an impious deed. But should he command it; can a father enjoin a cursed act? I was contracted to the son, can I wed the father?—No, madam, no; force should not drag me to Manfred's hated bed. I loathe him, I abhor him: divine and human laws forbid; and, my friend, my dearest Matilda, would I wound her tender soul by injuring her adored mother? my own mother—I never have known another."

"Oh, she is the mother of both," cried Matilda: "can we, can we, Isabella, adore her too much?"

"My lovely children," said the touched Hippolita, "your tenderness overpowers me; but I must not give way to it. It is not ours to make election for ourselves; Heaven, our fathers, and our husbands, must decide for us. Have patience until you hear what Manfred and Frederic have determined. If the marquis accepts Matilda's hand, I know she will readily obey. Heaven may interpose and prevent the rest. What means my child?" continued she, seeing Matilda fall at her feet with a flood of speechless tears.—"But no; answer me not, my daughter; I must not hear a word against the pleasure of thy father."

"Oh, doubt not my obedience, my dreadful obedience to him and to you!" said Matilda. "But can I, most respected of women, can I experience all this tenderness, this world of goodness, and conceal a thought from the best of mothers?"

"What art thou going to utter?" said Isabella, trembling. "Recollect thyself, Matilda."

"No, Isabella," said the princess, "I should not deserve this incomparable parent, if the inmost recesses of my soul harboured a thought without her permission—nay, I have offended her; I have suffered a passion to enter my heart without her avowal; but here I disclaim it; here I vow to Heaven and her——"

"My child! my child!" said Hippolita, "what words are these? what new calamities has fate in store for us? Thou, a passion! Thou, in this hour of destruction!"

"Oh, I see all my guilt," said Matilda. "I abhor myself, if

I cost my mother a pang: she is the dearest thing I have on earth. Oh, I will never, never behold him more!"

"Isabella," said Hippolita, "thou art conscious to this unhappy secret, whatever it is. Speak!"

"What!" cried Matilda, "have I so forfeited my mother's love, that she will not permit me even to speak my own guilt? Oh, wretched, wretched Matilda!"

"Thou art too cruel," said Isabella to Hippolita; "canst thou behold this anguish of a virtuous mind, and not commiserate it?"

"Not pity my child!" said Hippolita, catching Matilda in her arms. "Oh, I know she is good; she is all virtue, all tenderness and duty. I do forgive thee, my excellent, my only hope!"

The princesses then revealed to Hippolita their mutual inclination for Theodore, and the purpose of Isabella to resign him to Matilda. Hippolita blamed their imprudence, and showed them the improbability that either father would consent to bestow his heiress on so poor a man, though nobly born. Some comfort it gave her to find their passion of so recent a date, and that Theodore had had but little cause to suspect it in either. She strictly enjoined them to avoid all correspondence with him. This Matilda fervently promised; but Isabella, who flattered herself that she meant no more than to promote his union with her friend, could not determine to avoid him, and made no reply.

"I will go to the convent," said Hippolita, "and order new masses to be said for a deliverance from these calamities."

"Oh, my mother," said Matilda, "you mean to quit us: you mean to take sanctuary, and to give my father an opportunity of pursuing his fatal intentions. Alas! on my knees I supplicate you to forbear: will you leave me a prey to Frederic? I will follow you to the convent."

"Be at peace, my child," said Hippolita; "I will return instantly. I will never abandon thee, until I know it is the will of Heaven, and for thy benefit."

"Do not deceive me," said Matilda. "I will not marry Frederic until thou commandest it. Alas! what will become of me?"

"Why that exclamation?" said Hippolita. "I have promised thee to return."

"Ah, my mother," replied Matilda; "stay and save me from myself. A frown from thee can do more than all my father's severity. I have given away my heart, and you alone can make me recall it."

"No more," said Hippolita: "thou must not relapse, Matilda."

"I can quit Theodore," said she, "but must I wed another? Let me attend thee to the altar, and shut myself from the world for ever."

"Thy fate depends on thy father," said Hippolita: "I have ill bestowed my tenderness, if it has taught thee to revere aught beyond him. Adieu! my child, I go to pray for thee."

Hippolita's real purpose was to demand of Jerome, whether in conscience she might not consent to the divorce. She had oft urged Manfred to resign the principality, which the delicacy of her conscience rendered an hourly burden to her. These scruples concurred to make the separation from her husband appear less dreadful to her, than it would have seemed in any other situation.

Jerome, at quitting the castle overnight, had questioned Theodore severely why he had accused him to Manfred of being privy to his escape. Theodore owned it had been with design to prevent Manfred's suspicion from alighting on Matilda; and added, the holiness of Jerome's life and character secured him from the tyrant's wrath. Jerome was heartily grieved to discover his son's inclination for that princess; and leaving him to his rest, promised in the morning to acquaint him with important reasons for conquering his passion. Theodore, like Isabella, was too recently acquainted with parental authority to submit to its decisions against the impulse of his heart. He had little curiosity to learn the friar's reasons, and less disposition to obey them. The lovely Matilda had made stronger impressions on him than filial affection. All night he pleased himself with visions of love; and it was not till late after the morning office that he recollected the friar's commands to attend him at Alfonso's tomb.

"Young man," said Jerome, when he saw him, "this tardiness does not please me. Have a father's commands already so little weight?"

Theodore made awkward excuses, and attributed his delay to having overslept himself.

"And on whom were thy dreams employed?" said the friar sternly. His son blushed. "Come, come," resumed the friar, "inconsiderate youth, this must not be; eradicate this guilty passion from thy breast."

"Guilty passion!" cried Theodore: "can guilt dwell with innocent beauty and virtuous modesty?"

"It is sinful," replied the friar, "to cherish those whom Heaven has doomed to destruction. A tyrant's race must be swept from the earth to the third and fourth generation."

"Will Heaven visit the innocent for the crimes of the guilty?" said Theodore. "The fair Matilda has virtues enough——"

"To undo thee," interrupted Jerome. "Hast thou so soon forgotten that twice the savage Manfred has pronounced thy sentence?"

"Nor have I forgotten, sir," said Theodore, "that the charity of his daughter delivered me from his power. I can forget injuries, but never benefits."

"The injuries thou hast received from Manfred's race," said the friar, "are beyond what thou canst conceive. Reply not, but view this holy image! Beneath this marble monument rest the ashes of the good Alfonso; a prince adorned with every virtue; the father of his people; the delight of mankind! Kneel, headstrong boy, and list, while a father unfolds a tale of horror, that will expel every sentiment from thy soul, but sensations of sacred vengeance. Alfonso! much injured prince! let thy unsatisfied shade sit awful on the troubled air, while these trembling lips—— Ha! who comes there?"

"The most wretched of women," said Hippolita, entering the choir. "Good father, art thou at leisure? but why this kneeling youth? What means the horror imprinted on each countenance? Why at this venerable tomb?—alas! hast thou seen aught?"

"We were pouring forth our orisons to Heaven," replied the friar, with some confusion, "to put an end to the woes of this deplorable province. Join with us, lady: thy spotless soul may obtain an exemption from the judgments which the portents of these days but too speakingly denounce against thy house."

"I pray fervently to Heaven to divert them," said the pious princess. "Thou knowest it has been the occupation of my life to wrest a blessing for my lord and my harmless children. One, alas! is taken from me; would Heaven but hear me for my poor Matilda! Father, intercede for her."

"Every heart will bless her!" cried Theodore with rapture.

"Be dumb, rash youth," said Jerome. "And thou, fond princess, contend not with the powers above. The Lord giveth, and the Lord taketh away: bless His holy name, and submit to His decrees."

"I do most devoutly," said Hippolita; "but will He not

spare my only comfort? Must Matilda perish too?—Ah, father, I came—but dismiss thy son. No ear but thine must hear what I have to utter."

"May Heaven grant thy every wish, most excellent princess!" said Theodore, retiring. Jerome frowned.

Hippolita then acquainted the friar with a proposal she had suggested to Manfred, his approbation of it, and the tender of Matilda that he was gone to make to Frederic. Jerome could not conceal his dislike of the motion, which he covered under pretence of the improbability that Frederic, the nearest of blood to Alfonso, and who was come to claim his succession, would yield to an alliance with the usurper of his right. But nothing could equal the perplexity of the friar, when Hippolita confessed her readiness not to oppose the separation, and demanded his opinion on the legality of her acquiescence. The friar catched eagerly at her request of his advice; and without explaining his aversion to the proposed marriage of Manfred and Isabella, he painted to Hippolita, in the most alarming colours, the sinfulness of her consent, denounced judgments against her if she complied, and enjoined her, in the severest terms, to treat any such proposition with every mark of indignation and refusal.

Manfred, in the meantime, had broken his purpose to Frederic, and proposed the double marriage. That weak prince, who had been struck with the charms of Matilda, listened but too eagerly to the offer. He forgot his enmity to Manfred, whom he saw but little hope of dispossessing by force; and flattering himself that no issue might succeed from the union of his daughter with the tyrant, he looked upon his own succession to the principality as facilitated by wedding Matilda. He made faint opposition to the proposal; affecting, for form only, not to acquiesce unless Hippolita should consent to the divorce. Manfred took that upon himself. Transported with his success, and impatient to see himself in a situation to expect sons, he hastened to his wife's apartment, determined to extort her compliance. H learned with indignation that she was absent at the convent. His guilt suggested to him that she had probably been informed by Isabella of his purpose. He doubted whether her retirement to the convent did not import an intention of remaining there, until she could raise obstacles to their divorce; and the suspicions he had already entertained of Jerome made him apprehend that the friar would not only traverse his views, but might have inspired Hippolita with the resolution of taking sanctuary. Impatient to unravel this clue, and to defeat its success, Manfred hastened to the convent, and arrived there, as the friar was earnestly exhorting the princess never to yield to the divorce.

"Madam," said Manfred, "what business drew you hither? why did you not await my return from the marquis?"

"I came to implore a blessing on your councils," replied Hippolita.

"My councils do not need a friar's intervention," said Manfred; "and of all men living is that hoary traitor the only one whom you delight to confer with?"

"Profane prince!" said Jerome; "is it at the altar thou choosest to insult the servants of the altar?—but, Manfred, thy impious schemes are known. Heaven and this virtuous lady know them:—nay, frown not, prince. The Church despises thy menaces. Her thunders will be heard above thy wrath. Dare to proceed in thy cursed purpose of a divorce, until her sentence be known, and here I launch her anathema at thy head."

"Audacious rebel!" said Manfred, endeavouring to conceal the awe with which the friar's words inspired him; "dost thou presume to threaten thy lawful prince?"

"Thou art no lawful prince," said Jerome; "thou art no prince:—go, discuss thy claim with Frederic; and when that is done——"

"It is done," replied Manfred: "Frederic accepts Matilda's hand, and is content to waive his claim, unless I have no male issue."—As he spoke those words, three drops of blood fell from the nose of Alfonso's statue. Manfred turned pale, and the princess sunk on her knees.

"Behold!" said the friar; "mark this miraculous indication that the blood of Alfonso will never mix with that of Manfred!"

"My gracious lord," said Hippolita, "let us submit ourselves to Heaven. Think not thy ever obedient wife rebels against thy authority. I have no will but that of my lord and the Church. To that revered tribunal let us appeal. It does not depend on us to burst the bonds that unite us. If the Church shall approve the dissolution of our marriage, be it so—I have but few years, and those of sorrow, to pass. Where can they be worn away so well as at the foot of this altar, in prayers for thine and Matilda's safety?"

"But thou shalt not remain here until then," said Manfred. "Repair with me to the castle, and there I will advise on the proper measures for a divorce. But this meddling friar comes not thither: my hospitable roof shall nevermore harbour a traitor—and for thy reverence's offspring," continued he, "I banish him from my dominions. He, I ween, is no sacred personage, nor under the protection of the Church. Whoever weds Isabella, it shall not be Father Falconara's started-up son."

"They start up," said the friar, "who are suddenly beheld in the seat of lawful princes; but they wither away like the grass, and their place knows them no more."

Manfred, casting a look of scorn at the friar, led Hippolita forth; but at the door of the church whispered one of his attendants to remain concealed about the convent, and bring him instant notice if any one from the castle should repair thither.

CHAPTER V

EVERY reflection which Manfred made on the friar's behaviour conspired to persuade him that Jerome was privy to an amour between Isabella and Theodore. But Jerome's new presumption, so dissonant from his former meekness, suggested still deeper apprehensions. The prince even suspected that the friar depended on some secret support from Frederic, whose arrival coinciding with the novel appearance of Theodore seemed to bespeak a correspondence. Still more was he troubled with the resemblance of Theodore to Alfonso's portrait. The latter he knew had unquestionably died without issue. Frederic had consented to bestow Isabella on him. These contradictions agitated his mind with numberless pangs. He saw but two methods of extricating himself from his difficulties. The one was to resign his dominions to the marquis.—Pride, ambition, and his reliance on ancient prophecies, which had pointed out a possibility of his preserving them to his posterity, combated that thought. The other was to press his marriage with Isabella. After long ruminating on these anxious thoughts, as he marched silently with Hippolita to the castle, he at last discoursed with that princess on the subject of his disquiet, and used every insinuating and plausible argument to extract her consent to, even her promise of promoting, the divorce. Hippolita needed little persuasions to bend her to his pleasure. She endeavoured to win him over to the measure of resigning his dominions; but finding her exhortations fruitless she assured him, that, as far as her conscience would allow, she would raise no opposition to a separation, though without better founded scruples than what he yet alleged she would not engage to be active in demanding it.

This compliance, though inadequate, was sufficient to raise Manfred's hopes. He trusted that his power and wealth would easily advance his suit at the court of Rome, whither he resolved to engage Frederic to take a journey on purpose. That prince had discovered so much passion for Matilda, that Manfred hoped to obtain all he wished by holding out or withdrawing his daughter's charms, according as the marquis should appear more or less disposed to co-operate in his views. Even the absence of Frederic would be a material point gained, until he could take further measures for his security.

Dismissing Hippolita to her apartment, he repaired to that of the marquis; but crossing the great hall, through which he was to pass, he met Bianca. The damsel he knew was in the confidence of both the young ladies. It immediately occurred to him to sift her on the subject of Isabella and Theodore. Calling her aside into the recess of the oriel window of the hall, and soothing her with many fair words and promises, he demanded of her whether she knew aught of the state of Isabella's affections.

"I! my lord! no, my lord—yes, my lord—poor lady! she is wonderfully alarmed about her father's wounds! but I tell her he will do well; don't your highness think so?"

"I do not ask you," replied Manfred, "what she thinks about her father; but you are in her secrets. Come, be a good girl, and tell me; is there any young man—ha!—you understand me."

"Lord bless me! understand your highness, no, not I: I told her a few vulnerary herbs and repose——"

"I am not talking," replied the prince, impatiently, "about her father; I know he will do well."

"Bless me, I rejoice to hear your highness say so; for though I thought it not right to let my young lady despond, methought his greatness had a wan look, and a something—I remember when young Ferdinand was wounded by the Venetian——"

"Thou answerest from the point," interrupted Manfred; "but here, take this jewel, perhaps that may fix thy attention; nay, no reverences: my favour shall not stop here:—come, tell me truly, how stands Isabella's heart!"

"Well, your highness has such a way!" said Bianca, "to be

sure; but can your highness keep a secret? if it should ever come out of your lips——"

"It shall not, it shall not," cried Manfred.

"Nay, but swear, your highness. By my halidame, if it should ever be known that I said it—why, truth is truth, I do not think my Lady Isabella ever much affectioned my young lord, your son—yet he was a sweet youth, as one should see. I am sure, if I had been a princess—but bless me! I must attend my Lady Matilda; she will marvel what is become of me."

"Stay!" cried Manfred, "thou hast not satisfied my question. Hast thou ever carried any message, any letter?"

"I! good gracious!" cried Bianca; "I carry a letter? I would not to be a queen. I hope your highness thinks, though I am poor, I am honest—did your highness never hear what Count Marsigli offered me when he came a-wooing to my Lady Matilda?"

"I have not leisure," said Manfred, "to listen to thy tales. I do not question thy honesty; but it is thy duty to conceal nothing from me. How long has Isabella been acquainted with Theodore?"

"Nay, there is nothing can escape your highness," said Bianca: "not that I know anything of the matter. Theodore, to be sure, is a proper young man, and, as my Lady Matilda says, the very image of good Alfonso: has not your highness remarked it?"

"Yes, yes,—no,—thou torturest me," said Manfred: "where did they meet? when?"

"Who? my Lady Matilda?" said Bianca.

"No, no, not Matilda; Isabella. When did Isabella first become acquainted with this Theodore?"

"Virgin Mary!" said Bianca, "how should I know?"

"Thou dost know," said Manfred, "and I must know; I will."

"Lord! your highness is not jealous of young Theodore!" said Bianca.

"Jealous! no, no: why should I be jealous? perhaps I mean to unite them, if I were sure Isabella would have no repugnance."

"Repugnance! no, I'll warrant her," said Bianca: "he is as comely a youth as ever trod on Christian ground. We are all in love with him; there is not a soul in the castle but would be rejoiced to have him for our prince—I mean, when it shall please Heaven to call your highness to itself."

"Indeed," said Manfred, "has it gone so far? oh, this cursed friar! but I must not lose time:—go, Bianca, attend Isabella; but I charge thee, not a word of what has passed. Find out how she is affected towards Theodore: bring me good news, and that ring has a companion. Wait at the foot of the winding staircase: I am going to visit the marquis, and will talk further with thee at my return."

Manfred, after some general conversation, desired Frederic to dismiss the two knights his companions, having to talk with him on urgent affairs. As soon as they were alone, he began, in artful guise, to sound the marquis on the subject of Matilda; and finding him disposed to his wish, he let drop hints on the difficulties that would attend the celebration of their marriage, unless— At that instant Bianca burst into the room with a wildness in her look and gestures that spoke the utmost terror.

"Oh, my lord, my lord!" cried she; "we are all undone! it is come again! it is come again!"

"What is come again?" cried Manfred, amazed.

"Oh, the hand! the giant! the hand!—support me! I am terrified out of my senses," cried Bianca; "I will not sleep in the castle to-night. Where shall I go? my things may come after me to-morrow—would I had been content to wed Francesco! —this comes of ambition."

"What has terrified thee thus, young woman?" said the marquis. "Thou art safe here; be not alarmed."

"Oh, your greatness is wonderfully good," said Bianca, "but I dare not—no, pray let me go. I had rather leave everything behind me, than stay another hour under this roof."

"Go to, thou hast lost thy senses," said Manfred. "Interrupt us not; we were communing on important matters. My lord, this wench is subject to fits. Come with me, Bianca."

"Oh, the saints, no," said Bianca; "for certain it comes to warn your highness: why should it appear to me else? I say my prayers morning and evening. Oh, if your highness had believed Diego! 'Tis the same hand that he saw the foot to in the gallery chamber. Father Jerome has often told us the prophecy would be out one of these days. 'Bianca,' said he, 'mark my words——' "

"Thou ravest," said Manfred in a rage! "begone, and keep these fooleries to frighten thy companions."

"What, my lord!" cried Bianca, "do you think I have seen nothing? Go to the foot of the great stairs yourself— as I live I saw it."

"Saw what? Tell us, fair maid, what thou hast seen," said Frederic.

"Can your highness listen," said Manfred, "to the delirium of a silly wench, who has heard stories of apparitions until she believes them?"

"This is more than fancy," said the marquis; "her terror is too natural and too strongly impressed to be the work of imagination. Tell us, fair maiden, what it is has moved thee thus."

"Yes, my lord, thank your greatness," said Bianca. "I believe I look very pale; I shall be better when I have recovered myself. I was going to my Lady Isabella's chamber by his highness's order——"

"We do not want the circumstances," interrupted Manfred. "Since his highness will have it so, proceed; but be brief."

"Lord! your highness thwarts one so!" replied Bianca. "I fear my hair—I am sure I never in my life—well, as I was telling your greatness, I was going, by his highness's order, to my Lady Isabella's chamber. She lies in the watchet-coloured chamber, on the right hand, one pair of stairs. So when I came to the great stairs, I was looking on his highness's present here——"

"Grant me patience!" said Manfred; "will this wench never come to the point? What imports it to the marquis, that I gave thee a bauble for thy faithful attendance on my daughter; we want to know what thou sawest."

"I was going to tell your highness," said Bianca, "if you would permit me. So as I was rubbing the ring—I am sure I had not gone up three steps, but I heard the rattling of armour; for all the world such a clatter, as Diego says he heard when the giant turned him about in the gallery-chamber."

"What does she mean, my lord?" said the marquis: "is your castle haunted by giants and goblins?"

"Lord, what, has not your greatness heard the story of the giant in the gallery-chamber?" cried Bianca. "I marvel his highness has not told you—mayhap you do not know there is a prophecy——"

"This trifling is intolerable," interrupted Manfred. "Let us dismiss this silly wench, my lord; we have more important affairs to discuss."

"By your favour," said Frederic, "these are no trifles. The enormous sabre I was directed to in the wood, yon casque, its fellow—are these visions of this poor maiden's brain?"

"So Jaquez thinks, may it please your greatness," said Bianca. "He says this moon will not be out without our seeing some strange revolution. For my part, I should not be surprised if it was to happen to-morrow; for, as I was saying, when I heard the clattering of armour, I was all in a cold sweat: I looked up, and, if your greatness will believe me, I saw upon the uppermost banister of the great stairs a hand in armour, as big, as big—I thought I should have swooned—I never stopped until I came hither. Would I were well out of this castle! My Lady Matilda told me but yester-morning that her highness Hippolita knows something."

"Thou art an insolent!" cried Manfred. "Lord Marquis, it much misgives me that this scene is concerted to affront me. Are my own domestics suborned to spread tales injurious to my honour? Pursue your claim by manly daring; or let us bury our feuds, as was proposed, by the intermarriage of our children. But trust me, it ill becomes a prince of your bearing to practise on mercenary wenches."

"I scorn your imputation," said Frederic: "until this hour I never set eyes on this damsel. I have given her no jewel! My lord, my lord, your conscience, your guilt accuses you, and would throw the suspicion on me; but keep your daughter, and think no more of Isabella. The judgments already fallen on your house forbid me matching into it."

Manfred, alarmed at the resolute tone in which Frederic delivered these words, endeavoured to pacify him. Dismissing Bianca, he made such submissions to the marquis, and threw in such artful encomiums on Matilda, that Frederic was once more staggered. However, as his passion was of so recent a date, it could not at once surmount the scruples he had conceived. He had gathered enough from Bianca's discourse to persuade him that Heaven declared itself against Manfred. The proposed marriages, too, removed his claim to a distance; and the principality of Otranto was a stronger temptation than the contingent reversion of it with Matilda. Still he would not absolutely recede from his engagements; but purposing to gain time, he demanded of Manfred if it was true in fact that Hippolita consented to the divorce. The prince, transported to find no other obstacle, and depending on his influence over his wife, assured the marquis it was so, and that he might satisfy himself of the truth from her own mouth.

As they were thus discoursing, word was brought that the banquet was prepared. Manfred conducted Frederic to the great hall, where they were received by Hippolita and the young princesses. Manfred placed the marquis next to Matilda, and seated himself between his wife and Isabella. Hippolita comported herself with an easy gravity; but the young ladies were silent and melancholy. Manfred, who was determined to pursue his point with the marquis in the remainder of the evening, pushed on the feast until it waxed late; affecting unrestrained gaiety, and plying Frederic with repeated goblets of wine. The latter, more upon his guard than Manfred wished, declined his frequent challenges, on pretence of his late loss of blood; while the prince, to raise his own disordered spirits, and to counterfeit unconcern, indulged himself in plentiful draughts, though not to the intoxication of his senses.

The evening being far advanced, the banquet concluded. Manfred would have withdrawn with Frederic; but the latter, pleading weakness and want of repose, retired to his chamber, gallantly telling the prince, that his daughter should amuse his highness until himself could attend him. Manfred accepted the party, and, to the no small grief of Isabella, accompanied her to her apartment. Matilda waited on her mother, to enjoy the freshness of the evening on the ramparts of the castle.

Soon as the company were dispersed their several ways, Frederic, quitting his chamber, inquired if Hippolita was alone, and was told by one of her attendants, who had not noticed her going forth, that at that hour she generally withdrew to her oratory, where he probably would find her. The marquis, during the repast, had beheld Matilda with increase of passion. He now wished to find Hippolita in the disposition her lord had promised. The portents that had alarmed him were forgotten in his desires. Stealing softly and unobserved to the apartment of Hippolita, he entered it with a resolution to encourage her acquiescence to the divorce, having perceived that Manfred was resolved to make the possession of Isabella an unalterable condition, before he would grant Matilda to his wishes.

The marquis was not surprised at the silence that reigned in the princess's apartment. Concluding her, as he had been advertised, in her oratory, he passed on. The door was ajar; the evening gloomy and overcast. Pushing open the door gently, he saw a person kneeling before the altar. As he approached nearer, it seemed not a woman, but one in a long woollen weed, whose back was towards him. The person seemed absorbed in prayer. The marquis was about to return, when the figure, rising, stood some moments fixed in meditation, without regarding him. The marquis, expecting the holy person to come forth, and meaning to excuse his uncivil interruption, said:

"Reverend father, I sought the Lady Hippolita."

"Hippolita!" replied a hollow voice; "camest thou to this castle to seek Hippolita?" And then the figure, turning slowly round, discovered to Frederic the fleshless jaws and empty sockets of a skeleton, wrapt in a hermit's cowl.

"Angels of peace protect me!" cried Frederic, recoiling.

"Deserve their protection," said the spectre.

Frederic, falling on his knees, adjured the phantom to take pity on him.

"Dost thou not remember me?" said the apparition. "Remember the wood of Joppa!"

"Art thou that holy hermit?" cried Frederic, trembling; "can I do aught for thy eternal peace?"

"Wast thou delivered from bondage," said the spectre, "to pursue carnal delights? Hast thou forgotten the buried sabre, and the behest of Heaven engraven on it?"

"I have not, I have not," said Frederic; "but say, blest spirit, what is thy errand to me? what remains to be done?"

"To forget Matilda," said the apparition, and vanished.

Frederick's blood froze in his veins. For some minutes he remained motionless. Then falling prostrate on his face before the altar, he besought the intercession of every saint for pardon. A flood of tears succeeded to this transport; and the image of the beauteous Matilda rushing, in spite of him, on thoughts, he lay on the ground in a conflict of penitence and passion. Ere he could recover from this agony of his spirits, the Princess Hippolita, with a taper in her hand, entered the oratory alone. Seeing a man without motion on the floor, she gave a shriek, concluding him dead. Her fright brought Frederic to himself. Rising suddenly, his face bedewed with tears, he would have rushed from her presence; but Hippolita, stopping him, conjured him, in the most plaintive accents, to explain the cause of his disorder, and by what strange chance she had found him there in that posture.

"Ah, virtuous princess!" said the marquis, penetrated with grief, and stopped.

"For the love of Heaven, my lord," said Hippolita, "disclose the cause of this transport! What mean these doleful sounds, this alarming exclamation on my name? What woes has Heaven still in store for the wretched Hippolita?—yet silent!

By every pitying angel I adjure thee, noble prince," continued she, falling at his feet, "to disclose the purport of what lies at thy heart. I see thou feelest for me; thou feelest the sharp pangs that thou inflictest. Speak, for pity! Does aught thou knowest concern my child!"

"I cannot speak," cried Frederic, bursting from her. "Oh, Matilda!"

Quitting the princess thus abruptly, he hastened to his own apartment. At the door of it he was accosted by Manfred, who, flushed by wine and love, had come to seek him, and to propose to waste some hours of the night in music and revelling. Frederic, offended at an invitation so dissonant from the mood of his soul, pushed him rudely aside, and, entering his chamber, flung the door intemperately against Manfred, and bolted it inwards. The haughty prince, enraged at this unaccountable behaviour, withdrew in a frame of mind capable of the most fatal excesses. As he crossed the court, he was met by the domestic whom he planted at the convent as a spy on Jerome and Theodore. This man, almost breathless with the haste he had made, informed his lord, that Theodore and some lady from the castle were at that instant in private conference at the tomb of Alfonso, in St. Nicholas's church. He had dogged Theodore thither; but the gloominess of the night had prevented his discovering who the woman was.

Manfred, whose spirits were inflamed, and whom Isabella had driven from her on his urging his passion with too little reserve, did not doubt but the inquietude she had expressed had been occasioned by her impatience to meet Theodore. Provoked by this conjecture, and enraged at her father, he hastened secretly to the great church. Gliding softly between the aisles, and guided by an imperfect gleam of moonshine that shone faintly through the illuminated windows, he stole towards the tomb of Alfonso, to which he was directed by indistinct whispers of the person she sought. The first sounds he could distinguish were:

"Does it, alas! depend on me? Manfred will never permit our union."

"No, this shall prevent it!" cried the tyrant, drawing his dagger, and plunging it over her shoulder into the bosom of the person that spoke.

"Ah me, I am slain!" cried Matilda, sinking: "good Heaven, receive my soul!"

"Savage, inhuman monster, what hast thou done?" cried Theodore, rushing on him and wrenching his dagger from him.

"Stop, stop thy impious hand!" cried Matilda: "it is my father!"

Manfred, waking as from a trance, beat his breast, twisted his hands in his locks, and endeavoured to recover his dagger from Theodore to dispatch himself. Theodore, scarce less distracted, and only mastering the transports of his grief to assist Matilda, had now by his cries drawn some of the monks to his aid. While part of them endeavoured, in concert with the afflicted Theodore, to stop the blood of the dying princess, the rest prevented Manfred from laying violent hands on himself.

Matilda, resigning herself patiently to her fate, acknowledged, with looks of grateful love, the zeal of Theodore. Yet oft, as her faintness would permit her speech its way, she begged the assistants to comfort her father.

Jerome, by this time, had learnt the fatal news, and reached the church. His looks seemed to reproach Theodore; but turning to Manfred, he said, "Now, tyrant, behold the completion of woe fulfilled on thy impious and devoted head! The blood of Alfonso cried to Heaven for vengeance; and Heaven has permitted its altar to be polluted by assassination, that thou mightest shed thy own blood at the foot of that prince's sepulchre!"

"Cruel man," cried Matilda, "to aggravate the woes of a parent! may Heaven bless my father, and forgive him as I do! My lord, my gracious sire, dost thou forgive thy child? Indeed I came not hither to meet Theodore. I found him praying at this tomb, whither my mother sent me to intercede for thee, for her—dearest father, bless your child, and say you forgive her."

"Forgive thee, murderous monster," cried Manfred, "can assassins forgive? I took thee for Isabella; but Heaven directed my bloody hand to the heart of my child—oh, Matilda, I cannot utter it: canst thou forgive the blindness of my rage?"

"I can, I do, and may Heaven confirm it," said Matilda; "but while I have life to ask it—oh, my mother, what will she feel! will you comfort her, my lord, will you not put her away? indeed she loves you—oh, I am faint; bear me to the castle—can I live to have her close my eyes?"

Theodore and the monks besought her earnestly to suffer herself to be borne into the convent; but her instances were so pressing to be carried to the castle, that, placing her on a litter, they conveyed her thither as she requested. Theodore, supporting her head with his arm, and hanging over her in an agony of despairing love, still endeavoured to inspire her with

*G 856

hopes of life. Jerome on the other side comforted her with discourses of heaven; and holding a crucifix before her, which she bathed with innocent tears, prepared her for her passage to immortality. Manfred, plunged in the deepest affliction, followed the litter in despair.

Ere they reached the castle, Hippolita, informed of the dreadful catastrophe, had flown to meet her murdered child; but when she saw the afflicted procession, the mightiness of her grief deprived her of her senses, and she fell lifeless to the earth in a swoon. Isabella and Frederic, who attended her, were overwhelmed in almost equal sorrow. Matilda alone seemed insensible to her own situation: every thought was lost in tenderness for her mother. Ordering the litter to stop, as soon as Hippolita was brought to herself, she asked for her father. He approached, unable to speak. Matilda, seizing his hand and her mother's, locked them in her own, and then clasped them to her heart. Manfred could not support this act of pathetic piety. He dashed himself on the ground, and cursed the day he was born. Isabella, apprehensive that these struggles of passion were more than Matilda could support, took upon herself to order Manfred to be borne to his apartment, while she caused Matilda to be conveyed to the nearest chamber. Hippolita, scarce more alive than her daughter, was regardless of everything but her; but when the tender Isabella's care would have likewise removed her, while the surgeons examined Matilda's wound, she cried:

"Remove me! never! never! never! I lived but in her, and will expire with her." Matilda raised her eyes at her mother's voice, but closed them again without speaking. Her sinking pulse and the damp coldness of her hand soon dispelled all hopes of recovery. Theodore followed the surgeons into the outer chamber, and heard them pronounce the fatal sentence with a transport equal to frenzy.

"Since she cannot live mine," cried he, "at least she shall be mine in death! Father! Jerome! will you not join our hands?" cried he to the friar, who with the marquis had accompanied the surgeons.

"What means thy distracted rashness?" said Jerome; "is this an hour for marriage?"

"It is, it is," cried Theodore: "alas! there is no other!"

"Young man, thou art too unadvised," said Frederic: "dost thou think we are to listen to thy fond transports in this hour of fate? what pretensions hast thou to the princess?"

"Those of a prince," said Theodore, "of the sovereign of Otranto. This reverend man, my father, has informed me who I am."

"Thou ravest," said the marquis: "there is no prince of Otranto but myself, now Manfred, by murder, by sacrilegious murder, has forfeited all pretensions."

"My lord," said Jerome, assuming an air of command, "he tells you true. It was not my purpose the secret should have been divulged so soon; but fate presses onward to its work. What his hot-headed passion has revealed, my tongue confirms. Know, prince, that when Alfonso set sail for the Holy Land——"

"Is this a season for explanations?" cried Theodore. "Father, come and unite me to the princess; she shall be mine—in every other thing I will dutifully obey you. My life; my adored Matilda!" continued Theodore, rushing back into the inner chamber, "will you not be mine? will you not bless your——" Isabella made signs to him to be silent, apprehending the princess was near her end. "What, is she dead?" cried Theodore; "is it possible?" The violence of his exclamations brought Matilda to herself. Lifting up her eyes, she looked around for her mother.

"Life of my soul! I am here," cried Hippolita; "think not I will quit thee!"

"Oh, you are too good," said Matilda; "but weep not for me, my mother! I am going where sorrow never dwells;—Isabella, thou hast loved me: wo't thou not supply my fondness to this dear, dear woman?—Indeed I am faint!"

"Oh, my child, my child!" said Hippolita, in a flood of tears, "can I not withhold thee a moment?"

"It will not be," said Matilda: "commend me to Heaven—where is my father? Forgive him, dearest mother—forgive him my death; it was an error. Oh, I had forgotten, dearest mother, I vowed never to see Theodore more—perhaps that has drawn down this calamity, but it was not intentional—can you pardon me?"

"Oh, wound not my agonizing soul," said Hippolita; "thou never couldst offend me. Alas! she faints! help! help!"

"I would say something more," said Matilda, struggling, "but it wonnot be—Isabella—Theodore—for my sake—oh!" She expired. Isabella and her women tore Hippolita from the corse; but Theodore threatened destruction to all who attempted to remove him from it. He printed a thousand kisses on her clay-cold hands, and uttered every expression that despairing love could dictate.

Isabella, in the meantime, was accompanying the afflicted Hippolita to her apartment; but in the middle of the court they were met by Manfred, who, distracted with his own thoughts, and anxious once more to behold his daughter, was advancing towards the chamber where she lay. As the moon was now at its height, he read in the countenances of this unhappy company the event he dreaded.

"What! is she dead?" cried he in wild confusion: a clap of thunder at that instant shook the castle to its foundations; the earth rocked, and the clank of more than mortal armour was heard behind. Frederic and Jerome thought the last day was at hand. The latter, forcing Theodore along with them, rushed into the court. The moment Theodore appeared, the walls of the castle behind Manfred were thrown down with a mighty force, and the form of Alfonso, dilated to an immense magnitude, appeared in the centre of the ruins.

"Behold in Theodore the true heir of Alfonso!" said the vision; and having pronounced those words, accompanied by a clap of thunder, it ascended solemnly towards heaven, where the clouds parting asunder, the form of St. Nicholas was seen, and receiving Alfonso's shade, they were soon wrapt from mortal eyes in a blaze of glory.

The beholders fell prostrate on their faces, acknowledging the divine will. The first that broke silence was Hippolita.

"My lord," said she to the desponding Manfred, "behold the vanity of human greatness! Conrad is gone! Matilda is no more! in Theodore we view the true Prince of Otranto. By what miracle he is so, I know not—suffice it to us, our doom is pronounced! Shall we not—can we but—dedicate the few deplorable hours we have to live, in deprecating the further wrath of Heaven? Heaven ejects us: whither can we fly, but to yon holy cells that yet offer us a retreat?"

"Thou guiltless but unhappy woman! unhappy by my crimes!" replied Manfred, "my heart at last is open to thy devout admonitions. Oh, could—but it cannot be—ye are lost in wonder,—let me at last do justice on myself! To heap shame on my own head is all the satisfaction I have left to offer to offended Heaven. My story has drawn down these judgments: let my confession atone—but ah! what can atone for usurpation and a murdered child; a child murdered in a consecrated place? List, sirs, and may this bloody record be a warning to future tyrants!

"Alfonso, ye all know, died in the Holy Land—ye would interrupt me—ye would say he came not fairly to his end—it is most true—why else this bitter cup which Manfred must drink to the dregs? Ricardo, my grandfather, was his chamberlain—I would draw a veil over my ancestor's crimes, but it is in vain! Alfonso died by poison. A fictitious will declared Ricardo his heir. His crimes pursued him. Yet he lost no Conrad, no Matilda! I pay the price of usurpation for all. A storm overtook him. Haunted by his guilt, he vowed to St. Nicholas to found a church and two convents, if he lived to reach Otranto. The sacrifice was accepted: the saint appeared to him in a dream, and promised that Ricardo's posterity should reign in Otranto, until the rightful owner should be grown too large to inhabit the castle, and as long as issue-male from Ricardo's loins should remain to enjoy it. Alas! alas! nor male nor female, except myself, remains of all his wretched race!—I have done—the woes of these three days speak the rest. How this young man can be Alfonso's heir, I know not—yet I do not doubt it. His are these dominions: I resign them—yet I knew not Alfonso had an heir—I question not the will of Heaven—poverty and prayer must fill up the woeful space, until Manfred shall be summoned to Ricardo."

"What remains is my part to declare," said Jerome. "When Alfonso set sail for the Holy Land, he was driven by a storm to the coast of Sicily. The other vessel, which bore Ricardo and his train, as your *lordship* must have heard, was separated from him."

"It is most true," said Manfred; "and the title you give me is more than an outcast can claim—well! be it so—proceed."

Jerome blushed, and continued.

"For three months Lord Alfonso was wind-bound in Sicily. There he became enamoured of a fair virgin, named Victoria. He was too pious to tempt her to forbidden pleasures. They were married. Yet deeming this amour incongruous with the holy vow of arms by which he was bound, he determined to conceal their nuptials, until his return from the crusado, when he purposed to seek and acknowledge her for his lawful wife. He left her pregnant. During his absence she was delivered of a daughter; but scarce had she felt a mother's pangs, ere she heard the fatal rumour of her lord's death, and the succession of Ricardo. What could a friendless, helpless woman do?

would her testimony avail?—yet, my lord, I have an authentic writing——"

"It needs not," said Manfred; "the horrors of these days, the vision we have but now seen, all corroborate thy evidence beyond a thousand parchments. Matilda's death and my expulsion——"

"Be composed, my lord," said Hippolita; "this holy man did not mean to recall your griefs."

Jerome proceeded.

"I shall not dwell on what is needless. The daughter of which Victoria was delivered was, at her maturity, bestowed in marriage on me. Victoria died; and the secret remained locked in my breast. Theodore's narrative has told the rest."

The friar ceased. The disconsolate company retired to the remaining part of the castle. In the morning, Manfred signed his abdication of the principality, with the approbation of Hippolita, and each took on them the habit of religion in the neighbouring convents. Frederic offered his daughter to the new prince, which Hippolita's tenderness for Isabella concurred to promote. But Theodore's grief was too fresh to admit the thought of another love; and it was not until after frequent discourses with Isabella of his dear Matilda, that he was persuaded he could know no happiness, but in the society of one with whom he could for ever indulge the melancholy that had taken possession of his soul.

VATHEK:

AN ARABIAN TALE

BY
WILLIAM BECKFORD

WILLIAM BECKFORD

BECKFORD was born at Fonthill, Wiltshire, in 1760. He was educated privately, studying music under Mozart (at the age of five), painting under Alexander Cozens and architecture under Sir William Chambers. His father, a former Lord Mayor of London, owned considerable estates in Jamaica, and Beckford inherited a vast fortune at the age of nine. Chatham, his guardian, said that he was "all air and fire" and warned him against reading *The Arabian Nights*; George Selwyn predicted that he would end in a madhouse. He completed his education at Geneva. In 1780 and 1781 he made the grand tour of the Low Countries, Germany and Italy, and published an account of these travels anonymously in 1783 as *Dreams, Waking Thoughts and Incidents*, a work which he immediately suppressed with the exception of six copies. In the same year he married Lady Margaret Gordon. Next year he was involved in the Courtenay scandal and left England for Switzerland with his wife, who died two years later. From 1785 to 1798 Beckford travelled extensively in Portugal, Spain and France, and, on one of his longer visits to England in 1790, began to rebuild Fonthill as a vast Gothic abbey, with James Wyatt as his architect. It was completed in 1807, but so hurriedly constructed that its three-hundred-foot spire (modelled on the spire of Salisbury Cathedral) collapsed in a gale. Beckford furnished Fonthill with the treasures of the palaces of Europe—pictures by Raphael, Bellini, Breughel, Leonardo, Velasquez, and Rembrandt, an ebony cabinet designed by Bernini, a Cellini vase. The library was stocked on the same scale of splendour. Here Beckford shut himself up for the next twenty years, a seclusion broken only by visits to Paris and to London for the opera season, while legends circulated about his dark practices. By 1805 his income had fallen to a mere £30,000 a year and he was forced to sell estates in Jamaica, Bedfordshire, and St. Pancras. By 1821 his income was still further reduced and Beckford sold Fonthill itself and retired to Bath, where he built Lansdown Tower, a structure as classical in design as Fonthill was Gothic. *Italy, with Sketches of Spain and Portugal*, based on the suppressed *Dreams, Waking Thoughts and Incidents* and his travel-diaries of 1787–8, appeared in 1834, giving a remarkable picture of Europe before the French Revolution. At the age of seventy-four he published his masterpiece, *Recollections of an Excursion to the Monasteries of Alcobaça and Batalha*, based on a travel-diary of 1794. Beckford died at Bath on 2 May, 1844, his face, it is said, showing scarcely a trace of age. He left two daughters, one of whom married the tenth Duke of Hamilton.

G. Chapman and J. Hodgkin, *A Bibliography of William Beckford of Fonthill*, 1930; J. W. Oliver, *Life of William Beckford*, 1930; S. Sitwell, *Beckford and Beckfordism*, 1930; Guy Chapman, *Beckford*, 1937; new edition, 1952.

Editions of *Vathek*: First London edition, Henley's translation, 1786; French text published at Lausanne and Paris, 1787; definitive London edition of French text, 1815; ed. by Stephen Mallarmé, Paris, 1893; ed. by Dr. Richard Garnett (Henley's trans.), 1893; Nonesuch Press edition by H. E. Grimsditch (trans. of 1815 edition), 1929; *Episodes of Vathek*, French text ed. by Lewis Melville, 1912, English trans. by F. Marzials, 1912; *The Travel-Diaries*, ed. by Guy Chapman, 2 vols., 1928; *Vathek with the Episodes*, ed. by G. Chapman (from the Paris text of 1787), 2 vols., 1929; *The Vision* and *Liber Veritatis*, ed. by G. Chapman, 1930.

VATHEK

VATHEK, ninth caliph of the race of the Abassides, was the son of Motassem, and the grandson of Haroun al Raschid. From an early accession to the throne, and the talents he possessed to adorn it, his subjects were induced to expect that his reign would be long and happy. His figure was pleasing and majestic: but when he was angry, one of his eyes became so terrible, that no person could bear to behold it; and the wretch upon whom it was fixed instantly fell backward, and sometimes expired. For fear, however, of depopulating his dominions and making his palace desolate, he but rarely gave way to his anger.

Being much addicted to women and the pleasures of the table, he sought by his affability to procure agreeable companions; and he succeeded the better as his generosity was unbounded and his indulgences unrestrained: for he did not think, with the Caliph Omar Ben Abdalaziz, that it was necessary to make a hell of this world to enjoy paradise in the next.

He surpassed in magnificence all his predecessors. The palace of Alkoremi, which his father, Motassem, had erected on the hill of Pied Horses, and which commanded the whole city of Samarah, was, in his idea, far too scanty: he added, therefore, five wings, or rather other palaces, which he destined for the particular gratification of each of the senses.

In the first of these were tables continually covered with the most exquisite dainties; which were supplied both by night and by day, according to their constant consumption; whilst the most delicious wines and the choicest cordials flowed forth from a hundred fountains that were never exhausted. This palace was called *The Eternal or Unsatiating Banquet.*

The second was styled *The Temple of Melody, or the Nectar of the Soul.* It was inhabited by the most skilful musicians and admired poets of the time; who not only displayed their talents within, but dispersing in bands without, caused every surrounding scene to reverberate their songs, which were continually varied in the most delightful succession.

The palace named *The Delight of the Eyes, or the Support of Memory*, was one entire enchantment. Rarities, collected from every corner of the earth, were there found in such profusion as to dazzle and confound, but for the order in which they were arranged. One gallery exhibited the pictures of the celebrated Mani, and statues that seemed to be alive. Here a well-managed perspective attracted the sight; there the magic of optics agreeably deceived it: whilst the naturalist, on his part, exhibited in their several classes the various gifts that Heaven had bestowed on our globe. In a word, Vathek omitted nothing in this palace that might gratify the curiosity of those who resorted to it, although he was not able to satisfy his own; for, of all men, he was the most curious.

The Palace of Perfumes, which was termed likewise *The Incentive to Pleasure*, consisted of various halls, where the different perfumes which the earth produces were kept perpetually burning in censers of gold. Flambeaux and aromatic lamps were here lighted in open day. But the too powerful effects of this agreeable delirium might be alleviated by descending into an immense garden, where an assemblage of every fragrant flower diffused through the air the purest odours.

The fifth palace, denominated *The Retreat of Mirth, or the Dangerous*, was frequented by troops of young females, beautiful as the Houris, and not less seducing; who never failed to receive, with caresses, all whom the caliph allowed to approach them and enjoy a few hours of their company.

Notwithstanding the sensuality in which Vathek indulged, he experienced no abatement in the love of his people, who thought that a sovereign giving himself up to pleasure was as able to govern as one who declared himself an enemy to it. But the unquiet and impetuous disposition of the caliph would not allow him to rest there. He had studied so much for his amusement in the lifetime of his father, as to acquire a great deal of knowledge, though not a sufficiency to satisfy himself; for he wished to know everything; even sciences that did not exist. He was fond of engaging in disputes with the learned, but did not allow them to push their opposition with warmth. He stopped with presents the mouths of those whose mouths could be stopped; whilst others, whom his liberality was unable to subdue, he sent to prison to cool their blood, a remedy that often succeeded.

Vathek discovered also a predilection for theological controversy; but it was not with the orthodox that he usually held.

By this means he induced the zealots to oppose him, and then persecuted them in return; for he resolved, at any rate, to have reason on his side.

The great prophet, Mahomet, whose vicars the caliphs are, beheld with indignation from his abode in the seventh heaven the irreligious conduct of such a vicegerent. "Let us leave him to himself," said he to the Genii, who are always ready to receive his commands: "let us see to what lengths his folly and impiety will carry him: if he run into excess, we shall know how to chastise him. Assist him, therefore, to complete the tower which, in imitation of Nimrod, he hath begun; not, like that great warrior, to escape being drowned, but from the insolent curiosity of penetrating the secrets of heaven:—he will not divine the fate that awaits him."

The Genii obeyed; and, when the workmen had raised their structure a cubit in the daytime, two cubits more were added in the night. The expedition with which the fabric arose was not a little flattering to the vanity of Vathek: he fancied that even insensible matter showed a forwardness to subserve his designs; not considering that the successes of the foolish and wicked form the first rod of their chastisement.

His pride arrived at its height when, having ascended, for the first time, the fifteen hundred stairs of his tower, he cast his eyes below, and beheld men not larger than pismires; mountains, than shells; and cities, than bee-hives. The idea which such an elevation inspired of his own grandeur completely bewildered him: he was almost ready to adore himself; till, lifting his eyes upward, he saw the stars as high above him as they appeared when he stood on the surface of the earth.

He consoled himself, however, for this intruding and unwelcome perception of his littleness, with the thought of being great in the eyes of others; and flattered himself that the light of his mind would extend beyond the reach of his sight, and extort from the stars the decrees of his destiny.

With this view, the inquisitive prince passed most of his nights on the summit of his tower, till becoming an adept in the mysteries of astrology, he imagined that the planets had disclosed to him the most marvellous adventures, which were to be accomplished by an extraordinary personage, from a country altogether unknown. Prompted by motives of curiosity, he had always been courteous to strangers; but, from this instant, he redoubled his attention, and ordered it to be announced, by sound of trumpet, through all the streets of

Samarah, that no one of his subjects, on peril of his displeasure, should either lodge or detain a traveller, but forthwith bring him to the palace.

Not long after this proclamation, arrived in his metropolis a man so abominably hideous, that the very guards who arrested him were forced to shut their eyes as they led him along: the caliph himself appeared startled at so horrible a visage; but joy succeeded to this emotion of terror, when the stranger displayed to his view such rarities as he had never before seen, and of which he had no conception.

In reality, nothing was ever so extraordinary as the merchandise this stranger produced; most of his curiosities, which were not less admirable for their workmanship than splendour, had, besides, their several virtues described on a parchment fastened to each. There were slippers, which, by spontaneous springs, enabled the feet to walk; knives, that cut without motion of the hand; sabres, that dealt the blow at the person they were wished to strike; and the whole enriched with gems that were hitherto unknown.

The sabres especially, the blades of which emitted a dazzling radiance, fixed, more than all the rest, the caliph's attention; who promised himself to decipher, at his leisure, the uncouth characters engraven on their sides. Without, therefore, demanding their price, he ordered all the coined gold to be brought from his treasury, and commanded the merchant to take what he pleased. The stranger obeyed, took little, and remained silent.

Vathek, imagining that the merchant's taciturnity was occasioned by the awe which his presence inspired, encouraged him to advance, and asked him, with an air of condescension, who he was? whence he came? and where he obtained such beautiful commodities? The man, or rather monster, instead of making a reply, thrice rubbed his forehead, which, as well as his body, was blacker than ebony; four times clapped his paunch, the projection of which was enormous; opened wide his huge eyes, which glowed like firebrands; began to laugh with a hideous noise, and discovered his long amber-coloured teeth, bestreaked with green.

The caliph, though a little startled, renewed his inquiries, but without being able to procure a reply. At which, beginning to be ruffled, he exclaimed, "Knowest thou, wretch, who I am, and at whom thou art aiming thy gibes?"—Then, addressing his guards, "Have ye heard him speak?—is he dumb?"—

"He hath spoken," they replied, "but to no purpose."—"Let him speak then again," said Vathek, "and tell me who he is, from whence he came, and where he procured these singular curiosities; or I swear, by the ass of Balaam, that I will make him rue his pertinacity."

This menace was accompanied by one of the caliph's angry and perilous glances, which the stranger sustained without the slightest emotion; although his eyes were fixed on the terrible eye of the prince.

No words can describe the amazement of the courtiers, when they beheld this rude merchant withstand the encounter unshocked. They all fell prostrate with their faces on the ground, to avoid the risk of their lives; and would have continued in the same abject posture, had not the caliph exclaimed, in a furious tone, "Up, cowards! seize the miscreant! see that he be committed to prison, and guarded by the best of my soldiers! Let him, however, retain the money I gave him; it is not my intent to take from him his property; I only want him to speak."

No sooner had he uttered these words, than the stranger was surrounded, pinioned, and bound with strong fetters, and hurried away to the prison of the great tower, which was encompassed by seven empalements of iron bars, and armed with spikes in every direction, longer and sharper than spits. The caliph, nevertheless, remained in the most violent agitation. He sat down indeed to eat; but, of the three hundred dishes that were daily placed before him, he could taste of no more than thirty-two.

A diet to which he had been so little accustomed was sufficient of itself to prevent him from sleeping; what then must be its effect when joined to the anxiety that preyed upon his spirits? At the first glimpse of dawn he hastened to the prison, again to importune this intractable stranger; but the rage of Vathek exceeded all bounds on finding the prison empty, the grates burst asunder, and his guards lying lifeless around him. In the paroxysm of his passion he fell furiously on the poor carcasses, and kicked them till evening without intermission. His courtiers and viziers exerted their efforts to soothe his extravagance; but, finding every expedient ineffectual, they all united in one vociferation, "The caliph is gone mad! the caliph is out of his senses!"

This outcry, which soon resounded through the streets of Samarah, at length reached the ears of Carathis, his mother, who flew in the utmost consternation to try her ascendency on the mind of her son. Her tears and caresses called off his attention; and he was prevailed upon, by her entreaties, to be brought back to the palace.

Carathis, apprehensive of leaving Vathek to himself, had him put to bed; and, seating herself by him, endeavoured by her conversation to appease and compose him. Nor could any one have attempted it with better success; for the caliph not only loved her as a mother, but respected her as a person of superior genius. It was she who had induced him, being a Greek herself, to adopt the sciences and systems of her country, which all good Mussulmans hold in such thorough abhorrence.

Judicial astrology was one of those sciences in which Carathis was a perfect adept. She began, therefore, with reminding her son of the promise which the stars had made him; and intimated an intention of consulting them again. "Alas!" said the caliph as soon as he could speak, "what a fool I have been! not for having bestowed forty thousand kicks on my guards, who so tamely submitted to death; but for never considering that this extraordinary man was the same that the planets had foretold; whom, instead of ill-treating, I should have conciliated by all the arts of persuasion."

"The past," said Carathis, "cannot be recalled; but it behoves us to think of the future: perhaps you may again see the object you so much regret: it is possible the inscriptions on the sabres will afford information. Eat, therefore, and take thy repose, my dear son. We will consider, to-morrow, in what manner to act."

Vathek yielded to her counsel as well as he could, and arose in the morning with a mind more at ease. The sabres he commanded to be instantly brought; and, poring upon them, through a coloured glass, that their glittering might not dazzle, he set himself in earnest to decipher the inscriptions; but his reiterated attempts were all of them nugatory: in vain did he beat his head, and bite his nails; not a letter of the whole was he able to ascertain. So unlucky a disappointment would have undone him again, had not Carathis, by good fortune, entered the apartment.

"Have patience, my son!" said she: "you certainly are possessed of every important science; but the knowledge of languages is a trifle at best, and the accomplishment of none but a pedant. Issue a proclamation, that you will confer such rewards as become your greatness upon any one that shall interpret what you do not understand, and what is beneath you to learn; you will soon find your curiosity gratified."

"That may be," said the caliph; "but, in the meantime, I shall be horribly disgusted by a crowd of smatterers, who will come to the trial as much for the pleasure of retailing their jargon as from the hope of gaining the reward. To avoid this evil, it will be proper to add, that I will put every candidate to death, who shall fail to give satisfaction; for, thank Heaven! I have skill enough to distinguish, whether one translates or invents."

"Of that I have no doubt," replied Carathis; "but to put the ignorant to death is somewhat severe, and may be productive of dangerous effects. Content yourself with commanding their beards to be burnt: beards in a state are not quite so essential as men."

The caliph submitted to the reasons of his mother; and, sending for Morakanabad, his prime vizier, said, "Let the common criers proclaim, not only in Samarah, but throughout every city in my empire, that whosoever will repair hither and decipher certain characters which appear to be inexplicable, shall experience that liberality for which I am renowned; but that all who fail upon trial shall have their beards burnt off to the last hair. Let them add, also, that I will bestow fifty beautiful slaves, and as many jars of apricots from the Isle of Kirmith, upon any man that shall bring me intelligence of the stranger."

The subjects of the caliph, like their sovereign, being great admirers of women and apricots from Kirmith, felt their mouths water at these promises, but were totally unable to gratify their hankering; for no one knew what had become of the stranger.

As to the caliph's other requisition, the result was different. The learned, the half-learned, and those who were neither, but fancied themselves equal to both, came boldly to hazard their beards, and all shamefully lost them. The exaction of these forfeitures, which found sufficient employment for the eunuchs, gave them such a smell of singed hair as greatly to disgust the ladies of the seraglio, and to make it necessary that this new occupation of their guardians should be transferred to other hands.

At length, however, an old man presented himself, whose beard was a cubit and a half longer than any that had appeared before him. The officers of the palace whispered to each other, as they ushered him in, "What a pity, oh! what a great pity that such a beard should be burnt!" Even the caliph, when he saw it, concurred with them in opinion; but his concern was entirely needless. This venerable personage read the characters with facility, and explained them verbatim as follows: "We were made where everything is well made: we are the least of the wonders of a place where all is wonderful, and deserving the sight of the first potentate on earth."

"You translate admirably!" cried Vathek; "I know to what these marvellous characters allude. Let him receive as many robes of honour and thousands of sequins of gold as he hath spoken words. I am in some measure relieved from the perplexity that embarrassed me!" Vathek invited the old man to dine, and even to remain some days in the palace.

Unluckily for him, he accepted the offer; for the caliph, having ordered him next morning to be called, said: "Read again to me what you have read already; I cannot hear too often the promise that is made me—the completion of which I languish to obtain." The old man forthwith put on his green spectacles, but they instantly dropped from his nose, on perceiving that the characters he had read the day preceding had given place to others of different import. "What ails you?" asked the caliph; "and why these symptoms of wonder?"—"Sovereign of the world!" replied the old man, "these sabres hold another language to-day from that they yesterday held."—"How say you?" returned Vathek:—"but it matters not; tell me, if you can, what they mean."—"It is this, my lord," rejoined the old man: "'Woe to the rash mortal who seeks to know that of which he should remain ignorant; and to undertake that which surpasseth his power!'"—"And woe to thee!" cried the caliph, in a burst of indignation: "to-day thou art void of understanding: begone from my presence, they shall burn but the half of thy beard, because thou wert yesterday fortunate in guessing: —my gifts I never resume." The old man, wise enough to perceive he had luckily escaped, considering the folly of disclosing so disgusting a truth, immediately withdrew and appeared not again.

But it was not long before Vathek discovered abundant reason to regret his precipitation; for, though he could not decipher the characters himself, yet, by constantly poring upon them, he plainly perceived that they every day changed; and, unfortunately, no other candidate offered to explain them. This perplexing occupation inflamed his blood, dazzled his sight, and brought on such a giddiness and debility that he could hardly support himself. He failed not, however, though in so reduced a condition, to be often carried to his tower, as he flattered himself that he might there read in the stars, which he went to consult, something more congruous to his wishes: but in this his hopes were deluded; for his eyes, dimmed by the vapours of his head, began to subserve his curiosity so ill, that he beheld nothing but a thick, dun cloud, which he took for the most direful of omens.

Agitated with so much anxiety, Vathek entirely lost all firmness; a fever seized him, and his appetite failed. Instead of being one of the greatest eaters, he became as distinguished for drinking. So insatiable was the thirst which tormented him, that his mouth, like a funnel, was always open to receive the various liquors that might be poured into it, and especially cold water, which calmed him more than any other.

This unhappy prince, being thus incapacitated for the enjoyment of any pleasure, commanded the palaces of the five senses to be shut up; forbore to appear in public, either to display his magnificence or administer justice, and retired to the inmost apartment of his harem. As he had ever been an excellent husband, his wives, overwhelmed with grief at his deplorable situation, incessantly supplied him with prayers for his health, and water for his thirst.

In the mean time the Princess Carathis, whose affliction no words can describe, instead of confining herself to sobbing and tears, was closeted daily with the vizier Morakanabad, to find out some cure, or mitigation, of the caliph's disease. Under the persuasion that it was caused by enchantment, they turned over together, leaf by leaf, all the books of magic that might point out a remedy; and caused the horrible stranger, whom they accused as the enchanter, to be everywhere sought for with the strictest diligence.

At the distance of a few miles from Samarah stood a high mountain, whose sides were swarded with wild thyme and basil, and its summit overspread with so delightful a plain, that it might have been taken for the paradise destined for the faithful. Upon it grew a hundred thickets of eglantine and other fragrant shrubs; a hundred arbours of roses, entwined with jessamine and honeysuckle; as many clumps of orange trees, cedar, and citron; whose branches, interwoven with the palm, the pomegranate, and the vine, presented every luxury that could regale the eye or the taste. The ground was strewed with violets, harebells, and pansies; in the midst of which numerous tufts of jonquils, hyacinths, and carnations perfumed the air. Four fountains, not less clear than deep, and so abundant as to slake the thirst of ten armies, seemed purposely placed here to make the scene more resemble the garden of Eden watered by four sacred rivers. Here, the nightingale sang the birth of the rose, her well-beloved, and, at the same time, lamented its short-lived beauty: whilst the dove deplored the loss of more substantial pleasures; and the wakeful lark hailed the rising light that reanimates the whole creation. Here, more than anywhere, the mingled melodies of birds expressed the various passions which inspired them; and the exquisite fruits which they pecked at pleasure seemed to have given them a double energy.

To this mountain Vathek was sometimes brought, for the sake of breathing a purer air; and, especially, to drink at will of the four fountains. His attendants were his mother, his wives, and some eunuchs, who assiduously employed themselves in filling capacious bowls of rock crystal, and emulously presenting them to him. But it frequently happened that his avidity exceeded their zeal, insomuch that he would prostrate himself upon the ground to lap the water, of which he could never have enough.

One day, when this unhappy prince had been long lying in so debasing a posture, a voice, hoarse but strong, thus addressed him: "Why dost thou assimilate thyself to a dog, O caliph, proud as thou art of thy dignity and power?" At this apostrophe, he raised up his head, and beheld the stranger that had caused him so much affliction. Inflamed with anger at the sight, he exclaimed, "Accursed Giaour! what comest thou hither to do?—is it not enough to have transformed a prince remarkable for his agility into a water budget? Perceivest thou not, that I may perish by drinking to excess, as well as by thirst?"

"Drink, then, this draught," said the stranger, as he presented to him a phial of a red and yellow mixture: "and, to satiate the thirst of thy soul as well as of thy body, know that I am an Indian, but from a region of India which is wholly unknown."

The caliph, delighted to see his desires accomplished in part, and flattering himself with the hope of obtaining their entire fulfilment, without a moment's hesitation swallowed the potion, and instantaneously found his health restored, his thirst appeased, and his limbs as agile as ever. In the transports of his joy,

Vathek leaped upon the neck of the frightful Indian, and kissed his horrid mouth and hollow cheeks, as though they had been the coral lips and the lilies and roses of his most beautiful wives.

Nor would these transports have ceased had not the eloquence of Carathis repressed them. Having prevailed upon him to return to Samarah, she caused a herald to proclaim as loudly as possible: "The wonderful stranger hath appeared again; he hath healed the caliph; he hath spoken! he hath spoken!"

Forthwith, all the inhabitants of this vast city quitted their habitations, and ran together in crowds to see the procession of Vathek and the Indian, whom they now blessed as much as they had before execrated, incessantly shouting, "He hath healed our sovereign; he hath spoken! he hath spoken!" Nor were these words forgotten in the public festivals which were celebrated the same evening, to testify the general joy; for the poets applied them as a chorus to all the songs they composed on this interesting subject.

The caliph, in the meanwhile, caused the palaces of the senses to be again set open; and, as he found himself naturally prompted to visit that of taste in preference to the rest, immediately ordered a splendid entertainment, to which his great officers and favourite courtiers were all invited. The Indian, who was placed near the prince, seemed to think that, as a proper acknowledgment of so distinguished a privilege, he could neither eat, drink, nor talk too much. The various dainties were no sooner served up than they vanished, to the great mortification of Vathek, who piqued himself on being the greatest eater alive, and at this time in particular was blessed with an excellent appetite.

The rest of the company looked round at each other in amazement; but the Indian, without appearing to observe it, quaffed large bumpers to the health of each of them; sung in a style altogether extravagant; related stories, at which he laughed immoderately, and poured forth extemporaneous verses, which would not have been thought bad, but for the strange grimaces with which they were uttered. In a word, his loquacity was equal to that of a hundred astrologers; he ate as much as a hundred porters, and caroused in proportion.

The caliph, notwithstanding the table had been thirty-two times covered, found himself incommoded by the voraciousness of his guest, who was now considerably declined in the prince's esteem. Vathek, however, being unwilling to betray the chagrin he could hardly disguise, said in a whisper to

Babbabalouk, the chief of his eunuchs: "You see how enormous his performances are in every way; what would be the consequence should he get at my wives!—Go! redouble your vigilance, and be sure look well to my Circassians, who would be more to his taste than all of the rest."

The bird of the morning had thrice renewed his song, when the hour of the divan was announced. Vathek, in gratitude to his subjects having promised to attend, immediately arose from table and repaired thither, leaning upon his vizier, who could scarce support him; so disordered was the poor prince by the wine he had drunk, and still more by the extravagant vagaries of his boisterous guest.

The viziers, the officers of the crown and of the law, arranged themselves in a semicircle about their sovereign, and preserved a respectful silence; whilst the Indian, who looked as cool as if he had been fasting, sat down without ceremony on one of the steps of the throne, laughing in his sleeve at the indignation with which his temerity had filled the spectators.

The caliph, however, whose ideas were confused, and whose head was embarrassed, went on administering justice at haphazard; till at length the prime vizier, perceiving his situation, hit upon a sudden expedient to interrupt the audience and rescue the honour of his master, to whom he said in a whisper, "My lord, the Princess Carathis, who hath passed the night in consulting the planets, informs you that they portend you evil, and the danger is urgent. Beware lest this stranger, whom you have so lavishly recompensed for his magical gewgaws, should make some attempt on your life: his liquor, which at first had the appearance of effecting your cure, may be no more than a poison, the operation of which will be sudden. Slight not this surmise; ask him, at least, of what it was compounded, whence he procured it; and mention the sabres which you seem to have forgotten."

Vathek, to whom the insolent airs of the stranger became every moment less supportable, intimated to his vizier, by a wink of acquiescence, that he would adopt his advice; and, at once turning towards the Indian, said, "Get up, and declare in full divan of what drugs was compounded the liquor you enjoined me to take, for it is suspected to be poison: give also that explanation I have so earnestly desired concerning the sabres you sold me, and thus show your gratitude for the favours heaped on you."

Having pronounced these words in as moderate a tone

as he well could, he waited in silent expectation for an answer. But the Indian, still keeping his seat, began to renew his loud shouts of laughter, and exhibit the same horrid grimaces he had shown them before, without vouchsafing a word in reply. Vathek, no longer able to brook such insolence, immediately kicked him from the steps; instantly descending, repeated his blow; and persisted, with such assiduity, as incited all who were present to follow his example. Every foot was up and aimed at the Indian, and no sooner had any one given him a kick, than he felt himself constrained to reiterate the stroke.

The stranger afforded them no small entertainment; for, being both short and plump, he collected himself into a ball, and rolled on all sides at the blows of his assailants, who pressed after him, wherever he turned, with an eagerness beyond conception, whilst their numbers were every moment increasing. The ball, indeed, in passing from one apartment to another, drew every person after it that came in its way; insomuch that the whole palace was thrown into confusion, and resounded with a tremendous clamour. The women of the harem, amazed at the uproar, flew to their blinds to discover the cause; but no sooner did they catch a glimpse of the ball than, feeling themselves unable to refrain, they broke from the clutches of their eunuchs, who, to stop their flight, pinched them till they bled; but in vain: whilst themselves, though trembling with terror at the escape of their charge, were as incapable of resisting the attraction.

After having traversed the halls, galleries, chambers, kitchens, gardens, and stables of the palace, the Indian at last took his course through the courts; whilst the caliph, pursuing him closer than the rest, bestowed as many kicks as he possibly could; yet not without receiving now and then a few which his competitors, in their eagerness, designed for the ball.

Carathis, Morakanabad, and two or three old viziers, whose wisdom had hitherto withstood the attraction, wishing to prevent Vathek from exposing himself in the presence of his subjects, fell down in his way to impede the pursuit: but he, regardless of their obstruction, leaped over their heads, and went on as before. They then ordered the muezzins to call the people to prayers; both for the sake of getting them out of the way, and of endeavouring, by their petitions, to avert the calamity: but neither of these expedients was a whit more successful. The sight of this fatal ball was alone sufficient to draw after it every beholder. The muezzins themselves, though they saw it but at a distance, hastened down from their minarets, and mixed with the crowd; which continued to increase in so surprising a manner that scarce an inhabitant was left in Samarah except the aged; the sick, confined to their beds; and infants at the breast, whose nurses could run more nimbly without them. Even Carathis, Morakanabad, and the rest, were all become of the party. The shrill screams of the females, who had broken from their apartments and were unable to extricate themselves from the pressure of the crowd, together with those of the eunuchs jostling after them, and terrified lest their charge should escape from their sight; the execrations of husbands, urging forward and menacing each other; kicks given and received; stumblings and overthrows at every step; in a word, the confusion that universally prevailed, rendered Samarah like a city taken by storm, and devoted to absolute plunder. At last, the cursed Indian, who still preserved his rotundity of figure, after passing through all the streets and public places, and leaving them empty, rolled onwards to the plain of Catoul, and entered the valley at the foot of the mountain of the four fountains.

As a continual fall of water had excavated an immense gulf in the valley, whose opposite side was closed in by a steep acclivity, the caliph and his attendants were apprehensive lest the ball should bound into the chasm, and, to prevent it, redoubled their efforts, but in vain. The Indian persevered in his onward direction; and, as had been apprehended, glancing from the precipice with the rapidity of lightning, was lost in the gulf below.

Vathek would have followed the perfidious Giaour, had not an invisible agency arrested his progress. The multitude that pressed after him were at once checked in the same manner, and a calm instantaneously ensued. They all gazed at each other with an air of astonishment; and notwithstanding that the loss of veils and turbans, together with torn habits, and dust blended with sweat, presented a most laughable spectacle, yet there was not one smile to be seen. On the contrary, all with looks of confusion and sadness returned in silence to Samarah, and retired to their inmost apartments, without ever reflecting, that they had been impelled by an invisible power into the extravagance for which they reproached themselves; for it is but just that men, who so often arrogate to their own merit the good of which they are but instruments, should also attribute to themselves absurdities which they could not prevent.

The caliph was the only person who refused to leave the valley. He commanded his tents to be pitched there, and stationed himself on the very edge of the precipice, in spite of the representations of Carathis and Morakanabad, who pointed out the hazard of its brink giving way, and the vicinity to the magician that had so cruelly tormented him. Vathek derided all their remonstrances; and having ordered a thousand flambeaux to be lighted, and directed his attendants to proceed in lighting more, lay down on the slippery margin, and attempted, by the help of this artificial splendour, to look through that gloom, which all the fires of the empyrean had been insufficient to pervade. One while he fancied to himself voices arising from the depth of the gulf; at another, he seemed to distinguish the accents of the Indian; but all was no more than the hollow murmur of waters, and the din of the cataracts that rushed from steep to steep down the sides of the mountain.

Having passed the night in this cruel perturbation, the caliph at daybreak retired to his tent; where, without taking the least sustenance, he continued to doze till the dusk of evening began again to come on. He then resumed his vigils as before, and persevered in observing them for many nights together. At length, fatigued with so fruitless an employment, he sought relief from change. To this end, he sometimes paced with hasty strides across the plain; and as he wildly gazed at the stars, reproached them with having deceived him; but, lo! on a sudden, the clear blue sky appeared streaked over with streams of blood, which reached from the valley even to the city of Samarah. As this awful phenomenon seemed to touch his tower, Vathek at first thought of repairing thither to view it more distinctly; but, feeling himself unable to advance, and being overcome with apprehension, he muffled up his face in the folds of his robe.

Terrifying as these prodigies were, this impression upon him was no more than momentary, and served only to stimulate his love of the marvellous. Instead, therefore, of returning to his palace, he persisted in the resolution of abiding where the Indian had vanished from his view. One night, however, while he was walking as usual on the plain, the moon and stars were eclipsed at once, and a total darkness ensued. The earth trembled beneath him, and a voice came forth, the voice of the Giaour, who, in accents more sonorous than thunder, thus addressed him: "Wouldest thou devote thyself to me? adore the terrestrial influences, and abjure Mahomet? On these conditions I will bring thee to the Palace of Subterranean Fire. There shalt thou behold, in immense depositories, the treasures which the stars have promised thee; and which will be conferred by those Intelligences whom thou shalt thus render propitious. It was from thence I brought my sabres, and it is there that Soliman Ben Daoud reposes, surrounded by the talismans that control the world."

The astonished caliph trembled as he answered, yet he answered in a style that showed him to be no novice in preternatural adventures: "Where art thou? be present to my eyes; dissipate the gloom that perplexes me, and of which I deem thee the cause. After the many flambeaux I have burnt to discover thee, thou mayest at least grant a glimpse of thy horrible visage."—"Abjure then Mahomet!" replied the Indian, "and promise me full proofs of thy sincerity: otherwise, thou shalt never behold me again."

The unhappy caliph, instigated by insatiable curiosity, lavished his promises in the utmost profusion. The sky immediately brightened; and, by the light of the planets which seemed almost to blaze, Vathek beheld the earth open; and, at the extremity of a vast black chasm, a portal of ebony, before which stood the Indian, holding in his hand a golden key which he sounded against the lock.

"How," cried Vathek, "can I descend to thee? Come, take me, and instantly open the portal."—"Not so fast," replied the Indian, "impatient caliph! Know that I am parched with thirst, and cannot open this door, till my thirst be thoroughly appeased; I require the blood of fifty children. Take them from among the most beautiful sons of thy viziers and great men; or neither can my thirst nor thy curiosity be satisfied. Return to Samarah; procure for me this necessary libation; come back hither; throw it thyself into this chasm, and then shalt thou see!"

Having thus spoken, the Indian turned his back on the caliph, who, incited by the suggestions of demons, resolved on the direful sacrifice. He now pretended to have regained his tranquillity, and set out for Samarah amidst the acclamations of a people who still loved him, and forbore not to rejoice when they believed him to have recovered his reason. So successfully did he conceal the emotion of his heart, that even Carathis and Morakanabad were equally deceived with the rest. Nothing was heard of but festivals and rejoicings. The fatal ball, which no tongue had hitherto ventured to mention, was brought on

the tapis. A general laugh went round, though many, still
smarting under the hands of the surgeon from the hurts received
in that memorable adventure, had no great reason for mirth.

The prevalence of this gay humour was not a little grateful
to Vathek, who perceived how much it conduced to his project.
He put on the appearance of affability to every one; but
especially to his viziers and the grandees of his court, whom he
failed not to regale with a sumptuous banquet; during which
he insensibly directed the conversation to the children of his
guests. Having asked, with a good-natured air, which of them
were blessed with the handsomest boys, every father at once
asserted the pretensions of his own; and the contest imperceptibly grew so warm, that nothing could have withholden
them from coming to blows but their profound reverence for
the person of the caliph. Under the pretence, therefore, of
reconciling the disputants, Vathek took upon him to decide;
and, with this view, commanded the boys to be brought.

It was not long before a troop of these poor children made
their appearance, all equipped by their fond mothers with
such ornaments as might give the greatest relief to their beauty,
or most advantageously display the graces of their age. But,
whilst this brilliant assemblage attracted the eyes and hearts
of every one besides, the caliph scrutinized each, in his turn,
with a malignant avidity that passed for attention, and selected
from their number the fifty whom he judged the Giaour would
prefer.

With an equal show of kindness as before, he proposed to
celebrate a festival on the plain, for the entertainment of his
young favourites, who, he said, ought to rejoice still more than
all at the restoration of his health, on account of the favours
he intended for them.

The caliph's proposal was received with the greatest delight,
and soon published through Samarah. Litters, camels, and
horses were prepared. Women and children, old men and
young, every one placed himself as he chose. The cavalcade
set forward, attended by all the confectioners in the city and
its precincts; the populace, following on foot, composed an
amazing crowd, and occasioned no little noise. All was joy; nor
did any one call to mind what most of them had suffered when
they lately travelled the road they were now passing so gaily.

The evening was serene, the air refreshing, the sky clear, and
the flowers exhaled their fragrance. The beams of the declining
sun, whose mild splendour reposed on the summit of the

mountain, shed a glow of ruddy light over its green declivity, and the white flocks sporting upon it. No sounds were heard, save the murmurs of the four fountains, and the reeds and voices of shepherds, calling to each other from different eminences.

The lovely innocents, destined for the sacrifice, added not a little to the hilarity of the scene. They approached the plain full of sportiveness, some coursing butterflies, others culling flowers, or picking up the shining little pebbles that attracted their notice. At intervals they nimbly started from each other for the sake of being caught again and mutually imparting a thousand caresses.

The dreadful chasm, at whose bottom the portal of ebony was placed, began to appear at a distance. It looked like a black streak that divided the plain. Morakanabad and his companions took it for some work which the caliph had ordered. Unhappy men! little did they surmise for what it was destined. Vathek, unwilling that they should examine it too nearly, stopped the procession, and ordered a spacious circle to be formed on this side, at some distance from the accursed chasm. The body-guard of eunuchs was detached, to measure out the lists intended for the games, and prepare the rings for the arrows of the young archers. The fifty competitors were soon stripped, and presented to the admiration of the spectators the suppleness and grace of their delicate limbs. Their eyes sparkled with a joy, which those of their fond parents reflected. Every one offered wishes for the little candidate nearest his heart, and doubted not of his being victorious. A breathless suspense awaited the contests of these amiable and innocent victims.

The caliph, availing himself of the first moment to retire from the crowd, advanced towards the chasm; and there heard, yet not without shuddering, the voice of the Indian; who, gnashing his teeth, eagerly demanded, "Where are they?—where are they?—perceivest thou not how my mouth waters?" —"Relentless Giaour!" answerd Vathek, with emotion; "can nothing content thee but the massacre of these lovely victims? Ah! wert thou to behold their beauty, it must certainly move thy compassion."—"Perdition on thy compassion, babbler!" cried the Indian: "give them me; instantly give them, or my portal shall be closed against thee for ever!"—"Not so loudly," replied the caliph, blushing.—"I understand thee," returned the Giaour with the grin of an ogre; "thou wantest no presence of mind: I will for a moment forbear."

During this exquisite dialogue, the games went forward with all alacrity, and at length concluded, just as the twilight began to overcast the mountains. Vathek, who was still standing on the edge of the chasm, called out, with all his might, "Let my fifty little favourites approach me, separately; and let them come in the order of their success. To the first, I will give my diamond bracelet; to the second, my collar of emeralds; to the third, my aigret of rubies; to the fourth, my girdle of topazes; and to the rest, each a part of my dress, even down to my slippers."

This declaration was received with reiterated acclamations; and all extolled the liberality of a prince who would thus strip himself for the amusement of his subjects and the encouragement of the rising generation. The caliph in the meanwhile, undressed himself by degrees, and, raising his arm as high as he was able, made each of the prizes glitter in the air; but whilst he delivered it with one hand to the child who sprung forward to receive it, he with the other pushed the poor innocent into the gulf, where the Giaour, with a sullen muttering, incessantly repeated, "More! more!"

This dreadful device was executed with so much dexterity, that the boy who was approaching him remained unconscious of the fate of his forerunner; and, as to the spectators, the shades of evening, together with their distance, precluded them from perceiving any object distinctly. Vathek, having in this manner thrown in the last of the fifty, and, expecting that the Giaour, on receiving him, would have presented the key, already fancied himself as great as Soliman, and consequently above being amenable for what he had done; when, to his utter amazement, the chasm closed, and the ground became as entire as the rest of the plain.

No language could express his rage and despair. He execrated the perfidy of the Indian; loaded him with the most infamous invectives; and stamped with his foot, as resolving to be heard. He persisted in this till his strength failed him, and then fell on the earth like one void of sense. His viziers and grandees, who were nearer than the rest, supposed him at first to be sitting on the grass, at play with their amiable children; but at length, prompted by doubt, they advanced towards the spot, and found the caliph alone, who wildly demanded what they wanted? "Our children! our children!" cried they. "It is assuredly pleasant," said he, "to make me accountable for accidents. Your children, while at play, fell from the precipice, and I should have experienced their fate, had I not suddenly started back."

At these words, the fathers of the fifty boys cried out aloud; the mothers repeated their exclamations an octave higher; whilst the rest, without knowing the cause, soon drowned the voices of both with still louder lamentations of their own. "Our caliph," said they, and the report soon circulated, "our caliph has played us this trick, to gratify his accursed Giaour. Let us punish him for perfidy! let us avenge ourselves! let us avenge the blood of the innocent! let us throw this cruel prince into the gulf that is near, and let his name be mentioned no more!"

At this rumour and these menaces, Carathis, full of consternation, hastened to Morakanabad, and said: "Vizier, you have lost two beautiful boys, and must necessarily be the most afflicted of fathers; but you are virtuous, save your master." —"I will brave every hazard," replied the vizier, "to rescue him from his present danger, but afterwards will abandon him to his fate. Bababalouk," continued he, "put yourself at the head of your eunuchs: disperse the mob, and, if possible, bring back this unhappy prince to his palace." Bababalouk and his fraternity, felicitating each other in a low voice on their having been spared the cares as well as the honour of paternity, obeyed the mandate of the vizier; who, seconding their exertions to the utmost of his power, at length accomplished his generous enterprise; and retired, as he resolved, to lament at his leisure.

No sooner had the caliph re-entered his palace than Carathis commanded the doors to be fastened; but perceiving the tumult to be still violent, and hearing the imprecations which resounded from all quarters, she said to her son, "Whether the populace be right or wrong, it behoves you to provide for your safety; let us retire to your own apartment, and from thence through the subterranean passage, known only to ourselves, into your tower: there, with the assistance of the mutes who never leave it, we may be able to make a powerful resistance. Bababalouk, supposing us to be still in the palace, will guard its avenues for his own sake; and we shall soon find, without the counsels of that blubberer Morakanabad, what expedient may be the best to adopt."

Vathek, without making the least reply, acquiesced in his mother's proposal, and repeated as he went, "Nefarious Giaour! where art thou? hast thou not yet devoured those poor children? where are thy sabres? thy golden key? thy talis-

mans?" Carathis, who guessed from these interrogations a
part of the truth, had no difficulty to apprehend in getting at
the whole as soon as he should be a little composed in his tower.
This princess was so far from being influenced by scruples,
that she was as wicked as woman could be, which is not saying
a little; for the sex pique themselves on their superiority in
every competition. The recital of the caliph, therefore,
occasioned neither terror nor surprise to his mother: she felt
no emotion but from the promises of the Giaour, and said to
her son, "This Giaour, it must be confessed, is somewhat
sanguinary in his taste; but the terrestrial powers are always
terrible; nevertheless, what the one hath promised, and the
others can confer, will prove a sufficient indemnification. No
crimes should be thought too dear for such a reward: forbear,
then, to revile the Indian; you have not fulfilled the conditions
to which his services are annexed: for instance, is not a sacrifice
to the subterranean Genii required? and should we not be prepared to offer it as soon as the tumult is subsided? This charge
I will take on myself, and have no doubt of succeeding, by means
of your treasures, which, as there are now so many others in
store, may without fear be exhausted." Accordingly, the
princess, who possessed the most consummate skill in the art
of persuasion, went immediately back through the subterranean
passage; and, presenting herself to the populace from a window
of the palace, began to harangue them with all the address of
which she was mistress; whilst Bababalouk showered money
from both hands amongst the crowd, who by these united means
were soon appeased. Every person retired to his home, and
Carathis returned to the tower.

Prayer at break of day was announced, when Carathis and
Vathek ascended the steps which led to the summit of the
tower, where they remained for some time, though the weather
was lowering and wet. This impending gloom corresponded
with their malignant dispositions; but when the sun began to
break through the clouds, they ordered a pavilion to be raised,
as a screen against the intrusion of his beams. The caliph,
overcome with fatigue, sought refreshment from repose, at the
same time hoping that significant dreams might attend on his
slumbers; whilst the indefatigable Carathis, followed by a party
of her mutes, descended to prepare whatever she judged proper
for the oblation of the approaching night.

By secret stairs, contrived within the thickness of the wall,
and known only to herself and her son, she first repaired to the

mysterious recesses in which were deposited the mummies that had been wrested from the catacombs of the ancient Pharaohs. Of these she ordered several to be taken. From thence she resorted to a gallery where, under the guard of fifty female negroes, mute, and blind of the right eye, were preserved the oil of the most venomous serpents, rhinoceros' horns, and woods of a subtile and penetrating odour procured from the interior of the Indies, together with a thousand other horrible rarities. This collection had been formed for a purpose like the present, by Carathis herself, from a presentiment that she might one day enjoy some intercourse with the infernal powers, to whom she had ever been passionately attached, and to whose taste she was no stranger.

To familiarize herself the better with the horrors in view, the princess remained in the company of her negresses, who squinted in the most amiable manner from the only eye they had, and leered, with exquisite delight, at the skulls and skeletons which Carathis had drawn forth from her cabinets; all of them making the most frightful contortions, and uttering such shrill chatterings, that the princess, stunned by them and suffocated by the potency of the exhalations, was forced to quit the gallery, after stripping it of a part of its abominable treasures.

Whilst she was thus occupied, the caliph, who, instead of the visions he expected, had acquired in these unsubstantial regions a voracious appetite, was greatly provoked at the mutes. For having totally forgotten their deafness, he had impatiently asked them for food; and seeing them regardless of his demand, he began to cuff, pinch, and bite them, till Carathis arrived to terminate a scene so indecent, to the great content of these miserable creatures. "Son! what means all this?" said she, panting for breath. "I thought I heard as I came up the shrieks of a thousand bats, torn from their crannies in the recesses of a cavern; and it was the outcry only of these poor mutes, whom you were so unmercifully abusing. In truth, you but ill deserve the admirable provision I have brought you." —"Give it me instantly," exclaimed the caliph; "I am perishing for hunger!"—"As to that," answered she, "you must have an excellent stomach if it can digest what I have brought." —"Be quick," replied the caliph;—"but, oh heavens! what horrors! what do you intend?"—"Come, come," returned Carathis, "be not so squeamish; but help me to arrange everything properly; and you shall see that what you reject with such symptoms of disgust will soon complete your felicity. Let us get ready the pile for the sacrifice of to-night; and think not of eating till that is performed: know you not, that all solemn rites ought to be preceded by a rigorous abstinence?"

The caliph, not daring to object, abandoned himself to grief and the wind that ravaged his entrails, whilst his mother went forward with the requisite operations. Phials of serpents' oil, mummies, and bones, were soon set in order on the balustrade of the tower. The pile began to rise, and in three hours was twenty cubits high. At length darkness approached, and Carathis, having stripped herself to her inmost garment, clapped her hands in an impulse of ecstasy; the mutes followed her example; but Vathek, extenuated with hunger and impatience, was unable to support himself, and fell down in a swoon. The sparks had already kindled the dry wood; the venomous oil burst into a thousand blue flames; the mummies, dissolving, emitted a thick dun vapour; and the rhinoceros' horns, beginning to consume, all together diffused such a stench, that the caliph, recovering, started from his trance, and gazed wildly on the scene in full blaze around him. The oil gushed forth in a plenitude of streams; and the negresses, who supplied it without intermission, united their cries to those of the princess. At last the fire became so violent, and the flames reflected from the polished marble so dazzling, that the caliph, unable to withstand the heat and the blaze, effected his escape, and took shelter under the imperial standard.

In the meantime, the inhabitants of Samarah, scared at the light which shone over the city, arose in haste, ascended their roofs, beheld the tower on fire, and hurried, half naked, to the square. Their love for their sovereign immediately awoke; and, apprehending him in danger of perishing in his tower, their whole thoughts were occupied with the means of his safety. Morakanabad flew from his retirement, wiped away his tears, and cried out for water like the rest. Bababalouk, whose olfactory nerves were more familiarized to magical odours, readily conjecturing that Carathis was engaged in her favourite amusements, strenuously exhorted them not to be alarmed. Him, however, they treated as an old poltroon, and styled him a rascally traitor. The camels and dromedaries were advancing with water; but no one knew by which way to enter the tower. Whilst the populace was obstinate in forcing the doors, a violent north-east wind drove an immense volume of flame against them. At first they recoiled, but soon came back with redoubled zeal. At the same time, the stench of the horns and mummies increasing, most of the crowd fell backwards in a state of suffocation. Those that kept their feet mutually wondered at the cause of the smell, and admonished each other to retire. Morakanabad, more sick than the rest, remained in a piteous condition. Holding his nose with one hand, every one persisted in his efforts with the other to burst open the doors and obtain admission. A hundred and forty of the strongest and most resolute at length accomplished their purpose. Having gained the staircase, by their violent exertions, they attained a great height in a quarter of an hour.

Carathis, alarmed at the signs of her mutes, advanced to the staircase, went down a few steps, and heard several voices calling out from below, "You shall in a moment have water!" Being rather alert, considering her age, she presently regained the top of the tower, and bade her son suspend the sacrifice for some minutes; adding, "We shall soon be enabled to render it more grateful. Certain dolts of your subjects, imagining, no doubt, that we were on fire, have been rash enough to break through those doors which had hitherto remained inviolate, for the sake of bringing up water. They are very kind, you must allow, so soon to forget the wrongs you have done them; but that is of little moment. Let us offer them to the Giaour; let them come up; our mutes, who neither want strength nor experience, will soon dispatch them, exhausted as they are with fatigue."— "Be it so," answered the caliph, "provided we finish, and I dine." In fact, these good people, out of breath from ascending fifteen hundred stairs in such haste, and chagrined at having spilt by the way the water they had taken, were no sooner arrived at the top, than the blaze of the flames and the fumes of the mummies at once overpowered their senses. It was a pity! for they beheld not the agreeable smile with which the mutes and negresses adjusted the cord to their necks: these amiable personages rejoiced, however, no less at the scene. Never before had the ceremony of strangling been performed with so much facility. They all fell, without the least resistance or struggle: so that Vathek, in the space of a few moments, found himself surrounded by the dead bodies of the most faithful of his subjects; all which were thrown on the top of the pile. Carathis, whose presence of mind never forsook her, perceiving that she had carcasses sufficient to complete her oblation, commanded the chains to be stretched across the staircase, and the iron doors barricadoed, that no more might come up.

No sooner were these orders obeyed, than the tower shook; the dead bodies vanished in the flames, which at once changed from a swarthy crimson to a bright rose colour; an ambient vapour emitted the most exquisite fragrance; the marble columns rang with harmonious sounds, and the liquefied horns diffused a delicious perfume. Carathis, in transports, anticipated the success of her enterprise; whilst her mutes and negresses, to whom these sweets had given the colic, retired grumbling to their cells.

Scarcely were they gone, when, instead of the pile, horns, mummies, and ashes, the caliph both saw and felt, with a degree of pleasure which he could not express, a table covered with the most magnificent repast: flagons of wine and vases of exquisite sherbet reposing on snow. He availed himself, without scruple, of such an entertainment; and had already laid hands on a lamb stuffed with pistachios, whilst Carathis was privately drawing from a filigree urn a parchment that seemed to be endless, and which had escaped the notice of her son. Totally occupied in gratifying an importunate appetite, he left her to peruse it without interruption; which having finished, she said to him, in an authoritative tone, "Put an end to your gluttony, and hear the splendid promises with which you are favoured!" She then read as follows: "Vathek, my well-beloved, thou hast surpassed my hopes: my nostrils have been regaled by the savour of thy mummies, thy horns, and, still more, by the lives devoted on the pile. At the full of the moon, cause the bands of thy musicians, and thy timbals, to be heard; depart from thy palace, surrounded by all the pageants of majesty—thy most faithful slaves, thy best beloved wives, thy most magnificent litters, thy richest loaden camels —and set forward on thy way to Istakhar. There I await thy coming: that is the region of wonders: there shalt thou receive the diadem of Gian Ben Gian, the talismans of Soliman, and the treasures of the pre-Adamite sultans: there shalt thou be solaced with all kinds of delight.—But beware how thou enterest any dwelling on thy route; or thou shalt feel the effects of my anger."

The caliph, notwithstanding his habitual luxury, had never before dined with so much satisfaction. He gave full scope to the joy of these golden tidings, and betook himself to drinking anew. Carathis, whose antipathy to wine was by no means insuperable, failed not to pledge him at every bumper he ironically quaffed to the health of Mahomet. This infernal liquor completed their impious temerity, and prompted them to utter a profusion of blasphemies. They gave a loose to their wit, at the expense of the ass of Balaam, the dog of the seven sleepers, and the other animals admitted into the paradise of Mahomet. In this sprightly humour, they descended the fifteen hundred stairs, diverting themselves, as they went, at the anxious faces they saw on the square, through the barbacans and loopholes of the tower; and at length arrived at the royal apartments, by the subterranean passage. Bababalouk was parading to and fro, and issuing his mandates with great pomp to the eunuchs, who were snuffing the lights and painting the eyes of the Circassians. No sooner did he catch sight of the caliph and his mother, than he exclaimed, "Hah! you have then, I perceive, escaped from the flames; I was not, however, altogether out of doubt."—"Of what moment is it to us what you thought or think?" cried Carathis: "go, speed, tell Mora-kanabad that we immediately want him; and take care not to stop by the way to make your insipid reflections."

Morakanabad delayed not to obey the summons, and was received by Vathek and his mother with great solemnity. They told him, with an air of composure and commiseration, that the fire at the top of the tower was extinguished; but that it had cost the lives of the brave people who sought to assist them.

"Still more misfortunes!" cried Morakanabad, with a sigh. "Ah, commander of the faithful, our holy Prophet is certainly irritated against us! it behoves you to appease him." "We will appease him hereafter," replied the caliph, with a smile that augured nothing of good. "You will have leisure sufficient for your supplications during my absence, for this country is the bane of my health. I am disgusted with the mountain of the four fountains, and am resolved to go and drink of the stream of Rocnabad. I long to refresh myself in the delightful valleys which it waters. Do you, with the advice of my mother, govern my dominions, and take care to supply whatever her experiments may demand; for you well know that our tower abounds in materials for the advancement of science."

The tower but ill suited Morakanabad's taste. Immense treasures had been lavished upon it; and nothing had he ever seen carried thither but female negroes, mutes, and abominable drugs. Nor did he know well what to think of Carathis, who, like a chameleon, could assume all possible colours. Her cursed eloquence had often driven the poor Mussulman to his last shifts. He considered, however, that if she possessed but few good qualities, her son had still fewer; and that the alternative, on the whole, would be in her favour. Consoled, therefore, with this reflection, he went, in good spirits, to soothe the populace, and make the proper arrangements for his master's journey.

Vathek, to conciliate the spirits of the subterranean palace, resolved that his expedition should be uncommonly splendid. With this view he confiscated, on all sides, the property of his subjects; whilst his worthy mother stripped the seraglios she visited of the gems they contained. She collected all the sempstresses and embroiderers of Samarah and other cities, to the distance of sixty leagues, to prepare pavilions, palanquins, sofas, canopies, and litters for the train of the monarch. There was not left, in Masulipatan, a single piece of chintz; and so much muslin had been brought up to dress out Bababalouk and the other black eunuchs, that there remained not an ell of it in the whole Irak of Babylon.

During these preparations, Carathis, who never lost sight of her great object, which was to obtain favour with the powers of darkness, made select parties of the fairest and most delicate ladies of the city; but in the midst of their gaiety, she contrived to introduce vipers amongst them, and to break pots of scorpions under the table. They all bit to a wonder; and Carathis would have left her friends to die, were it not that, to fill up the time, she now and then amused herself in curing their wounds, with an excellent anodyne of her own invention; for this good princess abhorred being indolent.

Vathek, who was not altogether so active as his mother, devoted his time to the sole gratification of his senses, in the palaces which were severally dedicated to them. He disgusted himself no more with the divan, or the mosque. One half of Samarah followed his example, whilst the other lamented the progress of corruption.

In the midst of these transactions, the embassy returned, which had been sent, in pious times, to Mecca. It consisted of the most reverend mullahs, who had fulfilled their commission and brought back one of those precious besoms which are used to sweep the sacred Caaba; a present truly worthy of the greatest potentate on earth!

The caliph happened at this instant to be engaged in an apartment by no means adapted to the reception of embassies. He heard the voice of Bababalouk, calling out from between the door and the tapestry that hung before it, "Here are the excellent Edris al Shafei, and the seraphic Al Mouhateddin, who have brought the besom from Mecca, and, with tears of joy, entreat they may present it to your majesty in person."—"Let them bring the besom hither; it may be of use," said Vathek. —"How!" answered Bababalouk, half aloud and amazed.— "Obey," replied the caliph, "for it is my sovereign will; go instantly, vanish! for here will I receive the good folk who have thus filled thee with joy."

The eunuch departed muttering, and bade the venerable train attend him. A sacred rapture was diffused amongst these reverend old men. Though fatigued with the length of their expedition, they followed Bababalouk with an alertness almost miraculous, and felt themselves highly flattered, as they swept along the stately porticoes, that the caliph would not receive them like ambassadors in ordinary in his hall of audience. Soon reaching the interior of the harem (where, through blinds of Persian, they perceived large soft eyes, dark and blue, that came and went like lightning), penetrated with respect and wonder, and full of their celestial mission, they advanced in procession towards the small corridors that appeared to terminate in nothing, but, nevertheless, led to the cell where the caliph expected their coming.

"What! is the commander of the faithful sick?" said Edris al Shafei in a low voice to his companion.—"I rather think he is in his oratory," answered Al Mouhateddin. Vathek, who heard the dialogue, cried out, "What imports it you, how I am employed? approach without delay." They advanced, whilst the caliph, without showing himself, put forth his hand from behind the tapestry that hung before the door, and demanded of them the besom. Having prostrated themselves as well as the corridor would permit, and even in a tolerable semicircle, the venerable Al Shafei, drawing forth the besom from the embroidered and perfumed scarves in which it had been enveloped and secured from the profane gaze of vulgar eyes, arose from his associates, and advanced, with an air of the most awful solemnity, towards the supposed oratory; but with what astonishment! with what horror was he seized! Vathek, bursting out into a villainous laugh, snatched the besom from his trembling hand, and, fixing upon some cobwebs, that hung from the ceiling, gravely brushed them away till not a single one remained. The old men, overpowered with amazement, were unable to lift their beards from the ground; for, as

Vathek had carelessly left the tapestry between them half drawn, they were witnesses of the whole transaction. Their tears bedewed the marble. Al Mouhateddin swooned through mortification and fatigue, whilst the caliph, throwing himself backward on his seat, shouted and clapped his hands without mercy. At last, addressing himself to Bababalouk, "My dear black," said he, "go, regale these pious poor souls with my good wine from Schiraz, since they can boast of having seen more of my palace than any one besides." Having said this, he threw the besom in their face, and went to enjoy the laugh with Carathis. Bababalouk did all in his power to console the ambassadors; but the two most infirm expired on the spot: the rest were carried to their beds, from whence, being heart-broken with sorrow and shame, they never arose.

The succeeding night, Vathek, attended by his mother, ascended the tower to see if everything were ready for his journey; for he had great faith in the influence of the stars. The planets appeared in their most favourable aspects. The caliph, to enjoy so flattering a sight, supped gaily on the roof; and fancied that he heard, during his repast, loud shouts of laughter resound through the sky, in a manner that inspired the fullest assurance.

All was in motion at the palace; lights were kept burning through the whole of the night: the sound of implements, and of artisans finishing their work; the voices of women, and their guardians, who sung at their embroidery; all conspired to interrupt the stillness of nature, and infinitely delighted the heart of Vathek, who imagined himself going in triumph to sit upon the throne of Soliman. The people were not less satisfied than himself: all assisted to accelerate the moment which should rescue them from the wayward caprices of so extravagant a master.

The day preceding the departure of this infatuated prince was employed by Carathis in repeating to him the decrees of the mysterious parchment, which she had thoroughly gotten by heart; and in recommending him not to enter the habitation of any one by the way:—"For well thou knowest," added she, "how liquorish thy taste is after good dishes and young damsels: let me, therefore, enjoin thee to be content with thy old cooks, who are the best in the world; and not to forget that, in thy ambulatory seraglio, there are at least three dozen of pretty faces which Bababalouk has not yet unveiled. I myself have a great desire to watch over thy conduct, and visit the subterranean palace, which, no doubt, contains whatever can interest persons like us. There is nothing so pleasing as retiring to caverns: my taste for dead bodies, and everything like mummy, is decided; and, I am confident, thou wilt see the most exquisite of their kind. Forget me not then, but the moment thou art in possession of the talismans which are to open the way to the mineral kingdoms and the centre of the earth itself, fail not to dispatch some trusty genius to take me and my cabinet; for the oil of the serpents I have pinched to death will be a pretty present to the Giaour, who cannot but be charmed with such dainties."

Scarcely had Carathis ended this edifying discourse, when the sun, setting behind the mountain of the four fountains, gave place to the rising moon. This planet, being that evening at full, appeared of unusual beauty and magnitude in the eyes of the women, the eunuchs, and the pages, who were all impatient to set forward. The city re-echoed with shouts of joy and flourishing of trumpets. Nothing was visible but plumes nodding on pavilions, and aigrets shining in the mild lustre of the moon. The spacious square resembled an immense parterre variegated with the most stately tulips of the East.

Arrayed in the robes which were only worn at the most distinguished ceremonials, and supported by his vizier and Bababalouk, the caliph descended the great staircase of the tower in the sight of all his people. He could not forbear pausing, at intervals, to admire the superb appearance which everywhere courted his view; whilst the whole multitude, even to the camels with their sumptuous burdens, knelt down before him. For some time a general stillness prevailed, which nothing happened to disturb but the shrill screams of some eunuchs in the rear. These vigilant guards, having remarked certain cages of the ladies swagging somewhat awry, and discovered that a few adventurous gallants had contrived to get in, soon dislodged the enraptured culprits, and consigned them, with good commendations, to the surgeons of the serail. The majesty of so magnificent a spectacle was not, however, violated by incidents like these. Vathek, meanwhile, saluted the moon with an idolatrous air, that neither pleased Morakanabad, nor the doctors of the law, any more than the viziers and grandees of his court, who were all assembled to enjoy the last view of their sovereign.

At length, the clarions and trumpets from the top of the tower announced the prelude of departure. Though the instruments were in unison with each other, yet a singular dissonance was blended with their sounds. This proceeded from Carathis, who was singing her direful orisons to the Giaour, whilst the negresses and mutes supplied thorough-bass, without articulating a word. The good Mussulmans fancied that they heard the sullen hum of those nocturnal insects which presage evil, and importuned Vathek to beware how he ventured his sacred person.

On a given signal, the great standard of the Califat was displayed: twenty thousand lances shone around it; and the caliph, treading royally on the cloth of gold which had been spread for his feet, ascended his litter amidst the general acclamations of his subjects.

The expedition commenced with the utmost order, and so entire a silence, that even the locusts were heard from the thickets on the plain of Catoul. Gaiety and good humour prevailing, they made full six leagues before the dawn; and the morning star was still glittering in the firmament, when the whole of this numerous train had halted on the banks of the Tigris, where they encamped to repose for the rest of the day.

The three days that followed were spent in the same manner; but on the fourth the heavens looked angry: lightnings broke forth in frequent flashes; re-echoing peals of thunder succeeded; and the trembling Circassians clung with all their might to their ugly guardians. The caliph himself was greatly inclined to take shelter in the large town of Ghulchissar, the governor of which came forth to meet him, and tendered every kind of refreshment the place could supply. But, having examined his tablets, he suffered the rain to soak him almost to the bone, notwithstanding the importunity of his first favourites. Though he began to regret the palace of the senses, yet he lost not sight of his enterprise, and his sanguine expectation confirmed his resolution. His geographers were ordered to attend him; but the weather proved so terrible that these poor people exhibited a lamentable appearance: and their maps of the different countries, spoiled by the rain, were in a still worse plight than themselves. As no long journey had been undertaken since the time of Haroun al Raschid, every one was ignorant which way to turn; and Vathek, though well versed in the course of the heavens, no longer knew his situation on earth. He thundered even louder than the elements; and muttered forth certain hints of the bow-string, which were not very soothing to literary ears. Disgusted at the toilsome weariness of the way, he determined to cross over the craggy heights and follow the guidance of a peasant, who undertook to bring him in four days to Rocnabad. Remonstrances were all to no purpose: his resolution was fixed.

The females and eunuchs uttered shrill wailings at the sight of the precipices below them, and the dreary prospects that opened in the vast gorges of the mountains. Before they could reach the ascent of the steepest rock, night overtook them, and a boisterous tempest arose, which, having rent the awnings of the palanquins and cages, exposed to the raw gusts the poor ladies within, who had never before felt so piercing a cold. The dark clouds that overcast the face of the sky deepened the horrors of this disastrous night, insomuch that nothing could be heard distinctly but the mewling of pages and lamentations of sultanas.

To increase the general misfortune, the frightful uproar of wild beasts resounded at a distance; and there were soon perceived in the forest they were skirting the glaring of eyes, which could belong only to devils or tigers. The pioneers, who, as well as they could, had marked out a track, and a part of the advanced guard, were devoured before they had been in the least apprised of their danger. The confusion that prevailed was extreme. Wolves, tigers, and other carnivorous animals, invited by the howling of their companions, flocked together from every quarter. The crashing of bones was heard on all sides, and a fearful rush of wings overhead; for now vultures also began to be of the party.

The terror at length reached the main body of the troops which surrounded the monarch and his harem at the distance of two leagues from the scene. Vathek (voluptuously reposed in his capacious litter upon cushions of silk, with two little pages beside him of complexions more fair than the enamel of Franguestan, who were occupied in keeping off flies) was soundly asleep, and contemplating in his dreams the treasures of Soliman. The shrieks, however, of his wives awoke him with a start; and, instead of the Giaour with his key of gold, he beheld Bababalouk full of consternation. "Sire," exclaimed this good servant of the most potent of monarchs, "misfortune is arrived at its height; wild beasts, who entertain no more reverence for your sacred person than for a dead ass, have beset your camels and their drivers; thirty of the most richly laden are already become their prey, as well as your confectioners, your cooks, and purveyors; and unless our holy Prophet should protect us, we shall have all eaten our last meal." At the mention of eating, the caliph lost all patience. He began to bellow, and even beat himself (for there was no seeing in the dark). The rumour every instant increased; and Bababalouk, finding no good could be done with his master, stopped both his ears against the hurlyburly of the harem, and called out aloud, "Come, ladies and brothers! all hands to work: strike light in a moment! never shall it be said, that the commander of the faithful served to regale these infidel brutes." Though there wanted not, in this bevy of beauties, a sufficient number of capricious and wayward, yet, on the present occasion, they were all compliance. Fires were visible, in a twinkling, in all their cages. Ten thousand torches were lighted at once. The caliph himself seized a large one of wax; every person followed his example; and by kindling ropes' ends, dipped in oil and fastened on poles, an amazing blaze was spread. The rocks were covered with the splendour of sunshine. The trails of sparks, wafted by the wind, communicated to the dry fern, of which there was plenty. Serpents were observed to crawl forth from their retreats, with amazement and hissings; whilst the horses snorted, stamped the ground, tossed their noses in the air, and plunged about without mercy.

One of the forests of cedar that bordered their way took fire; and the branches that overhung the path, extending their flames to the muslins and chintzes which covered the cages of the ladies, obliged them to jump out, at the peril of their necks. Vathek, who vented on the occasion a thousand blasphemies, was himself compelled to touch, with his sacred feet, the naked earth.

Never had such an incident happened before. Full of mortification, shame, and despondence, and not knowing how to walk, the ladies fell into the dirt. "Must I go on foot?" said one. "Must I wet my feet?" cried another. "Must I soil my dress?" asked a third. "Execrable Bababalouk!" exclaimed all. "Outcast of hell! what hast thou to do with torches? Better were it to be eaten by tigers, than to fall into our present condition! we are for ever undone! Not a porter is there in the army, nor a currier of camels, but hath seen some part of our bodies; and, what is worse, our very faces!" On saying this the most bashful amongst them hid their foreheads on the ground, whilst such as had more boldness flew at Bababalouk; but he, well apprised of their humour, and not wanting in shrewdness, betook himself to his heels along with his comrades, all dropping their torches and striking their timbals.

It was not less light than in the brightest of the dog-days, and the weather was hot in proportion; but how degrading was the spectacle, to behold the caliph bespattered, like an ordinary mortal! As the exercise of his faculties seemed to be suspended, one of his Ethiopian wives (for he delighted in variety) clasped him in her arms, threw him upon her shoulder like a sack of dates, and, finding that the fire was hemming them in, set off with no small expedition, considering the weight of her burden. The other ladies, who had just learned the use of their feet, followed her; their guards galloped after; and the camel-drivers brought up the rear, as fast as their charge would permit

They soon reached the spot where the wild beasts had commenced the carnage, but which they had too much good sense not to leave at the approaching of the tumult, having made besides a most luxurious supper. Bababalouk, nevertheless, seized on a few of the plumpest, which were unable to budge from the place, and began to flay them with admirable adroitness. The cavalcade having proceeded so far from the conflagration that the heat felt rather grateful than violent, it was immediately resolved on to halt. The tattered chintzes were picked up; the scraps, left by the wolves and tigers, interred; and vengeance was taken on some dozens of vultures, that were too much glutted to rise on the wing. The camels, which had been left unmolested to make sal ammoniac, being numbered, and the ladies once more enclosed in their cages, the imperial tent was pitched on the levellest ground they could find.

Vathek, reposing upon a mattress of down, and tolerably recovered from the jolting of the Ethiopian, who, to his feelings, seemed the roughest trotting jade he had hitherto mounted, called out for something to eat. But, alas! those delicate cakes which had been baked in silver ovens for his royal mouth, those rich manchets, amber comfits, flagons of Schiraz wine, porcelain vases of snow, and grapes from the banks of the Tigris, were all irremediably lost! And nothing had Bababalouk to present in their stead but a roasted wolf, vultures *à la daube*, aromatic herbs of the most acrid poignancy, rotten truffles, boiled thistles, and such other wild plants as much ulcerate the throat and parch up the tongue. Nor was he better provided in the article of drink; for he could procure nothing to accompany these irritating viands but a few phials of abominable brandy which had been secreted by the scullions in their slippers. Vathek made wry faces at so savage a repast, and Bababalouk answered them with shrugs and contortions. The caliph, however, ate with tolerable appetite, and fell into a nap that lasted six hours.

The splendour of the sun, reflected from the white cliffs of the mountains, in spite of the curtains that enclosed Vathek, at length disturbed his repose. He awoke terrified, and stung to the quick by wormwood-colour flies, which emitted from their wings a suffocating stench. The miserable monarch was perplexed how to act, though his wits were not idle in seeking expedients; whilst Bababalouk lay snoring amidst a swarm of those insects that busily thronged to pay court to his nose. The little pages, famished with hunger, had dropped their fans on the ground, and exerted their dying voices in bitter reproaches on the caliph, who now, for the first time, heard the language of truth.

Thus stimulated, he renewed his imprecations against the Giaour, and bestowed upon Mahomet some soothing expressions. "Where am I?" cried he: "what are these dreadful rocks— these valleys of darkness? Are we arrived at the horrible Kaf? Is the Simurgh coming to pluck out my eyes, as a punishment for undertaking this impious enterprise?" Having said this he turned himself towards an outlet in the side of his pavilion; but, alas! what objects occurred to his view? on one side a plain of black sand that appeared to be unbounded; and, on the other, perpendicular crags, bristled over with those abominable thistles which had so severely lacerated his tongue. He fancied, however, that he perceived amongst the brambles and briars some gigantic flowers, but was mistaken; for these were only the dangling palampores and variegated tatters of his gay retinue. As there were several clefts in the rock from whence water seemed to have flowed, Vathek applied his ear with the hope of catching the sound of some latent torrent; but could only distinguish the low murmurs of his people, who were repining at their journey, and complaining for the want of water. "To what purpose," asked they, "have we been brought hither? hath our caliph another tower to build? or have the relentless afrits, whom Carathis so much loves, fixed their abode in this place?"

At the name of Carathis, Vathek recollected the tablets he had received from his mother, who assured him they were fraught with preternatural qualities, and advised him to consult them as emergencies might require. Whilst he was engaged in turning them over, he heard a shout of joy and a loud clapping of hands. The curtains of his pavilion were soon drawn back, and he beheld Bababalouk, followed by a troop of his favourites, conducting two dwarfs, each a cubit high; who had brought between them a large basket of melons, oranges, and pomegranates. They were singing in the sweetest tones the words that follow: "We dwell on the top of these rocks, in a cabin of rushes and canes; the eagles envy us our nest: a small spring supplies us with water for the Abdest, and we daily repeat prayers, which the Prophet approves. We love you, O commander of the faithful! our master, the good Emir Fakreddin, loves you also: he reveres, in your person, the vicegerent of Mahomet. Little as we are, in us he confides: he knows our hearts to be as good as our bodies are contemptible; and hath placed us here to aid those who are bewildered on these dreary mountains. Last night, whilst we were occupied within our cell in reading the holy Koran, a sudden hurricane blew out our lights, and rocked our habitation. For two whole hours a palpable darkness prevailed; but we heard sounds at a distance, which we conjectured to proceed from the bells of a cafila, passing over the rocks. Our ears were soon filled with deplorable shrieks, frightful roarings, and the sound of timbals. Chilled with terror, we concluded that the Deggial, with his exterminating angels, had sent forth his plagues on the earth. In the midst of these melancholy reflections, we perceived flames of the deepest red glow in the horizon; and found ourselves, in a few moments, covered with flakes of fire. Amazed at so strange an appearance, we took up the volume dictated by the blessed Intelligence, and, kneeling, by the light of the fire that surrounded us, we recited the verse which says, 'Put no trust in any thing but the mercy of Heaven: there is no help, save in the holy Prophet: the mountain of Kaf itself may tremble; it is the power of Allah only that cannot be moved.' After having pronounced these words, we felt consolation, and our minds were hushed into a sacred repose. Silence ensued, and our ears clearly distinguished a voice in the air, saying: 'Servants of my faithful servant! go down to the happy valley of Fakreddin: tell him that an illustrious opportunity now offers to satiate the thirst of his hospitable heart. The commander of true believers is, this day, bewildered amongst these mountains, and stands in need of thy aid.'—We obeyed with joy the angelic mission; and our master, filled with pious zeal, hath culled with his own hands these melons, oranges, and pomegranates. He is following us, with a hundred dromedaries, laden with the purest waters of his fountains; and is coming to kiss the fringe of your consecrated robe, and implore you to enter his humble habitation, which, placed amidst these barren wilds, resembles an emerald set in lead." The dwarfs, having ended their address, remained still standing, and, with hands crossed upon their bosoms, preserved a respectful silence.

Vathek, in the midst of this curious harangue, seized the basket; and, long before it was finished, the fruits had dissolved in his mouth. As he continued to eat, his piety increased; and, in the same breath, he recited his prayers and called for the Koran and sugar.

Such was the state of his mind when the tablets, which were thrown by at the approach of the dwarfs, again attracted his eye. He took them up; but was ready to drop on the ground when he beheld, in large red characters, inscribed by Carathis, these words—which were, indeed, enough to make him tremble: "Beware of old doctors and their puny messengers of but one cubit high: distrust their pious frauds; and, instead of eating their melons, impale on a spit the bearers of them. Shouldest thou be such a fool as to visit them, the portal of the subterranean palace will shut in thy face, with such force as shall shake thee asunder: thy body shall be spit upon, and bats will nestle in thy belly."

"To what tends this ominous rhapsody?" cries the caliph; "and must I, then, perish in these deserts with thirst, whilst I may refresh myself in the delicious valley of melons and cucumbers? Accursed be the Giaour with his portal of ebony! he hath made me dance attendance too long already. Besides, who shall prescribe laws to me? I, forsooth, must not enter any one's habitation! Be it so; but what one can I enter that is not my own?" Bababalouk, who lost not a syllable of this soliloquy, applauded it with all his heart; and the ladies, for the first time, agreed with him in opinion.

The dwarfs were entertained, caressed, and seated, with great ceremony, on little cushions of satin. The symmetry of their persons was a subject of admiration; not an inch of them was suffered to pass unexamined. Knick-knacks and dainties were offered in profusion; but all were declined with respectful gravity. They climbed up the sides of the caliph's seat, and, placing themselves each on one of his shoulders, began to whisper prayers in his ears. Their tongues quivered like aspen leaves; and the patience of Vathek was almost exhausted, when the acclamations of the troops announced the approach of Fakreddin, who was come with a hundred old grey-beards, and as many Korans and dromedaries. They instantly set about their ablutions, and began to repeat the Bismillah. Vathek, to get rid of these officious monitors, followed their example, for his hands were burning.

The good emir, who was punctiliously religious, and likewise a great dealer in compliments, made an harangue five times more prolix and insipid than his little harbingers had already delivered. The caliph, unable any longer to refrain, exclaimed, "For the love of Mahomet, my dear Fakreddin, have done! let us proceed to your valley, and enjoy the fruits that Heaven hath vouchsafed you." The hint of proceeding put all into motion. The venerable attendants of the emir set forward somewhat slowly, but Vathek having ordered his little pages, in private, to goad on the dromedaries, loud fits of laughter broke forth from the cages; for the unwieldy curvetting of these poor beasts, and the ridiculous distress of their superannuated riders, afforded the ladies no small entertainment.

They descended, however, unhurt into the valley, by the easy slopes which the emir had ordered to be cut in the rock; and already the murmuring of streams and the rustling of leaves began to catch their attention. The cavalcade soon entered a path, which was skirted by flowering shrubs, and extended to a vast wood of palm trees, whose branches overspread a vast building of freestone. This edifice was crowned with nine domes, and adorned with as many portals of bronze, on which was engraven the following inscription: "This is the asylum of pilgrims, the refuge of travellers, and the depository of secrets from all parts of the world."

Nine pages, beautiful as the day, and decently clothed in robes of Egyptian linen, were standing at each door. They received the whole retinue with an easy and inviting air. Four of the most amiable placed the caliph on a magnificent tecthtrevan; four others, somewhat less graceful, took charge of Bababalouk, who capered for joy at the snug little cabin that fell to his share: the pages that remained waited on the rest of the train.

Every man being gone out of sight, the gate of a large enclosure on the right turned on its harmonious hinges; and a young female, of a slender form, came forth. Her light brown hair floated in the hazy breeze of the twilight. A troop of young maidens, like the Pleiades, attended her on tiptoe. They hastened to the pavilions that contained the sultanas; and the young lady, gracefully bending, said to them, "Charming princesses! everything is ready; we have prepared beds for your repose, and strewed your apartments with jasmine. No insects will keep off slumber from visiting your eyelids; we will dispel them with a thousand plumes. Come, then, amiable ladies! refresh your delicate feet and your ivory limbs in baths of rosewater; and, by the light of perfumed lamps, your servants will amuse you with tales." The sultanas accepted with pleasure these obliging offers, and followed the young lady to the emir's harem; where we must, for a moment, leave them and return to the caliph.

Vathek found himself beneath a vast dome, illuminated by a thousand lamps of rock crystal: as many vases of the same material, filled with excellent sherbet, sparkled on a large table, where a profusion of viands were spread. Amongst others, were rice boiled in milk of almonds, saffron soups, and lamb à la crême; of all which the caliph was amazingly fond. He took of each as much as he was able; testified his sense of the emir's friendship by the gaiety of his heart; and made the dwarfs dance against their will, for these little devotees durst not refuse the commander of the faithful. At last, he spread himself on the sofa, and slept sounder than he ever had before.

Beneath this dome a general silence prevailed; for there was nothing to disturb it but the jaws of Bababalouk, who had untrussed himself to eat with greater advantage, being anxious to make amends for his fast in the mountains. As his spirits were too high to admit of his sleeping, and hating to be idle, he proposed with himself to visit the harem, and repair to his charge of the ladies: to examine if they had been properly lubricated with the balm of Mecca; if their eyebrows and tresses were in order; and, in a word, to perform all the little offices they might need. He sought for a long time together, but without being able to find out the door. He durst not speak aloud, for fear of disturbing the caliph; and not a soul was stirring in the precincts of the palace. He almost despaired of effecting his purpose, when a low whispering just reached his ear. It came from the dwarfs, who were returned to their old occupation, and, for the nine hundred and ninety-ninth time in their lives, were reading over the Koran. They very politely invited Bababalouk to be of their party; but his head was full of other concerns. The dwarfs, though not a little scandalized at his dissolute morals, directed him to the apartments he wanted to find. His way thither lay through a hundred dark corridors, along which he groped as he went, and at last began to catch, from the extremity of a passage, the charming gossiping of the women, which not a little delighted his heart. "Ah, ha! what, not yet asleep?" cried he; and, taking long strides as he spoke, "did you not suspect me of abjuring my charge?" Two of the black eunuchs, on hearing a voice so loud, left their party in haste, sabre in hand, to discover the cause; but presently was repeated on all sides, "'Tis only Bababalouk! no one but Bababalouk!" This circumspect guardian, having gone up to a thin veil of carnation-colour silk that hung before the doorway, distinguished, by means of the softened splendour that shone through it, an oval bath of dark porphyry, surrounded by curtains, festooned in large folds. Through the apertures between them, as they were not drawn close, groups of young slaves were visible; amongst whom Bababalouk perceived his pupils, indulgingly expanding their arms, as if to embrace the perfumed water and refresh themselves after their fatigues. The looks of tender languor; their confidential whispers, and the enchanting smiles with which they were imparted; the exquisite fragrance of the roses: all combined to inspire a voluptuousness, which even Bababalouk himself was scarce able to withstand.

He summoned up, however, his usual solemnity; and, in the peremptory tone of authority, commanded the ladies instantly to leave the bath. Whilst he was issuing these mandates, the young Nouronihar, daughter of the emir, who was as sprightly as an antelope, and full of wanton gaiety, beckoned one of her slaves to let down the great swing which was suspended to the ceiling by cords of silk; and whilst this was doing, winked to her companions in the bath, who, chagrined to be forced from so soothing a state of indolence, began to twist and entangle their hair to plague and detain Bababalouk, and teased him, besides, with a thousand vagaries.

Nouronihar, perceiving that he was nearly out of patience, accosted him, with an arch air of respectful concern, and said, "My lord! it is not by any means decent that the chief eunuch of the caliph, our sovereign, should thus continue standing; deign but to recline your graceful person upon this sofa, which will burst with vexation if it have not the honour to receive you." Caught by these flattering accents, Bababalouk gallantly replied, "Delight of the apple of my eye! I accept the invitation of your honeyed lips; and, to say truth, my senses

are dazzled with the radiance that beams from your charms."
—"Repose, then, at your ease," replied the beauty, as she
placed him on the pretended sofa, which, quicker than lightning,
flew up all at once. The rest of the women, having aptly conceived her design, sprang naked from the bath, and plied the
swing with such unmerciful jerks that it swept through the
whole compass of a very lofty dome, and took from the poor
victim all power of respiration. Sometimes his feet razed
the surface of the water; and, at others, the skylight almost
flattened his nose. In vain did he fill the air with the cries
of a voice that resembled the ringing of a cracked jar; the
peals of laughter were still predominant.

Nouronihar, in the inebriety of youthful spirits, being used
only to eunuchs of ordinary harems, and having never seen
anything so eminently disgusting, was far more diverted than
all the rest. She began to parody some Persian verses, and
sang, with an accent most demurely piquant, "Oh, gentle
white dove! as thou soar'st through the air, vouchsafe one kind
glance on the mate of thy love: melodious Philomel, I am thy
rose; warble some couplet to ravish my heart!"

The sultanas and their slaves, stimulated by these pleasantries,
persevered at the swing with such unremitted assiduity, that at
length the cord which had secured it snapped suddenly asunder;
and Bababalouk fell, floundering like a turtle, to the bottom of
the bath. This accident occasioned an universal shout. Twelve
little doors, till now unobserved, flew open at once; and the
ladies, in an instant, made their escape; but not before having
heaped all the towels on his head, and put out the lights that
remained.

The deplorable animal, in water to the chin, overwhelmed
with darkness, and unable to extricate himself from the wrappers
that embarrassed him, was still doomed to hear, for his further
consolation, the fresh bursts of merriment his disaster occasioned.
He bustled, but in vain, to get from the bath; for the margin was
become so slippery with the oil spilt in breaking the lamps,
that, at every effort, he slid back with a plunge which resounded
aloud through the hollow of the dome. These cursed peals
of laughter were redoubled at every relapse, and he, who thought
the place infested rather by devils than women, resolved to
cease groping, and abide in the bath; where he amused himself
with soliloquies, interspersed with imprecations, of which his
malicious neighbours, reclining on down, suffered not an accent
to escape. In this delectable plight the morning surprised him.

The caliph, wondering at his absence, had caused him to be sought for everywhere. At last he was drawn forth almost smothered from under the wisp of linen, and wet even to the marrow. Limping, and his teeth chattering with cold, he approached his master, who inquired what was the matter, and how he came soused in so strange a pickle.—"And why did you enter this cursed lodge?" answered Bababalouk. gruffly. "Ought a monarch like you to visit with his harem the abode of a grey-bearded emir, who knows nothing of life?— And with what gracious damsels doth the place too abound! Fancy to yourself how they have soaked me like a burnt crust; and made me dance like a jack-pudding, the livelong night through, on their damnable swing. What an excellent lesson for your sultanas, into whom I had instilled such reserve and decorum!" Vathek, comprehending not a syllable of all this invective, obliged him to relate minutely the transaction: but, instead of sympathizing with the miserable sufferer, he laughed immoderately at the device of the swing and the figure of Bababalouk mounted upon it. The stung eunuch could scarcely preserve the semblance of respect. "Ay, laugh, my lord! laugh," said he; "but I wish this Nouronihar would play some trick on you; she is too wicked to spare even majesty itself." These words made, for the present, but a slight impression on the caliph; but they not long after recurred to his mind.

This conversation was cut short by Fakreddin, who came to request that Vathek would join in the prayers and ablutions, to be solemnized on a spacious meadow watered by innumerable streams. The caliph found the waters refreshing, but the prayers abominably irksome. He diverted himself, however, with the multitude of calenders, santons, and dervishes, who were continually coming and going; but especially with the Brahmins, fakirs, and other enthusiasts, who had travelled from the heart of India, and halted on their way with the emir. These latter had each of them some mummery peculiar to himself. One dragged a huge chain wherever he went; another an orang-outang; whilst a third was furnished with scourges; and all performed to a charm. Some would climb up trees, holding one foot in the air; others poise themselves over a fire, and without mercy fillip their noses. There were some amongst them that cherished vermin, which were not ungrateful in requiting their caresses. These rambling fanatics revolted the hearts of the dervishes, the calenders, and santons; however, the vehemence of their aversion soon subsided, under the hope that the presence of the caliph would cure their folly, and convert them to the Mussulman faith. But, alas! how great was their disappointment! for Vathek, instead of preaching to them, treated them as buffoons, bade them present his compliments to Visnow and Ixhora, and discovered a predilection for a squat old man from the Isle of Serendib, who was more ridiculous than any of the rest. "Come!" said he, "for the love of your gods, bestow a few slaps on your chops to amuse me." The old fellow, offended at such an address, began loudly to weep; but, as he betrayed a villainous drivelling in shedding tears, the caliph turned his back and listened to Bababalouk, who whispered, whilst he held the umbrella over him, "Your majesty should be cautious of this odd assembly, which hath been collected I know not for what. Is it necessary to exhibit such spectacles to a mighty potentate, with interludes of talapoins more mangy than dogs? Were I you, I would command a fire to be kindled, and at once rid the estates of the emir, of his harem, and all his menagerie."—"Tush, dolt," answered Vathek, "and know that all this infinitely charms me. Nor shall I leave the meadow till I have visited every hive of these pious mendicants."

Wherever the caliph directed his course, objects of pity were sure to swarm round him; the blind, the purblind, smarts without noses, damsels without ears, each to extol the munificence of Fakreddin, who, as well as his attendant grey-beards, dealt about, gratis, plasters and cataplasms to all that applied. At noon, a superb corps of cripples made its appearance; and soon after advanced, by platoons, on the plain, the completest association of invalids that had ever been embodied till then. The blind went groping with the blind, the lame limped on together, and the maimed made gestures to each other with the only arm that remained. The sides of a considerable waterfall were crowded by the deaf; amongst whom were some from Pegû, with ears uncommonly handsome and large, but who were still less able to hear than the rest. Nor were there wanting others in abundance with hump-backs, wenny necks, and even horns of an exquisite polish.

The emir, to aggrandize the solemnity of the festival, in honour of his illustrious visitant, ordered the turf to be spread on all sides with skins and table-cloths; upon which were served up for the good Mussulmans pilaus of every hue, with other orthodox dishes; and, by the express order of Vathek, who was shamefully tolerant, small plates of abominations were prepared, to the great scandal of the faithful. The holy assembly began to fall to. The caliph, in spite of every remonstrance from the chief of his eunuchs, resolved to have a dinner dressed on the spot. The complaisant emir immediately gave orders for a table to be placed in the shade of the willows. The first service consisted of fish, which they drew from a river, flowing over sands of gold at the foot of a lofty hill. These were broiled as fast as taken, and served up with a sauce of vinegar and small herbs that grew on Mount Sinai; for everything with the emir was excellent and pious.

The dessert was not quite set on, when the sound of lutes from the hill was repeated by the echoes of the neighbouring mountains. The caliph, with an emotion of pleasure and surprise, had no sooner raised up his head, than a handful of jasmine dropped on his face. An abundance of tittering succeeded the frolic, and instantly appeared, through the bushes, the elegant forms of several young females, skipping and bounding like roes. The fragrance diffused from their hair struck the sense of Vathek, who, in an ecstasy, suspending his repast, said to Bababalouk, "Are the peris come down from their spheres? Note her, in particular, whose form is so perfect; venturously running on the brink of the precipice, and turning back her head, as regardless of nothing but the graceful flow of her robe. With what captivating impatience doth she contend with the bushes for her veil? could it be she who threw the jasmine at me?"—"Ay! she it was; and you too would she throw, from the top of the rock," answered Bababalouk, "for that is my good friend Nouronihar, who so kindly lent me her swing. My dear lord and master," added he, wresting a twig from a willow, "let me correct her for her want of respect: the emir will have no reason to complain; since (bating what I owe to his piety) he is much to be blamed for keeping a troop of girls on the mountains, where the sharpness of the air gives their blood too brisk a circulation."

"Peace! blasphemer," said the caliph; "speak not thus of her, who, over these mountains, leads my heart a willing captive. Contrive, rather, that my eyes may be fixed upon hers; that I may respire her sweet breath as she bounds panting along these delightful wilds!" On saying these words, Vathek extended his arms towards the hill; and directing his eyes with an anxiety unknown to him before, endeavoured to keep within view the object that enthralled his soul; but her course was as difficult to follow as the flight of one of those beautiful blue butterflies of Cashmere which are at once, so volatile and rare.

The caliph, not satisfied with seeing, wished also to hear Nouronihar, and eagerly turned to catch the sound of her voice. At last, he distinguished her whispering to one of her companions behind the thicket from whence she had thrown the jasmine: "A caliph, it must be owned, is a fine thing to see; but my little Gulchenrouz is much more amiable: one lock of his hair is of more value to me than the richest embroidery of the Indies. I had rather that his teeth should mischievously press my finger, than the richest ring of the imperial treasure. Where have you left him, Sutlememe? and why is he not here?"

The agitated caliph still wished to hear more; but she immediately retired with all her attendants. The fond monarch pursued her with his eyes till she was gone out of sight; and then continued like a bewildered and benighted traveller, from whom the clouds had obscured the constellation that guided his way. The curtain of night seemed dropped before him: everything appeared discoloured. The falling waters filled his soul with dejection, and his tears trickled down the jasmines he had caught from Nouronihar, and placed in his inflamed bosom. He snatched up a few shining pebbles, to remind him of the scene where he felt the first tumults of love. Two hours were elapsed, and evening drew on, before he could resolve to depart from the place. He often, but in vain, attempted to go: a soft languor enervated the powers of his mind. Extending himself on the brink of the stream, he turned his eyes towards the blue summits of the mountain, and exclaimed, "What concealest thou behind thee, pitiless rock? what is passing in thy solitudes? Whither is she gone? O heaven! perhaps she is now wandering in thy grottoes with her happy Gulchenrouz!"

In the meantime, the damps began to descend; and the emir, solicitous for the health of the caliph, ordered the imperial litter to be brought. Vathek, absorbed in his reveries, was imperceptibly removed and conveyed back to the saloon that received him the evening before. But let us leave the caliph immersed in his new passion, and attend Nouronihar beyond the rocks, where she had again joined her beloved Gulchenrouz.

This Gulchenrouz was the son of Ali Hassan, brother to the emir; and the most delicate and lovely creature in the world. Ali Hassan, who had been absent ten years on a voyage to the unknown seas, committed, at his departure, this child, the only survivor of many, to the care and protection of his brother.

Gulchenrouz could write in various characters with precision, and paint upon vellum the most elegant arabesques that fancy could devise. His sweet voice accompanied the lute in the most enchanting manner; and when he sang the loves of Megnoun and Leilah, or some unfortunate lovers of ancient days, tears insensibly overflowed the cheeks of his auditors. The verses he composed (for, like Megnoun, he, too, was a poet) inspired that unresisting languor, so frequently fatal to the female heart. The women all doted upon him; and, though he had passed his thirteenth year, they still detained him in the harem. His dancing was light as the gossamer waved by the zephyrs of spring; but his arms, which twined so gracefully with those of the young girls in the dance, could neither dart the lance in the chase, nor curb the steeds that pastured in his uncle's domains. The bow, however, he drew with a certain aim, and would have excelled his competitors in the race, could he have broken the ties that bound him to Nouronihar.

The two brothers had mutually engaged their children to each other; and Nouronihar loved her cousin more than her own beautiful eyes. Both had the same tastes and amusements; the same long, languishing looks; the same tresses; the same fair complexions; and, when Gulchenrouz appeared in the dress of his cousin, he seemed to be more feminine than even herself. If, at any time, he left the harem to visit Fakreddin, it was with all the bashfulness of a fawn, that consciously ventures from the lair of its dam: he was, however, wanton enough to mock the solemn old grey-beards, though sure to be rated without mercy in return. Whenever this happened, he would hastily plunge into the recesses of the harem; and, sobbing, take refuge in the fond arms of Nouronihar, who loved even his faults beyond the virtues of others.

It fell out this evening, that, after leaving the caliph in the meadow, she ran with Gulchenrouz over the green sward of the mountain that sheltered the vale where Fakreddin had chosen to reside. The sun was dilated on the edge of the horizon; and the young people, whose fancies were lively and inventive, imagined they beheld, in the gorgeous clouds of the west, the domes of Shaddukian and Ambreabad, where the Peries have fixed their abode. Nouronihar, sitting on the slope of the hill, supported on her knees the perfumed head of Gulchenrouz. The unexpected arrival of the caliph, and the splendour that marked his appearance, had already filled with emotion the ardent soul of Nouronihar. Her vanity irresistibly prompted her to pique the prince's attention; and this she before took good care to effect, whilst he picked up the jasmine she had thrown upon him. But when Gulchenrouz asked after the flowers he had culled for her bosom, Nouronihar was all in confusion. She hastily kissed his forehead, arose in a flutter, and walked with unequal steps on the border of the precipice. Night advanced, and the pure gold of the setting sun had yielded to a sanguine red, the glow of which, like the reflection of a burning furnace, flushed Nouronihar's animated countenance. Gulchenrouz, alarmed at the agitation of his cousin, said to her, with a supplicating accent, "Let us be gone; the sky looks portentous, the tamarisks tremble more than common, and the raw wind chills my very heart. Come! let us be gone; 'tis a melancholy night!" Then taking hold of her hand, he drew it towards the path he besought her to go. Nouronihar unconsciously followed the attraction; for a thousand strange imaginations occupied her spirits. She passed the large round of honeysuckles, her favourite resort, without ever vouchsafing it a glance; yet Gulchenrouz could not help snatching off a few shoots in his way, though he ran as if a wild beast were behind.

The young females seeing them approach in such haste, and, according to custom, expecting a dance, instantly assembled in a circle and took each other by the hand; but Gulchenrouz, coming up out of breath, fell down at once on the grass. This accident struck with consternation the whole of this frolicsome party; whilst Nouronihar, half distracted and overcome, both by the violence of her exercise and the tumult of her thoughts, sunk feebly down at his side, cherished his cold hands in her bosom, and chafed his temples with a fragrant perfume. At length he came to himself, and wrapping up his head in the robe of his cousin, entreated that she would not return to the harem. He was afraid of being snapped at by Shaban his tutor, a wrinkled old eunuch of a surly disposition; for, having interrupted the wonted walk of Nouronihar, he dreaded lest the churl should take it amiss. The whole of this sprightly group, sitting round upon a mossy knoll, began to entertain themselves with various pastimes, whilst their superintendents, the eunuchs, were gravely conversing at a distance. The nurse of the emir's daughter, observing her pupil sit ruminating with her eyes on the ground, endeavoured to amuse her with diverting tales; to which Gulchenrouz, who had already forgotten his inquietudes, listened with a breathless attention. He laughed, he clapped his hands, and passed a hundred little tricks on the whole of the company, without omitting the eunuchs, whom he provoked to run after him, in spite of their age and decrepitude.

During these occurrences, the moon arose, the wind subsided, and the evening became so serene and inviting, that a resolution was taken to sup on the spot. One of the eunuchs ran to fetch melons, whilst others were employed in showering down almonds from the branches that overhung this amiable party. Sutlememe, who excelled in dressing a salad, having filled large bowls of porcelain with eggs of small birds, curds turned with citron juice, slices of cucumber, and the inmost leaves of delicate herbs, handed it round from one to another, and gave each their shares with a large spoon of cocknos. Gulchenrouz, nestling, as usual, in the bosom of Nouronihar, pouted out his vermilion little lips against the offer of Sutlememe; and would take it only from the hand of his cousin, on whose mouth he hung, like a bee inebriated with the nectar of flowers.

In the midst of this festive scene, there appeared a light on the top of the highest mountain, which attracted the notice of every eye. This light was not less bright than the moon when at full, and might have been taken for her, had not the moon already risen. The phenomenon occasioned a general surprise, and no one could conjecture the cause. It could not be a fire, for the light was clear and bluish; nor had meteors ever been seen of that magnitude or splendour. This strange light faded for a moment, and immediately renewed its brightness. It first appeared motionless, at the foot of the rock; whence it darted in an instant, to sparkle in a thicket of palm-trees: from thence it glided along the torrent; and at last fixed in a glen that was narrow and dark. The moment it had taken its direction, Gulchenrouz, whose heart always trembled at anything sudden or rare, drew Nouronihar by the robe, and anxiously requested her to return to the harem. The women were importunate in seconding the entreaty; but the curiosity of the emir's daughter prevailed. She not only refused to go back, but resolved, at all hazards, to pursue the appearance.

Whilst they were debating what was best to be done, the light shot forth so dazzling a blaze that they all fled away shrieking. Nouronihar followed them a few steps; but, coming to the turn of a little by-path, stopped, and went back alone. As she ran with an alertness peculiar to herself, it was not long before she came to the place where they had just been supping. The globe of fire now appeared stationary in the glen, and burned in majestic stillness. Nouronihar, pressing her hands upon her bosom, hesitated, for some moments, to advance. The solitude of her situation was new, the silence of the night awful, and every object inspired sensations which, till then, she never had felt. The affright of Gulchenrouz recurred to her mind, and she a thousand times turned to go back; but this luminous appearance was always before her. Urged on by an irresistible impulse, she continued to approach it, in defiance of every obstacle that opposed her progress.

At length she arrived at the opening of the glen; but, instead of coming up to the light, she found herself surrounded by darkness; excepting that, at a considerable distance, a faint spark glimmered by fits. She stopped a second time: the sound of waterfalls mingling their murmurs, the hollow rustlings among the palm-branches, and the funereal screams of the birds from their rifted trunks, all conspired to fill her soul with terror. She imagined, every moment, that she trod on some venomous reptile. All the stories of malignant dives and dismal ghouls thronged into her memory; but her curiosity was, notwithstanding, more predominant than her fears. She therefore firmly entered a winding track that led towards the spark; but, being a stranger to the path, she had not gone far, till she began to repent of her rashness. "Alas!" said she, "that I were but in those secure and illuminated apartments, where my evenings glided on with Gulchenrouz! Dear child! how would thy heart flutter with terror, wert thou wandering in these wild solitudes, like me!" Thus speaking, she advanced, and coming up to steps hewn in the rock, ascended them undismayed. The light, which was now gradually enlarging, appeared above her on the summit of the mountain, and as if proceeding from a cavern. At length, she distinguished a plaintive and melodious union of voices, that resembled the dirges which are sung over tombs. A sound like that which arises from the filling of baths struck her ear at the same time. She continued ascending, and discovered large wax torches in full blaze, planted here and there in the fissures of the rock. This appearance filled her with fear, whilst the subtle and potent odour which the torches exhaled caused her to sink, almost lifeless, at the entrance of the grot.

Casting her eyes within in this kind of trance, she beheld a large cistern of gold, filled with a water, the vapour of which distilled on her face a dew of the essence of roses. A soft symphony resounded through the grot. On the sides of the cistern she noticed appendages of royalty, diadems and feathers of the heron, all sparkling with carbuncles. Whilst her attention was fixed on this display of magnificence, the music ceased, and a voice instantly demanded, "For what monarch are these torches kindled, this bath prepared, and these habiliments which belong not only to the sovereigns of the earth, but even to the talismanic powers?" To which a second voice answered, "They are for the charming daughter of the Emir Fakreddin." —"What," replied the first, "for that trifler, who consumes her time with a giddy child, immersed in softness, and who, at best, can make but a pitiful husband?"—"And can she," rejoined the other voice, "be amused with such empty toys, whilst the caliph, the sovereign of the world, he who is destined to enjoy the treasures of the pre-Adamite sultans, a prince six feet high, and whose eyes pervade the inmost soul of a female, is inflamed with love for her? No! she will be wise enough to answer that passion alone that can aggrandize her glory. No doubt she will, and despise the puppet of her fancy. Then all the riches this place contains, as well as the carbuncle of Giamschid, shall be hers."—"You judge right," returned the first voice; "and I haste to Istakar to prepare the palace of subterranean fire for the reception of the bridal pair."

The voices ceased; the torches were extinguished; the most entire darkness succeeded; and Nouronihar, recovering with a start, found herself reclined on a sofa in the harem of her father. She clapped her hands, and immediately came together Gulchenrouz and her women, who, in despair at having lost her, had dispatched eunuchs to seek her in every direction. Shaban appeared with the rest, and began to reprimand her, with an air of consequence: "Little impertinent," said he, "have you false keys, or are you beloved of some genius that hath given you a picklock? I will try the extent of your power: come to the dark chamber, and expect not the company of Gulchenrouz: be expeditious! I will shut you up, and turn the key twice upon you!" At these menaces, Nouronihar indignantly raised her head, opened on Shaban her black eyes, which, since the important dialogue of the enchanted grot, were considerably enlarged, and said, "Go, speak thus to slaves; but learn to reverence her who is born to give laws, and subject all to her power."

Proceeding in the same style, she was interrupted by a sudden exclamation of "The caliph! the caliph!" All the curtains were thrown open, the slaves prostrated themselves in double rows, and poor little Gulchenrouz went to hide beneath the couch of a sofa. At first appeared a file of black eunuchs trailing after them long trains of muslin embroidered with gold, and holding in their hands censers, which dispensed, as they passed, the grateful perfume of the wood of aloes. Next marched Bababalouk with a solemn strut, and tossing his head, as not overpleased at the visit. Vathek came close after, superbly robed: his gait was unembarrassed and noble; and his presence would have engaged admiration, though he had not been the sovereign of the world. He approached Nouronihar with a throbbing heart, and seemed enraptured at the full effulgence of her radiant eyes, of which he had before caught but a few glimpses; but she instantly depressed them, and her confusion augmented her beauty.

Bababalouk, who was a thorough adept in coincidences of this nature, and knew that the worst game should be played with the best face, immediately made a signal for all to retire; and no sooner did he perceive beneath the sofa the little one's feet, than he drew him forth without ceremony, set him upon his shoulders, and lavished him, as he went off, a thousand unwelcome caresses. Gulchenrouz cried out, and resisted till his cheeks became the colour of the blossom of pomegranates, and his tearful eyes sparkled with indignation. He cast a significant glance at Nouronihar, which the caliph noticing, asked, "Is that, then, your Gulchenrouz?" — "Sovereign of the world!" answered she, "spare my cousin, whose innocence and gentleness deserve not your anger!" — "Take comfort," said Vathek, with a smile: "he is in good hands. Bababalouk is fond of children, and never goes without sweetmeats and comfits." The daughter of Fakreddin was abashed, and suffered Gulchenrouz to be borne away without adding a word. The tumult of her bosom betrayed her confusion, and Vathek, becoming still more impassioned, gave a loose to his frenzy; which had only not subdued the last faint strugglings of reluctance, when the emir, suddenly bursting in, threw his face upon the ground at the feet of the caliph, and said, "Commander of the faithful! abase not yourself to the meanness of your slave."—"No, emir," replied Vathek, "I raise her to an equality with myself: I declare her my wife; and the glory of your race shall extend from one generation to another."— "Alas! my lord," said Fakreddin, as he plucked off a few grey hairs of his beard, "cut short the days of your faithful servant, rather than force him to depart from his word. Nouronihar is solemnly promised to Gulchenrouz, the son of my brother Ali Hassan: they are united, also, in heart; their faith is mutually plighted; and affiances, so sacred, cannot be broken."—"What then!" replied the caliph bluntly; "would you surrender this divine beauty to a husband more womanish than herself? and can you imagine that I will suffer her charms to decay in hands so inefficient and nerveless? No! she is destined to live out her life within my embraces: such is my will; retire, and disturb not the night I devote to the worship of her charms."

The irritated emir drew forth his sabre, presented it to Vathek, and stretching out his neck, said, in a firm tone of voice, "Strike your unhappy host, my lord: he has lived long enough, since he hath seen the Prophet's vicegerent violate the rights of hospitality." At his uttering these words, Nouronihar, unable to support any longer the conflict of her passions, sunk down into a swoon. Vathek, both terrified for her life and furious at an opposition to his will, bade Fakreddin assist his daughter, and withdrew; darting his terrible look at the unfortunate emir, who suddenly fell backward, bathed in a sweat as cold as the damp of death.

Gulchenrouz, who had escaped from the hands of Bababalouk, and was at that instant returned, called out for help as loudly as he could, not having strength to afford it himself. Pale and panting, the poor child attempted to revive Nouronihar by caresses; and it happened, that the thrilling warmth of his lips restored her to life. Fakreddin, beginning also to recover from the look of the caliph, with difficulty tottered to a seat; and, after warily casting round his eye, to see if this dangerous prince were gone, sent for Shaban and Sutlememe; and said to them apart, "My friends! violent evils require violent remedies; the caliph has brought desolation and horror into my family; and how shall we resist his power? Another of his looks will send me to the grave. Fetch, then, that narcotic powder which a dervish brought me from Aracan. A dose of it, the effect of which will continue three days, must be administered to each of these children. The caliph will believe them to be dead; for they will have all the appearance of death. We shall go as if to inter them in the cave of Meimouné, at the entrance of the great desert of sand, and near the bower of my dwarfs. When all the spectators shall be withdrawn, you, Shaban, and four select eunuchs, shall convey them to the lake; where provision shall be ready to support them a month: for one day allotted to the surprise this event will occasion, five to the tears, a fortnight to reflection, and the rest to prepare for renewing his progress, will, according to my calculation, fill up the whole time that Vathek will tarry; and I shall then be freed from his intrusion."

"Your plan is good," said Sutlememe, "if it can but be effected. I have remarked, that Nouronihar is well able to support the glances of the caliph, and that he is far from being sparing of them to her; be assured, therefore, that, notwithstanding her fondness for Gulchenrouz, she will never remain quiet, while she knows him to be here. Let us persuade her that both herself and Gulchenrouz are really dead, and that they were conveyed to those rocks, for a limited season, to expiate the little faults of which their love was the cause. We will add, that we killed ourselves in despair; and that your dwarfs, whom they never yet saw, will preach to them delectable sermons. I will engage that everything shall succeed to the bent of your wishes."—"Be it so!" said Fakreddin: "I approve your proposal: let us lose not a moment to give it effect."

They hastened to seek for the powder, which, being mixed in a sherbet was immediately administered to Gulchenrouz and Nouronihar. Within the space of an hour, both were seized with violent palpitations, and a general numbness gradually ensued. They arose from the floor where they had remained ever since the caliph's departure, and, ascending to the sofa, reclined themselves upon it, clasped in each other's embraces. "Cherish me, my dear Nouronihar!" said Gulchenrouz: "put thy hand upon my heart; it feels as if it were frozen. Alas! thou art as cold as myself! hath the caliph murdered us both, with his terrible look?"—"I am dying!" cried she, in a faltering voice: "press me closer; I am ready to expire!"—"Let us die, then, together," answered the little Gulchenrouz, whilst his breast laboured with a convulsive sigh; "let me, at least, breathe forth my soul on thy lips!" They spoke no more, and became as dead.

Immediately the most piercing cries were heard through the harem; whilst Shaban and Sutlememe personated, with great adroitness, the parts of persons in despair. The emir, who was sufficiently mortified to be forced into such untoward expedients, and had now, for the first time, made a trial of his powder, was under no necessity of counterfeiting grief. The slaves, who had flocked together from all quarters, stood motionless at the spectacle before them. All lights were extinguished, save two lamps, which shed a wan glimmering over the faces of these lovely flowers, that seemed to be faded in the spring-time of life. Funeral vestments were prepared; their bodies were washed with rose-water; their beautiful tresses were braided and incensed; and they were wrapped in cymars whiter than alabaster.

At the moment that their attendants were placing two wreaths of their favourite jasmines on their brows, the caliph, who had just heard the tragical catastrophe, arrived. He looked not less pale and haggard than the ghouls that wander at night among the graves. Forgetful of himself and every one else, he broke through the midst of the slaves; fell prostrate at the foot of the sofa; beat his bosom; called himself "atrocious murderer!" and invoked upon his head a thousand imprecations. With a trembling hand he raised the veil that covered the countenance of Nouronihar, and uttering a loud shriek, fell lifeless on the floor. The chief of the eunuchs dragged him off, with horrible grimaces, and repeated as he went, "Ay, I foresaw she would play you some ungracious turn!"

No sooner was the caliph gone, than the emir commanded biers to be brought, and forbade that any one should enter the harem. Every window was fastened; all instruments of music were broken; and the imans began to recite their prayers. Towards the close of this melancholy day, Vathek sobbed in silence; for they had been forced to compose with anodynes his convulsions of rage and desperation.

At the dawn of the succeeding morning, the wide folding doors of the palace were set open, and the funeral procession moved forward for the mountain. The wailful cries of "La llah illa Alla!" reached the caliph, who was eager to cicatrize himself and attend the ceremonial; nor could he have been dissuaded, had not his excessive weakness disabled him from walking. At the few first steps he fell on the ground, and his people were obliged to lay him on a bed, where he remained many days in such a state of insensibility as excited compassion in the emir himself.

When the procession was arrived at the grot of Meimouné, Shaban and Sutlememe dismissed the whole of the train, excepting the four confidential eunuchs who were appointed to remain. After resting some moments near the biers, which had been left in the open air, they caused them to be carried to the brink of a small lake, whose banks were overgrown with a hoary moss. This was the great resort of herons and storks, which preyed continually on little blue fishes. The dwarfs, instructed by the emir, soon repaired thither, and, with the help of the eunuchs, began to construct cabins of rushes and reeds, a work in which they had admirable skill. A magazine also was contrived for provisions, with a small oratory for themselves, and a pyramid of wood, neatly piled, to furnish the necessary fuel, for the air was bleak in the hollows of the mountains.

At evening two fires were kindled on the brink of the lake, and the two lovely bodies, taken from their biers, were carefully deposited upon a bed of dried leaves within the same cabin. The dwarfs began to recite the Koran, with their clear shrill voices; and Shaban and Sutlememe stood at some distance, anxiously waiting the effects of the powder. At length Nouronihar and Gulchenrouz faintly stretched out their arms; and, gradually opening their eyes, began to survey, with looks of increasing amazement, every object around them. They even attempted to rise; but, for want of strength, fell back again. Sutlememe, on this, administered a cordial, which the emir had taken care to provide.

Gulchenrouz, thoroughly aroused, sneezed out aloud; and, raising himself with an effort that expressed his surprise, left the cabin and inhaled the fresh air with the greatest avidity. "Yes," said he, "I breathe again! again do I exist! I hear sounds! I behold a firmament, spangled over with stars!" Nouronihar, catching these beloved accents, extricated herself from the leaves and ran to clasp Gulchenrouz to her bosom. The first objects she remarked were their long cymars, their garlands of flowers, and their naked feet: she hid her face in her hands to reflect. The vision of the enchanted bath, the despair of her father, and, more vividly than both, the majestic figure of Vathek, recurred to her memory. She recollected, also, that herself and Gulchenrouz had been sick and dying; but all these images bewildered her mind. Not knowing where she was, she turned her eyes on all sides, as if to recognize the surrounding scene. This singular lake, those flames reflected from its glassy surface, the pale hues of its banks, the romantic cabins, the bulrushes that sadly waved their drooping heads, the storks whose melancholy cries blended with the shrill voices of the dwarfs—everything conspired to persuade her that the angel of death had opened the portal of some other world.

Gulchenrouz on his part, lost in wonder, clung to the neck of his cousin. He believed himself in the region of phantoms, and was terrified at the silence she preserved. At length addressing her: "Speak," said he; "where are we? Do you not see those spectres that are stirring the burning coals? Are they Monker and Nekir who are come to throw us into them? Does the fatal bridge cross this lake, whose solemn stillness perhaps conceals from us an abyss, in which for whole ages we shall be doomed incessantly to sink?"

"No, my children," said Sutlememe, going towards them; "take comfort! the exterminating angel, who conducted our souls hither after yours, hath assured us, that the chastisement of your indolent and voluptuous life shall be restricted to a certain series of years, which you must pass in this dreary abode; where the sun is scarcely visible, and where the soil yields neither fruits nor flowers. These," continued she, pointing to the dwarfs, "will provide for our wants; for souls so mundane as ours retain too strong a tincture of their earthly extraction. Instead of meats, your food will be nothing but rice; and your bread shall be moistened in the fogs that brood over the surface of the lake."

At this desolating prospect, the poor children burst into tears, and prostrated themselves before the dwarfs; who perfectly supported their characters, and delivered an excellent discourse, of a customary length, upon the sacred camel which, after a thousand years, was to convey them to the paradise of the faithful.

The sermon being ended, and ablutions performed, they praised Alla and the Prophet, supped very indifferently, and retired to their withered leaves. Nouronihar and her little cousin consoled themselves on finding that the dead might lie in one cabin. Having slept well before, the remainder of the night was spent in conversation on what had befallen them; and both, from a dread of apparitions, betook themselves for protection to one another's arms.

In the morning, which was lowering and rainy, the dwarfs mounted high poles, like minarets, and called them to prayers. The whole congregation, which consisted of Sutlememe, Shaban, the four eunuchs, and a few storks that were tired of fishing, was already assembled. The two children came forth from their cabin with a slow and dejected pace. As their minds were in a tender and melancholy mood, their devotions were performed with fervour. No sooner were they finished than Gulchenrouz demanded of Sutlememe and the rest, "how they happened to die so opportunely for his cousin and himself?" —"We killed ourselves," returned Sutlememe, "in despair at your death." On this, Nouronihar, who, notwithstanding what had passed, had not yet forgotten her vision, said, "And the caliph! is he also dead of his grief? and will he likewise come hither?" The dwarfs, who were prepared with an answer, most demurely replied, "Vathek is damned beyond all redemption!"—"I readily believe so," said Gulchenrouz; "and am glad, from my heart, to hear it; for I am convinced it was his horrible look that sent us hither, to listen to sermons, and mess upon rice." One week passed away on the side of the lake unmarked by any variety; Nouronihar ruminating on the grandeur of which death had deprived her, and Gulchenrouz applying to prayers and basket-making with the dwarfs, who infinitely pleased him.

Whilst this scene of innocence was exhibiting in the mountains, the caliph presented himself to the emir in a new light. The instant he recovered the use of his senses, with a voice that made Bababalouk quake, he thundered out, "Perfidious Giaour! I renounce thee for ever! it is thou who hast slain my beloved Nouronihar! and I supplicate the pardon of Mahomet, who would have preserved her to me had I been more wise. Let water be brought to perform my ablutions, and let the pious Fakreddin be called to offer up his prayers with mine, and reconcile me to him. Afterwards, we will go together and visit the sepulchre of the unfortunate Nouronihar. I am resolved to become a hermit, and consume the residue of my days on this mountain, in hope of expiating my crimes."— "And what do you intend to live upon there?" inquired Bababalouk.—"I hardly know," replied Vathek; "but I will tell you when I feel hungry—which, I believe, will not soon be the case."

The arrival of Fakreddin put a stop to this conversation. As soon as Vathek saw him, he threw his arms around his neck, bedewed his face with a torrent of tears, and uttered things so affecting, so pious, that the emir, crying for joy, congratulated himself in his heart upon having performed so admirable and unexpected a conversion. As for the pilgrimage to the mountain, Fakreddin had his reasons not to oppose it; therefore, each ascending his own litter, they started.

Notwithstanding the vigilance with which his attendants watched the caliph, they could not prevent his harrowing his cheeks with a few scratches, when on the place where he was told Nouronihar had been buried; they were even obliged to drag him away, by force of hands, from the melancholy spot.

However, he swore, with a solemn oath, that he would return thither every day. This resolution did not exactly please the emir—yet he flattered himself that the caliph might not proceed farther, and would merely perform his devotions in the cavern of Meimouné. Besides, the lake was so completely concealed within the solitary bosom of those tremendous rocks, that he thought it utterly impossible any one could ever find it. This security of Fakreddin was also considerably strengthened by the conduct of Vathek, who performed his vow most scrupulously, and returned daily from the hill so devout, and so contrite, that all the grey-beards were in a state of ecstasy on account of it.

Nouronihar was not altogether so content; for though she felt a fondness for Gulchenrouz, who, to augment the attachment, had been left at full liberty with her, yet she still regarded him as but a bauble that bore no competition with the carbuncle of Giamschid. At times, she indulged doubts on the mode of her being; and scarcely could believe that the dead had all the wants and the whims of the living. To gain satisfaction, however, on so perplexing a topic, one morning, whilst all were asleep, she arose with a breathless caution from the side of Gulchenrouz; and, after having given him a soft kiss, began to follow the windings of the lake, till it terminated with a rock, the top of which was accessible, though lofty. This she climbed with considerable toil; and having reached the summit, set forward in a run, like a doe before the hunter. Though she skipped with the alertness of an antelope, yet, at intervals, she was forced to desist, and rest beneath the tamarisks to recover her breath. Whilst she, thus reclined, was occupied with her little reflections on the apprehension that she had some knowledge of the place, Vathek, who, finding himself that morning but ill at ease, had gone forth before the dawn, presented himself on a sudden to her view. Motionless with surprise, he durst not approach the figure before him trembling and pale, but yet lovely to behold. At length Nouronihar, with a mixture of pleasure and affliction, raising her fine eyes to him, said, "My lord! are you then come hither to eat rice and hear sermons with me?"—"Beloved phantom!" cried Vathek, "thou dost speak; thou hast the same graceful form; the same radiant features; art thou palpable likewise?" and, eagerly embracing her, added, "Here are limbs and a bosom animated with a gentle warmth!—What can such a prodigy mean?"

Nouronihar, with indifference, answered,—"You know, my lord, that I died on the very night you honoured me with your visit. My cousin maintains it was from one of your glances; but I cannot believe him; for to me they seem not so dreadful. Gulchenrouz died with me, and we were both brought into a region of desolation, where we are fed with a wretched diet. If you be dead also, and are come hither to join us, I pity your lot; for you will be stunned with the clang of the dwarfs and the storks. Besides, it is mortifying in the extreme, that you, as well as myself, should have lost the treasures of the subterranean palace."

At the mention of the subterranean palace, the caliph suspended his caresses (which, indeed, had proceeded pretty far), to seek from Nouronihar an explanation of her meaning. She then recapitulated her vision, what immediately followed, and the history of her pretended death; adding, also, a description of the place of expiation from whence she had fled; and all in a manner that would have extorted his laughter, had not the thoughts of Vathek been too deeply engaged. No sooner, however, had she ended, than he again clasped her to his bosom and said, "Light of my eyes, the mystery is unravelled; we both are alive! Your father is a cheat, who, for the sake of dividing us, hath deluded us both; and the Giaour, whose design, as far as I can discover, is that we shall proceed together, seems scarce a whit better. It shall be some time at least before he finds us in his palace of fire. Your lovely little person in my estimation is far more precious than all the treasures of the pre-Adamite sultans; and I wish to possess it at pleasure, and in open day, for many a moon, before I go to burrow underground, like a mole. Forget this little trifler, Gulchenrouz; and——"—"Ah, my lord!" interposed Nouronihar, "let me entreat that you do him no evil."—"No, no!" replied Vathek; "I have already bid you forbear to alarm yourself for him. He has been brought up too much on milk and sugar to stimulate my jealousy. We will leave him with the dwarfs; who, by the by, are my old acquaintances: their company will suit him far better than yours. As to other matters, I will return no more to your father's. I want not to have my ears dinned by him and his dotards with the violation of the rights of hospitality, as if it were less an honour for you to espouse the sovereign of the world than a girl dressed up like a boy."

Nouronihar could find nothing to oppose in a discourse so eloquent. She only wished the amorous monarch had discovered more ardour for the carbuncle of Giamschid; but flattered herself it would gradually increase, and therefore yielded to his will with the most bewitching submission.

When the caliph judged it proper, he called for Bababalouk, who was asleep in the cave of Meimouné, and dreaming that the phantom of Nouronihar, having mounted him once more on her swing, had just given him such a jerk, that he one moment soared above the mountains, and the next sunk into the abyss. Starting from his sleep at the sound of his master, he ran, gasping for breath, and had nearly fallen backward at the sight, as he believed, of the spectre by whom he had so lately been haunted in his dream. "Ah, my lord!" cried he, recoiling ten steps, and covering his eyes with both hands, "do you then perform the office of a ghoul? have you dug up the dead? Yet hope not to make her your prey; for, after all she hath caused me to suffer, she is wicked enough to prey even upon you."

"Cease to play the fool," said Vathek, "and thou shalt soon be convinced that it is Nouronihar herself, alive and well, whom I clasp to my breast. Go and pitch my tents in the neighbouring valley. There will I fix my abode, with this beautiful tulip, whose colours I soon shall restore. There exert thy best endeavours to procure whatever can augment the enjoyments of life, till I shall disclose to thee more of my will."

The news of so unlucky an event soon reached the ears of the emir, who abandoned himself to grief and despair, and began, as did his old grey-beards, to begrime his visage with ashes. A total supineness ensued; travellers were no longer entertained; no more plasters were spread; and, instead of the charitable activity that had distinguished this asylum, the whole of its inhabitants exhibited only faces of half a cubit long, and uttered groans that accorded with their forlorn situation.

Though Fakreddin bewailed his daughter as lost to him for ever, yet Gulchenrouz was not forgotten. He dispatched immediate instructions to Sutlememe, Shaban, and the dwarfs, enjoining them not to undeceive the child in respect to his state, but, under some pretence, to convey him far from the lofty rock at the extremity of the lake, to a place which he should appoint, as safer from danger, for he suspected that Vathek intended him evil.

Gulchenrouz, in the meanwhile, was filled with amazement at not finding his cousin; nor were the dwarfs less surprised:

but Sutlememe, who had more penetration, immediately guessed what had happened. Gulchenrouz was amused with the delusive hope of once more embracing Nouronihar in the interior recesses of the mountains, where the ground, strewed over with orange blossoms and jasmines, offered beds much more inviting than the withered leaves in their cabin; where they might accompany with their voices the sounds of their lutes, and chase butterflies. Sutlememe was far gone in this sort of description, when one of the four eunuchs beckoned her aside, to apprise her of the arrival of a messenger from their fraternity, who had explained the secret of the flight of Nouronihar, and brought the commands of the emir. A council with Shaban and the dwarfs was immediately held. Their baggage being stowed in consequence of it, they embarked in a shallop, and quietly sailed with the little one, who acquiesced in all their proposals. Their voyage proceeded in the same manner, till they came to the place where the lake sinks beneath the hollow of a rock: but as soon as the bark had entered it, and Gulchenrouz found himself surrounded with darkness, he was seized with a dreadful consternation, and incessantly uttered the most piercing outcries; for he now was persuaded he should actually be damned for having taken too many little freedoms in his lifetime with his cousin.

But let us return to the caliph, and her who ruled over his heart. Bababalouk had pitched the tents, and closed up the extremities of the valley with magnificent screens of India cloth, which were guarded by Ethiopian slaves with their drawn sabres. To preserve the verdure of this beautiful enclosure in its natural freshness, white eunuchs went continually round it with gilt water vessels. The waving of fans was heard near the imperial pavilion; where, by the voluptuous light that glowed through the muslins, the caliph enjoyed, at full view, all the attractions of Nouronihar. Inebriated with delight, he was all ear to her charming voice, which accompanied the lute; while she was not less captivated with his descriptions of Samarah, and the tower full of wonders, but especially with his relation of the adventure of the ball, and the chasm of the Giaour, with its ebony portal.

In this manner they conversed the whole day, and at night they bathed together in a basin of black marble, which admirably set off the fairness of Nouronihar. Bababalouk, whose good graces this beauty had regained, spared no attention, that their repasts might be served up with the minutest exactness: some exquisite rarity was ever placed before them; and he sent even to Schiraz, for that fragrant and delicious wine which had been hoarded up in bottles, prior to the birth of Mahomet. He had excavated little ovens in the rock, to bake the nice manchets which were prepared by the hands of Nouronihar, from whence they had derived a flavour so grateful to Vathek, that he regarded the ragouts of his other wives as entirely mawkish: whilst they would have died of chagrin at the emir's, at finding themselves so neglected, if Fakreddin, notwithstanding his resentment, had not taken pity upon them.

The Sultana Dilara, who, till then, had been the favourite, took this dereliction of the caliph to heart, with a vehemence natural to her character; for, duing her continuance in favour, she had imbibed from Vathek many of his extravagant fancies, and was fired with impatience to behold the superb tombs of Istakar, and the palace of forty columns; besides, having been brought up amongst the magi, she had fondly cherished the idea of the caliph's devoting himself to the worship of fire: thus his voluptuous and desultory life with her rival was to her a double source of affliction. The transient piety of Vathek had occasioned her some serious alarms; but the present was an evil of far greater magnitude. She resolved, therefore, without hesitation, to write to Carathis, and acquaint her that all things went ill; that they had eaten, slept, and revelled at an old emir's, whose sanctity was very formidable; and that, after all, the prospect of possessing the treasures of the pre-Adamite sultans was no less remote than before. This letter was entrusted to the care of two woodmen, who were at work in one of the great forests of the mountains, and who, being acquainted with the shortest cuts, arrived in ten days at Samarah.

The Princess Carathis was engaged at chess with Morakanabad, when the arrival of these woodfellers was announced. She, after some weeks of Vathek's absence, had forsaken the upper regions of her tower, because everything appeared in confusion among the stars, which she consulted relative to the fate of her son. In vain did she renew her fumigations, and extend herself on the roof, to obtain mystic visions; nothing more could she see in her dreams, than pieces of brocade, nosegays of flowers, and other unmeaning gewgaws. These disappointments had thrown her into a state of dejection, which no drug in her power was sufficient to remove. Her only resource was in Morakanabad, who was a good man, and endowed with a decent share of confidence; yet whilst in her company he never thought himself on roses.

No person knew aught of Vathek, and, of course, a thousand ridiculous stories were propagated at his expense. The eagerness of Carathis may be easily guessed at receiving the letter, as well as her rage at reading the dissolute conduct of her son. "Is it so?" said she; "either I will perish, or Vathek shall enter the palace of fire. Let me expire in flames, provided he may reign on the throne of Soliman!" Having said this, and whirled herself round in a magical manner, which struck Morakanabad with such terror as caused him to recoil, she ordered her great camel Alboufaki to be brought, and the hideous Nerkes, with the unrelenting Cafour, to attend. "I require no other retinue," said she to Morakanabad; "I am going on affairs of emergency; a truce, therefore, to parade! Take you care of the people: fleece them well in my absence; for we shall expend large sums, and one knows not what may betide."

The night was uncommonly dark, and a pestilential blast blew from the plain of Catoul, that would have deterred any other traveller, however urgent the call: but Carathis enjoyed most whatever filled others with dread. Nerkes concurred in opinion with her; and Cafour had a particular predilection for a pestilence. In the morning this accomplished caravan, with the woodfellers, who directed their route, halted on the edge of an extensive marsh, from whence so noxious a vapour arose as would have destroyed any animal but Alboufaki, who naturally inhaled these malignant fogs with delight. The peasants entreated their convoy not to sleep in this place. "To sleep," cried Carathis, "what an excellent thought! I never sleep, but for visions; and, as to my attendants, their occupations are too many to close the only eye they have." The poor peasants, who were not overpleased with their party, remained open-mouthed with surprise.

Carathis alighted, as well as her negresses; and, severally stripping off their outer garments, they all ran to cull from those spots where the sun shone fiercest the venomous plants that grew on the marsh. This provision was made for the family of the emir, and whoever might retard the expedition to Istakar. The woodmen were overcome with fear, when they beheld these three horrible phantoms run; and, not much relishing the company of Alboufaki, stood aghast at the command of Carathis to set forward, notwithstanding it was noon, and the heat fierce enough to calcine even rocks. In spite, however, of every remonstrance, they were forced implicitly to submit.

Alboufaki, who delighted in solitude, constantly snorted whenever he perceived himself near a habitation; and Carathis, who
was apt to spoil him with indulgence, as constantly turned him
aside: so that the peasants were precluded from procuring sub-
sistence; for the milch goats and ewes, which Providence had
sent towards the district they traversed to refresh travellers
with their milk, all fled at the sight of the hideous animal and
his strange riders. As to Carathis, she needed no common
aliment; for her invention had previously furnished her with
an opiate to stay her stomach, some of which she imparted
to her mutes.

At dusk Alboufaki, making a sudden stop, stamped with his
foot; which, to Carathis, who knew his ways, was a certain
indication that she was near the confines of some cemetery.
The moon shed a bright light on the spot, which served to
discover a long wall with a large door in it, standing ajar, and
so high that Alboufaki might easily enter. The miserable
guides, who perceived their end approaching, humbly implored
Carathis, as she had now so good an opportunity, to inter them,
and immediately gave up the ghost. Nerkes and Cafour, whose
wit was of a style peculiar to themselves, were by no means
parsimonious of it on the folly of these poor people; nor could
anything have been found more suited to their taste than the
site of the burying-ground, and the sepulchres which its precincts contained. There were at least two thousand of them on
the declivity of a hill. Carathis was too eager to execute her
plan to stop at the view, charming as it appeared in her eyes.
Pondering the advantages that might accrue from her present
situation, she said to herself, "So beautiful a cemetery must be
haunted by ghouls! they never want for intelligence: having
heedlessly suffered my stupid guides to expire, I will apply
for directions to them; and, as an inducement, will invite them
to regale on these fresh corpses." After this wise soliloquy,
she beckoned to Nerkes and Cafour, and made signs with her
fingers, as much as to say, "Go; knock against the sides of the
tombs, and strike up your delightful warblings."

The negresses, full of joy at the behests of their mistress,
and promising themselves much pleasure from the society of
the ghouls, went with an air of conquest, and began their
knockings at the tombs. As their strokes were repeated, a
hollow noise was made in the earth; the surface hove up into
heaps; and the ghouls, on all sides, protruded their noses to
inhale the effluvia which the carcasses of the woodmen began

to emit. They assembled before a sarcophagus of white marble, where Carathis was seated between the bodies of her miserable guides. The princess received her visitants with distinguished politeness; and, supper being ended, they talked of business. Carathis soon learned from them everything she wanted to discover; and, without loss of time, prepared to set forward on her journey. Her negresses, who were forming tender connections with the ghouls, importuned her, with all their fingers, to wait at least till the dawn. But Carathis, being chastity in the abstract, and an implacable enemy to love intrigues and sloth, at once rejected their prayer, mounted Alboufaki, and commanded them to take their seats instantly. Four days and four nights she continued her route without interruption. On the fifth, she traversed craggy mountains and half-burnt forests; and arrived on the sixth before the beautiful screens which concealed from all eyes the voluptuous wanderings of her son.

It was daybreak, and the guards were snoring on their posts in careless security, when the rough trot of Alboufaki awoke them in consternation. Imagining that a group of spectres, ascended from the abyss, was approaching, they all, without ceremony, took to their heels. Vathek was at that instant with Nouronihar in the bath, hearing tales, and laughing at Bababalouk who related them; but, no sooner did the outcry of his guards reach him, than he flounced from the water like a carp, and as soon threw himself back at the sight of Carathis; who, advancing with her negresses upon Alboufaki, broke through the muslin awnings and veils of the pavilion. At this sudden apparition, Nouronihar (for she was not at all times free from remorse) fancied that the moment of celestial vengeance was come, and clung about the caliph in amorous despondence.

Carathis, still seated on her camel, foamed with indignation at the spectacle which obtruded itself on her chaste view. She thundered forth without check or mercy, "Thou double-headed and four-legged monster! what means all this winding and writhing? Art thou not ashamed to be seen grasping this limber sapling, in preference to the sceptre of the pre-Adamite sultans? Is it then for this paltry doxy that thou hast violated the conditions in the parchment of our Giaour? Is it on her thou hast lavished thy precious moments? Is this the fruit of the knowledge I have taught thee? Is this the end of thy journey? Tear thyself from the arms of this little simpleton;

drown her in the water before me, and instantly follow my guidance."

In the first ebullition of his fury, Vathek had resolved to rip open the body of Alboufaki, and to stuff it with those of the negresses and of Carathis herself; but the remembrance of the Giaour, the palace of Istakar, the sabres, and the talismans, flashing before his imagination with the simultaneousness of lightning, he became more moderate, and said to his mother in a civil, but decisive tone, "Dread lady, you shall be obeyed; but I will not drown Nouronihar. She is sweeter to me than a Myrabolan comfit; and is enamoured of carbuncles, especially that of Giamschid, which hath also been promised to be conferred upon her: she, therefore, shall go along with us; for I intend to repose with her upon the sofas of Soliman: I can sleep no more without her."—"Be it so," replied Carathis, alighting, and at the same time committing Alboufaki to the charge of her black women.

Nouronihar, who had not yet quitted her hold, began to take courage; and said, with an accent of fondness to the caliph, "Dear sovereign of my soul! I will follow thee, if it be thy will, beyond the Kaf, in the land of the afrits. I will not hesitate to climb, for thee, the nest of the Simurgh; who, this lady excepted, is the most awful of created beings."—"We have here, then," subjoined Carathis, "a girl both of courage and science!" Nouronihar had certainly both; but, notwithstanding all her firmness, she could not help casting back a thought of regret upon the graces of her little Gulchenrouz, and the days of tender endearments she had participated with him. She even dropped a few tears, which the caliph observed; and inadvertently breathed out with a sigh, "Alas! my gentle cousin, what will become of thee?" Vathek, at this apostrophe, knitted up his brows, and Carathis inquired what it could mean. "She is preposterously sighing after a stripling with languishing eyes and soft hair, who loves her," said the caliph. —"Where is he?" asked Carathis. "I must be acquainted with this pretty child; for," added she, lowering her voice, "I design, before I depart, to regain the favour of the Giaour. There is nothing so delicious, in his estimation, as the heart of a delicate boy palpitating with the first tumults of love."

Vathek, as he came from the bath, commanded Bababalouk to collect the women and other movables of his harem, embody his troops, and hold himself in readiness to march within three days; whilst Carathis retired alone to a tent, where the Giaour solaced her with encouraging visions: but at length waking, she found at her feet Nerkes and Cafour, who informed her, by their signs, that having led Alboufaki to the borders of a lake, to browse on some grey moss that looked tolerably venomous, they had discovered certain blue fishes, of the same kind with those in the reservoir on the top of the tower. "Ah! ha!" said she, "I will go thither to them. These fish are, past doubt, of a species that, by a small operation, I can render oracular. They may tell me where this little Gulchenrouz is, whom I am bent upon sacrificing." Having thus spoken, she immediately set out with her swarthy retinue.

It being but seldom that time is lost in the accomplishment of a wicked enterprise, Carathis and her negresses soon arrived at the lake; where, after burning the magical drugs with which they were always provided, they stripped themselves naked, and waded to their chins; Nerkes and Cafour waving torches around them, and Carathis pronouncing her barbarous incantations. The fishes, with one accord, thrust forth their heads from the water, which was violently rippled by the flutter of their fins; and at length finding themselves constrained by the potency of the charm, they opened their piteous mouths, and said, "From gills to tail, we are yours; what seek ye to know?"—"Fishes," answered she, "I conjure you, by your glittering scales, tell me where now is Gulchenrouz?"—"Beyond the rock," replied the shoal, in full chorus; "will this content you? for we do not delight in expanding our mouths."—"It will," returned the princess; "I am not to learn that you are not used to long conversations; I will leave you therefore to repose, though I had other questions to propound." The instant she had spoken, the water became smooth, and the fishes at once disappeared.

Carathis, inflated with the venom of her projects, strode hastily over the rock, and found the amiable Gulchenrouz asleep in an arbour, whilst the two dwarfs were watching at his side, and ruminating their accustomed prayers. These diminutive personages possessed the gift of divining whenever an enemy to good Mussulmans approached; thus they anticipated the arrival of Carathis, who, stopping short, said to herself, "How placidly doth he recline his lovely little head! how pale and languishing are his looks! it is just the very child of my wishes!" The dwarfs interrupted this delectable soliloquy by leaping instantly upon her, and scratching her face with their utmost zeal. But Nerkes and Cafour, betaking themselves to the succour of their mistress, pinched the dwarfs so severely in return, that they both gave up the ghost, imploring Mahomet to inflict his sorest vengeance upon this wicked woman and all her household.

At the noise which this strange conflict occasioned in the valley, Gulchenrouz awoke, and, bewildered with terror, sprung impetuously and climbed an old fig-tree that rose against the acclivity of the rocks; from thence he gained their summits, and ran for two hours without once looking back. At last, exhausted with fatigue, he fell senseless into the arms of a good old genius, whose fondness for the company of children had made it his sole occupation to protect them. Whilst performing his wonted rounds through the air, he had pounced on the cruel Giaour, at the instant of his growling in the horrible chasm, and had rescued the fifty little victims which the impiety of Vathek had devoted to his voracity. These the genius brought up in nests still higher than the clouds, and himself fixed his abode in a nest more capacious than the rest, from which he had expelled the rocs that had built it.

These inviolable asylums were defended against the dives and the afrits by waving streamers; on which were inscribed in characters of gold, that flashed like lightning, the names of Alla and the Prophet. It was there that Gulchenrouz, who as yet remained undeceived with respect to his pretended death, thought himself in the mansions of eternal peace. He admitted without fear the congratulations of his little friends, who were all assembled in the nest of the venerable genius, and vied with each other in kissing his serene forehead and beautiful eyelids. Remote from the inquietudes of the world, the impertinence of harems, the brutality of eunuchs, and the inconstancy of women, there he found a place truly congenial to the delights of his soul. In this peaceable society his days, months, and years glided on; nor was he less happy than the rest of his companions: for the genius, instead of burdening his pupils with perishable riches and vain sciences, conferred upon them the boon of perpetual childhood.

Carathis, unaccustomed to the loss of her prey, vented a thousand execrations on her negresses, for not seizing the child, instead of amusing themselves with pinching to death two insignificant dwarfs from which they could gain no advantage. She returned into the valley murmuring; and, finding that her son was not risen from the arms of Nouronihar, discharged her ill-humour upon both. The idea, however, of departing next

day for Istakar, and of cultivating, through the good offices
of the Giaour, an intimacy with Eblis himself, at length
consoled her chagrin. But fate had ordained it otherwise.

In the evening, as Carathis was conversing with Dilara,
who through her contrivance had become of the party, and whose
taste resembled her own, Bababalouk came to acquaint her
that the sky towards Samarah looked of a fiery red, and seemed
to portend some alarming disaster. Immediately recurring
to her astrolabes and instruments of magic, she took the altitude
of the planets, and discovered, by her calculations, to her great
mortification, that a formidable revolt had taken place at
Samarah, that Motavakel, availing himself of the disgust
which was inveterate against his brother, had incited commo-
tions amongst the populace, made himself master of the palace,
and actually invested the great tower, to which Morakanabad
had retired, with a handful of the few that still remained faithful
to Vathek.

"What!" exclaimed she; "must I lose, then, my tower!
my mutes! my negresses! my mummies! and, worse than all,
the laboratory, the favourite resort of my nightly lucubrations,
without knowing, at least, if my hare-brained son will complete
his adventure? No! I will not be the dupe! immediately will I
speed to support Morakanabad. By my formidable art, the
clouds shall pour grape-shot in the faces of the assailants, and
shafts of red-hot iron on their heads. I will let loose my stores
of hungry serpents and torpedoes from beneath them; and we
shall soon see the stand they will make against such an explosion!

Having thus spoken, Carathis hasted to her son, who was
tranquilly banqueting with Nouronihar in his superb carnation-
coloured tent. "Glutton that thou art!" cried she; "were it
not for me, thou wouldst soon find thyself the mere commander
of savoury pies. Thy faithful subjects have abjured the faith
they swore to thee. Motavakel, thy brother, now reigns on
the hill of Pied Horses, and, had I not some slight resources in
the tower, would not be easily persuaded to abdicate. But,
that time may not be lost, I shall only add a few words: Strike
tent to-night; set forward; and beware how thou loiterest again
by the way. Though thou hast forfeited the conditions of the
parchment, I am not yet without hope; for it cannot be denied
that thou hast violated, to admiration, the laws of hospitality
by seducing the daughter of the emir, after having partaken
of his bread and his salt. Such a conduct cannot but be delightful to the Giaour; and if, on thy march, thou canst signalize

thyself by an additional crime, all will still go well, and thou shalt enter the palace of Soliman in triumph. Adieu! Alboufaki and my negresses are waiting at the door."

The caliph had nothing to offer in reply: he wished his mother a prosperous journey, and ate on till he had finished his supper. At midnight the camp broke up, amidst the flourishing of trumpets and other martial instruments; but loud indeed must have been the sound of the timbals, to overpower the blubbering of the emir and his grey-beards; who, by an excessive profusion of tears, had so far exhausted the radical moisture, that their eyes shrivelled up in their sockets, and their hairs dropped off by the roots. Nouronihar, to whom such a symphony was painful, did not grieve to get out of hearing. She accompanied the caliph in the imperial litter, where they amused themselves with imagining the splendour which was soon to surround them. The other women, overcome with dejection, were dolefully rocked in their cages; whilst Dilara consoled herself with anticipating the joy of celebrating the rites of fire on the stately terraces of Istakar.

In four days they reached the spacious valley of Rocnabad. The season of spring was in all its vigour; and the grotesque branches of the almond trees in full blossom, fantastically chequered with hyacinths and jonquils, breathed forth a delightful fragrance. Myriads of bees, and scarce fewer of santons, had there taken up their abode. On the banks of the stream, hives and oratories were alternately ranged; and their neatness and whiteness were set off by the deep green of the cypresses that spired up amongst them. These pious personages amused themselves with cultivating little gardens, that abounded with flowers and fruits; especially musk-melons of the best flavour that Persia could boast. Sometimes dispersed over the meadow, they entertained themselves with feeding peacocks whiter than snow, and turtles more blue than the sapphire. In this manner were they occupied when the harbingers of the imperial procession began to proclaim, "Inhabitants of Rocnabad! prostrate yourselves on the brink of your pure waters; and tender your thanksgivings to Heaven, that vouchsafeth to show you a ray of its glory: for, lo! the commander of the faithful draws near."

The poor santons, filled with holy energy, having bustled to light up wax torches in their oratories, and expand the Koran on their ebony desks, went forth to meet the caliph with baskets of honeycomb, dates, and melons. But, whilst they were advancing in solemn procession and with measured steps, the

horses, camels, and guards wantoned over their tulips and
other flowers, and made a terrible havoc amongst them. The
santons could not help casting from one eye a look of pity on
the ravages committing around them; whilst the other was
fixed upon the caliph and heaven. Nouronihar, enraptured
with the scenery of a place which brought back to her
remembrance the pleasing solitudes where her infancy had
passed, entreated Vathek to stop: but he, suspecting that these
oratories might be deemed by the Giaour an habitation,
commanded his pioneers to level them all. The santons stood
motionless with horror at the barbarous mandate, and at last
broke out into lamentations; but these were uttered with so
ill a grace, that Vathek bade his eunuchs to kick them from his
presence. He then descended from the litter with Nouronihar.
They sauntered together in the meadow; and amused themselves
with culling flowers, and passing a thousand pleasantries on
each other. But the bees, who were staunch Mussulmans,
thinking it their duty to revenge the insult offered to their
dear masters the santons, assembled so zealously to do it with
good effect, that the caliph and Nouronihar were glad to find
their tents prepared to receive them.

Bababalouk, who, in capacity of purveyor, had acquitted
himself with applause as to peacocks and turtles, lost no time
in consigning some dozens to the spit, and as many more to
be fricasseed. Whilst they were feasting, laughing, carousing,
and blaspheming at pleasure on the banquet so liberally
furnished, the moullahs, the sheiks, the cadis, and imans of
Schiraz (who seemed not to have met the santons) arrived;
leading by bridles of riband, inscribed from the Koran, a train
of asses which were loaded with the choicest fruits the country
could boast. Having presented their offerings to the caliph,
they petitioned him to honour their city and mosques with his
presence. "Fancy not," said Vathek, "that you can detain me.
Your presence I condescend to accept, but beg you will let me
be quiet, for I am not over-fond of resisting temptation. Retire,
then; yet, as it is not decent for personages so reverend to
return on foot, and as you have not the appearance of expert
riders, my eunuchs shall tie you on your asses, with the pre-
caution that your backs be not turned towards me; for they
understand etiquette."—In this deputation were some high-
stomached sheiks, who, taking Vathek for a fool, scrupled not
to speak their opinion. These Bababalouk girded with double
cords; and having well disciplined their asses with nettles

behind, they all started, with a preternatural alertness, plunging, kicking, and running foul of one another, in the most ludicrous manner imaginable.

Nouronihar and the caliph mutually contended who should most enjoy so degrading a sight. They burst out in peals of laughter to see the old men and their asses fall into the stream. The leg of one was fractured; the shoulder of another dislocated; the teeth of a third dashed out; and the rest suffered still worse.

Two days more, undisturbed by fresh embassies, having been devoted to the pleasures of Rocnabad, the expedition proceeded; leaving Schiraz on the right, and verging towards a large plain; from whence were discernible, on the edge of the horizon, the dark summits of the mountains of Istakar.

At this prospect the caliph and Nouronihar were unable to repress their transports. They bounded from their litter to the ground, and broke forth into such wild exclamations, as amazed all within hearing. Interrogating each other, they shouted, "Are we not approaching the radiant palace of light? or gardens, more delightful than those of Sheddad?"—Infatuated mortals! they thus indulged delusive conjecture, unable to fathom the decrees of the Most High!

The good genii, who had not totally relinquished the superintendence of Vathek, repairing to Mahomet in the seventh heaven, said, "Merciful Prophet! stretch forth thy propitious arms towards thy vicegerent; who is ready to fall, irretrievably, into the snare which his enemies, the dives, have prepared to destroy him. The Giaour is awaiting his arrival, in the abominable palace of fire; where, if he once set his foot, his perdition will be inevitable." Mahomet answered, with an air of indignation, "He hath too well deserved to be resigned to himself; but I permit you to try if one effort more will be effectual to divert him from pursuing his ruin."

One of these beneficent genii, assuming, without delay, the exterior of a shepherd, more renowned for his piety than all the dervishes and santons of the region, took his station near a flock of white sheep, on the slope of a hill; and began to pour forth from his flute such airs of pathetic melody, as subdued the very soul, and, wakening remorse, drove far from it every frivolous fancy. At these energetic sounds, the sun hid himself beneath a gloomy cloud; and the waters of two little lakes, that were naturally clearer then crystal, became of a colour like blood. The whole of this superb assembly was involuntarily drawn towards the declivity of the hill. With downcast eyes, they all stood abashed; each upbraiding himself with the evil he had done. The heart of Dilara palpitated; and the chief of the eunuchs, with a sigh of contrition, implored pardon of the women, whom, for his own satisfaction, he had so often tormented.

Vathek and Nouronihar turned pale in their litter; and, regarding each other with haggard looks, reproached themselves—the one with a thousand of the blackest crimes, a thousand projects of impious ambition; the other with the desolation of her family, and the perdition of the amiable Gulchenrouz. Nouronihar persuaded herself that she heard, in the fatal music, the groans of her dying father; and Vathek, the sobs of the fifty children he had sacrificed to the Giaour. Amidst these complicated pangs of anguish, they perceived themselves impelled towards the shepherd, whose countenance was so commanding that Vathek, for the first time, felt overawed; whilst Nouronihar concealed her face with her hands. The music paused; and the genius, addressing the caliph, said, "Deluded prince! to whom Providence hath confided the care of innumerable subjects, is it thus that thou fulfillest thy mission? Thy crimes are already completed; and art thou now listening towards thy punishment? Thou knowest that, beyond these mountains, Eblis and his accursed dives hold their infernal empire; and, seduced by a malignant phantom, thou art proceeding to surrender thyself to them! This moment is the last of grace allowed thee: abandon thy atrocious purpose: return: give back Nouronihar to her father, who still retains a few sparks of life: destroy thy tower with all its abominations: drive Carathis from thy councils: be just to thy subjects: respect the ministers of the Prophet: compensate for thy impieties by an exemplary life; and, instead of squandering thy days in voluptuous indulgence, lament thy crimes on the sepulchres of thy ancestors. Thou beholdest the clouds that obscure the sun: at the instant he recovers his splendour, if thy heart be not changed, the time of mercy assigned thee will be past for ever."

Vathek, depressed with fear, was on the point of prostrating himself at the feet of the shepherd, whom he perceived to be of a nature superior to man: but, his pride prevailing, he audaciously lifted his head, and, glancing at him one of his terrible looks, said, "Whoever thou art, withhold thy useless admonitions: thou wouldst either delude me, or art thyself deceived. If what I have done be so criminal as thou pretendest, there remains not for me a moment of grace. I have traversed a sea of blood to acquire a power which will make thy equals tremble; deem not that I shall retire when in view of the port, or that I will relinquish her who is dearer to me than either my life or thy mercy. Let the sun appear! let him illume my career! it matters not where it may end." On uttering these words, which made even the genius shudder, Vathek threw himself into the arms of Nouronihar, and commanded that his horses should be forced back to the road.

There was no difficulty in obeying these orders, for the attraction had ceased: the sun shone forth in all his glory, and the shepherd vanished with a lamentable scream.

The fatal impression of the music of the genius remained, notwithstanding, in the heart of Vathek's attendants. They viewed each other with looks of consternation. At the approach of night almost all of them escaped; and of this numerous assemblage there only remained the chief of the eunuchs, some idolatrous slaves, Dilara, and a few other women who, like herself, were votaries of the religion of the Magi.

The caliph, fired with the ambition of prescribing laws to the powers of darkness, was but little embarrassed at this dereliction. The impetuosity of his blood prevented him from sleeping; nor did he encamp any more as before. Nouronihar, whose impatience, if possible, exceeded his own, importuned him to hasten his march, and lavished on him a thousand caresses, to beguile all reflection. She fancied herself already more potent than Balkis, and pictured to her imagination the genii falling prostrate at the foot of her throne. In this manner they advanced by moonlight till they came within view of the two towering rocks that form a kind of portal to the valley, at the extremity of which rose the vast ruins of Istakar. Aloft on the mountain glimmered the fronts of various royal mausoleums, the horror of which was deepened by the shadows of night. They passed through two villages almost deserted, the only inhabitants remaining being a few feeble old men, who, at the sight of horses and litters, fell upon their knees, and cried out, "O Heaven! is it then by these phantoms that we have been for six months tormented? Alas! it was from the terror of these spectres, and the noise beneath the mountains, that our people have fled, and left us at the mercy of the maleficent spirits!" The caliph, to whom these complaints were but unpromising auguries, drove over the bodies of these wretched old men, and at length arrived at the foot of the terrace of

black marble. There he descended from his litter, handing
down Nouronihar. Both with beating hearts stared wildly
around them, and expected, with an apprehensive shudder,
the approach of the Giaour; but nothing as yet announced
his appearance.

A deathlike stillness reigned over the mountain and through
the air; the moon dilated on a vast platform the shades of the
lofty columns, which reached from the terrace almost to the
clouds; the gloomy watch-towers, whose number could not be
counted, were covered by no roof; and their capitals, of an
architecture unknown in the records of the earth, served as an
asylum for the birds of night, which, alarmed at the approach
of such visitants, fled away croaking.

The chief of the eunuchs, trembling with fear, besought
Vathek that a fire might be kindled. "No," replied he, "there
is no time left to think of such trifles. Abide where thou art,
and expect my commands." Having thus spoken, he presented
his hand to Nouronihar; and ascending the steps of a vast
staircase, reached the terrace, which was flagged with squares
of marble, and resembled a smooth expanse of water, upon
whose surface not a blade of grass ever dared to vegetate. On
the right rose the watch-towers, ranged before the ruins of an
immense palace, whose walls were embossed with various
figures. In front stood forth the colossal forms of four creatures,
composed of the leopard and the griffin, and though but of
stone, inspired emotions of terror. Near these were distinguished, by the splendour of the moon, which streamed full on
the place, characters like those on the sabres of the Giaour, and
which possessed the same virtue of changing every moment.
These, after vacillating for some time, fixed at last in Arabic
letters, and prescribed to the caliph the following words:
"Vathek, thou hast violated the conditions of my parchment,
and deservest to be sent back; but in favour to thy companion,
and as the meed for what thou hast done to obtain it, Eblis
permitteth that the portal of his palace shall be opened,
and the subterranean fire will receive thee into the number
of its adorers."

He scarcely had read these words before the mountain,
against which the terrace was reared, trembled, and the watch-
towers were ready to topple headlong upon them; the rock
yawned, and disclosed within it a staircase of polished marble,
that seemed to approach the abyss. Upon each stair were
planted two large torches, like those Nouronihar had seen in her

vision, the camphorated vapour of which ascended and gathered itself into a cloud under the hollow of the vault.

This appearance, instead of terrifying, gave new courage to the daughter of Fakreddin. Scarcely deigning to bid adieu to the moon and the firmament, she abandoned without hesitation the pure atmosphere, to plunge into these infernal exhalations. The gait of those impious personages was haughty and determined. As they descended, by the effulgence of the torches, they gazed on each other with mutual admiration, and both appeared so resplendent that they already esteemed themselves spiritual intelligences. The only circumstance that perplexed them was their not arriving at the bottom of the stairs: on hastening their descent with an ardent impetuosity, they felt their steps accelerated to such a degree, that they seemed not walking but falling from a precipice. Their progress, however, was at length impeded by a vast portal of ebony, which the caliph without difficulty recognized. Here the Giaour awaited them with the key in his hand. "Ye are welcome!" said he to them, with a ghastly smile, "in spite of Mahomet and all his dependents. I will now usher you into that palace where you have so highly merited a place." Whilst he was uttering these words he touched the enamelled lock with his key, and the doors at once flew open with a noise still louder than the thunder of the dog-days, and as suddenly recoiled the moment they had entered.

The caliph and Nouronihar beheld each other with amazement at finding themselves in a place which, though roofed with a vaulted ceiling, was so spacious and lofty, that at first they took it for an immeasurable plain. But their eyes at length growing familiar to the grandeur of the surrounding objects, they extended their view to those at a distance, and discovered rows of columns and arcades, which gradually diminished, till they terminated in a point radiant as the sun when he darts his last beams athwart the ocean. The pavement, strewed over with gold dust and saffron, exhaled so subtle an odour as almost overpowered them. They, however, went on, and observed an infinity of censers, in which ambergris and the wood of aloes were continually burning. Between the several columns were placed tables, each spread with a profusion of viands, and wines of every species sparkling in vases of crystal. A throng of genii and other fantastic spirits of either sex danced lasciviously at the sound of music which issued from beneath.

In the midst of this immense hall, a vast multitude was incessantly passing, who severally kept their right hands on their hearts, without once regarding anything around them: tney had all the livid paleness of death. Their eyes, deep sunk in their sockets, resembled those phosphoric meteors that glimmer by night in places of interment. Some stalked slowly on, absorbed in profound reverie; some, shrieking with agony, ran furiously about like tigers wounded with poisoned arrows; whilst others, grinding their teeth in rage, foamed along more frantic than the wildest maniac. They all avoided each other; and, though surrounded by a multitude that no one could number, each wandered at random unheedful of the rest, as if alone on a desert where no foot had trodden.

Vathek and Nouronihar, frozen with terror at a sight so baleful, demanded of the Giaour what these appearances might mean, and why these ambulating spectres never withdrew their hands from their hearts? "Perplex not yourselves with so much at once," replied he bluntly; "you will soon be acquainted with all: let us haste and present you to Eblis." They continued their way through the multitude: but, notwithstanding their confidence at first, they were not sufficiently composed to examine with attention the various perspectives of halls and of galleries that opened on the right hand and left; which were all illuminated by torches and braziers, whose flames rose in pyramids to the centre of the vault. At length they came to a place where long curtains, brocaded with crimson and gold, fell from all parts in solemn confusion. Here the choirs and dances were heard no longer. The light which glimmered came from afar.

After some time, Vathek and Nouronihar perceived a gleam brightening through the drapery, and entered a vast tabernacle hung round with the skins of leopards. An infinity of elders with streaming beards, and afrits in complete armour, had prostrated themselves before the ascent of a lofty eminence; on the top of which, upon a globe of fire, sat the formidable Eblis. His person was that of a young man, whose noble and regular features seemed to have been tarnished by malignant vapours. In his large eyes appeared both pride and despair: his flowing hair retained some resemblance to that of an angel of light. In his hand, which thunder had blasted, he swayed the iron sceptre that causes the monster Ouranbad, the afrits, and all the powers of the abyss to tremble. At his presence, the heart of the caliph sunk within him; and he fell prostrate on his face. Nouronihar, however, though greatly dismayed, could not help admiring the person of Eblis; for she expected to have seen some stupendous giant. Eblis, with a voice more mild than might be imagined, but such as penetrated the soul and filled it with the deepest melancholy, said, "Creatures of clay, I receive you into mine empire: ye are numbered amongst my adorers: enjoy whatever this palace affords: the treasures of the pre-Adamite sultans, their fulminating sabres, and those talismans that compel the dives to open the subterranean expanses of the mountain of Kaf, which communicate with these. There, insatiable as your curiosity may be, shall you find sufficient objects to gratify it. You shall possess the exclusive privilege of entering the fortresses of Aherman, and the halls of Argenk, where are portrayed all creatures endowed with intelligence; and the various animals that inhabited the earth prior to the creation of that contemptible being whom ye denominate the father of mankind."

Vathek and Nouronihar, feeling themselves revived and encouraged by this harangue, eagerly said to the Giaour, "Bring us instantly to the place which contains these precious talismans."—"Come," answered this wicked dive, with his malignant grin—"come and possess all that my sovereign hath promised, and more." He then conducted them into a long aisle adjoining the tabernacle; preceding them with hasty steps, and followed by his disciples with the utmost alacrity. They reached, at length, a hall of great extent, and covered with a lofty dome; around which appeared fifty portals of bronze, secured with as many fastenings of iron. A funereal gloom prevailed over the whole scene. Here, upon two beds of incorruptible cedar, lay recumbent the fleshless forms of the pre-Adamite kings, who had been monarchs of the whole earth. They still possessed enough of life to be conscious of their deplorable condition. Their eyes retained a melancholy motion; they regarded one another with looks of the deepest dejection, each holding his right hand, motionless, on his heart. At their feet were inscribed the events of their several reigns, their power, their pride, and their crimes; Soliman Raad, Soliman Daki, and Soliman, called Gian Ben Gian, who, after having chained up the dives in the dark caverns of Kaf, became so presumptuous as to doubt of the Supreme Power. All these maintained great state, though not to be compared with the eminence of Soliman Ben Daoud.

This king, so renowned for his wisdom, was on the loftiest elevation, and placed immediately under the dome. He appeared to possess more animation than the rest. Though, from time to time, he laboured with profound sighs; and, like his companions, kept his right hand on his heart, yet his countenance was more composed, and he seemed to be listening to the sullen roar of a cataract visible in part through one of the grated portals. This was the only sound that intruded on the silence of these doleful mansions. A range of brazen cases surrounded the elevation. "Remove the covers from these cabalistic depositories," said the Giaour to Vathek, "and avail thyself of the talismans which will break asunder all these gates of bronze, and not only render thee master of the treasures contained within them, but also of the spirits by which they are guarded."

The caliph, whom this ominous preliminary had entirely disconcerted, approached the vase with faltering footsteps; and was ready to sink with terror when he heard the groans of Soliman. As he proceeded, a voice from the livid lips of the prophet articulated these words: "In my lifetime I filled a magnificent throne; having, on my right hand, twelve thousand seats of gold, where the patriarchs and the prophets heard my doctrines: on my left, the sages and doctors, upon as many thrones of silver, were present at all my decisions. Whilst I thus administered justice to innumerable multitudes, the birds of the air, hovering over me, served as a canopy against the rays of the sun. My people flourished; and my palace rose to the clouds. I erected a temple to the Most High, which was the wonder of the universe; but I basely suffered myself to be seduced by the love of women, and a curiosity that could not be restrained by sublunary things. I listened to the counsels of Aherman and the daughter of Pharaoh; and adored fire and the hosts of heaven. I forsook the holy city, and commanded the genii to rear the stupendous palace of Istakar, and the terrace of the watch-towers; each of which was consecrated to a star. There, for a while, I enjoyed myself in the zenith of glory and pleasure. Not only men but supernatural beings were subject also to my will. I began to think, as these unhappy monarchs around had already thought, that the vengeance of Heaven was asleep; when, at once, the thunder burst my structures asunder, and precipitated me hither: where, however, I do not remain, like the other inhabitants, totally destitute of hope; for an angel of light hath revealed that in consideration of the piety of my early youth my woes shall come to an end, when this cataract shall for ever cease to flow. Till then

I am in torments, ineffable torments! an unrelenting fire preys on my heart."

Having uttered this exclamation, Soliman raised his hands towards heaven, in token of supplication; and the caliph discerned through his bosom, which was transparent as crystal, his heart enveloped in flames. At a sight so full of horror, Nouronihar fell back, like one petrified, into the arms of Vathek, who cried out with a convulsive sob, "O Giaour! whither hast thou brought us! Allow us to depart, and I will relinquish all thou hast promised. O Mahomet! remains there no more mercy?"—"None! none!" replied the malicious dive. "Know, miserable prince! thou art now in the abode of vengeance and despair. Thy heart, also, will be kindled like those of the other votaries of Eblis. A few days are allotted thee previous to this fatal period: employ them as thou wilt; recline on these heaps of gold; command the infernal potentates; range, at thy pleasure, through these immense subterranean domains: no barrier shall be shut against thee. As for me, I have fulfilled my mission: I now leave thee to thyself." At these words he vanished.

The caliph and Nouronihar remained in the most abject affliction. Their tears were unable to flow, and scarcely could they support themselves. At length, taking each other despondingly by the hand, they went faltering from this fatal hall, indifferent which way they turned their steps. Every portal opened at their approach. The dives fell prostrate before them. Every reservoir of riches was disclosed to their view; but they no longer felt the incentives of curiosity, of pride, or avarice. With like apathy they heard the chorus of genii, and saw the stately banquets prepared to regale them. They went wandering on, from chamber to chamber, hall to hall, and gallery to gallery; all without bounds or limit; all distinguishable by the same lowering gloom; all adorned with the same awful grandeur; all traversed by persons in search of repose and consolation, but who sought them in vain; for every one carried within him a heart tormented in flames. Shunned by these various sufferers, who seemed by their looks to be upbraiding the partners of their guilt, they withdrew from them to wait, in direful suspense, the moment which should render them to each other the like objects of terror.

"What!" exclaimed Nouronihar; "will the time come when I shall snatch my hand from thine?"—"Ah!" said Vathek, "and shall my eyes ever cease to drink from thine long draughts of enjoyment? Shall the moments of our reciprocal ecstasies be reflected on with horror? It was not thou that broughtest me hither; the principles by which Carathis perverted my youth have been the sole cause of my perdition! it is but right she should have her share of it." Having given vent to these painful expressions, he called to an afrit, who was stirring up one of the braziers, and bade him fetch the Princess Carathis from the palace of Samarah.

After issuing these orders, the caliph and Nouronihar continued walking amidst the silent crowd, till they heard voices at the end of the gallery. Presuming them to proceed from some unhappy beings, who, like themselves, were awaiting their final doom, they followed the sound, and found it to come from a small square chamber, where they discovered, sitting on sofas, four young men of goodly figure, and a lovely female, who were holding a melancholy conversation by the glimmering of a lonely lamp. Each had a gloomy and forlorn air; and two of them were embracing each other with great tenderness. On seeing the caliph and the daughter of Fakreddin enter, they arose, saluted, and made room for them. Then he who appeared the most considerable of the group, addressed himself thus to Vathek: "Strangers! who doubtless are in the same state of suspense with ourselves, as you do not yet bear your hand on your heart, if you come hither to pass the interval allotted, previous to the infliction of our common punishment, condescend to relate the adventures that have brought you to this fatal place; and we, in return, will acquaint you with ours, which deserve but too well to be heard. To trace back our crimes to their source, though we are not permitted to repent, is the only employment suited to wretches like us!"

The caliph and Nouronihar assented to the proposal; and Vathek began, not without tears and lamentations, a sincere recital of every circumstance that had passed. When the afflicting narrative was closed, the young man entered on his own. Each person proceeded in order; and, when the third prince had reached the midst of his adventures, a sudden noise interrupted him, which caused the vault to tremble and to open.

Immediately a cloud descended, which, gradually dissipating, discovered Carathis on the back of an afrit, who grievously complained of his burden. She, instantly springing to the ground, advanced towards her son, and said, "What dost thou here, in this little square chamber? As the dives are become subject to thy beck, I expected to have found thee on the throne of the pre-Adamite kings."

"Execrable woman!" answered the caliph; "cursed be the day thou gavest me birth! Go, follow this afrit; let him conduct thee to the hall of the prophet Soliman: there thou wilt learn to what these palaces are destined, and how much I ought to abhor the impious knowledge thou hast taught me."

"Has the height of power, to which thou art arrived, turned thy brain?" answered Carathis: "but I ask no more than permission to show my respect for Soliman the prophet. It is, however, proper thou shouldst know that (as the afrit has informed me neither of us shall return to Samarah) I requested his permission to arrange my affairs, and he politely consented. Availing myself, therefore, of the few moments allowed me, I set fire to the tower, and consumed in it the mutes, negresses, and serpents, which have rendered me so much good service; nor should I have been less kind to Morakanabad, had he not prevented me, by deserting at last to thy brother. As for Bababalouk, who had the folly to return to Samarah, to provide husbands for thy wives, I undoubtedly would have put him to the torture; but being in a hurry, I only hung him, after having decoyed him in a snare, with thy wives, whom I buried alive by the help of my negresses, who thus spent their last moments greatly to their satisfaction. With respect to Dilara, who ever stood high in my favour, she hath evinced the greatness of her mind, by fixing herself near, in the service of one of the magi; and, I think, will soon be one of our society."

Vathek, too much cast down to express the indignation excited by such a discourse, ordered the afrit to remove Carathis from his presence, and continued immersed in thoughts which his companions durst not disturb.

Carathis, however, eagerly entered the dome of Soliman, and without regarding in the least the groans of the prophet, undauntedly removed the covers of the vases and violently seized on the talismans. Then, with a voice more loud than had hitherto been heard within these mansions, she compelled the dives to disclose to her the most secret treasures, the most profound stores, which the afrit himself had not seen. She passed, by rapid descents, known only to Eblis and his most favoured potentates; and thus penetrated the very entrails of the earth, where breathes the sansar, or the icy wind of death. Nothing appalled her dauntless soul. She perceived, however, in all the inmates who bore their hands on their heart, a little singularity not much to her taste.

As she was emerging from one of the abysses, Eblis stood

forth to her view; but notwithstanding he displayed the full effulgence of his infernal majesty, she preserved her countenance unaltered, and even paid her compliments with considerable firmness.

This superb monarch thus answered: "Princess, whose knowledge and whose crimes have merited a conspicuous rank in my empire, thou dost well to avail thyself of the leisure that remains; for the flames and torments, which are ready to seize on thy heart, will not fail to provide thee soon with full employment." He said, and was lost in the curtains of his tabernacle.

Carathis paused for a moment with surprise; but, resolved to follow the advice of Eblis, she assembled all the choirs of genii, and all the dives, to pay her homage. Thus marched she, in triumph, through a vapour of perfumes, amidst the acclamations of all the malignant spirits, with most of whom she had formed a previous acquaintance. She even attempted to dethrone one of the Solimans, for the purpose of usurping his place; when a voice, proceeding from the abyss of death, proclaimed, "All is accomplished!" Instantaneously the haughty forehead of the intrepid princess became corrugated with agony; she uttered a tremendous yell, and fixed, no more to be withdrawn, her right hand upon her heart, which was become a receptacle of eternal fire.

In this delirium, forgetting all ambitious projects, and her thirst for that knowledge which should ever be hidden from mortals, she overturned the offerings of the genii; and, having execrated the hour she was begotten and the womb that had borne her, glanced off in a rapid whirl that rendered her invisible, and continued to revolve without intermission.

Almost at the same instant, the same voice announced to the caliph, Nouronihar, the four princes, and the princess, the awful and irrevocable decree. Their hearts immediately took fire, and they, at once, lost the most precious gift of heaven— HOPE. These unhappy beings recoiled, with looks of the most furious distraction. Vathek beheld in the eyes of Nouronihar nothing but rage and vengeance; nor could she discern aught in his but aversion and despair. The two princes who were friends, and, till that moment, had preserved their attachment, shrunk back, gnashing their teeth with mutual and unchangeable hatred. Kahlah and his sister made reciprocal gestures of imprecation; all testified their horror for each other by the most ghastly convulsions, and screams that could not be smothered.

All severally plunged themselves into the accursed multitude, there to wander in an eternity of unabating anguish.

Such was, and such should be, the punishment of unrestrained passions and atrocious deeds! Such shall be the chastisement of that blind curiosity, which would transgress those bounds the wisdom of the Creator has prescribed to human knowledge; and such the dreadful disappointment of that restless ambition, which, aiming at discoveries reserved for beings of a supernatural order, perceives not, through its infatuated pride, that the condition of man upon earth is to be—humble and ignorant.

Thus the caliph Vathek, who, for the sake of empty pomp and forbidden power, had sullied himself with a thousand crimes, became a prey to grief without end, and remorse without mitigation; whilst the humble, the despised Gulchenrouz passed whole ages in undisturbed tranquillity, and in the pure happiness of childhood.